Regency Rebels

by

Colin Yardley

Grosvenor House
Publishing Limited

The right of Colin Yardley to be identified as the author of this
work has been asserted in accordance with Section 78
of the Copyright, Designs and Patents Act 1988

This book is published by
Grosvenor House Publishing Ltd
Link House
140 The Broadway, Tolworth, Surrey, KT6 7HT.
www.grosvenorhousepublishing.co.uk

This book is a work of fiction. Any resemblance to
people or events, past or present, is purely coincidental.

A CIP record for this book
is available from the British Library

ISBN 978-1-80381-537-4

Thanks to Cath Green for copy-editing,
Bill Metson for the photographs and Martha Allen
and Susie Taylor, his models.

1815

"When I am Prime Minister, such things will not be allowed. When I 'm Prime Minister, people will be kinder, have more sympathy. People will be less selfish. My laws will not have it otherwise.

Calista Reed, is having yet another rant, addressing her parents and the whole world, in the sitting room.

"But I may never be elected Prime Minister, because so many people have wrong ideas or no idea at all how to live a civilised life. They know nothing beyond their own little world. So many people are pitifully insular, because their experience is limited and they may not even be able to read. Or their life may be totally dominated and distorted by poverty and the most basic need to find enough to eat. That makes them no better than any of the other animals, who spend their entire lives searching for a mate, escape from a predator, or for something for the belly.

"Father, it is disgraceful" Cally's head was thrust forward as she stentoriously repeated, "Disgraceful."

"With my friends I walked to the Vauxhall Gardens this afternoon and I was horrified. Fixed at the gates there was a big sign, reading: 'No dogs and no soldiers in uniform'. I was tempted to turn round and come straight home. My disgust I first made clear to the guard at the gate, a local constable, a man familiar to me.

"His response was insolent and dismissive. He said: 'Never mind, dearie, from next week the one shilling entrance fee will keep them all out. You and your friends don't want your promenade spoilt by the annoyance of beggars and the sight of scruffy peg-legs back from the war.'

"*I* then had another thought, so I went back to the guard and demanded, "Tell me, do you stop officers in uniform from entering?"

"'No, never,'" said he, 'Officers are gentlemen. They know how to behave.'"

"I told him that many officers are definitely not gentlemen and have no idea how to behave, as many a lady could attest". He was sneering at me. Had I a weapon, I would have hit his silly head.

"I was so incensed by now that I tore down the paper sign and trod it underfoot. My friends then grabbed me and tried to rush me away, before the constable could use the weight of the law against me."

"But I noticed a group of ex-soldiers along the street. They were trying to make music, of a sort, and begging. They had a battered trumpet, a fife and a side drum. I offered them thrupence each if they could play the Marseillaise for me. After some la la la-ing from me, they had some idea of the tune.

"So, in the remnants of their filthy uniforms, the little band led the way and my lovely friends joined in the fun. We all marched through the gate, our arms and legs swinging in exaggerated military style, leaving the guard with an open mouth and gesticulating wildly. No passer-by joined us, but some on-lookers applauded us and all were amused.

"There, that was my day's revolutionary defiance, a tiny blow struck for liberty and justice.

"The French anthem is so much more uplifting than our own funereal jeremiad and its message is as fittingly directed at the people of London as at the people of Paris."

She impatiently pushes her hair from her face and continues her rant.

"Father, It is only weeks since Waterloo. The Duke has dismissed half of his army, getting their measly shilling a day off the government's pay-roll as quickly as possible. The soldiers have come home, some three hundred thousand of them, with nothing but the clothes on their backs – their ragged red coats. Many are maimed for life, with only a pittance of a pension. The sacrifices they have made on behalf of the nation are quickly forgotten. They are now put in the same category as dogs and banished from one of the few free entertainments in London. It makes me question whether the right side won the war. That sign manifests the opposite of equality and fraternity – a motto of the French, but also a worthy aspiration of all right-thinking people"

"Given a choice between Bonaparte and Wellington, I pick the Corsican, rather than the man in fancy boots.

In the Reed family it was ever Father and Mother. 'Papa' and 'Mama' were considered antiquated and meet only for the pompous gentry.

Calista Reed is always quick to anger and now her temper is red-hot. Her father knows of old that he is well advised not to interrupt his daughter's eruption, but simply to let the lava flow. Her eyes are wide and glaring. Like her mother's eyes, strikingly emerald green, they are remarkable at any time; now wide and glistening, they transfix any observer.

She was not given to tantrums as a young child. This righteous anger has come with her growing awareness of the dreadful state of the world, resulting from the moral turpitude of the men who control it.

Calista's mother, Ananya, is Indian. Born in Calcutta, she was brought to England, when still a child, as a personal servant to the wife of Major General Stibbert of the British Indian Army. She remembers that her family had too many daughters and so she was either given away to the Mem Sahib, or perhaps sold. Lavender Reed, of the Bow Street Runners, met her when investigating a suspicious death at the Woolwich Artillery Depot. Their only child, known by family and friends as Cally, has her mother's raven hair, coffee skin colour and those unusual emerald eyes, all the more mysterious and exotic for being deep-set. From a couple of paces, the eye colour is noticeable, but up-close, for anyone newly meeting her, the eyes are fascinating and one cannot help staring.

Her best friend since her earliest days at school was Eliza, known to all as Ellie. Their routine was to meet each other for the walk to and from school, often using a circuitous route coming home, in order to prolong their time together. They both liked the sorts of games boys played, which involved running, jumping, kicking and throwing things, but they had no patience with girlish pastimes, which usually involved foolish pretending; pretending to be mothers, teachers or princesses, dressing up in adult clothes, cuddling dolls and incessantly combing and plaiting one another's hair.

Mother raised Cally to be bilingual in English and Bengali and so she could vent her spleen in either language, but finds her English to have a bigger range of vehement words and she finds so much in the world that makes her angry, especially the idiocy of most people. Her misanthropy is mitigated by her sympathy for the poor and distressed and her concern that there should be fairness for all.

Fully occupied with her studies and the problems of the world, she is unselfconscious and surprisingly unaware, even at fifteen, of her striking looks and the impact they have on others.

Her arms are stretched straight, as if standing to attention, with clenched fists and her shoulders are pumping. This indicates that her anger has not yet subsided.

"I shall write to Mr Tyers of the family I understand still to be the owners of the Gardens, demanding that no such offensive notice should be displayed. I shall also write to the Duke of Wellington, asking what he intends to do about this insult to the battle-scarred veterans of his army. He should immediately come to their defence."

"Cally, I am sure the bastions of the State quail when they see your signature on yet another demanding missive."

"Father, your sarcasm does not blunt my anger at injustice."

"Cally, sweet child, If I were not fully aware of that, I would hold my peace. You know I am proud of your compassion and your agitation on behalf of the poor and oppressed.

"But you also know that, like your mother, I am concerned that, should there be a sudden, bigger surge in the tide against English Jacobinism; if the Prince Regent and the Earl of Liverpool take a sudden fit to quell all opposition, you might be swept up by their hysteria, just as many have already suffered." With a waft of her hand, Cally dismisses the idea. Just like most others of her age, she is unassailable, even immortal.

Before taking up her determined pen, Calista makes her father and herself a conciliatory cup of tea. Then she writes her letter and goes back to her Latin prep.

In her early years, when Cally saw her parents reading books, she was impatient to know the secret of it. Being taught at home, as well as at school, she came quickly to reading and writing. Silly games had no appeal, but as soon as she heard of the existence of other languages, lessons in Latin and Greek appeared on her wanted list. Father found the money to pay the Rector for private tuition. This eagerness for learning was heightened as soon as she read that women were not allowed admission to English universities. That gross unfairness would not stand in her way.

Her determination became even sterner when she found that there were women professors of Greek and mathematics in Italy. If in Italy, why not in England?

Ellie was not as bookish as Cally, who was reputed to be the cleverest pupil in the school, but this did not distance them. Ellie valued being known as the best friend of Cally Reed and, for her part, Cally was glad to have a partner in her tomboyish activities, which distanced some other girls from her.

At school they had to wear skirts, but whenever possible they appeared in a version of boys' breeches, often showing bandaged or scabby knees. When Ellie reached ten, her mother insisted she must always be seen in petticoats. In sympathy, Cally dressed likewise and cared not that boys could see up her skirts when she fell over or climbed trees. "Secrets of any value I keep under my hat, not under my skirts." it was Ellie's mother who heard this remark and, knowing Cally, she was not shocked. Friends and teachers accepted that the girls were inseparable and largely good for one another. Ellie tried to emulate Cally's scholarship, whilst acting as a brake on her friend's more reckless adventurousness. Their mutual fondness was obvious. Each afternoon, when having to part for several hours until the following morning, they hugged each other and kissed on the lips, which they had seen grown-ups do.

It was mid-June when the news reached London that the allied armies under Wellington and Blücher had routed the French Imperial Guard at Waterloo and that Boney had leapt from his battle carriage on to Marengo, his horse, and galloped off into the sunset. In the eyes of most people, Napoleon was the devil incarnate. Cally was not so sure.

Most saw Waterloo as a glorious English victory and there was much rejoicing.

Cally regretted that England and Prussia had won. She looked upon Waterloo as the calamitous defeat of the French Revolution and its noble principles. Bonapartism had been crushed and in France and elsewhere, decrepit and corrupt monarchies would continue, "Another opulent and dissolute Louis in Paris to match our dissipated Charlie, closely followed by the imported mad German George, in London."

In the following days, captured regimental banners, imperial eagles and even Napoleon's coach were brought to London and those with nothing better to do went along to gawp. In Parliament there was talk of erecting a celebratory monument. Cally derided all this nonsense, urging that any money that might be spent on a statue of the Duke of Wellington would be better spent on the poor. The war had left thousands in dire poverty. The peace alone was not sufficient to provide for the relief of their distress. Peace was a new condition abroad, in Europe. Hunger was a continuing condition, here in England.

No. Cally would not go to the celebratory bonfire and fireworks in the Pleasure Gardens and she would not go to see the military victory parade. Her friends called her an inveterate Jacobin, which label she accepted with pride, claiming this put her in the same circle as Lord Byron and Percy Shelley, her favourite poets.

Prime Minister, Lord Liverpool and the Prince Regent were not best pleased to hear that the defeat of Napoleon was not unanimously celebrated around the country. The caricaturists, Cruikshank and Gilray were much in demand for mischievous comment. When they heard that Prinny was happy to let it be thought that he was present, in command, on the field of battle for the glorious victory, their venom knew no bounds.

This day, in late summer sunshine, Cally enjoys walking through Kennington Common to the Glebeland for her next Latin lesson with the Rector, the Reverend Arthur Onslow. She has a boyish sort of stride in her laced leather boots, which kick up a little dust from the gravel footpath in this dry weather. She has no time for the thin-soled, satin-topped slippers that are currently more fashionable for young ladies, forcing them to trip along daintily, avoiding stones, mud and puddles. She wears her summer pelisse and her usual single concession to her obvious oriental heritage, a long silk scarf. Today she is in equable mood and so the scarf is orange. When it is red, best take care. On one side of the road there is a hedge of, ragwort, bracken and bramble, with the occasional hawthorn tree. Beyond the hedge, the stubble indicates that the harvest is in on the few commoners' strip fields left by the encroaching enclosures. She walks through a gap in the hedge and picks a poppy and a knapweed flower from among the stubble She pushes the stalks under the band of her straw bonnet. Feeling a little more decorative and at one with nature, she walks on. The other side of the road has gardens busy with people harvesting vegetables, most of which will be sold at local markets, or carted as far as Covent Garden. This being a lane not much walked, there are no beggars. In contrast, the busier thoroughfares have many distressing homeless and hungry people, including children, with hands outstretched, repetitively pleading to passers-by. She overtakes and greets Mary from the farm, who supplies their milk. The girl is labouring under her heavy yoke with a canister hanging on each side.

Cally has her books and pencils in a satchel and the Rector's teaching fee is in the pocket of her dress. At the Rectory, on the edge of the Glebeland, she is admitted by the maid, who takes her bonnet and gloves. welcomed by Mrs Onslow, as usual, she is led into the library, which has two walls lined with shelves of leather-bound volumes, most of them, as Mr Onslow has explained, a rich inheritance from his father, who was Dean of Worcester. The room smells pleasantly of the books, with an admixture of beeswax candles and tobacco. The Reed household could afford only tallow candles, which give off an unpleasant, heavy smell that has to be expelled each morning, by opening the doors and windows for a while, regardless of the weather. Cally hopes Mrs Onslow has her housemaid salvage and remould the unburnt stumps of the altar and votive candles from the church. After all, beeswax is costly and too good to waste.

She keeps on her pelisse, as this north-facing room is usually chilly, even in summer, unless the fire has been lit.

For formal occasions and going about the parish on his chestnut horse, the rector wears his shovel-hat, frock coat, waistcoat, breeches and gaiters, all in black. Today he has dispensed with the frock coat and his Geneva bands overlap the front of his waistcoat. This is as informal as he is ever seen. When younger, he had jet black hair, which prematurely turned grey and then white. His clean-shaven youthful face indicates that he is in his forties. He greets Cally with a half-bow and she makes a polite bob. Teacher and pupil sit at opposite ends of the table, set in the bay window, which has always served for their lessons. It has a pile of books in the middle, including the Bible and various collections of sermons. This is where the Rector works on his orders of service and sermons for much of the week. He is a busy man, because he preaches at several churches in this part of the Rochester diocese.

"Does the Rector start your lessons with a prayer?" Cally was once asked by an inquisitive school friend. Taken aback by such an idea, she assured her friend that, "There was no such time-wasting. After all, my father is paying for the Rector's tuition.

"And, No. At home, we do not say grace before meals, we are usually too hungry to delay eating, but we always thank the cook for our food and for her skill in preparing it. We are aware that people, not God, had to grow the food for us." Her friend was left aghast.

Cally has been working her way through Cicero's *Philippics* and her prep was to start a translation of speech number seven. In her discourse and letter-writing, she is trying to mirror Cicero's rhetoric, although not his grisly end that she has read about (head and hands chopped off for public display at the behest of Mark Anthony). She has tried hard to emulate Cicero's five canons of rhetoric in this preparation and is hopeful that her teacher notices this effort. She has even followed the final canon by learning her translation, in order to speak it from memory, having handed her teacher a written copy. Mr Onslow, without a word, registers the departure from their previous practise, but he has become used to this girl's surprises and idiosyncrasy. Best not to comment, because today he can do without time-consuming distractions. She notes her teacher's corrections and comments with pencilled marginal notes on her copy. Nowadays, at meetings of the Friends and the Hampden Club, Cally's frequent contributions are delivered from memory, unless she is quoting someone else. Because she has to memorise her speeches, they are succinct. Cally would admit that she finds concision a difficult process; verbosity comes more easily.

She is aware that since the Civil War, Southwark has maintained its tradition as a dissenting stronghold, as have the villagers around Kennington Common, and that the Rector sometimes feels besieged by Baptists, Quakers and other dissenters. She once heard an aged Quaker speculate that, but for Wesley's Methodism spreading during the 1790s among the lower classes of towns and countryside, especially here, in the country south of London, there might have been another revolution. Some of her political friends aver that, in light of the mounting unrest around the country, another revolution is on the way. This is not Cally's reading of the temper of the people and she feels she has more contact with ordinary people than the theoretical revolutionists who hold forth without leaving their houses, failing to test their theories against the reality of the streets. She is not happy that most of the lower orders are tractable and unpredictable, but that is the position and it is as well to be realistic, even if disappointed.

As is often the case, with her prep examined and further work set, the interview is elongated by Cally engaging poor Mr Onslow in discussion of the matters currently crowding her mind. Firstly, she tells him about the scandalous notice at the entrance to Vauxhall Gardens. Then come the matters arising from her latest reading. It was always her assumption that, provided her concerns had an ethical dimension, the Rector would have nothing more demanding of his time than consideration of her thoughts on the state of the world. Sometimes Master Onslow's wife, Elizabeth, rescues him from this earnest and prolix young woman by interrupting the exchange to remind him of an imminent appointment (real or illusory). For his part, Onslow is ever hopeful of breaking Cally's adherence to the Quakers and winning her whole-heartedly for The Church of England and its Book of Common Prayer. She is proving a tough nut to crack. If she graced his congregation more often than once or twice each year, she would detect in his sermons an occasional reference to a social problem she had brought to his attention. He finds the girl intellectually precocious, opinionated, aggravating, even confrontational, but a valuable source of stimulating conversation; not to mention his appreciation of those unique emerald eyes. Set in her light brown face; no better choice of complementary colours could have been created by nature, Mrs Onslow once suggested.

"It is from books you kindly lent me that I have learned about the preachings of John Lilburne and Gerrard Winstanley, who are among the inspirers of the Quakers, the Friends, as we call ourselves."

"That is my concern, Miss Reed (It was always Miss Reed, rather than Cally, when she has vexed him), "Your inspiration should be the holy word of God; not the secular rantings of these revolutionaries, who are as one with the Levellers and Diggers of the Commonwealth period and the later Jacobins"

"You do them and the Friends, a grave injustice, Sir. Their views are well founded. George Fox has handed down our principles, which I would call our Three Commandments writ on tablets of stone, if you would not accuse me of plagiarism of the Book of Exodus and blasphemy. George Fox did not lead us out of the desert to storm the walls of Jericho and we do not consider England to be a land of milk and honey, certainly not in its present state, but we have firm ethical principles, which have as good standing as those of the Church of England.

"Firstly, charity. Treat all human life as sacred, helping those who are less fortunate. Charity a religious obligation and a social duty. Thus our sensitiveness to oppression and injustice, our wish to overthrow class distinctions, our aims to end the horror of slavery, to give women their rightful place of equality with men, to rectify the disgraceful conditions in our prisons and ending the cruelty of excessive punishments for petty felonies."

"Secondly, sincerity of behaviour and honesty in all our dealings, eschewing false servilities, flattery, dissembling and crafty practice.

"Surely, these are all good things."

"Thirdly, in contradistinction to the example of the gross and repugnant Prince Regent, temperance, avoiding luxuries and excesses in food, drink, dress, self-pampering and recreations.

Noticing that the Rector winced at her scathing reference to Prince George, she could not resist repeating herself: "The Prince Regent's egregiously sinful self-indulgence sets an appalling example for the rest of the country. I am sure James Gilray's savage depictions of Prinny are only slight caricatures of the real man.

"Not content with importunately draining the Exchequer to build Carlton House for himself, he is having his ridiculous Indian-Chinese seaside pavilion enlarged at great expense, so that he can entertain Mrs Fitzherbert, his spare wife. How many wives is he allowed? Is he a secret Mohameden, do you think? How many wives will he be allowed when he becomes King and Supreme Governor of the Church?" The Rector was looking down at the table, hearing this *lèse magisté*, but not wishing to respond. Cally realised she was now being tormenting and decided to say no more about the king's prodigal son. She knows the Rector to be a loyal royalist. Presumably, Mr Onslow wished not to hear adverse comment on the Regent. On a previous occasion she had taxed Mr Onslow on the Prince's slipshod attitude to his marriage vows, taking at least one mistress, blessed by a secret marriage, rumour has it, if her friends are to be believed.

"Is there not so much in these Quaker codes I have detailed that is familiar from any reading of the scriptures?

"And, as she reached across the table, tapping on the Bible, "Therefore laudable in any Christian's eyes?

"If we are charged with being upholders of Levelling principles, it is a description we bear with pride. "So many of the country's problems, particularly poverty and ignorance, would be eliminated if Levellers had any influence. The aristocracy hate the ideas of the Levellers and Diggers, because they fear being dispossessed, brought down to the level of the rest of us".

At that, Cally challengingly spread her open hands and fixed the Rector's eyes, as if to say, "There: an unanswerable case".

"From the Friends' Meeting House library, I have read contemporaneous transcriptions, of some of the 1647 Putney debates, held in your sister church of St Mary.

"It is clear that, even before the Restoration of the Crown, soldiers of the New Model Army were expressing fears that the political and religious achievements of the revolution were being betrayed.

"It was Oliver Cromwell himself who undermined the entirely reasonable demand that every male adult not disqualified by having a criminal record or incapacitated by lack of reason should have the vote. Regrettably, he argued that only men of property, albeit a modest quantity, could have sufficient interest in the stability of the state, as if the stability of the present dispensation brings us heaven on earth.

"Utter nonsense." With a swipe of her hand, Cromwell's conservatism was swept aside and she continued her demolition of him. "The so-called Lord Protector was intent on protecting, first and foremost, the nobleman, the gentleman and the yeoman, preserving England from 'That levelling principle', which he condemned as – I quote – 'reducing all men to an equality.' Surely, the achievement of equality in society would imply no reduction. It would represent a major ethical elevation.

"Regrettably, even some Levellers, at the time, betrayed their principles by subscribing to the notion that the likes of day labourers, poor husbandmen, retailers and copy-holders who owned no land, should have no voice nor authority and no account should be taken of them, but to be ruled, because 'there is something of great value peculiar only to the genius of a gentleman'".

"The genius of a gentleman," Shaking her head in disbelief, Cally went on, "The king was executed by the will of the people, but among the people, the age of deference was not over. The tentacles of serfdom still held their grip. Fearful of the discontent and turmoil still evident here, in England, and aware of the revolutionary example across the channel, from the government and misguided mobs there went up the cry for servile, unquestioning loyalty, 'Church and King'.

"The extraordinary, almost mystical belief lingers on that property and political understanding are indissolubly joined. Forty shillings-worth of freehold is associated with superior intellect, or at least sufficient intellect to use the vote responsibly. By 'responsibly' is meant, in order to secure the status quo.

"It is not possession of a house or ground that gives a man morality, common sense and a conscience, but a modicum of learning, beginning with literacy. The property qualification is merely a ruse to restrict the franchise to the propertied, excluding the majority. That is the opposite of democracy. Cicero would not have tolerated it for one minute.

"Some soldiers of the New Model Army disagreed with Cromwell and Ireton and continued to demand universal suffrage. They were ostracised as 'ultra-Levellers'. I stand with the ultra-Levellers, or, as we have more recently been called, the red Levellers, or irredeemable Jacobins. Proudly we stand."

As Cally paused for breath, The Rector leapt to interrupt her: "You must be aware that the Puritans were never reconciled to the Restoration, but they did not represent the majority of the people. With the death of Cromwell came the end of 'sword government' and the restoration of monarchy and episcopacy. The Puritans – many of them erstwhile Ironsides of the New Model Army – along with the Quakers, were dismissed by most people as fanatics."

When speaking in conversation, even when seated, the Rector usually had the palms of his hands firmly pressed together at waist level; not quite as if in prayer, but giving the impression that he was being thoughtful, sincere and earnest in all that he said. It is a pose that Cally would dearly love to mimic as a joke, but she knew that would be in shockingly bad taste. Good manners, which are merely showing due consideration for others, have been drilled into her by her parents.

"You Quakers, together with the Anabaptists and Fifth Monarchists have consistently refused to conform to the doctrines and practices of the Church of England, making yourselves a threat of more mischief to this kingdom." Strong words, but not delivered in an unfriendly tone.

The Rector was now in his stride and, ignoring Cally's open-mouthed impatience to interrupt, he would not give way.

"Why! He cried, "When a proclamation was issued in 1661 prohibiting meetings of these sects, who continued to propagate seditious Leveller notions of turning the world upside down, in order to bring in their idea of economic equality, the defiant response was to convene even bigger gatherings.

"Small wonder that many Quakers landed in gaol. Of course, they then complained of being persecuted."

Cally emitted an impatient sigh and in her most emollient tone, she recounted: "Sir, over four thousand Quakers were put under lock and key.

"Here, in Southwark, the White Lion prison was filled to capacity. To add to their woes, the Friends were thrown among common felons, who stripped and robbed them, watched by the prison guards, who stood idly by, enjoying the spectacle and benefitting from the spoils.

"I was proud when I read that in Bristol, where the mayor required of the wives of prisoners sureties for desisting from meeting, he was met with an answer typical of the Quaker spirit, that he might as well think to hinder the sun from setting, or the tide from turning as persuading the Lord's people from meeting; 'for where two or three are gathered together in my name, there am I in the midst of them'; Matthew 18, verse 20." Cally was happy to show off her knowledge of the Bible from the dreadfully boring school scripture lessons.

Now, her face a picture of innocence, she resumed in her gentlest tone: "Sir, regarding Leveller ideas, do you see nothing in the present social order that cries out to be rectified?"

"You disparage the likes of John Lilburne and Gerrard Winstanley, who were merely honouring the noble ideals of the 1642 Revolution. William the Conqueror, having won a battle and ruthlessly put down all opposition, claimed to own the whole country. He stole it, using military force, from its rightful owners, the commoners of England. Lilburne and other former soldiers of the New Model Army, who became Quakers, sought to remain true to the aim of distributing the land to its former owners; not to the

Church, gentry and squires; no − to the bereft poor. Even as we speak, all over the country, enclosures are stealing the commons from the commoners".

Mr Onslow was by now a little exasperated: "We know, Miss Reed, that there are many injustices and iniquities, which is why we meet each Sabbath in worship and prayer and why we collect tithes for the relief of the poor."

"Sir, you malign Quakers for what you perceive as extremist views, but our principles are based on those of the early Christians, whose communities had no contrast between rich and poor, holding everything in common."

"And there is Thomas Paine's Declaration of the Rights Man. Let's remember that he was from a Quaker family. His seventeen Articles could not be bettered in any Christian sermonizing."

"As I have said, I consider myself a Leveller. Two hundred years ago, the Levellers were cruelly routed by Cromwell, but their principles live on.

"Edmund Burke has disdainfully written-off most people, asserting that 'the occupations of hair-dresser or tallow-chandler, to say nothing of even more servile employments, cannot be a matter of honour to any person. Such lowly men ought not to suffer oppression from the state, but the state suffers oppression, if such as they, either individually or collectively, are permitted to rule'.

"I presume that his argument would run that, as most people are wage-earners, who as servants of their masters, are deemed to have no will of their own, voting in polls according to their masters' instructions, allowing them the vote would negate the virtue of universal suffrage.

"Burke is wrong. Wage-earners, if allowed to organise collectively, are not tyros of the masters. The hard discipline of their daily work makes them conscious of their place in society and of the exploitation of their labour.

"For example, In 1649, soldiers of the New Model Army mutinied demanding their arrears of pay. Three of their leaders were shot on 16th May, in Burford Churchyard. Cornet Thomson, Corporal Perkins and Private Church. Christians all, they live on in the memory of every radical. When we win constitutional reform, their sacrifice will be vindicated."

At this point, Mrs Onslow brought welcome relief for the Rector, in the form of a reminder that his afternoon was promised to poor Mrs Saunders, who was expected not to out-live the day. Cally wished the Rector's wife had rather brought both of them some tea, because her walk and the Latin lesson, followed by all this talking, had left her parched.

On her way home, Cally sees a palfrey coming towards her, bearing the whey-faced, black-clad Master Roland Brown, one of the Rector's curates. "Good day, Miss Reed," as he salutes by lifting his hat, Cally half-turns and bows. Thankfully, he is not tempted to converse. She finds him sanctimonious and mundane; his conversation is limited to facile ecclesiastical parish gossip and his little world extends no further than the boundaries of the diocese. He has a chubby, wobbly face and, for such a young man, a more than ample frame. Cally might shrink from the rudeness of describing him as fat, but when talking of him, she once suggested he is well nourished.

There was the time when the curate visited St Mary's school, while Cally was teaching, leading the children in reciting in unison, from memory, Wordsworth's recently published poem composed on Westminster Bridge.

Mr Brown made a mildly derogatory remark about Wordsworth. This was a costly mistake, because the poet was one of Cally's favourites. She countered him with, "Mr Wordsworth's genius is a pure emanation of the spirit of the age. So says William Hazlitt and I agree with him."

The pitiable curate now damned himself forever by retorting that, "Both Wordsworth and Hazlitt are Whigs; what is worse, they are not even yellow; they are unashamed *red* Whigs. His chubby cheeks wobbled as he emphasised the disgrace of being *red*; in other words, having a reputation for radicalism. It was no surprise that the curate was discomfited by any mildly reformist idea, always flaunting his deference to the monarchy and episcopacy, anyone higher up the tree than himself.

With no wish for further words with this lickspittle silly man, Cally sharply turned her back on him and signalled to the children to repeat their lines. Making a lifting action with her hands, she bid them voice the words louder and louder. Coming to the final lines, "Dear God, the very houses seem asleep/And all that mighty heart is lying still," Cally claps her hands, while smiling and nodding encouragement that the class should applaud themselves, which they are always happy to do, with great energy.

She was pleased with their enunciation. By virtue of her tutoring, their glottal stops were largely replaced by consonants which exaggeratedly snapped like minor explosions. Their strangulated London vowels were now elongated and rounded, just like her father's Yorkshire dialect, which his daughter has inherited, diluted by her mother's gentler enunciation, a legacy of her time in a middle class household. The curate was too insular and self-absorbed to notice the children's performance. He simply left, without a word for his youngest parishioners, but he did give them a contemptuous glance over his shoulder. Cally, on the other hand, can be touched to tearfulness by children's good performance.

The curate's stilted outlook would not allow him to appreciate or applaud mere children, especially children as unkempt as some of these London urchins.

"*So much for Jesus's words, suffer little children to come unto me*", thought Cally, "*That curate is an insufferably cold fish.*"

Almost at home, she was shocked to come upon a sad sight that was almost an apparition. An ex-soldier beggar had wandered into her street, probably from nearby Newington Place. His ragged, filthy and faded coatee had no more red about it than his pallid face. His cheek-bones had the sharpness of hunger and his grimey begging hand was skeletal. Mindful of the suffering of the troops over the months leading up to

Waterloo, as described in the little on-the-spot reporting that had filtered through – no shelter from the driving rain, no sleep and little food – usually no pay and then the return to an unwelcoming England – Cally mustered a sixpence for him. His shocked gratitude was pitiful.

Dinner that afternoon is finished and the girls have cleared the dishes to the scullery. Now they reappear, dancing a somewhat restrained minuet around the table, humming Beethoven's Minuet in G. This being one of Cally's current practice pieces, it is fixed in their brains.

Cally flops on the chair next to her father, faces him almost nose to nose and asks in a voice exuding sympathy: "Oh, what doth ail thee, knight at arms, alone and palely loit'ring? Father, dear, you are not alone in the world. You are not the only sufferer. Man that is born of woman has but a short span, a life full of woe.

"Father, Your face never betrays a jolly mood, but today your look is so doleful, nay, funereal.

"I know your profession cannot bring you much good cheer, but would you be happier as a grave-digger, a man ever close to death and corpses? Perhaps you and I could form a partnership, you doing the hefting and me sitting beside the frightful pit, keening, as a paid mourner and condoler. You might even unearth another Yorick skull. And from the skull might creep a toad with a diamond in his mouth and then we should be rich."

Lavender is well used to his daughter's nonsense and dismisses it by shaking his head in mock despair. "Do you really think Yorick had two heads?"

"No. Of course not father. But if I plagiarise an old joke, I might suggest that one skull was that of Yorick as a boy and one was his head at the point of death." Lavender portrays more mock despair and kisses the hand of his daughter. Cally, this wonderful gift from his wife, is the pride and joy of his life.

He is a tall, lean man in mid-life. He has a mop of black hair and a matching well-groomed beard. As with many a Yorkshireman, it takes a lot to make him laugh. He is useless at small-talk and even bland niceties, such as "How are you?"or "Pleasant weather." Rarely pass his lips. When asked by one he meets, "How are you?" he is tempted to respond: "Still alive, as well you can observe for yourself, thinking *"What a fatuous greeting I have to suffer several times a day"*.

When in company, he rarely engages more than minimally in casual conversation, although he is happy to contribute to discussion on anything serious. He quickly loses patience with a person who has an abundance of words and scarcity of matter. He finds it easy to cut himself off from pointless chitchat, allowing his thoughts to wander elsewhere. Those who know him, simply accept that he is a quiet man, with little or nothing to say until he wishes to interject something he considers worthy of consideration. Even then, it is as if brevity is his watchword. He rarely says anything twice; not even for the sake of emphasis; so, unless you pay close attention, you may fail to understand his utterances. He always has something on his mind or a task to perform, which tends to make him intolerant of any interruption; hence his frequently affected deafness or his cursory response to a greeting or comment. He has two vices. He makes no secret of his liking for Whisky.

And nobody knows, although Ananya suspects, that in his most depressed moods, he resorts to a few drops of laudanum. Like King James 1st and 6th, he detests the foul habit of tobacco-smoking.

As a policeman, he is a good interrogator, posing a question and then remaining silent, his eyes challenging the other party to speak. At Bow Street he has a high reputation as a crime solver. He closely examines any crime scene, ferreting out clues. He has no secret methods, he emphasises; he merely detects whatever hints there are, pointing towards the felon. He has earned himself the title of Detective Reed, the only Runner of that rank in the force.

Some people have a face which relaxes into an automatic, inane half-smile, or an honest, kindly smile and that is the countenance by which they are remembered and recognised.

Reed's face, for those who know him well enough to read it, invariably betrays his changing moods, be it boredom, bemusement – rarely amusement – contempt or melancholy. It is usually the latter, which is no surprise, because for the greater part of his adult life, he has been a Bow Street officer, dealing with the unwashed, the arse-end of humanity. No more heartening has he found the rich, well-washed, scented, powdered and powerful, who can be just as venal or stupid as the poor and downtrodden and much more prone to hypocrisy. Such is Lavender's experience and summation of the frailty and hopelessness of the human race. Mankind is essentially selfish and wicked. Morality and civilisation, wherever found, are but a thin veneer. His permanent pessimism shows in his face. Some say he always looks miserable. The truth is that, if there is no immediate cause for mirth, his face will slip by default into the arrangement of facial muscles which betrays his typically lugubrious mien. Some would describe him as taciturn, but he is far from humourless; family and friends know he has a sharp wit. But he will not waste his wit on any he deems too witless to appreciate it. Thus even in a rare jolly mood, he is sparing with his words.

Cally, having borrowed Robert Burton's *Anatomy of Melancholy* from the Rector's library, has diagnosed her father's permanently doleful appearance and laconic responses as due to melancholia. When in a happy or contented mood, he merely looks wistful, but it is melancholy that wins. Those who know him well can interpret his face and have no need of his strictly rationed utterances. His bland face betrays no reaction even when he is hearing a confession or accusation of murder and so the interlocutor continues divulging information, in case the policeman has not been listening or has not understood. His placid face receives denunciations of adultery and counter-denunciations, without apparent judgement. Thus he is a recipient, absorber and accumulator of intelligence that the more typical gormless-looking, prolix, prating officer would never invite.

It is a rarity for Lavender to bring home his daily work, but his daughter is persuasive.

"Cally, I can't get it out of my mind. I have told you of a particular prisoner in Newgate, awaiting possible execution or transportation, although I am sure she is innocent. She may be hanged for theft. One would think she had stolen the Crown Jewels, but no, nothing more than a pineapple. If the case ever comes to court, for a semblance of a trial, and she is convicted and sentenced to death, the sentence might be commuted, but then she would probably spend the rest of her life as a work-horse, no more than a slave, in Botany Bay.

"There are scores of petty felonies for which the poor, weak and friendless may pay the ultimate price. For them our legal system has little justice. It exists principally to protect the property of the rich."

"Deborah Jones, a housemaid, is accused of theft from her master's house by a footman in the same household, whose evidence is flimsy or non-existent. Deborah is in such a state of despair that I fear for her sanity.

"I have tried to press her case with the Bow Street Bench, but they give me no hearing, because the aggrieved party is no less than Lord Sidmouth, Minister of the Home Department, renowned for having a heart of stone, if he has a heart at all."

"The poor woman could be left to rot in Newgate for years, such is the law's delay.

"In the hands of our judges and magistrates, the law proceeds as if the Magna Carta never existed. These eminences no doubt go to church of a Sunday, but their consciences show not a ha'p'orth of Christian sympathy, let alone respect for habeas corpus. Such is the insolence of office."

"Father, you have quoted Shakespeare twice in a single breath. That shows that your deep concern for this young woman's predicament has moved you to greater eloquence."

"Truly, that was a lot of words from one normally so laconic.

"I feel that I should visit this poor woman," said Cally. "She might welcome me as a friend. You are doing your best to help her, but I am in a better position to befriend her. Please will you use your position, at Bow Street, to see that I am allowed into her cell. It will help if you describe me as one of Mrs Fry's helpers.

"As you know, I am forewarned. I am familiar with the appalling conditions in Newgate, having been there many times with Mrs Fry".

So it is that Cally is allowed into the condemned cell. Although rebuilt as recently as 1783, Newgate retains all the antiquated features of the original medieval bastille and its formidable counterpart in Paris, which, following the Revolution of 1789, is now a pile of rubble, an appropriate symbol of the fate of the *ancien régime*. Just as the Paris Bastille was demolished in the heat of revolution, the original Newgate building was attacked and largely demolished by the London mob, in the turmoil of the Gordon riots of 1780.The hurried rebuilding of Newgate was in the French *architecture terrible* style, which deliberately made the structure look sinister and repulsive, the idea being that the mere sight of the prison would deter potential offenders.

The government was seriously underestimating the resilience of the hardened criminal and ignoring the fact that many inmates of its prisons were immured through no fault of their own, being innocents or petty felons fallen victim to an unjust and malevolent system.

The cell appears to be below ground, having no window. The walls are of grey granite, as is the arched ceiling and most of the floor, apart from a boarded area covered by a little straw. The cold stone is all damp with condensation. There is neither bed nor chair. In one corner there is a leather bucket of water for drinking and washing. For all other purposes there is a wooden pail. The familiar, but no less shocking stench which hit Cally at the main entrance, pervades the entire prison, the stink of unwashed bodies, slop buckets and open drains. There are few windows and those few are small, high in the walls and fixed closed. The cells and corridors are crepuscular and airless. Only in the exercise yard can there be sight of the sky or sunshine. There is overwhelming noise: Shrieking, hysterical cackling laughter, incessant, painful bronchitic coughing and hawking, desperate groaning, incoherent shouting, the jangling of chains and the clanging of iron gates. The inmates suffer this din, without let-up, throughout the day and night. One can never be sure whether the night-time scuffling is hungry prisoners stealing others' food, or scavenging rats.

A warder stands at the door and remains there all day and all night, as required for prisoners awaiting execution.

The only glimmer of relief in the gloom is a sulphurous yellow, coming through the bars of the cell door from the sputtering gas mantle in the corridor. As Cally's eyes adjust to the dismal light, she sees the prisoner, her ragged dress leaving her half naked, sitting on the wooden floor, back against the wall, with her arms clutching her legs to her chest, so that she is in as tight a ball as possible. How else to retain some bodily warmth in this dank chill? She is rocking to and fro, making a low whining sound, like a fretting animal. She does not register the entry of a visitor. Her eyes, set deep in her pallid face, surrounded by the blue-blackness of sleeplessness, are vacant. The woman is not yet twenty, but she could pass for fifty and more, so haggard and worn is she.

Cally kneels to one side of Deborah, holds her shoulders and draws her into an embrace. The shock of sudden gentle human contact immediately brings sobbing. As the two women rock back and forth, Cally can feel the prominent bones of a starveling. She can smell the body and sour breath of a poor soul denied the most basic hygiene. She knows that, as usual, she may collect a dose of fleas or lice during this visit. That is of no great matter. She is here to bring a little comfort to a victim of a cruel, vindictive and hypocritical, so-called Christian society. For fear of typhus, gaol fever, thought to come from fleas and lice, she will wash her clothes and herself as soon as she gets home.

The bigger killer in prisons, as in the outside world, is probably consumption, which is not caught during a short visit.

"Deborah, my name is Cally. My father is a Bow Street Runner."

Deborah tenses at that.

"No. Please have no fear. My father is a good man. He knows you are innocent and is doing all he can to have the court accept that. But do not yet have too much hope. You are already the victim of hard-heartedness. I am here to bring you some comfort. I am your friend.

"In this bundle there is a woollen frock, stockings and a cap. Nothing grand, because the guards would strip you and steal everything. At least these things will make you a little warmer.

"Also here, some rags and some soap. There is some bread and cheese and an apple.

"I can see those cruel leg-irons have made your ankles sore. I am going to smooth some ointment into your skin. Here, sniff the box; It smells of rose water. I will leave it with you.

"Here some coins to buy from the guards as you will. Perhaps to empty and refresh your bucket today.

"I will be back to visit you in a few days."

With that, Cally presses her lips to Deborah's sallow cheek, disregarding the prison grime, while stroking her lank hair. An arm is stretched out in speechless thanks as Cally moves to the door. She is sad for the prisoner, but glad to leave the musty sweet smell of bed-bugs, noticeable even above the all-pervading insanitary stench. *This place is hell on earth; unfit for animals, let alone humans. When it is torn down, England may be able to consider itself a mite more civilised.*

Coming to the guard in the corridor, Cally says, in her firmest tone: "Do not mistreat or steal from this prisoner. I will be back to inspect her condition. She is a prisoner of particular interest to Lavender Reed of the Bow Street Court police.

"Here, tuppence for a generous bundle of fresh straw for her floor.

"Officer Reed and I, like Mrs Elizabeth Fry, are only too well aware of the evils of this place and ever watchful."

It is a few months since Cally became interested in Newgate. Throughout her childhood she was aware of this forbidding monstrosity of a building which her father often had to visit, but until she heard Mrs Fry speaking of it at a Quaker meeting, she was unaware of the gruesome extent of the evil hidden within its walls. At the end of the meeting she introduced herself to Mrs Fry and asked if she might accompany her on one of her visits to the prison. Thinking the young woman's interest was probably frivolous and even ghoulish, she politely, but firmly declined. Cally was disappointed, but not defeated; she was aware that Newgate was a source of morbid entertainment for some Londoners, who paid the Governor for admission, in order to see, some with relish, the disgusting conditions visited upon the inmates and to witness the demented antics of the most disturbed prisoners.

She wrote a letter to Mrs Fry, introducing herself anew, Calista Reed, the daughter of a senior Bow Street Runner, concerned for the welfare of the prisoners, having questioned her father and having read the book by John Howard, *An Account Of The state Of The Houses of Correction*.

Appreciating that this was not a voyeur, but a woman of serious intentions, Elizabeth Fry invited Cally to accompany her on her next visit to Newgate and the nearby Giltspur street Compter.

Even on a summer's day, the Compter was cold. Its few prisoners, awaiting a magistrates' hearing and possible transfer to Newgate, men and women were thrown together in a single chamber. There was a little daylight from a high slit window.

The inmates were fed, or not, at the whim of the guards. The prisoners who survived winter cold and starvation were those with friends who could afford to bring them food and clothing and to bribe the guards not to snatch it for themselves, as what they considered to be their rightful 'garnish' to top-up their pitiful pay.

Being remanded to a compter was a temporary confinement lasting hours, days or weeks, whereas a Newgate sentence could entail years of ill-treatment and misery. England's prisons contained scores of inmates who were simply forgotten by the system and were left to rot in custody for years.

The 1789 revolution, just across the Channel, sent the British aristocracy running for cover. The wars against Napoleon had ravaged the economy and with Wellington's final victory came the discharge of as many as half a million workless soldiers and sailors on to the streets of London and the country byways. A harsh and heartless state had employed them in battle and now could dispense with the survivors.

Cally's father, in philosophical mood, has a bleak view of his profession. Most of the law concerns the protection of private property, and yet most people have next to no property, apart from the rags on their backs. He has to spend much of his time apprehending hungry people who have stolen for a crust, sometimes with violence. "Desperate hunger can break down stone walls", he was not the first to have said.

He is not a devout man, but he knows his Bible: "Empty stomachs do not honour the seventh of the Ten Commandments handed down by the Almighty: Thou shalt not steal." At dinner one afternoon, he was responding to his wife's question, "Why is everybody talking of the increasing lawlessness of London?"

"The great wen. That's what William Cobbett calls London, the disease carbuncle on the face of the nation." Having delivered this nugget, Cally took another potato. She always has a healthy appetite, belied by her slender build, a legacy of her diminutive mother.

Lavender finishes chewing, takes a sip of ale, sits back and pronounces: "With all due humility" – he winks at his listeners to indicate that his humility is not so very humble – "I recommend another list of commandments, created by humanity here on Earth and handed up to God, who is in need of our help in this world of sin.

"Firstly, eliminate poverty. It is an abomination, which is at the root of much crime, including murder. God may be grateful for helpful advice on how to go about putting an end to poverty.

"He should start by using His power to curb the pervasive sin of greed. Some, who consider themselves higher and mightier than the rest of us, are in a position to satisfy their greed, their intense desire for more than a fair ration of land, of money, of shelter, of food. And even of women.

"The wretched local dipper is not satisfying greed as he goes about his nefarious business of craftily fingering the bags and pockets of gentlefolk; no, he is merely in search of the means to sate his hunger for the day. Dipping is never going to make him a rich man.

"In sharp contrast, when the Prince Regent is feeling peckish, he bids a servant bring him meat. He downs more than enough fodder in a single day, into his voluminous, weskit-bursting bulge, to satisfy our dipper's shrunken belly for a week or more."

Cally giggles and mimes clapping her hands. She always appreciates her father's acerbic wit.

"As often promised in the scriptures," Lavender continues, "God's creation is plenteous, giving us a land of milk and honey. If that were so, there would be enough to go round and so every man and woman would receive their fair share. That would be nothing but justice, which the Almighty should dispense."

Lavender has not yet finished his sermon. With characteristic mordant humour, He quotes the prophet, Job, a man like himself, a melancholic: "Shall mortal man be more just than God? Shall a man be more pure than his Maker?"

"Well", says Lavender – again enlisting his audience in the conspiracy, by raising his eyebrows.

"Speaking as a Bow Street policeman, a guardian of the peace and an ensnarer of criminals, "Yes, God can look after heavenly justice and I can advise Him on what justice is needed on the streets of London.

"To quote the play-writer, George Farquhar: 'There is no scandal like rags, nor any crime so shameful as poverty'.

"Eliminate greed; bring fair shares for all, then poverty and its attendant crimes will subside."

"Will that leave you with nothing to do? Does it mean that you will join those without employment, Father?" Cally asks, affecting a face of wide-eyed innocence.

"Sadly, no, sweet child. The wickedness of men and women has no bounds. There will still be murders; perhaps more of them crimes of passion and fewer of them murderous robberies."

"There will still be secret duellers, lost, abducted and abandoned children, counterfeiters, coin-clippers, dropped purses and fraudulent bankers, suspicious fires and accidents on the roads. I fear that greed cannot be completely eliminated and there is no limit to human folly. The Runners will still be needed, dealing more, I suggest, with a better class of clientele, if – dare we hope? – the passage of time sees a reduction in the number of abject poor.

"There will always be the well-to-do who are willing to offer a reward to the Runners for solving a crime, including entrapment of a wayward husband or wife. There will always be cuckolds and cuckqueans, victims of marriage partners who are greedy for more than their marriage vows allow."

"There is a man who avers that the Prince Regent's London is Satan's stronghold, with 50,000 street-strutting harlots, 5,000 publicans and 10,000 thieves, as well as receivers of stolen goods, coiners and bludgeon-men, all out of a population of less than one million. This suggests there will always be plenty of business for the Runners.

"By the way, Cally, the gent of whom I speak, Patrick Colquhoun, a lawyer and diplomat, founder of the Thames River Police some fifty years after the Runners, considers that entitlement to vote should be denied to any man out of steady employment and without property, because, in that state, he must be maintaining himself by illicit means. That's the kind of sweeping indictment one expects of rich men and government ministers.

"Why he is so disparaging of publicans, I do not know. After all, this is a man who established a distillery in Scotland, making me one of his customers.

"Into the mix of miscreants he throws Strolling minstrels, gypsies, pedlars, the one million poor people in receipt of parish relief and all who co-habit without marriage. As you can see, he considers few to be on the side of the angels.

"Methinks," said Cally, "that he is unlikely to be a blithesome blighter, not a jocose gent."

"He has an equally lugubrious colleague, William Wilberforce," said Lavender, "who is founder of the overly solemn Society for the Suppression of Vice and Encouragement of Religion. It aims to influence chiefly the labouring poor, for whom it prescribes uncomplaining patience, conscientious labour, sobriety and frugality. There are no such ordinances for members of his own class, who are presumably all God's Chosen, being in no need of improvement."

"I understand," said Cally, jumping up and shaking her head and wagging an admonitory finger in emphasising each key word, "Be patient enough not to have your poverty or distress relieved until you reach heaven. And be grateful to the government and your employers for helping you to be sober and frugal by keeping you so poor that you cannot afford to be otherwise."

This little speech brightened her eyes, coloured her cheeks and had her hair and ear-rings shaking.

"Mr Colquhoun", said Lavender, "Has facts at his command, but little morality. It is men of means and property who rule this land, which is marred by the enormous divide between the very rich and the very poor".

"The swinish multitude", threw in Cally, "I remember reading that was Edmund Burke's contemptuous term for the majority of the people.

"Intended as a humiliating insult, 'swinish multitude' has provided rich meat (forgive the stretched pun) for the ironic titles of the satirical and radical pamphlets and papers I read: *Hog's Wash* and *Pig's Meat*, not to mention William Cobbett's *Twopenny Trash*.

"Talking of the milk of human kindness", continued Lavender, "I must not overlook the Reverend Thomas Malthus. He writes that human populations will inevitably grow faster than food supply and so starvation for some is unavoidable and valuably serves to bring supply and demand into appropriate balance. He argues that over-large families result from too early marriage and from parish relief being too generous. He considers the Corn Laws to be a good means of insuring us against over-consumption. This is another man of the cloth, with a heart of stone.

"Oddly", added Lavender, "The morality of the labouring poor was, in the last century, a serious concern of both an influential Puritan tendency among the Jacobins and the straight-laced Methodist dissenters. The Methodists wanted everything joyous to be prohibited, while the more zealous reformers considered that removal of the distraction of sports, amusements, excessive drink and any other licentiousness would give the lower orders greater earnestness and gravity, better facilitating the reception of the radicals' demanding Jacobin tenets.

"Face it, Cally, this puritanical tendency lingers on in the corresponding societies. Although you meet in coffee houses, ale houses and tap-rooms, you earnestly encourage literacy and thrift and thunder against inebriation."

"Father, dear, I know that po-faced Oliver Cromwell, no less, warned that the people were led into sin by too much frivolity and so theatres, dancing, spooning and even Christmas were proscribed. I think your information and philosophising have earned you a glass of port; if you dare such self-indulgence. Please allow me."

With the occasional nod or grunt of agreement, the family sat at the table, absorbing all this talking. At its completion, Mrs Reed indicated to the maid that the table may now be cleared. Cally stood up to help.

The maid must be introduced. Her name is Polly, Polly Forester, daughter of another Bow Street officer. Her mother died in childbirth when Polly was twelve years old. Her father turned to Lavender with a heart-felt plea: "My wife's death has left me with Polly and four younger children. I am concerned that Polly has already become a drudge, looking after me and her younger brothers and sisters. She has the right to some sort of childhood, a life of her own and some schooling. I have relatives who will take the babes. Would you offer Polly, who is coming up to thirteen, a position in your household? Mrs Reed would find her a hard worker as a housemaid."

Thus it was that Cally came to have a sisterly companion of much the same age. Although arriving as no more than a live-in maidservant, Polly quickly endeared herself to the family. Mrs Reed instructed her in her daily tasks, on which she worked alongside Cally, who continued to help about the house, just as before Polly came. Much to her delight, She was sent off to school with Cally and for extra tuition with the Rector.

At first, clearly still distressed by the loss of her mother and separation from her father and siblings, Polly went about her daily routine in subdued mood, timid and nervous. Mrs Reed already had a cook and a washerwoman and now two excellent live-in housemaids. On arrival, Polly's one frock was drab and well-worn. She immediately acquired smarter clothes that had once been Cally's. Cally was immediately attracted to this pretty companion and her feelings were shyly reciprocated. Polly was as pale as Cally was dark

Although expecting to be no more than a servant in this household, Polly found herself doted on by the parents and closer to Cally than she had ever been to anyone.

The girls shared a bedroom at the top of the house, which could be an ice-box in winter, and so they soon came to cuddle for warmth in the same bed, just as girls and women and young brothers and sisters did all over England. There is nothing as warming as another body. The girls were delighted in their intimacy.

Most of her friends at school were from large families and Cally had long held a secret wish for a brother or sister. Then suddenly her wish is fulfilled.

At this time, girls of Cally's social level, neither genteel, nor so lowly, are generally confined to the home, engaged in ladylike pursuits, including music, sewing, cross-stitch and occasional good works outside the home, as well as undertaking domestic tasks of the gentler type, if there are not servants enough.

From her early years, Cally made it clear that she would conform to no standard pattern. Needlework she always abhorred. The needlewoman of the household was Mrs Reed, who kept her girls, now numbering two, in the latest styles, favouring Polly no less than Cally. At this time, many young women felt no need to wear restrictive stays. The high-waisted skirt and short

Spencer jacket were *de rigeur*, as well as variable *décolletage* for those who dared. The slender Reed girls' embonpoint was, as yet, too unimpressive for display.

One day, in Vauxhall Pleasure Gardens, near their home, Cally and Polly dismounted and sat on a bench in the sunshine. They watched the promenaders and passing phaetons and broughams, commenting to one another on the ladies' fashions, on the towering powdered and decorated wigs still favoured by some ladies of substance and on the many large crazy hats. They were aware of courtesans and when they saw an older man, obviously mismatched in age with a pampered younger woman, they speculated on her likely status as a spare wife. They soon gave up on this exercise, agreeing that it made them rather bitchy.

"You re looking sad today", said Cally; quite the diagnostician, following her studies in Robert Burton's book.

There was a silence in which Cally sensed that Polly was mustering her thoughts. So, by way of encouragement, she took her hand.

"I am very happy living with you, but I miss my family," Said Polly, her eyes beginning to brim.

Cally kissed away the tears, while stroking Polly's hair and neck and then, perhaps for the first time, kissed her on the mouth. With her lips still moist and salty, that seemed excitingly intimate. It marked their growing affection."Please, Polly, not just a member of the family, I love you and want to consider you my sister. "Her kiss was returned.

"Polly, precious, you have another family now, an extra family, who love you dearly, but you must not go without seeing your first family. You must visit them often."

Slight and short, Polly is the smallest in the class at school, although not the youngest. She gives the impression of being timid, although her nature is resilient. Her movements tend to be twitchy and she scuttles hither and thither, as if always on urgent business. Noticing this, and in light of her size, she acquired the nickname. Mouse, which soon became the endearment, Sugar-Mouse, reflecting the children's favourite sweetmeat.

It was from the circulating library that Cally borrowed *Pride and Prejudice*, written anonymously by 'a lady'. It was passed on to Polly and then to Mother and Father. Now devoted readers of the Lady, they all read more books by her as they appeared. Cally is grateful that her mother is nothing like the fictional Mrs Bennet created by the Lady, being under no pressure to seek "a good match". On the contrary, Mrs Reed wants her daughter to continue being the free spirit that has enlivened and entertained the household since she first could walk and talk.

She helps about the house and works at her studies of Latin, Greek, algebra and Euclid. Since she was little, she has accompanied her mother on her visits to the poor of the parish, taking food, clothing, or medicine. Her family is not rich, but has enough to be able to share. Thus she knew what was expected of her when, with Quaker Friends, she visited the local Poor

House. Since Polly arrived on the scene, it is the two Reed girls, as they are known, who together engage in charitable activities. When they walk out, they are invariably arm-in-arm or hand-in-hand. For their good works and occasional surprises in behaviour and dress, they are well-known about the parish. Cally wears her heart on her sleeve and is no retiring violet. Her conversation with acquaintances on the street is always energetic and would-be eavesdroppers have no difficulty in picking up the gist of her radical views. Given opportunity, she will express her opinion on any subject under the sun. There are now two Reed girls who ride their horses astride, rather than side-saddle, bringing elderly ladies close to swooning. Mrs Reed enjoys dressing the girls *à la mode* and they seem always to add a certain piquancy all their own. The times are changing. The gathered silhouette of the Empire line is gradually being replaced by fuller skirts, supported by voluminous petticoats for those who can afford them. The Reed girls are no longer the only ones to ride astride, with their skirts bundled around each leg and the stirrup straps. This mode of riding is now commonplace among younger women. The side-saddle is now for high-born ladies, who prize appearance and out-dated propriety over comfort and safety.

Cally is conscience-stricken, appreciating that her new, obvious attachment to Polly must make Ellie feel rejected after their close friendship of five or six years. She explained this predicament to Polly, not wanting there to be any secrets or reservations between them.

Polly fully understood that, as the newcomer to Cally's family and to the school, she could be looked upon as the intruder, the spoiler. However, she felt happy and secure enough in her new situation to be able to do the right thing. "Cally, please let us embrace Ellie as the friend of both of us. She is pretty, cheerful and kindly and so I will love to have her as a new friend." This close-knit trio goes on to benignly dominate the academic, creative and social life of the school.

When she discovered the 18th century writings of Mary Astell, Cally found revealed another field of injustice to concern her. "I have often wondered," said she to a circle of girls in her class, sitting at their desks after lessons had finished, "Why it was always men who possessed all the places of power, trust and profit, making laws and occupying the magistracy as a male preserve.

"Well, Mary Astell correctly points out that 'It is men who have all the swords and all the blunderbusses, which gives them the title to all they are pleased to claim'. Who shall be brave enough to contend with them?"

"We shall. We are the ones to do so. The girls were used to Cally's challenging rhetoric and knew how to respond. Agree or disagree, but do it with conviction and be prepared to stand your ground. It was Polly who now took up the baton. "In every generation, fathers and their sons have taught and practised superiority over the physically weaker sex and consequently it has been handed down through the centuries that women are by nature inferior. Patriarchy is not inevitable.

There have been successful matriarchal societies. I learned that in my lessons about ancient Greece.

"And we should deny our being physically weaker," asserted Ellie, "It is women who have the courage and strength to give birth to babies, suffering all that pain. I heard my mother screaming in agony when she had our youngest. And lots of women die in childbearing.

"Who is to say that the Amazon warriors were mythological, rather than real?" continued Ellie, "They beat the men at archery and sword-fighting."

"I am convinced that much of the problem lies with education, or lack of it".

Cally is retaining her audience as she raises her volume and vehemence.

"Mary Astell points out that boys in a family have much time and pains, care and cost bestowed on their education, whereas their sisters have little or none.

"It undeniably follows that men's understandings are often superior to women's. It is not nature, but lack of learning that leaves women the subordinate sex in the affairs of the State.

"I will not have our sex so demeaned. We girls are fortunate in attending school and we know that we are just as clever in lessons as any of the boys. We must commit ourselves to acquiring knowledge and understanding, so that we are self-supporting and assertive and can stand up to any man.

"We are the lucky ones. Our parents are sending us to school. We must each make the most of this education and ensure that, during our lives, we make our mark on sit calmly and join the contemplative mood. They have learned that, although there are Friends with prominent positions in society, as a whole they are far from rich and often ostracised by their neighbours, who take exception to their sombre dress, their ignoring of the Sabbath, their pacifism and teetotalism. Some Anglicans were perturbed that Quakers took their belief in universal equality to the extreme of demanding an end to slavery and even for men and women to have equal rights before the law.

Cally decided to ask the Rector at a future lesson, "Why are we Quakers so vilified?"

Lavender and Ananya Reed are not devout, but they attend services at the parish church of St Mary, Newington Butts, at Christmas and Easter, seldom accompanied by their even less devout daughters. The truth is that Lavender wants his wife to be fully accepted in the neighbourhood and church attendance is a way of achieving that, because the St Mary's congregation is the biggest and most influential body of people in Newington. Although she normally wears English clothes and speaks perfect English, Ananya has brown skin, which marks her as foreign and unusual. Black and brown people are found in many parts of England, usually working as menials, but few in this part of London.

There have been whispers of consternation in the congregation that Cally and Polly are not compelled to attend church. Lavender would have reminded any complainants that Sabbath attendance is no longer required by law and, although his girls are not part of the Sabbath congregation, they attend Quaker meetings and furthermore, he would insist, no child is born a Christian, even if born to Christian parents. The girls were born with no religion, just as they were born unable to walk and talk. They will find their own way to belief, or not, as the case may be.

At school the girls learned reading and writing, arithmetic, drawing and geography. Scripture lessons entailed laboriously reading aloud the Bible from cover to cover and then starting again. Polly attended needlework lessons, but Cally had created such a rumpus of objection to the subject that the teacher allowed her to sit on her own, reading instead of sewing. For extra fees, the girls had lessons in dancing and singing, which they greatly enjoyed. Cally had received piano lessons since she was quite little.

The Reed parents are stalwarts of the St Mary's Vestry meetings and sponsors of the Workhouse, which is run by the Vestry.

A rather forbidding building, the St Mary's Workhouse has a varying number of inmates, sometimes up to 200 men, women, babes and 'scholars', the latter meaning children of school age.

Several parishioners are regular workhouse visitors, including the whole Reed family. They hand out little extras and such comforts as second-hand clothes and blankets. They also keep a judicious eye on the Poor Relief overseers, who are sometimes more parsimonious than necessary. The inmates have to work hard for their food and shelter, making oakam, sewing burlap sacks, or canvas sails. It is hard, repetitive work, hard on the hands and the dim light of the workhouse strains the eyes.

Teasing out the strands of old jute rope, prior to oiling it, so that it could be used as oakam for caulking between the timbers and decking of wooden ships, made the finger-tips raw and bloodied.

"Father", said Cally, "As you know, I have met poor Deborah Jones in Newgate. Please tell me more about the case. For example, who are the other servants in Lord Sidmouth's household?"

"There is the butler, called Cranston, an imperious fellow, who rules the Servants' Hall with a rod of iron. He has an under-butler, who is spineless and cowed, but uses Cranston's reflected glory to bully the other servants, who all despise him. There are footmen and housemaids. I suppose there is a coachman and groom. Rather than cooks, the house has a French chef, because his lordship cossets his ample belly with haute cuisine."

"Which servant would you judge is closest to Lord Sidmouth?" asked Cally.

"Two of them," suggested Lavender. "Definitely the chef, who has to consult the gormandiser daily on his lordship's culinary fancies and, of course, the valet, who has to keep the conceited senior minister immaculately suited."

"You told me, Father, that Deborah's accuser is a footman. Why is he putting her in such mortal danger? What has he against her?"

"You have seen her. After a few months in Newgate, the poor woman is a ghost, a shadow of her former self.

But she entered the prison still a girl and an averagely comely one at that.

"It takes not much imagination to see a possible explanation for a young woman falling foul of a malevolent, vengeful man in the same household."

"Tell me, Father, what precisely is the accusation against Deborah?"

It is not a short story. Stop me if I bore you"

"Your crime stories are never boring, father. One day you must write them in a book. Or I shall be your amanuensis and become a famous author."

"Well, Lord Sidmouth has a country seat in Devon, at a place called Upottery. There he has glasshouses, taking advantage of the mildness of the weather in that country. As you know, two centuries ago, there was tulip-mania. people with more money than sense were paying bagfuls of sovereigns for new varieties of tulips. Like many of the landed gentry, who boast a hot-house, a glasshouse kept comfortably warm all year long, his gardeners have mastered the art of raising exotic fruit and, in particular, pineapples. That is this century's mania. There is not an aristocrat in the land who does not covet a pineapple to grace the epergne at the centre of his dining table. The nearest I have been to a pineapple is a picture of one in last year's Royal Academy Summer Exhibition. You saw it, too, because you and Polly came with me, showing off your latest frocks. The name notwithstanding, it looks nothing like an apple and it does not come from a pine tree. It stands about a foot high. They say it is worth its weight in gold. I don't know, but I am sure it would be worth stealing, especially if the thief could then sell it. The few who have tasted it, say it is the fruit of heaven. It comes expensive.

"Lord Sidmouth has a pineapple dispatched express from his estate most weeks when the fruit is in season.

"It was 30th May, that he invited many of the Quality to dinner, marking his birthday.

"The gathering was at his London house in Grosvenor Square. You can imagine his consternation on entering the dining salon, before his guests arrived, to find no pineapple; starched linen, crockery, glassware and silverware galore, but not as much as a smell, of Ananas, the queen of the crop. The epergne was heavy with an abundance of grapes, apricots and cherries, a veritable cornucopia but lacking its crowning glory.

"Close to apoplexy, as he ever is, without discrimination between the smallest and largest of matters, his lordship demanded of his servants an explanation. 'Twould be better for them that they offer up a pineapple, but at least he must have an explanation for its absence.

"Affairs of state, for the present are set aside. The Home Office, the Foreign Office, the Treasury, the Commons, the Lords Temporal and the Lords Spiritual, all have their place under the Firmament, but today we are pinioning whomsoever is responsible for the truancy of the pineapple. There has been no such crisis since Boney threatened imminent invasion.

"His Lordship first taxed the butler, who carpeted the under-butler, who in turn gave the footmen a blistering. By now, the entire household was aquiver.

With all eyes on him, the second footman, Huggins, stumbled forth with the explanation that housemaid Jones was today responsible for collecting the fruit brought up from the estate. The trembling Jones was called forth."

"Yes, that morning, after cleaning the fire-grates, she walked to La Belle Sauvage Inn at Ludgate Hill, where the Exeter stagecoach made its weekly halt. There were apricots and grapes, which she brought to the house, but no pineapple. The second footman whispered in the ear of the first footman, who passed on the message to the Under-Butler, who pointed a condemnatory finger at Jones, with the verdict: "She must've stole it. She's a pincher.""

"All present heard this terrible conclusion. Nevertheless, it was repeated to his Lordship. Momentarily, Lord Sidmouth was speechless, but then the whole of Grosvenor Square must have heard his thunderous order: "Call the constables.""

Poor Deborah Jones was hurled into Giltspur Street Compter within the hour. In this case there was no question of the law's delay. Indeed, there was no legal process, merely alleged crime and immediate punishment. Being the victim of larceny, the Home Secretary had circumvented due process. He considered it to be his right to do this; he has suffered grievously and he has his hands on the guilty party.

"As I have told you," said Lavender, "Laws grind the poor and it is rich men who lay down the laws."

Cally is incensed. "But, Father, Deborah Jones has not even been questioned. The constables have lamely obeyed the unjust instructions of a rich and powerful man.

"Tell me, Where did you come into this sorry story?"

"I received a message to report to Bow Street urgently. The Home Secretary had suffered larceny – nay, as the stolen item was valued at much more than a shilling – *grand* larceny, a capital offence, and he had himself solved the crime, with the culprit now behind bars. I was bidden to collect the fearsome prisoner and bring him in irons from the Compter to the Court. I was surprised to discover the dangerous felon was a timorous young woman.

"Irons were not necessary. My hand on her arm was restraint enough as we walked the small distance to the Court. Along the way, I questioned her and ascertained her short story as already recounted to you. At the Inn on Ludgate Hill, she had collected a wooden crate containing the fruit that she carried to the house and handed to the chef. Both were surprised to find no pineapple.

"The courtroom was in its usual manic state of confusion and the magistrates were clearly bound up with bellicose petitioners and obfuscating lawyers for hours to come and so I sent a junior Runner to bring second footman, Bevis Huggins, to the Court.

"Before two magistrates (one of them asleep for the duration), I first questioned Deborah Jones, whose well-trodden story you have heard.

"Huggins then confirmed his name, address and occupation. The only impressive aspect of this witness was his footman's elaborate livery. He had difficulty stringing a sentence, could not offer his place of work without my prompting and his eyes were certainly not the only shifty thing about him.

"I addressed him thus: 'Huggins, you accused Jones of the theft of a pineapple and with sufficient fervour to convince no less a legal authority than Lord Sidmouth. What, precisely, is your evidence against Jones?'

"This was too much for him.

"'Have you ever had reason to suspect Jones of stealing before this incident?'

Silence.

"When Jones arrived at the house, after meeting the Exeter stagecoach, she handed the crate of fruit to the chef. There was no pineapple. If she stole it, where was it?

"Huggins was again severely challenged, but he managed to blurt out:'She fenced the booty along the way from Ludgate Hill, or it was hidden under her clothes.'

"'A pineapple is a large, heavy fruit, I said, 'With its foliage, it is at least a foot long. It would fit in no pocket. How could Jones hide it in her clothes?'"

"Huggins' brain was labouring under the strain. Eventually he managed a mental leap: 'She held it against her belly, under her apron. It's no surprise if sluts like her are again with child.

Or she fenced it to a fruit-seller in Covent Garden Square'"

"I could see that the one wakeful magistrate had now succumbed to his lunchtime beverage and so we had a totally comatose Bench about to pronounce a verdict on a capital offence. The poor woman could be hanged on the word of a worthless reprobate. I stepped up to the Bench and did my best to wake them from their post-prandial torpor: 'Your Honours, I shouted above the general din,'The accused has a previously unblemished record and now faces a capital charge. Surely, a trial before her peers is warranted.'

"The duo of bewigged dolts mumbled at each other in a huddle, until one of them emerged with an almost coherent pronouncement: 'Pending trial, to Newgate with her.'he mustered just enough energy to wave his hand, dismissing us."

"That, my dear Cally, illustrates the state of the law in this benighted country after seven hundred years of practising the legacies of King Henry I and the Magna Carta."

As she listened to her father, Cally was breathing heavily, as if restraining some irresistible force.

At last, she was able to burst forth:" Firstly, can we be certain that a pineapple was sent from Devon? Secondly, was the wooden crate secure, or could any thieving hand snatch the pineapple along the way? Thirdly, How many stage stations are there between Devon and London? At any of them there could be thievery. Four, How many were overnight stops? That is when any luggage would be most vulnerable. How was the crate secured overnight?

"Finally, footpads are common on our roads. Was this stagecoach robbed along the way? There is much here to be investigated before Deborah Jones could be fairly tried, let alone condemned.

"It is your case, Father, so why have you not investigated these questions?

"If I were in charge of Bow Street, there is much that would be done differently. As far as the Bench is concerned, Lord Sidmouth has solved the crime and so I have been assigned to other cases."

The following day, Cally was champing at the bit when her father arrived home for his dinner.

"Father, I will go to the Belle Sauvage Inn and find the coachman who drove the Exeter coach into London on the last day of May. I fear that I may have to make more than one visit before I find him, but I am determined. It is a long way, so may I ride Alexia?"

"Of course, and I will ride with you. I cannot think of a more formidable interlocutor than you. So, unless he has disappeared from the face of the earth, he will suffer a pitiable ordeal when you confront him."

"Cally, my dear, not sparing your blushes, I tell you that you are a beautiful woman and well able to twist any man around your little finger. if you, in large-eyed innocence, go asking questions, they may try to fool you – a ruse you would detect – or they may give some honest information, thinking that you are powerless to do them any harm.

"Whereas, If I, a Bow Street Runner, were to initiate this investigation, there is a danger that any felons would close up like clams, especially if this theft is part of a regular scheme of larceny afflicting this stage coach service, which I suspect could be the case.

"But you, my clever girl, need not resort to flirtatiousness, because your open, honest, pretty face will be sufficient to draw out truths, while you are astute enough not be fooled by specious stories, blatant lies and obfuscatory nonsense."

Unlike his loquacious daughter, Lavender is a man of few words. He admits to being lugubrious, but claims he has ample excuse for this condition. As a Bow Street officer for many years, dealing with the unwashed of the lower depths, he has a jaundiced view of humanity. Morality and civilisation are but a thin veneer; mankind is essentially venal, frail and stupid. The man is not without sympathy for the poor and downtrodden, whose sins are often understandable in light of the conditions they have to bear. London has thousands of people who, through poverty and ignorance are cruel, neglectful of their children, drunken and dishonest. The rich, well-washed, scented and powerful can be just as venal as the poor and much more hypocritical. His despondency at the doomed destiny of humanity shows in his face, which invariably betrays his mood, be it boredom, bemusement, contempt, or simply melancholy.

He is wearied to death if, in company, he has to endure small talk, the drifting hither and thither of shallow minds, endlessly entertaining themselves with trivialities and the vacuity of petty scandal. He finds it easy to disengage from such mindless meandering, allowing his thoughts to wander. He may suddenly re-enter such conversation if he detects the hint of a more serious turn, but even then, brevity invariably marks his contributions. He never repeats or paraphrases himself and so his words may be wasted on those not paying close attention.

Cally has diagnosed her father's condition as melancholia. Her prescription for his cure is to provide him with the medicine of her distractive jollity, which she dispenses liberally.

Travelling about London in the early years of the 19th century was no easy matter. Some people took to the Thames, hiring a boatman and trusting his skill and knowledge of the river's hazards. The rich would own a four-in-hand, or would hire one, for as little as a pound a day, from any of the numerous livery stables distributed around the City. Most people travelled on horse-back, or their own two feet.

Men usually lived at their place of work – sleeping under their workbench, if necessary – or close enough to make the daily journey on foot.

Even people who lived within a day's journey of London, in the counties of Essex, Kent and Surrey, may never have visited the City, unless as an excursion of two or three days. Taking a mail coach from London to the coast, for example, would be a whole day's journey and cost as much as £4 for an inside seat.

Lavender Reed had a horse provided by Bow Street Court and Alexia, a horse of his own, both stabled next to the family home in Kennington. Together with two neighbouring families, they employed a stable lad.

Cally felt that Alexia carried her exceedingly well. She was teaching Polly to ride, with the horse on a leading rein, circling the paddock to the rear of the houses in their street.

Until something even more disturbing arose, it was the talk of the street that Calista Reed did not use a side-saddle, but wore a split skirt and straddled her horse like a boy. "Before long you will see her in breeches – and yet her father's a Bow Street Runner. You would expect him to discipline the girl."

The gossips were newly aghast when both Reed girls were seen in their baggy Zouave breeches, drawn in at the waist and below the knee. Mrs Reed's needle had been busy, following a picture of French infantrymen in a broadsheet, shown her by Cally.

Father, not in his uniform, rode his police horse and Cally was mounted on Alexia, a sweet-tempered animal she loved dearly, wearing her Soave breeches and her long riding habit. They made for Southwark, with the river on their left. The further eastward they rode, the more they were aware of the acrid stink of smoke from Newcastle sea-coal drifting from the hundreds of chimneys in the City and its environs. That smell was soon overtaken by the sickening stench from the river, which from time to time, forced Cally to hold her handkerchief over her nose and mouth. Father had warned her that in this warm weather, the river would stink even more than usual. They crossed the Thames at London Bridge, having passed the site of the new granite bridge, that will commemorate Waterloo. Making their way to St Paul's Cathedral and on to

Ludgate Hill, this was all familiar territory for Lavender. Cally, on the other hand, realised she was really just a rustic country girl. Coming from Kennington, with its gardens and surviving fields, she was overwhelmed by the density of the buildings, the crowds of people, the chaotic clamour, the rubbish and the foul open drains on the streets and the unfamiliar smell and sound of too many unwashed people living in closely packed decaying rookeries. There was the constant overlay of coal smoke, made even worse in places where there had been a chimney fire. She felt more than a little unsafe in this turbulent place and very glad that she had not attempted the journey on her own. On her father's recommendation, she wore her large-brimmed bonnet, tied under her chin, so that her face was largely hidden. He explained that coarse and ignorant people remark anybody looking the least out of the ordinary and let loose foul insults. A brown young woman, dressed like a boy, would be bound to attract attention.

She kept Alexia close behind her father's horse as he weaved among the chaos of coaches, wagons, sedan chairs, dog-carts, walkers and even sheep, pigs and cattle on their way to the butchers for slaughter. Almost every pedestrian seemed to be carrying a heavy load. There were women with baskets on their heads, children pushing wheelbarrows. Pedlars loaded with their wares, such as pots and pans; laden sellers of food and drink. Above the clatter of horses' hooves and the rumble of iron-rimmed wheels on the cobbles, she could hear a hurdy-gurdy player and the oaths of coachmen battling to get the better of one another in the melee. Church bells seemed to be ringing incessantly. There were crossing-sweepers, who earned the occasional pittance by clearing a path through the horse-droppings and general filth for ladies and their trailing skirts. They passed sellers of pamphlets and broadsheets and a balladeer, outside a taproom, who had attracted an uproariously responsive audience. Cally caught enough of his voice to hear lewd references to the Prince. A butcher advertised his shop by having a dripping pig's head hanging over his door. Riding clear of the narrow pavements, they were probably safe from slops ejected from upstairs windows. They rode a little of Fleet Street and, in the vicinity of the Cathedral there were scores of black-clad clerics, looking like so many great ravens.

There were sellers of pies, baked potatoes and Whitstable oysters, all shouting their wares. There and then, Cally made a vow never to touch an oyster. She called up from memory the geography of the Thames and its estuary. This ordure-laden river flowed past Whitstable on its way to the North Sea. This was the putrid water on which the oysters fed. Cally's concern for hygiene and disease was much more than average for that time. Considering that oysters were so cheap and eaten in such vast quantity, it was amazing that so little disease resulted from them.

The Belle Sauvage Inn was easy to find by its massive coloured sign and the dense clutter of coaches lined up, awaiting entry, or simply refreshing the horses with fodder and water. Lavender and Cally rode through the arched entrance, into the courtyard, which was surrounded by doors, windows and balconies. There was a strong smell of horses and ale. For a few pence, their mounts were handed over to a groom. Beside a door, there was a sign announcing: 'London, Reading, Swindon, Bath, Bristol, Exeter, Cornwall'. The door led into a sordid little office, with a man sleeping and snoring in a chair beside a glowing coal fire. The weather was mild that day and so the overheated room would have made Cally drowsy, had she not important business in hand. Lavender had to kick the man's boots twice before he stirred. Coughing and spluttering, he woke enough for Cally to address him: "My good sir, I see from the sign at your door that, you have knowledge of the express to and from Exeter."

"Yes, my Lady, you wish to travel today. With the passengers gathered, the coach leaves here at three this afternoon."

"No, not today, but I wish to speak with the driver of the Exeter coach that arrived here on the last day of May."

"Oh, dear, there are so many coaches and coachmen."

"Would a shilling help your memory, sir? Cally held out her hand with the coin and his grubby fingers took it.

"Let me see." He rifled through a bundle of dog-eared papers.

"That could be Amos Pentlow."

He held out his hand and, for another sixpenny piece, he yielded:

"If he be here to drive today's coach, thou'll find him in the chop-house over the corner."

Cally followed his finger to the corner of the Courtyard, following the smell of cooking mutton.

A legacy of her mother's Hinduism is not eating meat and so she finds the scent of roasting meat to be both intense and sickening.

In a room made dim by the haze of burnt fat and tobacco smoke, Cally can see a few men lounging, eating, drinking, smoking or drowsing.

She breathes deep, despite the acrid air, in preparation for a bellow. "Is Amos Pentlow here?"

One of the somnolent carcasses stirs: "Is it the Exeter coach you're wanting? Here's your man, milady."

The man was heavy with the weight of fat from too much sitting on the driver's seat and too little exercise. His eyes were leaky and he had the enlarged red snout of a drinker. His Inverness greatcoat, in which he undoubtedly slept, bore the traces of his last several meals. He was the unfortunate owner of a large mouth, with lips that reminded Cally of a well-worn leather purse, upper and lower working independently, sometimes revealing a single central blackened tooth.

"Another day for travelling, sir," says Cally, "But my immediate question is: were you the driver of the Exeter coach arrived here on the last day of May?"

"I maybe was, I maybe weren't." Cally held out a shilling, but her father intervened, closing her palm.

"Now, listen to me, Pentlow, I have been a passenger on your coach. On more than one journey, you have been held up by a footpad, who robbed the passengers. Either you are a most unlucky driver, or you stopped by arrangement with your criminal friend." Lavender had made up this story on the spur of the moment, but the coachman was in no position to gainsay him.

"No doubt, you took a share of the spoils. Now, if you do not wish me to report this to the Bow Street Court, you will answer my wife's questions without further prevarication. You could be locked up for a long time, transported or hanged. Bear that in mind."

"Listen to me carefully, your life could depend on this" said Cally, fixing his eyes and showing just a hint of an enticing smile. He visibly melted a little. "Are you listening?" He nodded obediently. "Regular cargo on the Exeter coach, is a crate of fruit from Lord Sidmouth's estate. There was such a crate on the last day of May. What happened to it? Some of its contents went missing. You are the most likely thief" As she said those last few words, "You are the most likely thief," her index finger ominously moved across her throat." That's something more for the Bow Street police."

"I'll tell you what I know, milady," said Pentlow, now eager to off-load any blame.

"Not for t'first time, among the passengers was William Addington, His Lordship's son. He was again on his way back to Westminster School. He spent the night at Bath with a doxy, who travels reg'lar from

Exeter to Bristol, where she serves sailors. In the morning she was screaming at him for his lack of gold to give her and so he quieted her by grabbing a pineapple from a crate in the luggage basket and pressing it on her. She was well satisfied with that."

Stepping outside, leaving the thick smelly fug behind, The frosty fresh air caught Cally's throat and left her coughing.

"Cally, you have been brilliant, magical. I only hope you do not decide to make deception your profession, by becoming an actor. Your mother would be distressed by that. But do you feel able to play this game a little further?"

"If it will help Deborah, yes, of course."

Early the following day, at the porter's lodge of Westminster School, Lavender, now in uniform, asked to see Mr William Addington. The young man arrived at the Lodge, looking a little mystified, but otherwise very much the man-about-town. His hair was short, but he had side-whiskers, which were generous in size for one so young. He wore a brown velvet cut-away coat, fawn breeches and tan-topped riding boots. His linen looked starched and spotless. His black satin stock was immaculately tied. His appearance bespoke 'no expense spared'. This schoolboy was very much of the entitled aristocracy.

Lavender's uniform was a cut-away blue coat with silver buttons and a leather belt. The low top hat had a silver badge showing two crossed truncheons. He dispensed with the red waistcoat, except in the coldest weather. His full accoutrements would have been a short sword, pistol, a spinning rattle for summoning help, a truncheon and a notebook. He rarely bothered with more of this clutter than the notebook. Instead of the rattle, which he considered to be a child's toy, he carried a thunderer whistle, made by the Birmingham Acme company. This innovation was soon copied by the rest of the force.

"Do you remember me?" said Cally, following her father's briefing. Her coy smile could hardly be seen, because the brim of her bonnet was pulled down and tied under her chin, obscuring much of her face. She affected a country rhotic accent, which she had practiced when entertaining the family with readings from Henry Fielding's Tom Jones. The Reed women never resorted to make-up, apart from a little rouge on the cheeks. Only actors and tarts used more than that. But for this special enactment, Cally had dabbed her lips with some carmine that her mother used for her bindi.

"You have forgotten me, you callous man", said Cally coquettishly, with head to one side.

"Too many libations have blunted your memory of it and the room was dark, because you had no money for candles, having lost at cards, you said. We spent the night together, in the stage inn, at Bath, at the end of May."

The poor lamb was confused and nervous, to such an extent that it did not enter his head to exert his superiority by damning this girl and sending her packing. Of course, the inexplicable presence of the Bow Street Runner urged caution.

"You had no coins for me and so I took the pineapple you offered. Surely, you remember the night and the pineapple, you wicked man. All I want you to do is counter-sign this receipt for my payment, namely one pineapple. You are a gentleman and so it was proper payment. I need the receipt as proof, because I had no coins to give to my fancy man and he was not impressed by the fruit. Please would you sign the receipt and we can consider the matter closed, until we happily meet again at the Bath coaching inn.

Mr Addington, totally addled, toddled away, baffled still. Enjoying the entitlements befitting an aristocrat of his station, he was un-used to being called to account, especially by a common harlot, even if unaccountably accompanied by a Runner.

Lavender and Cally mounted and rode home. Most unusually, several times, her father could not stop himself giggling. They reached home in twilight. Their three-storey house, one of a small terrace, was built from yellow London stocks, now more than a little darkened by London's perpetual pall of smoke.

"Father, do you think I could become the first woman Bow Street police officer?"

"You know, Cally, that I consider this country to be conservative, heartless and backward.

"We have not even women magistrates, let alone judges. We have no woman in government and no women members of Parliament. The first step surely has to be to win for women the right to vote.

"I fear that is a long way off and so, my clever girl, although you are an exceptional specimen of your sex, the answer to your question is an emphatic "No".

"However, I'm sure you will do wonderful things in your life, without the need of being in the police.

"The life of a thief-taker is endlessly disheartening."

"But, Father, said Cally, "Bow Street considers you their thief-taker and killer-capturer extraordinaire."

"I know, said he, "That while I am catching the pathetic small-fry, the bigger fish are getting away, scot-free, protected by the laws enacted by the government they control."

The following day, Lavender sought an interview with Lord Sidmouth on a matter concerning his son. When the Minister heard it was a Bow Street Runner waiting on him, he had the officer immediately ushered in. Lavender explained that the Minister's son had perhaps been a little indiscreet ("Oh, the waywardness of youth.") and this slip of paper shows that there was a brief intercourse best covered up. Sidmouth readily agreed, accepted Jones's innocence, instructed an underling to go to Bow Street and see to her release and, on Reed's suggestion, wrote her a one-sentence recommendation for future employment. The sisters waited outside Newgate for Deborah on the following day. Her imprisonment had taken place regardless of habeas corpus. Her release was similarly without any record being made. Such was the Home Minister's regard for the law and due process. They took Deborah home with them, helped her to have a bath, found her a set of clothes and led her to a happy reunion with her mother. Having a good character, from Lord Sidmouth, no less, she would soon find another position.

Lavender was, of course, pleased with the outcome, but downcast when considering the detective work and connivance to which he and Cally had to resort in order to free an innocent girl.

"The poor girl suffered weeks in Newgate and justice delayed is justice denied. Said many times, but every example makes the statement even truer." He slammed his hand on the table in his frustration.

"I wish I could put Sidmouth and all magistrates in prison for just two or three nights. That would surely be enough to pound some sense of justice into their pudding brains.'" suggested Cally

"For the aristocracy, justice equals punishment; not fairness; not equality before the law, certainly not redemption, simply rigorous punishment. The more cruel, the better."

The war which began in 1793 and continued through Cally's childhood, before she became socially and politically aware, is now over. There is peace abroad, but little peace in England. The discharged troops and paid-off ships' crews find their home villages are in such disarray that many of those returning find no heroes' warm home-coming. Their jobs have been filled by others or have completely disappeared. Peasant subsistence farming is too precarious to welcome more mouths to feed. By enclosures, many men's ancestral plots have been stolen. The only visible residue of the ancient strip fields, which covered the commons for centuries, is the pattern of parallel ridges which marked the boundaries. People are now replaced by sheep.

The French, after their revolution, are again in the power of the Bourbons, as the English were again under the Stuarts and then under foreign kings from Hanover. The Church, its bishops and the old nobility are all restored. In both countries, the hopes of their revolutions are retreating into history.

There came about a mildly erotic episode in Cally's rather protected life.

Rising in the morning has to be a fast process, especially in winter. Washing in cold water at the bedroom wash-stand and dabbing on plenty of lavender water or rose water. Then putting on some clothes, with extra layers in winter. Dressing each other's hair was a weekly exercise undertaken in a warmer room.

This particular morning, standing behind her adopted sister, Cally has her hands on Polly's shoulders and kisses the nape of her neck. This much happens every day as a morning greeting. But this time there is a memorable event, which Cally has been contemplating, with some trepidation, for days, fearful of Polly's possible reaction. "I love you, I love you, my beautiful Polly," Cally whispers as her hands slowly slide down Polly's arms and around to cup and caress her tiny breasts. This is a shock for both of them. Polly twists round and kisses Cally's lips. Now Cally's breasts are being touched and she, too, finds it ecstatic, a novel sensation coursing through her body. Since they first developed, she has touched her own breasts, but to have someone else being so intimate, is a new and exciting experience.

New territory has been discovered and more exploration follows. The girls are both enraptured and not a little aghast. They exchange more wordless kisses while finishing their dressing.

Mother has always been Cally's close confidante and now she must hear this, in case it is a reprehensible thing. Something as joyous as this is bound to be suspect, says her Puritan tendency. It is not often that Cally has such a pessimistic outlook.

Mother holds her girls' hands and nods encouragement to speak their minds. They came to her with such an apprehensive approach that she wonders what has happened to make them so anxious. Cally takes the lead, falteringly telling what happened this morning; this unprecedented and remarkably enjoyable experience. "Are we unusual? Are we misbehaving?" asks Polly.

This sweet child is not her own, but has become beloved, as precious as if she were a real sister to Cally. The morning and goodnight greetings between Mother and Polly evolved from a perfunctory peck to a kiss on the cheek and a quick embrace.

There is no shyness between Ananya and her girls. They share their nakedness and scrub one another's backs on weekly bath days. This practice, consistent with Ananya's Hindu influence, dated from Cally's infancy

"There is nothing new under the sun," Mother says, raising her hands as if to the sun and letting them fall to her lap, "Apart from each new generation, who have to discover some things for themselves".

"You are both now as beautiful as you will ever be in your lives. It is a gift from nature, a gift of fate. While you have such beauty, enjoy it. The passing years will steal it. Enjoy it in your own eyes and in the eyes of others.

"Men will enjoy looking at you." As she said this, Mother nodded, as if to assure them of the truth of her words, "And so will other women."

"Most men and women are attracted to the opposite sex but there are men and women who love others of the same sex," explained Mother. "Enjoying and adoring one another's bodies will bring no harm."

"This kind of love is common enough at your age. It may not last a life-time. We'll see."

Her girls' love for one another may be more than typically sisterly and perhaps long-lasting. She will talk with them again and make sure they understand themselves. They must be prepared for those who look askance at loving relationships such as theirs. She knows her girls have ample resilience.

"I have no doubt that, if you speak of this morning's discovery in one of your tête à têtes with your friends, you will find them surprised that you have come to this revelation so late".

Mother was right. Cally's tentative mention of the subject, when next the usual gaggle of young women met, brought a flood of accounts of their friends' experiences. It appeared that Polly and Cally, at 15 and 16 respectively, were between two and five years behind the pack. Their friends were bemused and loved them the more for their innocence.

The sisters could find nothing in their books and so they went to see the local fount of all wisdom on matters female and carnal, the local midwife. They learned a lot. When they stood at her door, Mrs Downing's first thought was that one of them might be with child and she was shocked, for here were the girls rarely seen in church, but often seen horse-riding, daringly astraddle, like boys. Their purpose once made clear, she was patient with their naïve questions and helpful, assuring them that such touching is not a sin. That men do it to women, Cally found distasteful.

On pondering her new knowledge, as well as her recollection of mother's explanation when her monthlies ('cousin's visits') began, she was now even more certain that she would never want to marry. There was now an additional reason: marriage meant having children and although little children are adorable, the means by which they are conceived and born are extraordinary and unthinkable. Worse still, having a husband might entail the displacement of her beloved Polly.

This sister of hers had grown not a jot since joining the Reed family. She could still pass for a 12-year old, with hardly existent breasts and lean limbs. Although she ate little, her energy was boundless. More than once, early in the morning, Cally was woken by Polly prancing and twisting in a spirited dance around the bedroom. Her walk was always fast-paced. Her laughter came easily and in infectious shrieks, leaving her companions laughing more at Polly and her laugh than at the subject.

In August of 1815, Lavender hired a brougham and coachman to take the family on excursion to the village of Chertsey, westward along the Thames. There they took two rooms at the inn for a week. They travelled in fine weather and the coachman knew the country well enough to select smooth roads and well kept turnpikes. It is said that if rain falls on St Swithin's birthday, 15th July, it will fall on forty days successively thereafter. The month of June had seen plenty of rainy weather, starting with a storm on 26th June. That means it rained for nineteen days before the crucial date. If those days can be deducted from the folklore's prediction, then the saint owes us dry weather in August. Cally reasoned thus as they made their way. In reality, she was no more convinced than her listeners. They saw fields which should have been harvested by now, but the crop was too wet. If the farmers are unlucky, this will be the second successive year of poor yield. They passed two hay-ricks which had apparently been damaged by fire. Lavender suggested they might have been deliberately set alight; such arson had been reported from various parts. The coachman stopped at a pond to water the horses. From a cottage nearby two little children ran out. They were thin, ragged, grubby and, of course, bare-foot Their hands were outstretched for pennies. Polly gave them coins from her purse. This part of the north Surrey Weald showed no signs of prosperity.

Cally had visited Chertsey before and proposed a picnic and bathing at a nearby secluded pond as the day was so warm. Leaving Father, the ever-hopeful angler, fishing the river, Mother accompanied the girls as chaperone. They were aware that, although men and boys invariably swam naked, women who entered the sea at the Prince Regent's resort of Brighthelmstone, went to extraordinarily prudish lengths to protect their modesty, with bathing machines, attendants and cumbersome costumes. Here, closely hemmed in by bushes and trees and distant from any footpath, they felt safe in walking into the pond naked. They had brought soap and so the dip served a dual purpose.

Cally was the more accomplished swimmer, having been taught by her father, from her earliest years, in this very pond. Swimming underwater, although her eyes were closed, she sensed the shadows of Polly and mother when she passed underneath them as they floated at the surface, in the sunshine. From near the edge of the pond she picked a waterlily flower and pushed its stalk into the wet hair behind Polly's ear. The girls embraced. Mother noted this. There cannot be too much love in the world and women loving women was not alien to Hindu culture. On the contrary, it is considered natural and joyful.

Polly was the first out of the water and stood on the bank towelling herself, feeling extraordinarily liberated and daring in her nakedness in the open air for the first time in her life, although safe in this secluded place. Cally and Mother enjoyed more wallowing and splashing. They then emerged and Polly could not help thinking of beautiful mermaids rising from the waves and she told them this, much to their amusement. She had once had to assure a girl at school that Cally was, indeed, that colour all over.

She could have added that so is her mother, although distinctly a shade darker. The girl was additionally grateful for Polly's assurance that, under her clothes, Cally had all the parts that other girls had. Polly felt that she had valuably expanded the girl's education. There were black and brown people seen in London, but Cally was the only such girl in the school.

Dried and dressed, they took themselves back to the inn. Cally, her damp hair bobbing in rats' tails, led the way, swaying and singing a slightly nautical song by Rabbie Burns'

> *Come boat me o'er,*
> *Come row me o'er,*
> *Come boat me o'er to Charlie.*

On the way home from their excursion to Chertsey, again in a hired brougham, Cally and Polly noted numerous indications of the poverty-stricken state of the nation. They often overtook men and even whole families, carrying pathetic bundles of belongings, presumably traipsing from farm to farm in search of casual work, somewhere dry to spend the night, or looking for discarded fruit or vegetables, anything edible that could be taken. At one point, at the roadside, they saw labourers erecting a fence, apparently overseen by other men holding carbines. The coachman told them this country was part of Epsom Common. So this was enclosure in action. The fence builders were being protected, by armed guards, from a crowd of loudly protesting people, presumably displaced commoners, who were losing their fields and their ancient rights of sustenance from the land. More people were being added to the hungry vagrants, who were often forced to choose between starvation and theft. Lavender, incensed by what they had seen, had much to say when they reached home. That afternoon, at the dinner table, he gave vent to his feelings.

"Rich men, lords of the manors, title-holders by virtue of dubious inheritance centuries ago, or more recent proprietors, rewarded with land for their mercenary support of Charles I or his unspeakable son, are now stealing the commons which have sustained commoners for hundreds of years. Those enclosing fences we have seen, deny poor people their ancient right to graze their animals and grow barley and potatoes. All too soon, many of those people, forced by hunger to steal a crust, will find themselves in the hands of the law.

"Magistrates in parts of England are invoking the viciously vengeful Black Act passed in the last century. A man found poaching can be hanged. A man found with his face blackened as a disguise, or to be obscured at night, or carrying a weapon, even if without prey, can be hanged. A threat to burn a haystack, as a means of threatening a landowner, is a capital offence. No other laws appoint the punishment of death for so many offences, some of them really quite trivial. First passed in 1723, the Act had been strengthened over the years. A suspect who has been named, but refuses to give himself up, can be summarily judged guilty *in absentia* and sentenced to execution. Villages that fail to surrender a named suspect, can be subject to collective punishment. The vindictiveness of landowners knows no bounds.

"This year, the richest landowners have celebrated Waterloo by continuing to exercise their greed, at the expense of the poor. Having got a taste for the fortunes they can make when corn is in short supply and its price is high, as it was during the war, they want to keep it that way. Parliament has passed Acts banning Imports from France and Poland, so that the corn from the land they have recently enclosed makes as much money as possible. The Corn Laws have facilitated unmitigated greed.

"The high price of bread drives more people into the local workhouse, where they at least have shelter and a little food".

St Mary's Church, Newington, opened a school for boys from 1710 and some years later a girls' school was established in an adjacent building. This was the school attended by the sisters. In 1816, the two schools were united, together with the Sunday schools. Newington workhouse was built early in the 18th century.

There came a day when an inflated pig's bladder, which the boys kicked around in their school play area, found its way over the hedge into the girls' area and happened to trickle towards Cally's feet. Her move appeared to come naturally in response to a challenge. She positioned the bladder, stepped back two or three paces, then advanced and belted it back to the boys. They were astounded and delighted and so was Cally. The teachers were happy to leave the children to their own devices for unsupervised play, otherwise there might have been an intervention before girls came to mix regularly with the boys after school, playing this game, known as football, on the paddocks where local people grazed their horses. The horses were not perturbed and only the most mean-spirited, rigid and severe grown-ups would have complained.

Girls found that their leather boots were good for kicking, but their long skirts flapped around their legs and impeded their running and kicking.

The Reed sisters had a solution. They first tried playing in their divided skirts and then resorted to stockings and the horse-riding breeches mother had made for them. The sisters already caused quite enough outrage in the parish, without this football playing. When the matter was raised at a Vestry meeting, to the mild disquiet of Lavender and Ananya, by an ill-tempered pernikety old baggage whose house overlooked the ground where the children played, the Rector (bless him for his spirit of forgiveness) pleaded that the sisters had redeeming behaviours. They helped at the school for mothers and children in Newgate Prison and they provided a similar service in St Mary's Workhouse, as well as other good works.

Until the national government took over the cost of poor relief, in 1834, the burden fell on local rate-payers and so the Poor Law Overseers, who were appointed and remunerated by the Vestry meeting of parishioners, were always tempted to keep costs as low as possible. Inmates of workhouses all around England tended to be under-fed, ill-clad and overworked. Many overseers – not those at the St Mary's Workhouse – skimmed for themselves some of what should have gone to the inmates. Mrs Reed and her daughters were among those who collected clothes, bedding, food and other comforts for the Workhouse and visited the sick.

Considering the risks they took, regularly visiting Newgate and the Workhouse, the girls were unusually healthy. But theirs was a house that maintained good sanitary and hygiene standards in a teeming and increasingly sordid city. Every room in the Reed household had a chamber pot, or peepot, to use the girls' name for it. In most cases, the pot was modestly hidden in a wooden chamber-box. In the dining room and the sitting room there was a curtained corner for the discreet use of the pot.

In these days, few people were embarrassed by the noises and smells of natural functions, which, after all, paupers could be seen performing on the street every day of the week.

In the scullery – a small room at the rear of the basement – there was a close stool. A task falling to the housemaids, was the emptying of all of this crockery, every morning, either into the privy pit –also known as the 'necessary' – in the backyard, or in the sluice sink in the scullery, which had an earthenware pipe emptying into the privy pit. Over the sluice stood the household's source of water, a lift-pump, which was connected by a pipe to the well in the backyard. Ananya insisted that water was never drunk unless first boiled. There was always a kettle singing on the kitchen range, ever ready to make tea. And there was always home-brewed small beer in a barrel in the kitchen.

There was wine or beer with every meal apart from breakfast, but never enough was taken for intoxication.

Unfortunately, not every family knew it to be unwise to draw water from a well which was close to privies and consequently abdominal infections were common. Most families had no option.

Each bedroom had its wash-stand and the slops were carried to the scullery, except for the girls' wash-basin and pee-pot, which they emptied on to the sloping roof just below their bedroom window. This concession was most advantageous, because their room was at the top of three flights of stairs.

The girls had both received Dr Jenner's calf lymph variolation to protect them from smallpox.

On their regular prison visits they risked collecting fleas and lice. As a precaution, over their clothes, they wore aprons, which were put to be washed, when they got home. They sometimes competed with one another over the number of bug bites received. Newgate was riddled with bed bugs, making Prisoners' lives an itching misery. Simple hygiene could so easily have controlled them. The guards tied string round their trousers at the ankle, so that bugs could not climb up their legs.

In all prisons and workhouses, gaol fever, phthisis, was rife, just as it was throughout the nation. The Reed family was less likely to contract the disease, because their household was not overcrowded, it was hygienic and in this semi-rural part of London they had fresh air and could afford a healthy diet.

The whole family bathed each Saturday, using the metal bath placed in front of the kitchen range. Water was heated in kettles and pans. The girls shared the first bath and then mother and father shared fresh water. The bath had to be bailed out until it was light enough to be lifted to the sluice.

The women of the house washed their hair just once each month, using warm, soapy water. They never wore wigs, never used pomade or other greasy creams and certainly never powdered their hair, a practice continued by some men and women of the older generation, who doused their hair or wig with white powder. At this time, some elaborate wigs had little flea traps embedded in them.

The girls eschewed curling their hair, despite the fashion of wearing the hair piled up, with bunches of curls at each ear. Such curls were laboriously created each evenng, before bed, using heated tongs and paper curlers. Even with the help of a maid, this took ages. Such time-wasting was not to the sisters' taste and so their hair was always 'down', in a style which was becoming increasingly popular with the more liberated young women of the Regency period, although scorned as wanton by some older women.

Father had bought toothbrushes of William Addis, at his workshop in Covent Garden. The brush was a length of bone in which were embedded small bundles of stiff bristles shaved from a pig. The girls shared one brush and mother and father shared another. Mother made a special mixture for teeth, using soft soap, ground pumice as an abrasive and crushed peppermint leaves for the flavour. Wooden toothpicks were also used. For themselves the girls washed and dried the rags and under-skirts they wore for their monthly courses. Cally was astounded when Mother explained to her, when her courses started, that this was her body preparing itself every month, with a fresh egg, for a baby to be born. Cally had to be reassured not to worry, because there could be no baby without the contribution of a man. For the present, that was enough carnal information; Cally had Latin prep. to do.

Even upper class people often had dirty finger nails, grave-digger's nails, Cally commented, when she noticed them. Not so the Reed girls.

Despite no longer being at war abroad, England was at war within itself. Food prices were constantly rising. Tens of thousands were under-nourished or starving. Enclosures of common land continued apace and landowners, who had control of Parliament, passed more punitive laws in order to protect themselves and their property from the ire of displaced commoners. This was the aftermath of the conflict with Napoleon, but nobody was yet aware that this troubled year of 1815 was but the harbinger of a yet worse year to come.

Just as the family's excursion to Chertsey had enjoyed fine weather, so had the farmers' harvest, but early autumn brought unusually fierce westerly winds, heavy rain and unseasonally cold days and freezing nights.

In April of 1815, on the other side of the world, Mount Tambora, a quiescent volcano, on the island of Sumbawa, in the Dutch East Indies, suddenly erupted. Some three years earlier, the ancient crater atop the mountain issued smoke and more recently there had been rumblings in the earth. All of this was ignored because there had been no eruptions in living memory. When the lusciously vegetated green mountain exploded, losing half of its height, lava flowed down all sides into the sea, overwhelming hundreds of people in its path. Ten thousand islanders were killed at this time and thousands more on neighbouring islands died after the failure of their crops. On the day of the eruption, a few hundred miles to the west, near Makassar, on the British naval vessel, HMS Benares, the officers interpreted the distant explosions as canons firing, possibly pirate attacks on merchant shipping. This must be investigated. Benares set sail and headed into inexplicable conditions. Daytime could be as dark as moonless night. Sunrise was no more than a deep red glow on the eastern horizon which refused to brighten. At midday it was sometimes as dark as midnight. There was constant precipitation as of snowfall. It was not snow, but white, powdery ash. The air was increasingly foul with it, causing all the crew to cough and wheeze. The ship's surgeon was inundated with sick men. The daylight hours were foreshortened and persistently dimmed, as by a thick haze. Sunset, like sunrise, was blood-red. There came a point when the ship's hull was hitting floating objects, as if making way through ice-floes. But these were tropical waters. A boat was launched to investigate and brought back boulders of rock which had been floating. The ship's surgeon reported to the captain that the rock was buoyant by virtue of being porous. It was pumice, which must have been ejected from a volcano. The ash landed on the decks relentlessly, to a depth of two or more feet, despite the crew being set to clear it overboard. It started to rain and the deposit was turned into a sort of white mud.

It was not known at the time, that at great height, a dense cloud of ash was girdling the northern hemisphere, blocking the sunlight and bringing about an early, cold autumn, to be followed by a premature and elongated winter. The following Year, 1816 became known as 'the year without a summer.'

In the summer of 1815, in unseasonably low temperatures, the artist, John Constable, left the Blue Boar Inn, in Aldgate, on his way home, by mailcoach, to East Bergholt on the Essex-Suffolk border. At the roadside, he passed a sign saying,' Poachers beware. Any foul poacher caught on this land or anyone breaking down fences will be punished severely or shot and no mercy show'd'. In order to save money, he had chosen to ride in the luggage basket at the back of the coach, exposed to the weather.

It rained solidly for the whole journey. Soaked to the skin and cold, he swore that henceforth he would always pay the extra fare for sitting inside, risking the cramped company being smelly, or in some other way objectionable. The journey was made longer than usual by the state of the roads. Even the turnpikes were awash with mud from the overflowing ditches, making hard going for the horses and sometimes the wheels of the coach slid sideways, causing the passengers to fear they might tip over.

The common about Dedham and East Bergholt was abustle with fences going up. Cattle, that had been free to roam the commons, were now enclosed in small fields. What applied to the beasts applied equally to men. Legally or otherwise, the rich were appropriating more land and the poor were being caged in prisons if they acted against the enclosures. Constable painted a fast-changing world, as did his contemporary, J M W Turner.

It was a fellow Quaker and acquaintance of Cally's, Luke Howard, of the Tottenham Friends, who kept careful records of the extraordinary weather of 1816, which well earned its reputation as the year without a summer. It was Howard's classification of clouds, published in 1803, and his almanac of London weather conditions between 1807 and 1819, as well as his collection of data from correspondents all over Europe that earned him the title, 'Father of Meteorology', a science taken further by Admiral Robert Fitzroy later in the century.

The winter of 1815-1816 brought the first indications of the historically cold temperatures and heavy rains that would afflict the country through all of 1816 and beyond. The daytime temperature, in London, on 9th February 1816 never exceeded 6 degrees on the Celsius temperature scale, falling that night to 5 degrees below zero. Howard recorded that all across Europe there were crops buried under snow, or drowned by flooding, and elsewhere, parched by drought. Some Quakers saw this *annus horribilis* as the vengeance of the Lord. All across England, October 1816 saw whole fields of potatoes, barley or oats buried and rotting under early snow which lingered until the following spring. There had been nothing to harvest. Thousands of starving poor went from the countryside, scavenging in the towns, where they were shown no sympathy.

In April 1816, just when the sisters were looking forward to warmer weather brightening the outlook, Cally woke one morning, complaining of a severe headache. Mother felt her forehead and confirmed a fever. Coughing and sneezing suggested a cold, but later in the day, the patient complained that the light from the window was hurting her eyes and Polly could see a pink rash on Cally's face, neck and chest. Mother diagnosed measles. Polly agreed, having seen the same condition when her younger brothers and sisters caught the illness. Furthermore, as the girls were aware, measles was running through the children in their school in Newgate

Cally suggested that Mr John Lettsom, the Quaker physician might be consulted, but recalled that he had recently died. Cally's fever continued for a week and when delirium set in, Polly became fearful and frantic. She slept on a truckle bed near Cally and could not have been a more conscientious nurse.

It was shocking to see Cally, this intelligent and rational girl so disorientated. Her mind was rambling and her speech was angry and incoherent. Efforts to calm her and cool her burning brow met with squirming, struggling and grinding her teeth.

Polly ran along the street for Mrs Downing, sobbing that Cally was dying.

The midwife and Ananya conferred and agreed that the delirium was probably due to the prolonged high temperature and took the drastic action of opening the window and allowing the room to grow cold, hoping that this would cool the patient. Additionally, Cally was given a few drops of laudanum. Giving Polly some reassurance was not so easy; she was in a desperate state of desolation. When Mrs Downing learned that measles had worked its way through the Forrester family some years ago, she concluded that this explained why Polly had not caught the disease. Being normally a picture of good health, Cally would quickly shake off the illness.

Hearing all this wisdom, Polly determined to temper her concern, lest she distract from Cally's needs.

True enough, surprisingly quickly, the fever and rash subsided, although the patient was left exhausted. She had the most attentive of nurses, who was still recovering from the harrowing ordeal of thinking she might lose her precious sister.

With Cally now well on the mend, Polly decided the housemaids would celebrate her recovery by having a week of spring-cleaning.

Of course, there had to be some fun as well as drudgery.

Polly clapped her hands for attention and submitted the dinner table to some doggerel:

"We clear and tidy, dust and clean.

Wherever we've been, you can see the gleam.

The pee-pot queens are we;

Daily they're whisked away, with nary a spillage of the wee".

Father and Mother were delighted that their adopted daughter was coming out of her shell.

She had not Cally's *éclat*, but Lavender and Ananya enjoyed this addition of youthful energy to the household and Cally obviously loved her.

1816

The early months of 1816 were bitterly cold. The sisters had the great excitement of crossing the frozen Thames on horse-back and sharing a mug of mulled wine, bought from a stall at the centre of the river. Severe frosts lasted for several weeks. When spring eventually came, it was disappointing. The weather remained cold, the sky was permanently iron-grey and it appeared to rain every day, without cease.

Looking out of the window one day, Polly pulled a face and declaimed, "Rain, rain, go away, come again on washing day"

"You had better not recite that in Mother's hearing; she is sick of having every room festooned with damp washing. She is praying for just one dry and windy day.

Cally told the Hampden Club officers that May of 1816 would see the 167th anniversary of the execution, at Burford, of the three New Model Army soldiers who led a mutiny demanding their arrears of pay. She offered to present a lecture in their honour.

On 16th May she addressed the Club, from memory, of course.

"The three men, Levellers, set in train more than they could know. They were being exploited by the

Army. Rations were poor and irregular, so that the troops had to fend for themselves as best they could, which usually entailed requisitioning food from the pitifully poor people among whom they were billeted. Promised uniforms failed to arrive. Often they were short of weapons and ammunition and they had not been paid for months. The officers took the best billets, strutted around in fancy uniforms and looked well fed.

"Refusal to accept exploitation we see among our correspondents in the northern centres.

"The Combination Acts of 1799 and 1800 and the threat of imprisonment have not been allowed to prevent trade unions in the spinning and weaving mills from demanding shorter hours and higher pay, backed by withdrawal of labour if demands are not met.

Ruthless exploitation will not be eliminated until those who suffer most are protected by laws enacted in Parliament.

"But Parliament at present represents the propertied, to the exclusion of the majority, who, owning neither house nor land, pay no local rate to their Vestry.

"How has this fixation with property come about? Even the Levellers were in thrall to this ancient stricture. Perhaps it stems from our agrarian beginnings, our dependence on a plot of land for our sustenance, without which men were indigent and on the parish.

"Why did our Leveller predecessors have such a backward idea about the rights of property?

"We no longer believe ourselves to be the puppets of the gods. We have freewill. We make our own decisions.

"Men mould the history of the time in which they live". Cally felt she was saying something of significance and so she repeated herself. "Men mould the history of the time in which they live. Their collective actions create the events of the passing days. But they are not able to make that unfolding history just as they please.

"No. They are limited by the circumstances in which they live and by the legacies of the past, the handed down understanding and traditions of dead generations, which set boundaries to our thinking. Of course, intellectual leaps do take place, breaking the bonds that tie us to the past, but those revolutions are few and far between. Humanity prefers a staid existence and will stoically endure the status quo long after it has become intolerable. It appears to require a sudden, major convulsion for the sleeping giant to awake and discard its mental shackles.

"When, during the Civil War, Levellers demanded manhood suffrage, their thinking was limited by the context of their time. They did not intend literally that every adult male should have the vote. They took it for granted that it would be understood that the franchise could not be extended to the poor and the servant class, nor to wage-earners, who were servilely dependent on their employers for their livelihood and therefore could not be considered to have a will of their own. Many were unlettered. "This ignorance and their subservient status was seen as incapacitating them from being fully conversant with public affairs and able to think independently.

"This manner of thinking was made explicit in the Army Council's Agreement Of The People, drawn up in 1647 during the Putney Debates. The document allowed the franchise to rate-payers, those who paid local taxes to the Vestry, but withheld it from the poor and the servant class.

"This strict definition of the franchise suited Cromwell, ever the protector of the propertied class, whereas the Levellers were intent on relaxing the definitions of property requirements.

"Over time, Leveller thinking evolved. The servant or wage-earner's capacity to labour was now considered to be his property, available to a master or employer for hire. Thus, apart from those unable to work because they are too old, ill or disabled, every man holds property in the form of his potential to sell his labour. The sweat of his brow is worth money, or at least can be bartered.

"Still the idea lingered on that the man who hires himself out by putting his hand to the plough or spade, has a head which is seldom elevated to sublime notions. Some have stretched this to say that the manual worker's head does not extend to politics and public affairs. This travesty can even be found in the Biblical Apocrypha. But if I read on a bit further, I find reference to the skilled worker, who, I quote, 'Is wise in his own art and without him a city is not built.'"

"If all men hold property, be it land, a house, or the capacity to labour, then all men should have the right to vote. There should be universal male suffrage.

"And the day is not far off when our demand will be for universal suffrage, above a certain age, for men *and women* alike."

There was applause at this, but support was not unanimous. The reference to women was not to everyone's liking. As usual, Cally was attempting to extend the thinking of her listeners to new horizons.

"From reports that Polly and I receive from around the country, it is clear that membership of trade unions is spreading. This is surely no surprise. When men and women in a factory are undertaking similar work under similar rules. They are bound to have shared interests and will join together for mutual support and protection. An advantage of this solidarity is that they will develop a common consciousness of their conditions and interests. As a consequence, they will collectively make their demands for better wages, shorter hours and better conditions. They will see the need for their interests to be expressed by politicians in Parliament. For that to happen, men must be able to elect representatives from their ranks, who must therefore receive a wage In other words, economic justice requires universal suffrage.

"I suggest to you that the trade unions are becoming the biggest force for such constitutional reform.

"The workers in the manufactures will be the vanguard of our movement. Their class will eventually establish a political party to represent them in parliament. Those members of parliament will be unlike any previous MPs. They will not covet high office, nor use their positions to feather their own nests. They will loyally pursue the interests of the workers who elected them.

"Brothers and sisters, that is our vision of the future."

Cally sat to applause and the customary vote of thanks from the vice-chairman, who urged her to make a transcription of her speech and send it for publication to Black Dwarf or Cobbett's Two-Penny Trash. "A contribution as thoughtful and inspiring as that deserves much wider circulation."

That evening, in the warmth of home, Polly handed Cally a cup of mulled wine, sat close to her and placed a hand on her lap.

Cally was able to read the signs that her sister had something serious to impart.

"Dear heart, you know that I trust your political judgement above all others, but I find it hard to have your faith in a new crop of MPs, worker MPs, carrying us through to the Elysian Fields.

"Yes, we certainly must have parliamentary reform, but most men are such shallow creatures, that I do not see worker MPs, nor any new workers' party having sufficient moral fibre to keep to our reformist programme and bring in the fundamental changes that are needed.

"Face it;the few radical MPs we have now are ever at sixes and sevens, the Whigs are divided and unpredictable. Members of the Commons appear so quickly and easily to be seduced by the power they wield.

"In the hands of most men, power corrupts. It is so tempting for them to abuse their entrusted influence for private gain, be it money, or favour from the mighty.

"Even with the new, reformed parliament you picture, most land will still be in the hands of the gentry and the aristocracy. The mines, the mills, all the other factories and the workers' houses and the banks will still be held by their present owners. There will still be the monarchy." All these powerful people will resist the changes we want to see and will do their best to seduce the new MPs who support our cause.

Like Cally, Polly was up to her neck with her teaching duties, as well as maintaining her studies. She would never have any trouble in supporting herself, even if marriage was an unlikely prospect for both girls. They could continue as teachers, their parents thought, or become governesses, or pioneer their way into journalism, or other professions. They could not be described as domesticated.

Mother made her daughters' clothes, assisted by Polly, who was becoming an able seamstress. Cally would have been better at a forge, making needles, suggested Mother, smiling in order to soften the sarcasm, rather than impatiently trying to wield one.

In May 1816, news reached London of riots in the East Anglian counties and Yorkshire, where armed labourers marched with banners saying 'Bread or Blood'. There was much more disorder in 1817, with the Riot Act being frequently read and the army called out to quell disturbances. The government responded in predictably draconian fashion. Prime Minister, Lord Liverpool, suspended habeas corpus. With due process abandoned and magistrates being hand-picked as the landowners' biddable sychophants, gaols were quickly filled to overflowing, as were the Thames hulks, with prisoners awaiting transportation to Botany Bay or Virginia. Nevertheless, desperate beggars lost all fear of the law. Waves of assault, robbery and arson swept the countryside and the towns. The years 1817 to 1819 saw a new kind of harvest of widespread economic hardship: the first substantial voluntary emigration to the North American colonies.

The London Corresponding Society was greatly exercised by all this tumult and grew in membership, another unintended consequence of Lord Liverpool's swingeing and punitive policies. Groups of workers organised clandestinely. In order to thwart police spies, they swore loyalty oaths to secret societies, forerunners of trade unions eventually representing every trade and industry in the country.

In July of 1815, Mary Godwin, daughter of Mary Wollstonecraft Godwin, had eloped with Percy Bysshe Shelley to Europe. Their love affair had begun in 1814, when Mary was only 16 and Shelley 21. The crossing to Calais, even in summer, was rough. They could not afford cabin seats in the dry and so they suffered soaking sea spray, as well as nausea. Mary was carrying her newborn, William, known as Wilmouse. She had difficulty in keeping him warm. Shelley was not a noticeably caring companion, always preoccupied with his own concerns. On landing, the journey became worse. They had expected mild late summer weather, but it was more like an early winter.

Unable to afford a coach, they and their luggage were carried mostly by mules. Post-war France was just as wretched and disorganised as England. The weather continued to be harsh. They had to traverse the mountains of eastern France and increasing height brought worsening cold and all too soon they met snow. From Calais To Geneva took ten painful days, occasionally with money expended on a coach to carry the mother and baby and additional men to help the horses haul up to the highest passes. On arrival, the resort was found to be hardly warming after the premature winter's cold. The dark Lake appeared to swallow any warmth into its freezing depths.

Cally is not one for making confessions, although from infancy she observed the rule that one must always tell the truth. Her imminent statement is a confession to the extent that she feared the information might not be welcome to her parents. Seated at the table after dinner, Cally announces that she and Polly are now members of the local Hampden Club. This news is received in silence, making the girls apprehensive. Then Lavender explains to Ananya what the Hampden clubs are. He pours himself some ale and speaks his mind.

"My dears, I am proud of you both, but I have not heard your information. You have not told me. I am unaware of your new affiliation. Your political friends would not be easy with knowing you both to be closely related to police officers and my employers would see me, on the one hand, as a risk to the government's security and, on the other hand, a potential spy on the government's behalf.

"What you must constantly bear in mind is that the clubs are riddled with government spies and *agents provocateurs* and this is probably true of all the reformist organisations.

"There is a man, John Reeves, responsible for distributing Treasury funds to the various magistrates' offices for the employment of informers. In his spare time, he founded the Association for Preserving Liberty and Property Against Republicans and Levellers. In other words, the association of the devil's disciples. When such a man speaks of liberty, beware; the word turns to poison in his mouth. He has money enough to bribe a growing army of spies and trouble-makers. They will be among you. They will have money to spare on blandishments, as they seek to wheedle their way into positions of influence. Beware, my dears. "Lavender was looking at the sisters and nodding, in order to emphasise the wisdom of his words.

"The forerunners of the Hampden clubs were the corresponding societies," Lavender explains to his wife.

"The London Corresponding Society was formed in 1792 and made links with similar societies all over the country. Tom Hardy, a shoe-maker, founding secretary of the London Society, together with the Society's other leaders was seized and thrown into the Tower and then Newgate, charged with seditious practices.

"The charge then became high treason and they were all put on trial. If found guilty they could have suffered execution in public, being hanged, sometimes then beheaded, drawn and quartered.

"The judge and jury must have considered that Prime Minister Liverpool and Home Minister, Sidmouth had been too zealous and vengeful, because Hardy and his colleagues – printers, engravers, cabinet-makers, pamphleteers and book-sellers – on the strength of the subtle arguments of their lawyers, were all aquitted. On their release, there were celebrations and demonstrations of support from the people of London. The arrest of Tom Hardy, in 1794, had been a great palaver.

"This was a few years before I became a Bow Street Runner, but his arrest was still talked about when I was appointed. For the arrest of this one man, there turned up at his house the King's Messenger, no less, the secretary to the Home Minister, who was then Henry Dundas, several Runners and constables and Minister's clerks. This army of officials and police ransacked his house, damaging it greatly, taking away sacks of letters, pamphlets and books. This was not just the arrest of a man. This was the government rattling its sabres, displaying its might and issuing a warning to all radicals and reformers that the long arm of the law will invade your home, destroy your privacy and take you down. A special committee of the House of Commons was formed to undertake the task of examining the considerable volume of confiscated documents. It was dubbed the Committee of Secrecy. The joke among the

Runners was that the Committee assembled those members of the House who were able to read and it was secret in case the membership leaked out, because that could mean any members of the House not on the Committee were illiterate or permanently without their wits. The actual reason for its title was that the Committee was responsible for collating and analysing the information now flowing in from the government's many spies. Hardy was questioned several times by the Privy Council in full session; all those aristocrats with nothing better to do than harangue and grill a boot-maker reformist. However, the government's efforts were not wasted; a consequence of its blundering, heavy-handed action was that the LCS was severely weakened. Intimidation had worked and now that the Hampden clubs have seriously taken up the reformist cause, they have become the target of the government's displeasure and scrutiny. Their moderate agenda for parliamentary reform, sought by non-violent means, is seen as revolutionary and treasonous by the government. As a police officer, I would be commended for betraying you to the office of the Home Minister. You, Cally, have experience of the Minister, yes, petulant Lord Sidmouth, he of the world-shattering case of the disappearing pineapple." The girls smiled at each other and stood to clear the dishes. They returned to the table and Polly, who was always a little shy when addressing Lavender, although he invariably gave her an encouraging smile, said: "Sir, we hear from members of the Hampden Club the same philosophy that we have learned from your own lips. The Club stands for the reform of Parliament. A recent speaker said that the government rules by three instruments. Firstly, its soldiers, who are by profession slaughterers. Secondly, Church of England clergyman, who bless, with the sanction of divinity, state robbery. Thirdly, the lawyers, who rake in fortunes by tyrannically defending the private property of the greedy rich." These words are close to those I first heard from you."

"Impressed by the simplicity and obvious fairness of these ideas, we presented them to our Quaker Friends at a recent meeting", reported Polly, "There were some present who might have found this Spencian philosophy too radical, verging on Jacobinism, but it was not contended; all were aware of the widespread wretchedness being caused by the Corn Laws and the current waves of heartless enclosures of common land".

Lavender, touching Polly's hand, said "Polly, I am pleased to hear a young woman motivated by such ethical politics, but I must advise you to be careful of who may be listening when you repeat such ideas.

"A colleague of mine, not a friend, another Bow Street officer, John Stafford, is a favourite of Lord Sidmouth. His sole function is to linger covertly wherever he might collect information on what the Hampden clubs and other radicals are planning. He passes this, together with any names he can gather, directly to Sidmouth."

"You know of Oliver the Spy, also known as William Oliver, or William Richards. Another dangerous man to watch out for is one often called John Castle".

"Father", said Cally, "Polly is such a quick thinker. When we joined, she asked the Secretary of the Club whether he wanted our real names. On his advice, Polly instantly adopted the name of Poppy Mouse and I am not Calista Reed, I am Calpernia Wright. Members' addresses are never written down."

Lavender smiled, shaking his head in disbelief. He said, "If you are Calpernia, then I pity Julius Caesar. You girls are well ahead of me. If either of you ever decides to make spying your profession, I will give you a recommendation."

The girls had seen enough of London to know that their lives were privileged. They had a secure home and they never went hungry. They lacked nothing and were being educated. They took the view that they must do all in their power to help those less fortunate; not only material help – as with their prison visiting – also political action, in order to create a better world.

During the abysmal summer of 1816, the girls went to a Hampden meeting in the courtyard of the Elephant and Castle Inn, in Newington Butts, not far from home. Thomas Spence, the radical writer, had died in 1814 and this was a memorial meeting in his honour. The Spenceans were renowned, and often rebuked, for always meeting in ale-houses and inns. They considered themselves to be the truest heirs of Jacobin ideology and were certainly seen by the authorities as the most dangerous of the radicals for their advocacy of the dispossession of all land-owners, as preached by Spence.

The sisters were aware that two women entering a taproom, not even accompanied, might cause consternation. Only a certain type of woman did that. But by now they enjoyed their bravado. Entering these male domains with such confidence, their presence and respectability were never questioned.

The speaker opened his address with an ironic warning: "Dear friends, we have come to expect that our esteemed Prime Minister, the Earl of Liverpool, takes such close interest in our discussions that he sends a note-taking scribe to each of our meetings, so be polite and, as usual, speak nothing but the truth. We have much to teach Lord Liverpool.

"I will paraphrase the late, great, Tom Spence: Philosophers talk of the time when we were in a state of nature; in other words, before rulers and rich men and their laws existed. At that time, each man's property in land and liberty were surely equal. Taking this for granted, the territory of any people is properly their common, in which each of them has an equal share, enough to sustain himself and his family with the animals, fruits and other products thereof.

"Thus such people reap jointly the advantages of their country or neighbourhood, without having their right in so doing called in question by any, not even by the most greedy and corrupt.

"Hence it is plain that the land in any neighbourhood, with everything in or on the same, or pertaining thereto, belongs at all times to the inhabitants living there.

"But if we look back to the origin of the nations of the world, we shall see that the land, with all its appurtenances, was claimed by a few and divided among themselves, in as assured a manner as if they had manufactured it and it had been the work of their own hands. The law-makers consider their first and foremost duty to be the defence of landowners' property. Thus our birthright has been stolen. But there will come the day, when, even if we have to buy it back, the land will again be ours and every man will be allotted his rightful share.

"In a rational society, how should things be? We should go back to the land being held in common. The nominal owner should be the parish, with each man within the parish given an equal share, for which he must pay a manner of rent. The rent is paid to the parish in order that teachers and clergymen may be remunerated and roads and bridges maintained.

"Yes, the present owners will be dispossessed, so that every commoner will have his share.

"That is the gospel of the great Tom Spence."

The speaker sat down to loud cheers and hammering on the tables.

Gazing out at the relentless drizzle, one morning, Polly was moved to poetize her frustration at the prospect of being kept indoors for another day, creating games to keep Tilly amused:

"Rain, rain, again and again,
Rain running down the window pane,
Gives me pain in my belly and brain."

"Veritably," commented Cally, "You are a poet and nobody knows it."

"So my artistry is not appreciated," complained Polly. Feigning a hurt moue. "You love your Shelley, your Byron, your Southey and your Keats, but not your resident poet. I am miffed. More than that, I am deeply hurt.

She pulled another exaggerated face in mock chagrin.

"You should not be," said Cally, cuddling her sister. "Your whole body contains rather less poetry than pee, my love. It is true that I read the poems of the greats, but it is pretty Polly Forester of Kennington Common, that I take into my bed each night."

It was during 1816, that Elizabeth Fry explained to the Reed sisters that she needed to devote more time to her own several children and hoped that Cally and Polly might be willing to take on some of her work, spending more time visiting Newgate prison, in particular. Of course, they agreed and this became their chief occupation. As well as continuing their teaching of children and mothers, they gathered around them several helpers from among the Quaker Friends and from the congregation of St Mary's Church. This allowed for more teaching sessions and the wider collection of clothes, shoes, bedding and other comforts for the prisoners. A system introduced by Mrs Fry was continued. She had already won from the Governor the unofficial concession of the separation of men from women and children. The adult prisoners were now divided into groups of ten or a dozen and required to appoint a monitor from among their number. It was the monitor's task to make sure each prisoner received a fair share of prison food and of the clothing and other comforts brought in by the visitors. The monitors' hardest challenge was to make sure each prisoner had a fair share of space. For example, the womens' accommodation was a hall big enough for about 60, into which up to 300 were often crammed – some with children – varying according to how many were sent down by the Bow Street magistrates, who had no regard for the overcrowding their sentencing might create in Newgate.

The sisters thought long and hard about this problem. Could the magistrates be persuaded to make occasional visits, so that they could be shown the cruel consequences of their insouciant committal of prisoners to Newgate? Overcrowding led to more arguments and violence between prisoners and worsened the problems of poor sanitation and the spread of vermin and disease. But in order to send fewer prisoners to Newgate, the Bench might decide to send more to the Thames hulks, where conditions were even more inhumane.

The root of the problem was the government's penal policies, which incarcerated too many people. The law was too harsh. For so many petty offences, people were sent to gaol, transported, or even sentenced to death. Capital sentences were often commuted to transportation, or long terms in prison

This ostensibly Christian society was locking up and abandoning thousands of people for lack of a little charity, which if applied, might see them reformed and redeemed.

There came a day when all hell was let loose among the women. This was now most unusual. There was shouting, screaming and fighting, made more frenetic by the gin they had somehow obtained. One of the monitors explained to Cally that a group of prisoners had learned that they were to be transported to Botany Bay for varying terms, torn from family and friends and likely never to return. They were to leave Newgate in just a few days. To make matters worse, they knew that they would be taken from the prison to the hulks at Deptford, in open carts, manacled and chained to one another. The riff-raff on the London streets, having been denied the spectacle of a public flogging or execution for some time, would enjoy treating the prisoners with screaming calumny and pelting them with all manner of rubbish and filth. In this supposedly Christian nation, empathy was in short supply. For the sake of the women and their children who were due to be transported, the monitor agreed to accompany Cally to the governor, Major Cathcart, in order to see whether there might be some mitigation for this transport.

"Major", said Cally", this is Miss Sarah Webb, one of our valued monitors among the women prisoners. She will explain to you the cause of the disorder just broken out, which is nowadays most unusual and could, we suggest, be easily calmed.

Sarah spoke first and then Cally added: "This news of transportation has been sprung upon the prisoners, who understandably fear they may not survive the sea journey, or may die at Botany Bay and never again see England. Furthermore, Sir, you know what horrors will be inflicted on the women, at the hands of the street mob, on the journey from here to Deptford. A herd of sheep passing through the City would suffer no hurt, unlike these wretched women and children, who fear being pelted with stones, all manner of filth and opprobrium.

"When spotting a prisoner transport, the street mob shows no mercy, especially if, of late, there has been no public execution to entertain them.

"When they leave on the morrow, may they not be in a covered cart or in Hackney carriages from here to the quay? If cost is the impediment, I will see that you are fully reimbursed. If you agree to this concession, I think the women's wing can be quickly returned to its customary calm."

The governor, out of respect for Cally and her good works, agreed and this set a precedent for future transportations, at least of women and children, from Newgate.

That afternoon, Cally was missing from the Reed family dinner table.

Polly explained the concession over the journey to Deptford that Cally had won for the women. She added that she had little doubt that her sister would travel with the women and be there for their leave-taking at the dockside.

"She was sure you would not be angry. She sent me home without her, because she is spending tonight with the women who are to be transported in the morning. She is writing letters for them to their relatives, who they fear they will never see again. The prisoners doubt they will ever return to England. She is trying to reassure them about the long sea journey and what to expect at Botany Bay.

"She has learned from Mrs Fry how to speak calmingly to the women. I think she will relieve their distress. Although she considers it a vacuous occupation for herself, she will kneel with them and lead them in prayer, just as Mrs Fry would. I know the prisoners will value her presence through the long hours of darkness. They might otherwise cause a great deal of clamour and have the guards giving them a cruel last night in Newgate."

Father and mother were not worried for their daughter. They knew her to be strong and resilient, but in the absence of the vivacious Cally, the family was in sombre mood.

Lavender broke the silence:"In his Sermon on the Mount, Jesus said, 'I was in prison and you came unto me.' One of the righteous answered him, 'When saw we thee in prison?'

"Jesus explained, 'Verily I say unto you: inasmuch as ye have done that for one of the least of these, my brethren, ye have done it unto me.'"

Polly said: "Sir, as a preacher, you are superior to the Rector. You are more sincere, more convincing. You are, to be sure, the most Christian unbeliever I know."

""Polly, dear", said Mother, "You must not reserve for him a place in heaven. He does not believe in it."

They turned to making arrangements to collect Cally from Deptford Quay on the morrow.

As soon as they heard of the impending transport, the prison visitors and helpers had assembled a bundle for each prisoner, containing, along with their personal possessions, spare clothes, an apron, a Bible, a thimble and scissors, a little money and remnants of fabric donated by local haberdashers, thread, tape, ribbon and needles, so that the women had some occupation during the voyage and perhaps something to sell on arrival in Brazil, the half-way point, or Australia.

At Deptford, Cally saw the weeping women aboard, carrying their pathetic bundles and saw to her dismay that the women from other parts of the country were not nearly as well served as those from Newgate. She resolved to tell this to Mrs Fry, so that their good practices might be spread to other prisons.

Cally climbed down into the hold which would be the quarters for most of the prisoners. It was on two levels. She asked to meet the captain and explained to him the Newgate monitorial system and its benefits in ensuring fair shares of food and space and encouraging group cohesion, self-control and calm. The captain expressed his thanks for this advice and said he would ensure his officers and crew knew of it and would implement it."

He seemed a humane man. He agreed to keep the men on the lower level and the women, with their children, on the upper level. He suggested dividing the prisoners into groups of 12, including their children and would recognise whoever each group put forward as their monitor. Cally felt she could ask no more and pleaded that he might write to her and Mrs Fry on his arrival at Botany Bay. It would be good to hear of their safe arrival. The prisoners in this transport were unaware how relatively fortunate they were. Their conviction and sentencing had coincided with a Botany Bay ship being due to depart from Deptford and consequently they went straight from prison to embarkation. Most transports left their prisons and had to await a sailing, held on a prison hulk moored on the Thames. These were rotting decommissioned naval ships, anchored off-shore, at Woolwich or Greenhithe, with the prisoners held, sometimes for several months, in conditions even worse than the prisons from which they came. Cally decided to urge Mrs Fry to press the Home Minister so to arrange transportations that direct embarkation was possible, avoiding incarceration in the hulks. In addition, during the long voyages, the prisoners need useful occupation. There should be books available to them. It is wrong to assume they are all illiterate.

Lavender and Polly rode to Deptford and met an exhausted and tearful Cally on the dockside. There was a bitter wind and she wore no coat, having given it to Sarah Webb. Huddled in a saddle blanket, She rode home pillion behind her father.

At their next meeting, the ever-patient Rector listened to Cally's comments on the transportation punishment, its gratuitous cruelty and what the bishops in Parliament should do about it.

The rector said he would be happy to write to the Bishop of London, the Very Reverend William Howley, but he would first like more information. Cally agreed to consult with Elizabeth Fry and perhaps assemble an essay on the matter; in English, rather than Latin, she hastened to affirm.

There was to be a meeting of the Hampden Club at the Saracen's Head in Fore Street, overlooking the Thames. This presented a problem for the girls. They went there for a meeting once before, when they were new to the Club and not yet known to the other members. The publican had seen two unaccompanied young women enter and thought the worst. He drove them out, shouting that he was having no trollops in this respectable house.

The sisters planned this second visit carefully. They went to the extravagance of hiring a gig, with a canopy, for the short journey. On arrival they bid the driver to wait for them. They donned long sackcloth aprons before entering the dim, smoke-filled taproom. They started collecting the empty tankards and pots. Provided they were doing menial tasks, women were quite acceptable, so it seemed. When they had both hands full and there were no more empties on the tables, they made for the door at rear of the room, rightly guessing that it led to a balcony. This is where men stood, relieving their beer-filled bellies into the river. All the mugs and pots were dropped on to the slime and mud below. They now went back through the taproom, into the gig, telling the driver to make haste back to Kennington.

They were elated. This was their first demonstrative action for the rights of women. The rude man who had insulted them was now the hapless landlord of a pot-less tavern.

The spring of 1816 seemed never to warm, but the rain was incessant. When rarely not obscured by lowering dark clouds the sunsets were fantastic in yellow, orange, blood-red and purple.

Then came late snow, which freezing nights turned to ice. Daytime brought blue skies and sunshine which was not warm enough to relieve the frozen earth. One day, the sisters rode to Wimbledon and Putney Common. There came a point when smoke-grey cloud obscured the sun and, for lack of grey shadows, the fields and woods became a starkly black and white world. Then, in the late afternoon, the cloud dispersed and the sunset turned the western sky into a wonder of red, orange, yellow and lilac, with these colours reflected in the icy covering of the rising ground of the Chilterns.

It was a breathtaking sight. "Perhaps it is such wonders as this that lead some to seek explanation in a god-figure," suggested Polly, lost in thought.

In August, 1816, in weather that was more like late autumn than late summer, Cally and Polly Had decided to tackle the Rector on the existence of God.

The routine business of their lesson finished, Cally broached the subject. "Mr Osmond, it is now more than a year since the eruption of Mount Tambora. Tens of thousands of islanders were killed within hours, in the initial lava flows. I have read in the newspaper that thousands more are dyingall over the world, even now, as a consequence of harvests failing in the year which had no summer and the continuing dark and cold weather.

"Why has God allowed this to happen?"

The Rector sat with his hands pressed together, in his usual composed manner, looking down intently at the table, as if the polished mahogany might contain a revelation. He made no answer and so Cally repeated her challenge.

"If there is an omnipotent and beneficent god, how can such slaughter of innocents be allowed?

"The most likely explanation is that, contrary to popular belief, there is no god."

At this, the Rector riled. "You are denying God by reason of his creation not being perfect.

"But God never claimed perfection. Even the greatest part of his creation, Man, was flawed from the outset. Despite the clear admonitions, which came directly from God, Adam and Eve committed sins in the Garden of Eden. They allowed themselves to be seduced by the enticement of the serpent, eating the fruit of the tree of knowledge of good and evil and trying to know the mind of God.

"The serpent had, of course, misled them. Having eaten of the forbidden fruit, they became no wiser, but now saw themselves for what they were: not on a par with the angels, but naked, no better than the other animals and fallen from God's grace.

"You see," said the Rector, with a smile for the sisters, which was intended to be benign, but which Polly interpreted as patronising, "We are as imperfect as the rest of God's creation."

"Not good enough." Polly rounded on Mr Osmond with such vigour that both he and Cally were momentarily taken aback."Still you can offer no reason for the death toll inflicted by such catastrophes as Mount Tambora."And why do so many have to suffer the evil that some powerful men inflict, such as the recent wars across Europe and the hunger caused in this country by the Corn Laws?

"Surely, an omnipotent god has the power to intervene and stop the evil-doers.

The rector fidgeted, shifting his chair so that he directly faced both sisters. His voice now took on that solemn delivery and slightly up and down timbre he usually reserved for the Sunday pulpit. Polly saw this as meaning that Mr Osmond had now had enough of calm philosophical discussion with these self-confessed unbelievers and was about to make better use of his time, by changing to serious preaching mode.

In his measured evangelizing voice, the Rector patiently explained that God had chosen not to exert His dominion by pre-determining the unfolding history of His creation. His work of six days, as described in the *Book of Genesis*, being completed, the Earth and mankind have been left to their own devices. Man is not a slave or automaton. Man has been given free will, but has to be accountable on the Day of Judgement, either heaven or hell being the fate in store.

"Accountable eventually,"Polly scoffed, "But meanwhile, so much suffering can be inflicted on innocent people.

"And it seems to me that the richest people always enjoy the greatest amount of free will, while the poor and weak have little or no free will. They are left to be the victims of other people's free will.

Cally was becoming impatient at this turn in the discussion.

"I know, Mr Osmond, that there are eminent men who are deists, believing in an omnipotent god who created the world, but who stands aloof, making no attempt to have further influence.

"There have also been natural philosophers, who, despite their profound interest in secular matters, have been devout Catholics. I have in mind Gallilei Gallileo and Nicolaus Copernicus. Between them they proved the Ptolemaic model of our solar system to be mistaken. Ptolemy pictured the Earth at the centre of the system, with the sun and planets in fixed positions relative to one another, on a nest of celestial domes, slowly turning, with Earth at the centre of the circle. If God was the creator, this is not the system he created and yet he tolerated generations of men believing it to be so. He even stood by while the authorities of his Church persecuted men who questioned the validity of Ptolemy's system, proposing an alternative system which more closely conformed to observed reality.

"Empirical studies, especially since the invention of the telescope, have shown that the sun, not Earth is at the centre of our planetary system. If there is a creator god, that is the system he created, the heliocentric universe.

"I cannot believe in an omnipotent god who shows no omnipotence, not even intervening when his one sentient creation, man, is labouring, for generations under erroneous ideas and not even when those who reveal the true nature of God's creation are persecuted by the authorities of his Church. "It makes no sense. It is not just. Did he not care when the Pope and his other representatives on Earth were proscribing truthful depictions of his universe and prescribing Ptolemy's false depiction?

"Another crazy state of affairs. In brief, I see no reason for assuming the existence of god.

Among the deists there are some great thinkers, to whom I bow, but in accepting the hypothesis that god exists, there being no other explanation for the creation of Earth, the sea, night and day, the sun, moon and planets and mankind, I consider them to be wrong. Let them show patience, rather than embracing a mythological explanation of Creation. The time will come when discoveries will reveal the truth of the origin of Earth and human life. Meanwhile, god is merely a hypothesis and a hypothesis I do not require. I am prepared to await the empirical findings of the natural philosophers"

As Mrs Osmond entered the room in order to rescue her embattled husband, Cally and Polly stood and moved towards the door. "Thank you, Rector", said Polly, making a slight bob, "For such a stimulating discussion. I fear it may be some time before we see eye to eye on these matters."

The Rector said not a word, but looked up to the ceiling, as if he could see through it, to the seat of God. Was he looking for divine consolation? Or perhaps more helpful revelation.

On the way home, Cally said, "I am sure you realise that, as committed atheists, we are probably among a minority of reformist activists. From our correspondents' letters, we can tell that most of them have at least some residual religious belief, or may even be deeply involved in the Baptists, or Evangelical Methodism, they may be Quakers or the Scots may be Episcopalians. I have yet to come across an Anglican reformist, but they may exist. Why are there so many believers?

"Could it be simply that people want an after-life? Complete nonsense. There is neither heaven nor hell, no after-life.

"I am sure the biggest influence is your childhood," said Polly. "Few young children would stand firm against their parents and few would be more strongly influenced outside the family than within it.

"I hear there is a chapel in Camberwell that conducts conversions and baptisms every week," said Cally. "it would take us no more than an hour to ride there and see what it is all about"

Accordingly, the next Sunday saw them seating themselves in a recently-built bleak building full of people. The ascetic nature of the church was matched by the formidable dourness of the congregation. St Mary's Church had stained glass windows, paintings, banners, memorial plaques and the clergy and choir in liturgical vestments. Some of this decoration had miraculously survived from the time when this and all other churches owed allegiance to Rome.

No such frivolous decoration or clutter here, in Camberwell's Ebenezer Strict Baptist Church. although there were serious and sanctimonious-looking congregants.

There was no organ. The mournful hymns, each appearing to drone on for a score or more of repetitious verses, every single one a dismal dirge going on forever. The accompaniment was provided by a man with a concertina and a woman energetically foot-pumping a harmonium.

There were enthusiastic singers, who appeared to aspire to grand opera. Their voices were audible above all others. There were embarrassed mumblers, mainly men, and there were several women trying to make the most of their feeble, piping high-pitched voices. Cally could have whispered scathing comments to Polly about the performance, but she knew the people were taking the service very seriously and she respected their right to do so.

A man in a surplice – the chapel's sole concession to traditional ecclesiastical dress – mounted the platform. In a sepulchral voice, which battered the bare walls, he delivered the sermon. He reminded the congregation that the Christmas season was approaching. It should be a time of pious contemplation and celebration. Instead, it was for many a time for intemperance and licentiousness.

True believers should meet as families and sing the well known Christmas hymns, not the coarse popular songs of the day. Dancing is often a suspect activity. Bringing a man and a woman into close contact, it can

lead to spooning and other sinful behaviour, bringing
the evil-doers to the edge of the fiery pit.

Polly was aware of Cally's increasing agitation. She
was fidgeting on the seat and she was licking a finger
and vigorously rifling through the pages of a Bible
from beside her on the pew.

A grunt of satisfaction indicated that Cally's hunt
had been successful. Up she stood and imperiously
interjected: "Sir, am I right in thinking that the Bible is
the fount of all wisdom?"

Disapproving looks and mumbles around the chapel
indicated widespread resentment at this intrusion by a
complete stranger, a brown woman, who has the
audacity to interrupt the minister's sermon. It has never
been known.

"The good book is the word of God and, of course,
totally without errancy. The minister smiled benignly
on Cally and took a deep breath in order to continue his
homily, but before he uttered another word, Cally leapt
in, turning this way and that, in order to address the
whole congregation from her place near the centre of
the chapel: the word of God says, "To everything there
is a season and a time to every purpose under the
heaven." She held up the bible so that everybody could
see the impeccable source of her reading.

Her voice was loud and clear. "A time to be born and
a time to die. A time to plant and a time to pluck up that
which was planted. A time to kill, A time to heal … a
time to weep and a time to laugh.

"A time to mourn and a time to dance. A time to
embrace and a time to refrain from embracing".

"Sir, you admonish us for contemplating dancing at Christmas and for the bodily contact that dancing implies.

"And yet, in the scriptures without errancy, in the appropriate season, there is a time to dance, a time to embrace and a time for laughing."

The minister'sresponse was a dire warning. "Beware temptation" he warned, his voice melodramatically trembling, as if to emphasise how frightening was his warning.

"Dance if you must, but members of the same sex and in broad daylight, not in evening light.

"By all means gather at the family hearth, in order to share holy readings and to sing hymns.

Christmas is a season of great temptation. In sinfulness we teeter on the edge of the fiery pit.

On the way home, "That book of Ecclesiastes," said Cally, "really is the most meaningless drivel.

"I can't see the workers of Camberwell sitting at their firesides on Christmas Day, reading from the Bible. I am sure the ban on dancing and popular songs will be as effective as it was in Cromwell's time. Only die-hard puritans will pay it any regard.

By the autumn of 1816, there was considerable disorder in all parts of the country. The distress caused by unemployment and the high price of bread was aggravated by another poor harvest and the abolition of income tax. The tax on earnings from professions, profits and investments had been introduced by Pitt the Younger in 1798 and ran for the duration of the

Napoleonic wars. On its abolition, the Government replaced it as a source of income by duties on various goods, including salt, sugar, soap, candles and leather, causing the prices of these commodities to rise unprecedentedly. Thus the burden of taxation was moved from the better-off to the poor. The Riot Act was being read by magistrates in many towns where, for example, during an election poll, disputatious groups might resort to fisticuffs, which escalated to looting and arson, revenge being meted out on greedy landlords, merchants or magistrates. Militias were frequently called out and gaols were bursting.

A tax had long been levied according to the number of hearths in a house. A new tax depended on the number of windows in a house. A desperate government had put a price on God's heavenly light. Would the air we breathe be the next target?

A coalition of radical groups, led by the Spenceans, assessed that, such was the mood of the people, they were ready for demonstrative action. They called for a mass gathering, in November, at Spa Fields, a common at Clerkenwell.

Cally and Polly were eager to go to the gathering, but how to get there? It was a long way and it would probably be raining, as usual. Disappointed by their feebleness, they decided to stay at home. The Spa Fields crowd was addressed by Henry Hunt, the greatest radical orator of the day. Proceedings ended with the crowd's agreement, by acclamation, that Hunt should take to the Prince Regent a petition seeking relief of the distress of the people and parliamentary reform. At the gates of Carlton house, Hunt was twice denied admittance. This calculated snub illustrated the extent of Prince George's egregious arrogance and contempt for his subjects and his reckless uncouthness. It would have cost him nothing to graciously receive the delegation and their petition and then to ignore it, as was the fate of all such pleas and representations. After all, there is nothing to be feared from such mass gatherings. With the crowds dispersed and the demonstrators left confronting the problems of their everyday lives, memories of the up-lifting speeches and petitions fade and the ship of state sails on undisturbed and the demonstrators expend their remaining energy and anger in traipsing home in the interminable rain.

As word spread, the insulting treatment of Hunt cut deeply. The organisers of the meeting decided on another mass gathering in the following month. On 2nd December, another enormous crowd gathered. The members of the various organisations were now in angrier mood, providing fertile ground for the spies and provocators, who induced a large section of the crowd to march on the Tower, aiming to take control of it, with its great armoury. Others were intent on capturing the Royal Exchange, where the nation's wealth was kept (so they mistakenly thought). The men were well armed from cart-loads of pikes, swords and guns which had been drawn to Spa Fields. On their way to the Tower, men collected additional weapons by looting gunsmiths' shops on Snow Hill.

The spies and *agents provocateur* earned a lot of money that day by forewarning the army and Bow Street magistrates of the likelihood of armed insurgency.

Confronted by Soldiers and police, who were beating and arresting the vanguard of the march, the demonstrators first hesitated and then started dispersing in confusion, many more of them being pursued, beaten and taken into custody.

It became known among the Hampden Club members that it was the radical zealot, young Doctor Jem Watson, again in drink, who initiated the break-away from the main demonstration, providing opportunity for the spy, John Castle, to provoke a riot.

1817

For those who could be bothered with such nonsense, which occasionally included Lavender and Ananya, Prinny continued to be an endless source of amusement. In 1794, while Regent, he had married his first cousin, Princess Caroline of Brunswick, although he was already secretly married to Maria Fitzherbert and so he was committing bigamy. As his detractors in the satirical sheets pointed out, he was being a thoroughly naughty boy. He should not have married Maria without the permission of the king, his father, George III, He should not have married a Catholic, as that would penalise him by removing him from the line of succession. But Lord Liverpool's government was unlikely to suggest that the laws of the land, least of all the law against bigamy, should apply to blue-bloods. After all, a royal marriage has nothing to do with love or religion and everything to do with politics and preservation of the monarchy.

In some lower class communities, first cousin marriage was frowned upon, but it was common among the royal families of Europe. After all, there was not an enormous supply of nobility and it was absolutely out of the question that a prince or princess might stoop to marrying a commoner.

Lords Liverpool and Sidmouth saw the Spa Fields disturbance as proof that armed revolution was in preparation and imminent. In this febrile state, the government resurrected every repressive measure in its armoury, rushing through Parliament renewal of legislation from the previous century, the so-called Gagging Acts. Meetings of over 50 people, unless for legitimate purpose, such as vestry meetings, were banned and magistrates were empowered to arrest anyone suspected of spreading sedition. Henceforth, anyone making a speech, writing an article or making organisational arrangements, which could be interpreted as tending to encourage insurrection against the established order, should be arrested. The Treason Act, 1817 made it a crime of high treason, punishable by being hanged, beheaded, eviscerated and quartered, to plan or cause any physical harm to the Prince Regent, although he was not the monarch. "I remember the Easter hymn, said Cally, "that refers to 'His precious blood.' I suppose every drop of Prinny's blue blood is considered too precious to be spilt."

In January 1817, the sisters attended a meeting of their Hampden Club, held in a local tavern. After the initial formalities, the meeting quickly became a lengthy post mortem of the recent Spa Fields demonstrations held at the end of the previous year. Cally's thinking had been dwelling on the meetings and the massive defeat they represented for the aims of the Hampden clubs and the whole reformist movement.

She leapt into the discussion as soon as there was a pause.

"I have read Henry Hunt's words and there is a sharp contrast between what he advocated and the behaviour of a large section of the crowd.

"Mr Hunt demanded universal male suffrage, secret ballots, equal-sized electoral areas and annual elections. He stressed that these aims would be achieved not by insurrection, but by exerting the sheer weight of opinion of the vast majority of the people, whose support would be won by the power of our arguments and the obvious justice of our cause.

"He eschewed violence and yet hundreds of our supporters, overcome by excitement, and vulnerable to incitement, allowed themselves to be led like sheep by the government's perfidious agitators planted amongst them.

I side with Henry Hunt's words, but not with his trust in petitioning the hard–hearted men of power. Neither do I side with the demonstrators who fell for the trickery of the infiltrated spies and agitators, acting on the silly notion that after dinner, they could enjoy the afternoon taking over the nation's seats of power."

It was clear that Cally was merely getting into her stride, with much more to say. A man dragged an up-turned box towards her and handed her on to it. Now she could be seen as well as heard.

"Have we learned nothing since 1381 and the peasants' rising of that year?

This rhetorical question drew shouts of support from some and looks of bafflement from others.

"In 1381, Wat Tyler mustered an army of thousands, putting our few hundred at Spa Fields in the shade. They made no feeble toy soldier march on the Tower. No. By brute force and strength of numbers, they took over the City and captured and punished the evil men of the Church and State who had oppressed the people. That was revolution in word and deed."

"Hear, hear" was heard from around the room, as well as foot stamping and fists banging on the tables. Cally's voice had been rasping and now she was coughing and struggling to continue. Polly knew the stuffiness and dense tobacco smoke was seriously irritating her sister's throat. She rushed to the outer door and threw it open, ignoring the protests of men now sitting in the draught. She handed Cally her pot of small beer and ordered her to take some. Cally now had a second wind and carried on with gusto.

"Despite the strength of his army's position, Wat Tyler fell for the king's trickery. Those were the days when monarchs were thought to rule by divine right and were close to God. Simple folk would wait for days for an opportunity to receive the royal touch, which was thought to cure disease. Since that time we have seen that Kings are nothing more than mortal men. We have even executed an evil king and we beheaded Charles I over 100 years before the French beheaded Louis XVI." There were cheers around the room and pots banged on the tables.

"Wat Tyler accepted the invitation to meet King Richard II, in order to receive confirmation of the royal concession of most of the rebels' demands. Beguiled by this apparent success, Tyler went to the king, as arranged and was attacked and severely wounded by the king's henchmen and was then beheaded. Now leaderless, Tyler's followers dispersed in panic and confusion. Hundreds were hunted down and gaoled or killed.

"Kings, when seeing their power threatened, cannot be trusted to behave in a civilised manner.

"That is the bitter lesson of 1381, which should never be forgotten; yet our leaders went from Spa Fields, lamely sought to petition Prince George and were disappointed by his predictable response. There should be no more obsequious petitions. There should be nothing less than a stern remonstrance. We should state our case in detail and demand, I repeat, *demand* our rights. No more weak supplications. There are so many of us and so few of them, that there must come the day when we mobilise hundreds of thousands, rather than hundreds. There will then be less need of weapons; with such strength of numbers, no government could dismiss or ignore our demands. Government intransigence would be countered by the people immobilising the entire country until all demands are met.

"Our Hampden clubs and other organisations are in agreement over our aims. Disagreements over strategy are not so great that we are benumbed. Ignoring the government'S gagging laws, we continue our education of the people; we publish our pamphlets and books, including the writings of Tom Spence, Thomas Paine, Richard Carlile and William Cobbett. We continue our readings for those who cannot read for themselves"

With a fist raised in the air, Cally declared: "We defy Lords Liverpool, Sidmouth and Castlereagh and the sycophants around them, who stand in the way of reform, progress and justice."

That Cally's polished prose was delivered off the cuff, made it all the more impressive.

Polly took her hands and she stepped down to loud applause, shouts of support and stomping.

During 1817, Calpurnia Wright was much in demand to speak at meetings and conduct public readings. Her sister, Polly, usually accompanied her.

In May 1817, Cally spoke at another Hampton Club meeting. She referred to her previous speech, in which she excoriated the Prince Regent for his contempt of the people. She had now received word, confirmed in the newspapers, of a body of starving spinners and weavers, leaving Manchester on 10th March, intent on parading the 165 Miles to London, in order meet and petition the Regent. Intelligence must have reached Carlton House, because the Prince had arranged a reception for his subjects in usual style. Not eleven miles along their route, the marchers were halted by the army, with the customary arrests and beatings.

"How many lessons do we reformists need in order to learn that the Prince and the entire government are contemptuous of us and our cause?" she stormed.

"How can we Spencians give wise leadership to the poor and downtrodden if we are ourselves in a permanent state of confusion? There can be no lasting solution to the plight of the hungry until we have some power in Parliament.

"That requires constitutional reform; reform that limits the power of the aristocracy and propertied classes and limits the power of the monarchy.

"Some of us would go further. Tom Spence has written that 'Thirst for absolute power is the natural disease of monarchy.' Let us rid the land of this diseased institution, this abomination of hereditary succession."

In January 1817 a new publication appeared. *Black Dwarf* was published by Thomas Jonathan Wooler. It came out weekly at 4 pence, giving news of radical meetings and satirising the government, its ministers and its policies. Wooler, speaking as the eponymous Black Dwarf, explained his aims: "To expose every species of vice and folly with which this virtuous age abounds. Neither the Throne, nor the altar will be sanctuary against the Dwarf's intrusion."

This was challenge, indeed, to the distrustful and uneasy government and within three months Wooler was arrested and charged with seditious libel. With Wooler imprisoned, there was no lack of substitute editors stepping forward to take his place, including Richard Carlile. In 1819, in an attempt to stifle all radical papers, the government imposed a tax, which forced *black Dwarf*'s price up to six pence a week, but still each issue amazingly sold 12,000 copies. The sisters were frequently called upon to read the paper, cover to cover, for gatherings in taverns or at family hearths.

1818 saw gas lighting installed on some of the streets of central London. This innovation was detested by the dippers and put some of the link-boys out of a job, but it helped to make the sisters feel safer when away from home longer than planned and on the rare occasions they were out and about in the evening.

Lavender, who tried to keep abreast of modern developments, made their house the first one in the street to have gas lighting in some of the rooms. This bookish family found the bright light a great boon on dark evenings and they quickly became used to the constant murmuring of the gas mantles, finding it much to be preferred to the flickering yellow light, smoke and heavy smell of tallow candles. The housemaids, that is, Cally and Polly, no longer had the daily task of airing the rooms and scraping dripped wax from the furniture and floors.

The sisters were now among the most familiar figures in the radical organisations of London and their attendance at meetings and their wide reading, made them as erudite as any other activists.

During the sisters' childhood and adolescence – roughly the first quarter of the new century – the country became industrialised at great pace. Small-scale masters gave way to bigger manufacturers. Weavers, stockingers and nail-makers became wage-earning out-workers, their employment being as precarious as the varying demands of the market.

From around 1817, their correspondence with Hampden Clubs in all parts helped the sisters form a picture of developments in the Midlands and North. The discipline of the factory system, with its fixed hours and required work rates, was becoming widespread. Now working in large groups, rather than singly in their cottages, the manufacturing population, as it was sometimes termed, became aware of their exploitation and the social cohesion of groups of employees led to resistance and collective action, which employers met with oppressive measures, always able to call on the coercive arms of the state, the police, magistrates and militias.

The industrial discipline imposed by the masters was increasingly countered by the collective consciousness of the working class.

Concluding her remarks, when invited to deliver a speech at the Deptford Political Union, Cally said, "We reformers are continually lambasted by government ministers and bishops, who keep harping on about violence during the the Spa Fields events in 1816 and alleged disorder at other gatherings, but no matter how demonstratively and violently the anger of the poor and distressed may be expressed, it will never match the murderous levels of the state and the slaughterers it employs. As she spoke, she was unaware how painfully valid her words would prove in Derbyshire, a few months hence.

"The poor are learning the value of mutual support and organisation in trade unions.

"Brought together in factories and mines, men, women and children, in large numbers, suffer long working hours, dangerous conditions and pitiful wages from the masters. In the few hours they are not at work, they are thrown together in over-crowded, insanitary, jerry-built houses, in the shadow of the mill or pit-wheel, owing rent to the same master and even having no choice but to buy their necessities in the masters' truck shops. Among the factory-hands of the Midlands and North, a new kind of political awareness is evolving, solidarity among the manual workers. The more far-sighted among them come to the conclusion that their lives will not be improved unless they gain influence over the law-making of Parliament."

Where the sisters lived, apart from ship-building, there were no great manufactures. Radical politics continued to draw its strongest influence from London's artisans, the Spitalfields weavers, the printers and book-sellers, shoe-makers, saddlers, building workers, Jewish tailors, dissenting lay preachers and even some professional men, including writers, doctors and lawyers, who had become enlightened by their reading of Cobbett or Henry Hunt's speeches, or their own observation of the privations of the poor, among whom they lived and worked.

Hampden Clubs, in centres like Leicester, Birmingham, Manchester, Sheffield and Derby, had tentacles extending into surrounding villages.

Particularly well organised were the stocking frame weavers of the Nottingham area. The knitting machine was invented around the turn of the 19th century, enormously speeding the production of stockings and making the clothiers, the middle-men, rich. Priced out of work, the grievances of the cottage hand-knitters reached a peak from around 1811 to 1816, when the Luddite frame-breakers resorted to smashing the machines they saw as destroying their livelihoods. The surviving frame-knitters were skilled men. The frame demanded complex manual operation, using both hands and both feet simultaneously. Some likened their skill to playing a cathedral organ, with its many keys, stops and pedals.

The legacy of the Luddite struggles and awareness of the wealth being created for the clothiers by the sweat of the operator's brow led these workers towards militancy.

During 1816, a new Hampden Club had been added to the sisters' list of correspondents. It was in Royton, a short distance from Manchester. This was a most valuable addition to the Hampden Club network, being a source of news from the fastest-growing industrial centre in the country.

It was known that the war years, with the need of uniforms, blankets and tents for the army and sail canvas for the navy, had been a boom time for the spinners and weavers of the cotton, wool and linen industries of the North, West Country and East Anglia. The possibility of a steady income led to rapid growth in the textile industry. Small farmers, agricultural labourers, returning soldiers and immigrants entered the mills or set up looms in their homes.

Lingering memories of the good times were described in the letters from Royton. The spinners and weavers were increasingly aware that it was by their being exploited that the mill-owners and clothiers had so quickly become rich men, bequeathing churches and building big houses for themselves. The embryonic trade unions, seeking a shorter working week and better pay, organised strikes and protests, which were strenuously put down. The Royton correspondent recorded the general jaundiced view of their local magistrates and employers (usually much the same people), backed by the local Anglican clergy, These worthies all shared the firm conviction that depressed earnings encouraged harder work, whereas too much money in the pocket led to unwillingness to work and to drunkenness.

For a working week of six 14-hour days, dawn to dusk, with only the Sabbath free, the workers in the Manchester area received an average of six shillings. Their dilemma was that a reduction in these torturous hours would entail a loss of pay. Such was the growing strength of feeling at this gross injustice that the matter had reached the House of Commons in the form of the Minimum Wage Bill, 1808, moved by George Rose MP, Vice president of the Board of Trade, who had received representations, from all levels within society, concerning the hardship peculiar to the cotton weaving trade. Cally read that opposition to the Bill in parliament was led by a member who perversely argued that much of the distress arises not from wages being too low, but because at one time they were too high. Reading this caused her blood pressure to rise and the dinner table was treated to her diatribe against the mill-owners and their lackeys at Westminster.

The 1808 Bill was rejected and five days later, there was a strike and a demonstration by 6,000 weavers on St George's Field. The magistrates called out the dragoons and the crowd was dispersed with the customary arrests and bloodshed.

When Cally and Polly, at their Hampden Club drew attention to the problem of excessive working hours detailed in letters from the spinning and weaving districts, one of the members reported the ideas of Robert Owen and the humane working conditions he had created at his New Lanark Mills.

Established by Owen's father-in-law beside the River Clyde, the factories used water-power to drive machinery invented by Richard Arkwright. When management passed to Owen, he implemented his ideas for hygienically planned housing for the workers, recreational amenities and schools. New Lanark demonstrated that inhuman working conditions were not necessary for a business to turn a profit. As steam engines replaced fluctuating water as the source of power, Productivity increased, excessive working hours were no longer necessary for employees to receive an adequate wage and child-labour could be dispensed with. Advancing production methods should have allowed higher wages and better conditions for the workers, but the discontent of growing bodies of craftsmen, concentrated in manufactures, combined with political Jacobinism, terrified the employers' class and the government into taking drastic action. The previous century's legislation, in the form of the Combination Acts was called upon by Pitt and

Wilberforce to counter the nascent trade unions when taking action to improve pay and conditions. Strikes and any other restrictive practices were branded subversive conspiracies. Combination leaders were identified by magistrates, with the help of Sidmouth's retinue of spies. Then, as described by Francis Place, of the London Corresponding Society, "betrayed, prosecuted, convicted, sentenced and monstrously severe punishments inflicted on them, they were reduced to a most wretched state of existence and kept there"

If hailing from London and the southern counties, they might be thrown into Clerkenwell's Cold Bath Fields House of Correction, of which the poets, Southey and Coleridge, wrote in their poem, The Devil's Walk, quoted by Cally at a meeting:"As he went through Cold Bath Fields/ He saw a cell/ And the Devil was pleased/ For it gave him a hint/ for improving prisons in hell."

When the suspension of habeas corpus was declared, many clubs gave their members protection from arbitrary arrest, by retreating into secrecy. That this cloak-and-dagger manoeuvre was in order to lay plans for revolution, was the authorities' paranoid suspicion.

Cally conjectured that the virtual warfare between the employers and the workers was an innate characteristic of the modern economy and would not be resolved until the economy and society as a whole are organised along the lines of the socialist principles advocated b y Robert Owen.

One of the best known middle class radicals of the day was John Cartwright. From a wealthy family, he had a successful career in the navy, which ended when he relinquished his commission, refusing to fight against the American colonists, whose struggle to free themselves from British rule he supported. He was a founder of the London Corresponding Society and the Hampden clubs, which he named in honour of a leading Parliamentarian in the Civil War. He was a founding sponsor of *Black Dwarf*.

1817

In an attempt to test the possibility of establishing nation-wide coordination of the Hampden clubs and other reformist organisations, convinced, as were some Spenceans, that the people were ready for concerted radical action, Cartwright wrote to all of his contacts, inviting them to a meeting, in January 1817, at the Crown and Anchor Inn, Arundle Street, off the Strand. The sisters were agreed as delegates from their local club. They rode there. They left home in surprising unseasonally brilliant sunshine, but the weather quickly cooled. Cally pointed to what she called the "watery sun", struggling as it was, to be seen through the dulling blanket of cloud.

"Not watery", said Polly, "It's drowndead. The sunk sun has had its flames put out, but after a day or two, it will float back to the surface, as corpses always do"

"Where do you get your crazy ideas? asked Cally, shaking her head in disbelief. "Why, from this sad, mad world," answered Polly, "As Earth spins on its axis, it jumbles my brain."

Reviewing the meeting on their way home, Cally expressed her dismay at the disarray of the reformist movement. Some delegates from Northern parts, described the distress and discontent in their regions and spoke as if the country were on the verge of rising up in revolutionary ardour. They claimed the people were eager and only awaiting the signal from London when it was time to mobilise and overthrow the government. The sisters considered that London was, in reality, a long way from sending any such signal.

There was one valuable outcome from the meeting. Cally was instantly alerted when she heard a delegate introduce himself as William Richards. "*By the pricking of my thumbs, something evil this way comes*", was her immediate thought. She recalled this infamous name from her father's advice that government spies abounded. Knowing this to be the man also known as Oliver the Spy, or John Castle, she concentrated on studying his face and his voice, memorising them for future reference.

It was particularly galling that Richards offered himself to accompany representatives of the London meeting in touring Midland and Northern cities, drumming up support for a revolutionary call later in the year. Before going home, Cally sought out John Cartwright and warned him, that taking Richards to meet the reformist movement's leaders was inviting a viper into the nest. Cartwright was phlegmatic. Fortunately, he did not ask what proof Cally had of Richards' link to the government. He would not have been reassured to learn that this London delegate, to whom he was speaking, was closely related to a Bow Street Runner. "We know," he assured Cally, "That there are spies and agitators in our midst and that is why we do all that we can to protect the identity of our leaders and to ensure that our plans for action are based on real potential, rather than mere hope or ambition". Cally made a mental note of those confident words: "Our plans for action are based on real potential, rather than mere hope or ambition."

"If only that were so", she thought.

True to form, Richards earned his Judas silver by Following Lord Sidmouth's suggested ploy, that he should make the most of agitation in the North by encouraging uprisings with the promise of support from London. His first target was Pentrich and its neighbouring villages in the Amber Valley of Derbyshire. He rode there in the early summer and promised the principal local organiser, Thomas Bacon, who had been a delegate at the January London meeting, instant support from Nottingham and London for any initiative taken by the radical movement in Derbyshire.

Richards then advised Sidmouth that an insurrection was planned for the night of 9th June. The Nottingham magistrates and the 15th Light Dragoons regiment were forewarned accordingly.

At the appointed time and place, 200 to 300 men assembled, comprising quarrymen, pitmen, stockingers, ironworkers and farm labourers. They were armed with farm implements and a few guns. They were convinced that more men and arms would augment their force along the way and that Nottingham would probably be in rebel hands by the time they reached it. London would be their next objective, with hundreds of thousands following their example, by taking up arms. There would be uproarious welcome in the capital. There would befood, drink and guineas aplenty for every brave rebel. This new campaign offered hope for the hopeless, sight of the wider world for the confined villagers and great adventure for the downtrodden.

Before they moved off, following the tradition of the New Model Army, they sang the 23rd Psalm.

Bitter reality struck all too soon. At Eastwood, some fourteen miles from Nottingham, the vanguard saw a solid phalanx of soldiers ahead of them. In disordered panic, they threw down their weapons and fled. There had been just one death, probably accidental. Forty five of those captured were put on trial for high treason. A few were hanged and others were transported.

Lord Sidmouth was embarrassed when the crucial role of his creature, Oliver the Spy, came to light during the trials.

As the news of this sad episode filtered through to London, Cally became very depressed.

She was disappointed that men could be so easily duped and misled by an obvious scoundrel. She was angry that the January meeting in London had so chaotic an outcome that a tragedy such as Pentrich could occur and most of all she was angry with herself for failing to convince John Cartwright that Oliver was an influential agent, about whom the entire movement must be informed and warned.

"What was the point? She ground out in desperation, "Of having a nation-wide network if it fails to convey the most essential information to all principal activists?

"This is a major set-back. Scores of lives have been ruined; hundreds have been disillusioned and probably lost from the reformist cause". Lord Sidmouth's intentions are clear to see. By being provoked into insurrectionary activity that is bound to fail, our supporters become disillusioned and the general populace can be persuaded that we are intemperate, dangerous anarchists, who must be put down for the good of the nation.

Cally did what she always did when in a state of despair, invariably caused by political adversities. She went to the pianoforte and thundered again and again through Bach's Toccata and Fugue, transcribed for pianoforte. Her sight-reading was not good and so there were lots of mistakes, but she rolled on regardless. The entire street must have heard her anger being played out. Having pounded the piano, she now put on her boots and pounded the roads. She eschewed company on her walks. She returned home only when too tired to carry on. She ate hardly anything and said very little. She slept badly, because her mind was constantly rehearsing what might have been and what should have been. If a visitor came into the house, she would disappear to the bedroom. Feeling guilty that she might be casting gloom on the household, without a word, she kissed Polly and her parents several times a day, just to show that the usual Cally was still inside there, somewhere. Polly was sure that Cally had inherited from her father her tendency to melancholia. Of course, Father and Mother noticed Cally's depressed mood, asked Polly what was wrong and were not surprised by her explanation. The more she dwelt on the matter, the more convinced was Cally that the chief burden of responsibility for the repercussions of Pentrich fell on her.

It was unfortunate that, during this bleak time, Cally had an appointment with the Rector for a lesson. She asked that she might be excused early, as she was feeling low. Without probing, Mr Onslow readily agreed and, seeing that Cally was out of sorts, said he would pray for her. This was not the first time he had made such a pledge and Cally wondered how she would benefit from being the subject of a prayer. Would she experience anything particular? Would she feel a cosy glow? Would the Rector's intercession result in God shining a sunbeam of enlightenment on her? She shook off these trivial thoughts, knowing that, if God existed, he would be receiving far too many requests to bother with her self-indulgent maudlin state, verging on self-loathing.

Not until the next meeting of their Hampden Club, the first following Pentrich, did the old sparkle return. It was noticeable that each member walked in, saluting or mumbling greetings, paying the one penny subscription, then sitting and, with a gloomy countenance looking round at all the other dismal faces. The beer and wine had not yet lightened the subdued mood. The usual camaraderie was missing.

From their first days in the London Corresponding Society and in the Hampden Club, without hesitation, the sisters had taken it for granted that they had the same speaking and voting rights as the men. There had initially been murmurs of discontent at the forwardness of these precocious young women, met by a look of withering disdain from those unique eyes. As the proportion of women members grew, their rights were never questioned and their superior skills in reading, piano-playing, handwriting and creating banners were increasingly appreciated.

Until she became used to it, Cally was invariably amused by the strict formality of these meetings. The Chairman would announce that a speaker "Has the floor". He would hammer with his gavel and shout "Order, Order", if anyone interrupted the speaker, or commented derogatively on an earlier speaker, and would come down in terrible wrath on any member who uttered a profanity.

Today, there was the standard formal opening procedure: election of a chairman and minuting secretary, reports from the secretary and treasurer and the laborious reading of the minutes of the previous meeting.

Today, before anyone else, Cally Stood up and indicated that she wished to speak. She had removed her bonnet, but kept on her cloak, because the room was cold.

"Miss Wright is recognised," announced the Chairman, "And has the floor. Attention, please." Her *nom de guerre* was how she was always known in the Club.

"I want to speak about romanticism and realism, because some here present, as in other clubs, appear not to know the difference."

Such a challenging opening struck some as perverse. It was not typical of Hampden Club speakers, but Cally was well known to be not a typical sort of member; a woman; a black woman of striking looks and with much to say. Most of her audience were still fidgeting, mumbling to their neighbours, not yet settled into listening mode, being still preoccupied with the problems of their everyday lives, but eventually content just to sit and be entertained by the usual sort of political discussion at Club meetings. They were quiet, supping from their pots and many puffing on their pipes.

Cally continued: "I freely confess to being a romantic. I love the poetry of Lord Byron and John Keats and Shelley. Speaking as was her wont, without notes, her face was held high and her eyes roamed the room, engaging every listener

"The poets, the composer, Beethoven and the artists John Constable and Joseph Turner have framed the time in which we live − despite the war-torn state of Europe − as the age of romanticism. Our poets and painters are intent on capturing the fugitive phenomena of nature. They depict the sea, the sky and the pinnacle of creation, we humans. In the works they create, they plumb the depths of their imagination. In so doing, they have liberated the imagination of all of us, as never before in human history. Our imagination enables us to simulate objects and situations that stretch well beyond the limitations of the real world. This liberation of imagination enabled our forebears, nearly two hundred years ago, to visualise an England without a despotic king. Hence our Revolution and our continuing struggle for the betterment of our people's lives. As a child, with a child's imagination, I loved fairy stories, but I no longer believe in fairies and I hope I know the difference between what is real and what is make-believe. It was fairy stories told by a government spy and projected by provocators that led to the recent tragic, abortive uprising in Derbyshire. Scores of men were duped into thinking that London was in revolutionary mood and ready to send a citizens' army to the North country to join similar forces from Nottingham, Sheffield and other centres.

"It was even put about that Manchester would be a Moscow, to be razed by fire, as was the Russian city during the war against Napoleon.

"Who concocted such a crazed idea? The government would not have been disadvantaged by such a scorched earth strategy, but thousands of workers would have lost their homes and their livelihoods. That was all a creation of unbridled imagination, imagination gone wild, far removed from reality, with predictably tragic results.

"The men of Derbyshire know little or nothing at first-hand about London, but the plot contrived between Lord Sidmouth and his agents and spread by such as Oliver the Spy was made believable by the kind of silly talk that was heard at January's conference of Hampden Club delegates from around England, when some present, grossly exaggerated the people's readiness for insurrection.

"Now let me ask you: which parts of London are presently under the control of revolutionaries?"

Cally paused, as if waiting for a response, And then answered her own question: "None."

In composing this speech, she had recalled the rhetorical devices used by the great Cicero.

"Which towns and villages around London have been successfully taken over by armed citizens?"

"None."

"Has the House of Commons declared in favour of the constitutional reforms we seek and pledged to support us by having the army take over the Tower of London and Carlton House?"

Has the Prince Regent been interned?"

Is the Lord Chancellor in the Tower and the House of Peers forbidden to meet?

"Are peers and bishops excluded from Parliament?

"No."

"How many army regiments and militias have overridden their officers and declared in favour of a revolutionary parliamentarian army?

How many naval ships are in the hands of their crews, anchored in the Thames with guns trained on the Tower?

"Again, none, but these would be the essential signs that reformists have become revolutionaries. "These were the kinds of developments that presaged the outbreak of civil war in 1642 and, until we see them again, let none of us indulge in silly, childish make-believe.

"Under the Gagging Acts, I could be arrested for seditious libel in merely posing these questions, because the power resides still with Liverpool and Sidmouth, who recline undisturbed, confident that they remain unchallenged.

"Yes, the repressive Gagging Acts remain in force and we are in no position to repeal them, because we have no representation in Parliament worthy of the name.

"We may find it disappointing that most people are prepared to do no more for the cause than sign our petitions. Even that, betrays, on their part – and ours – a romantic trust in the honour and good intentions of the Prince Regent and the rest of the aristocracy, just as our forbears placed their trust in King Charles 1st before the Civil War, during the war and even after his execution, believing that his successor, the dissolute Charles Stuart would, as he had undertaken, exact no retribution from those responsible for the regicide.

"But we know that brave revolutionaries paid with their lives for carrying out the ultimate aim of the Revolution. John Cooke and Thomas Harrison were brutally butchered at Charing Cross for carrying out the will of the New Model Army and Parliament. The new king's word was worth no more than his father's.

"Psalm 146 says, with the wisdom of ages: 'Put not your trust in princes.'

"It makes no sense that we put our trust in the evil men we seek to displace. Many, perhaps most of the people of England remain in thrall to royalty; obedient to the monarch, the bishops and the squires, who all stand in the way of progress.

"That nexus must be broken.

"There is the grotesque myth that hereditary succession, rule by monarchy, preserves a nation from civil war and internal strife. Tom Paine has discredited that gross falsity, pointing out that, since the Norman Conquest, thirty kings and two minors have ruled England, during which time there have been no fewer than eight civil wars and nineteen rebellions. Monarchies have laid low this country and others, in blood and ashes.

"This country is ruled by barbarism. Dressed up as Christianity, the government's rule is a devastating daily assault against the poorest and most vulnerable.

"By means of our meetings, readings and newspapers, we must continue popularising the works of Paine, Spence and Carlile,

"Like **you,** I find it frustrating that so many people fail to grasp the good sense, the justice of the reforms we seek. For some of them, the difficulty is ignorance born of illiteracy; others are ground down by the chronic poverty which blights their lives and dominates their concerns to the **exclusion** of all else.

"If recent events should have taught us anything, it is that there are no short cuts to constitutional reform. It may not come about during our generation. Not until the majority of the people are won to our side, can there be fundamental change". As usual, Cally was speaking from memory. With no need to look down at notes, her eyes were roving the room, from person to person and engaging directly with every one present.

"So please let us hear no more wishful thinking, no more fairy tales about London being in insurrectionary mood.

"Alexander Pope wrote, 'Hope springs eternal in the human breast,' It is natural that we should have our hopes, but hope alone will not change the world. Another poet, Francis Bacon, warned us, 'Hope is good for breakfast, but it is a bad supper'.

"Hope is not long-lived. Our movement needs achievements, steps forward, bearing in mind that great leaps forward will be rarities. That is a reality with which we have to live.

"I have a guilty conscience. At the end of the January conference, I went to John Cartwright and warned him lest he underestimated the capacity of government agents to infiltrate our organisations and lead them into chaos. He countered that I underestimated the wisdom of our leaders. I remember his words: 'We ensure our plans for action are based on real potential, rather than hope or ambition.'

"It was not for me to question the superiority of his knowledge, but I wish I had pressed my argument with him. I might have saved much misery and some lives. It is clear that the insurrection planned in Derbyshire was based on too little real potential and much too much Hope and ambition.

"John Cartwright, over many years, has visited what he terms 'the disturbed districts', in order to see 'the actual condition of a starving people. Better than anyone else, he knows the people's problems, their leaders and their opinions. And yet we came asunder at Pentrich.

"Grand hopes built on false foundations will soon fall to bits, with many casualties.

There were nods and murmurs of agreement around the room.

"But all is not bleak. Let us take what encouragement we can from the fact that, if even a blatant, transpicuous scoundrel, such as Oliver the spy can muster men willing to take action in the cause of reform, then that reservoir of potential is there for us to lead, when we have prepared the ground and the time is right."

Her hands, with her fingers interlocked, had been at waist level, rather like the Rector's mannerism She now brought them up to each side of her face, rather as one would if in despair. Looking round at her listeners, she dropped her voice to little more than a whisper for her concluding words.

"The news from Derbyshire made me very sad. Sad that we suffered yet another defeat. Sad for the men now in custody, awaiting trial and God knows what harsh sentences. Bitter for their distressed fatherless families. Guilt-ridden that we were responsible, in large part, for their being vulnerable to the machinations of an infamous agent of a malevolent government. We must never repeat such errors.

We typically underestimate the duplicity, the venality of the government. They take us for simpletons. Mr Cartwright and, I fear, too many other reformist leaders have underestimated Lord Sidmouth's spies and the extent to which they have burrowed into our organisations like woodworms. The most successful of them do not have to monitor and inform on organisations from outside; they are embedded in our clubs as members, some of them having inveigled themselves into leading positions. They are able to help frame our policies and the details of our demonstrations, leading us into the arms of our enemies. They have no need of a Trojan horse; they are already inside Troy, undermining the city's defences from within.

Still in hardly more than a whisper, she concluded: "Brothers and sisters, thank you for listening to me."

Cally sat down and Polly took and squeezed her hand. Apart from a few members saying, "Hear, hear", or "Well said," there was silence for one or two minutes and then applause broke out. It was subdued at first, but rose to a crescendo, with the usual stomping. The message had been wounding, but thought-provoking and salutary.

Other speakers, for the most part, took a leaf from Cally's book and thanked her for her perceptive analysis of the lessons from the failed Pentrich rising.

The meeting broke up in a better mood than it started. From across the room came Tabitha Maxton, wife of a local notary, known to the sisters as a regular face at the Friends' Meeting House. "Bless you, Cally, for your wise words."

Reviewing the afternoon, Cally expressed to her sister a determination to keep track of Oliver the spy and his aliases and his despicable fellow agitator, John Castle, doing all in her power to thwart their dealings and eventually bring them down. "That project may take a few years."

"Please let us do that together," said Polly.

"Welcome back to the world," she continued. "I've been missing you, my darling girl.

"I know you feel all the woes of the world on your shoulders, all the living, loving, crying and dying. I know you fret in frustration over things you cannot control."

Cally pulled Polly into a cuddle. "I know I have been a moody beast for the past weeks. I have been in a dark desert; no oases, no light and no hope."

"I only wish I could reach you in that dark desert," said Polly, "I think you have inherited something of your father's melancholia.

"In your desert, just remember that I love you, body and soul, moods and all."

"In future," said Cally, "Lead me to the broom cupboard, box my ears and instruct me to stop moping and start mopping."

A good pun earns a long kiss.

The reverberations of Pentrich went on for months. It became known that The Lord Lieutenant of Yorkshire, Earl Fitzwilliam, the Monarch's representative in the county, had written to Lord Sidmouth, after the trials, in angry mood, regarding the involvement of his lordship's agent in tricking distressed workmen into conspiracy. He wrote of the defendants: "All the misled mischievous men, have erroneously considered themselves as subordinate members of a great leading body of revolutionists in London. Had not then a person, pretending to come from that body, made his appearance ... it is not assuming too much to say probably no insurrectionary trouble would have been seen in my patch."

Sidmouth's weasel words in response were that Oliver was required to do no more than monitor and report on events and that, to the extent that he was responsible for fomenting disturbance, he was exceeding his brief. When Lavender read Sidmouth's preposterous fabrication in *The Times*, he shared his exasperated disbelief with his girls. It was obvious that the authorities all knew in advance about the Pentrich rising − Oliver having taken a hand in the detailed planning − and so there was a detachment of soldiers strategically positioned. The sisters kept to themselves their resolve to disable Oliver and John Castle and somehow bring about the spies' permanent neutralisation. They did not underestimate the size of such an undertaking.

From many quarters, after Pentrich, there was a surprising and encouraging reaction. People found the government's employment of spies and *provocateurs* to be unfair, sneaky and un-English. This attitude was reflected in the various trials under the Gagging Acts. Judges and juries acquitted defendants or handed down sentences more lenient than expected. Oliver became infamous, a byword for corruption, government intrigue and underhand dealing.

The sisters shared the work of maintaining correspondence with Hampden Club members in northern counties, many of whom were home-working artisans in various trades and often leading lights in trade unions. Ever sensitive to the machinations of lord Sidmouth and his spies, the sisters had their voluminous mail delivered to the house of Mrs Wallace, a few doors along the street. They made sure Mrs Wallace was kept in generous credit, because the cost of postage had to be paid on delivery. Of course, Mrs Wallace was remunerated for this service. Better by far that the known address of a Bow Street Runner did not attract attention by having an unusually large volume of postal traffic.

Chiefly motivating Cally and Polly in their commitment to their Club was their radical politics. It therefore came as a surprise – and even a disappointment – that for many of their correspondents, it was religion that motivated their reformism.

It was clear that in North Country villages, charismatic lay preachers and fire-and-brimstone doom-mongers in the pulpits had families flocking to the Primitive Methodists, their Spartan chapels and their stripped-down ceremonials. One of the legacies of the failed Pentrich rising, for people still suffering hunger and poverty, was the consolation and food for hope in the Millennarian promise of Christ's return, ushering in a thousand-year Golden Age.

The sisters saw that it was a mixed and confusing picture. The solidarity of some chapel congregations translated into the communitarian spirit of trade unionism and yet, some Methodist zealots were branded as employers's narks, to be ostracised.

Desperate men may come to extreme solutions. There was a revival of some of the Puritan sectaries of which the sisters knew nothing apart from their reading about the Civil War. Born out of the Reformation were the Antinomians, Muggletonians and Ranters, as well as groups of Quakers, with varying degrees of discipline, some stern in the extreme.

Polly suggested they could find some gratification, even amusement, in the competitive tension, especially in rural areas, between the lower orders in their austere chapels on the one hand, and on the other hand, the relative grandeur of the Church of England, with its elaborate rituals, regalia and adherents among the farmers, merchants and gentry.

From their conversations with educated men among the Quakers and Hampden Club members, the sisters appreciated that most of them were deists, finding a god-figure necessary to explain Creation and the after-life, but that did not necessarily entail being pious.

"Some in the educated and upper classes consider it part of their duty to society to set an example to the lower orders by attending church and going through the motions, whilst being sceptical in private about the whole rigmarole, ventured Polly

"The working class, you see, need religion, otherwise all sorts of immorality would lead them astray, even into the arms of revolutionaries. Such patronising thinking comes easily to those with money". Polly was oozing sarcasm.

The family was in the sitting room, after dinner. Polly continued to regale them.

"Even non-believing men-folk think it best that their ladies should be at least a little religious, lest they be thought wanton, in any degree careless of their marriage-vows.

"Piety, purity and propriety are seen as natural virtues appropriate to the fairer sex. "Just as pride, pomposity and hypocrisy come so easily to men, excepting those present." Polly stood, put her hands together, as if in prayer, and bowed, as if acknowledging a crowd's expected applause for her speech. Her audience was highly amused by this clinical dissection of the Church of England and its followers and applauded in appreciation.

"You may not have been born with a silver spoon in your mouth, dear Polly, but you have a silver tongue." Ananya blew a kiss across the table.

It was their support for the secular aims of the English and French revolutions and their reading of Voltaire in translation and Richard Carlile, in particular, as well as their awareness of the social unorthodoxy of their guilt-free sapphism which brought Cally and Polly to the realisation that they had no religious belief. They were unequivocal atheists.

This need not prevent their attending Friends' meetings. Eventually they discovered other atheist Quakers.

"Is it possible to be ethical without having religion?" Not for the first time, this question was put by Polly at the dinner table. Cally took up the baton:"Let me ask a similar question, "Is it possible to be unethical, although professing to be a true believer?" Then, answering her own question: "Decidedly so. We could name scores of men in prominent positions, who go through all the motions of piety, whilst flouting the most basic principles of ethical behaviour. Hypocrisy comes naturally to them as if it were the main requirement for entry into their class.

"We could also name scores of people who profess no religion, but go through life as if guided by the

Sermon on the Mount, ever ready to defend the interests of others, regardless of the cost to themselves.

You and I, sweet sister, battle for fundamental constitutional reform, because that is essential if we are all to live in a just and ethical society.

Over the course of time, the London Hampden Clubs came to understand the major social changes taking place around the country. The villages were being drained of their cottage crafts as the new industrial centres expanded over the countryside, becoming hubs for circles of industrialisation. As the farmlands and enclosed commons were covered with brick, they became the suburbs of the manufacturing centres, some of them dark, satanic mills in every sense. As the Reed sisters rode to meetings in Kent and Surrey towns and villages, they saw this spreading urbanization for themselves. Near to home, the market gardens and fields that once abutted the streets of Newington and Kennington were now being gobbled up by streets of new houses, all brick-built, some stuccoed, in terraces, or as individual villas and occasionally in a pretentious miniaturised Palladian style, all interspersed with the sooty black trunks of surviving venerable lime and oak trees The spreading streets represented spreading wealth, although the foul rookeries of St Giles and Seven Dials were within walking distance.

Dr Jem Watson, junior, had been lying low, dodging arrest, since the second Spa Fields riot. During the summer of 1817, it became known that he had escaped arrest with the help of a gun, taking ship for

Pennsylvania, from Gravesend, in the guise of a Quaker pilgrim.

On a rare mild day, The sisters took their mounts to Vauxhall Gardens. Polly wore her new, highly fashionable Pamela hat, replete with silk flowers and ribbons. As there was not a hint of breeze, instead of tying the ribbons under her chin, she left them loose and dangling. Of a sudden, a young scoundrel leapt up alongside Polly's horse, yanked one of the ribbons and ran off with her hat. Like many other Londoners, he had a sickly complexion that closely matched the dappled mud colour of the Thames. She jerked her horse into a gallop, in order to give chase. The boy darted into a dim alley leading to a rabbit warren of narrow passages and houses. Polly gave up the hopeless cause, uttering a volley of most unladylike invective. Cally congratulated her sister on the extensive profane vocabulary she was able to call up at a moment's notice and sympathised at her loss. Ever after, they both held tight to their bonnets.

1818

In the late summer of 1818 there was a General Election. At the following meeting of the Hampden Club, Cally was asked to give an analysis of the outcome.

"This country considers itself to be a democracy. Nothing could be further from the truth.

"In ancient Athens, the whole population of men – not including slaves – met in the agora, in order to decide the policies of the state. As populations grew and became geographically wider spread, meetings of the entire *demos* became less practicable and representative government developed, which is acceptable provided the whole *demos* elect their representatives, for a fixed term, and provided those they elect remain answerable to the electors.

"When we took from King Charles 1st his head and his hereditary power to govern, we took away from him that which he had no right to possess – Hereditary power.

"Be it monarchical rule over a country, or an aristocrat's ownership of an estate, such power should not exist.

"Tom Paine says his arguments against the hereditary system are chiefly based on the absurdity of it.

"Here, in Southwark, a borough within the County of Surrey, we are entitled to two Members of Parliament, as is the rest of the County, regardless of the enormous disparity in population numbers between this borough and all the rest of Surrey.

"One of our MPs is Sir William Brougham, a Master of the Court of Chancery, an institution stuffed with sinecurists and responsible, more than any other body within our judicial system, for the notorious, lawyer-enriching, time – consuming, suicide-inducing, law's delay.

"The other Member is Sir Robert Wilson, General of Hussars, diplomat and favourite of the Prince Regent. As an officer in the 15th Light Dragoons, later the 15th Hussars, he has his troopers practice their sabre-wielding on the heads and backs of demonstrating workers in Northern parts.

"Neither man will be inclined to study the interests of the distressed of Southwark, while they have bigger fish to fry, further feathering their own nests.

"We now have a Parliament of 280 Tories, led by the Earl of Liverpool and an opposition of 175 Whigs, led by George Tierney, who has circulated around a number of parliamentary seats, including Southwark. No doubt he professed to be dedicated for life to each of them. Some years ago he fought a duel with William Pitt. They both missed. Doubly unfortunate.The Tories include the richest people, the staunchest supporters of the Monarchy and the Church and they attract the most gullible, ill-informed and unawakened of the rural population, who manifest their rustic idiocy by supporting these aristocrts. We can summarise Liverpool's patronage and following as 'throne, altar and cottage'.

"The Whigs include the merchants, factory owners and the most powerful of the landed aristocracy.

"Would it be an exaggeration, a slander, to call this Parliament a den of thieves? No. That is what William Cobbett calls it and rightly so.

"It is the product of a corrupt system which has no universal male suffrage, grossly unequal electoral areas, the ability of the rich to buy seats and to blatantly bribe voters.

"Old Sarum, in Wiltshire, became an abandoned village centuries ago. It has no human inhabitants, but several fields and flocks of sheep. Under the terms of our benighted constitution, it has just returned two Members of Parliament. We can imagine them being kept very busy by the demands of their woolly constituents.

"Gatton, in Surrey, a tiny village, has a Member, although just two electors. That is corruption on an egregious scale.

"Meanwhile, Birmingham, a centre of metal and engineering industries, with a population of seventy-five thousand and fast-growing, is entitled to no representation whatsoever in Parliament.

"Manchester, the biggest industrial centre in Britain, with a population of four hundred thousand and still growing, is another densely populated area denied any representation in Parliament. That is how this unscrupulous government wants it. If workers had the vote, they would assuredly throw out Liverpool, Sidmouth, Castlereagh and the rest.

"This Parliament is, indeed, like its forerunner, a den of thieves. It has stolen the people's right to choose by whom they should be governed. It has stolen the peoples' dignity.

"In this election, only five in one hundred men had the vote, owning freehold property worth at least two pounds.

"So far I have spoken only of the House of Commons".

Cally cleared her throat and sipped her drink.

"Let us now look at the House of Peers, the preserve of the highest aristocracy.

"As Thomas Paine has written – she was now reading from a book – 'The origin of aristocracy was robbery. The first aristocrats were brigands. Those of latter times, sycophants.

'The great landed estates, now held in descent, were plundered from their quiet, English inhabitants at the Conquest. That part of government that is called the House of Lords, was originally composed of persons who had committed the robberies led by William of Normandy. The House of peers remains an association for the protection of the property their ancestors stole from the commoners of England.'

"Thus spoke the great Tom Paine". Cheers around the room.

Cally acknowledged the cheers and continued.

"When Queen Elizabeth freed the last remaining serfs in 1574, she failed to complete the task. She should also have discharged from their aristocratic titles, the last of the serf-owning class."

Shouts and stamping at this point, around the assembly.

"We must continue to press our demands for constitutional reform.

"Nobody should be in government unless elected to be so. Just as seats in the Commons should no longer be heritable, neither should seats in the other House.

"That brings me to the bishops, who sit in ecclesiastical splendour in the House of Peers. When the monarchy was restored, reversing the achievement of our great Revolution, there was indemnity for the royalist aristocrats, who resumed their seats in the House of Lords, and there was episcopal restoration, too. The bishops no longer have the power to act as princelings in their dioceses, but they do possess powers for good or ill in the House of Lords. They have no rightful place there.

Applause around the room.

"Let's reiterate our demands for constitutional reform:

"All men over 18, should have the vote, with no need of property ownership;

"Electoral areas should be of equivalent size and no more rotten boroughs like Old Sarum;

"No more buying of Commons seats;

"Secret ballots and annual parliaments are what we want.

"Men elected to the House of Commons should receive a salary. Otherwise, as now, only rich men will be able to afford to forfeit their previous employment.

"Our struggle is to achieve a parliament representative of the people, so that we become the power in the land, making decisions for the good of the majority of the people, at the expense of the rich.

"Let's start with the repeal of the Corn Laws." Cally paused for the expected shouts of approval.

"Let's determine a shorter working week, such as 40 hours, a minimum hourly wage, below which no employer could go.

"Let's ensure everybody has a secure home at affordable rent"

"And, having won all these basic rights, let us further improve our lives through schooling for all

children and a pension for those too old to work.

"And I take it for granted that this reformed parliament, not any monarch, will take decisions over peace and war.

"A final word of wisdom from Tom Paine: I quote, 'Holland without a king hath enjoyed more peace for this last century than any of the monarchical governments in Europe.'"

Cally sat down to loud applause and Polly handed her a pot of small beer for her parched throat.

The Chairman called on his deputy to move a vote of thanks to Cally, which was agreed by acclamation.

One morning, Cally announced that she had woken up with a good idea. She called it demonstrative dressing. She explained it as she ran her soft warm fingertips down Polly's backbone, with a special caress for that bullet wound scar. Demonstrative dressing entailed recruiting Mother toundertake some needlework. Then came implementation in public. The sisters rode to Rotten Row, the *route du Roi* in Hyde Park, there to join the monied classes in their carriages, or on palfreys, all there to see and to be seen.

Polly wore a wide-brimmed straw bonnet, the crown adorned with silk flowers. The front of the brim was bent upwards, displaying the embroidered words, VOTES FOR ALL. Cally wore a large shawl, which draped her back, displaying the large embroidered words, REFORM PARLIAMENT. There was no indication that anyone had noticed their little remonstrance until they were waved down by two of the Park constables, accompanied by a mounted Lifeguard officer in full rig, sword drawn to boot.

"What's the meaning of this? demanded the soldier. Then, shouting at the open-mouthed constables, rather than the ladies,"We cannot allow the hoi polloi to parade their slogans here.

"Here of all places, where the king might see them." The constables were still at a loss and looking gormless and so Cally addressed them directly: "Is there a law about what ladies may and may not wear in the Park?

Provided we are not naked, like Lady Godiva, surely, we may dress as we wish."

The charlies remained mute and flustered, but the officer responded to the artful question of the brown woman with the remarkable eyes: "It is the Provocative decoration that causes offence."

By now, this little altercation had drawn the attention of enough walkers and riders to assemble a small cluster of spectators. Never one to disappoint an audience, Cally addressed the officer: "Sir, you seek to admonish my sister and me for an un-named offence. I shall quote the great Tom Paine: 'Power which hath endeavoured to subdue us is of all others, the most improper to defend us,'

"Not that we are in need of any gentleman's protection. We shall wend our way." Urging their horses, they continued their sedate promenade, leaving the officer and constables to continue chewing air.

They considered this episode to be a success. Henceforth, they seldom rode without displaying a reformist quotation or demand, on their clothing, or a hand-held placard. It could soundly be claimed that they were the inventors of this form of political publicity.

In January of 1818, Sidmouth had felt it was safe enough to restore habeas corpus and two months later, the Attorney General introduced the Indemnity Bill, 1818. It indemnified ministers and magistrates who had locked up people, without proper legal process, acts they had done "for suppressing insurrections and guarding against imminent danger to the State". In other words, anyone detained during the suspension of habeas corpus could not sue for redress. Taking no risks, the government declared that whether the Bill passed or not, the conduct of ministers could never be called in question in any court of justice for having done what parliament had declared it should be legal for them to do. Of course, the Bill was enacted.

"These autocrats," said Cally, speaking at the next meeting of her Hampden Club, "Use their home-made laws like suits of armour to protect themselves and their interests.

"Laws should be based on ethical principles, but Liverpool, Sidmouth and the rest have no ethics and their only principles are self-protection and self-aggrandisement, in other words, self, self, self. Yet, to be sure, they consider themselves good Christians. Parliament must be wrested from them."

During 1818, the Reed family suffered a veritable earthquake; not world-shaking, but perhaps a little Southwark-shaking. its repercussions would be felt by the Reed family for the next twenty years and more.

Father arrived home one day, unusually flustered and carrying a blanketed bundle. "I apologise for this," said he, "But as you know, we have no women police and I was at a loss what else to do. It's just for tonight. Tomorrow I will take it to the new orphanage at Bonner Road, Bethnal Green, or perhaps the Coram Foundling Hospital"

Mother took the bundle, which was now issuing whimpering sounds. She put it on the table and started to unwrap it, with Cally and Polly all eyes. "You can stop referring to 'it', Lavender. You have brought home a 'she'. This is a baby girl."

Now came the story. That afternoon, Bow Street Runners had been called to a tenement near the Elephant and Castle Inn, where there had been screams and shouts of 'bloody murder'. Unfortunately, Lavender and his colleagues arrived too late to avert disaster. Amidst much blood, there was a black woman, presumably from Africa, lying on the floor, with her throat cut. It was as gruesome a scene as found by the police in many a month, even in this violent part of the Capital.

Held by several excited and shouting men – presumably neighbours – was an Englishman with his clothes blood-splashed. With the apparent murderer handcuffed and his captors calmed down, it was possible to elicit some sense from the men. According to them, the dead woman was a prostitute, by the name of Serenity. She lived with the Englishman, name of Richards, who was her fancy-man, living off her earnings. The neighbours reported that the couple were constantly at war, the trouble being that Serenity did not bring in enough money to satisfy her pimp. Things had come to a head during the morning, to such an extent that a neighbour was sent for the Runners, while others entered the room in an attempt to calm the worsening struggle. They were too late, finding the woman in a pool of blood, already mortally wounded and clearly beyond saving.

Towards the end of this confused interrogation, with the room calmed down, babyish wailing was heard from a bundle in the corner of the room. "It's not mine. It's nothing to do with me. She was already expecting when I took her in," shouted Richards. The colour of the baby's skin appeared to confirm this disclaiming of paternity.

Richards was taken off to Bow Street and things look very bad for him.

Lavender, the only married Runner present, was left literally holding the baby. He agreed to look after it until next day.

"Tomorrow, I can take it to an orphanage".

By now the baby had been thoroughly inspected and cuddled and quietened. Her skin was darker than Cally's, but Cally could probably pass as the child's real mother. Ananya expressed the view that the baby had been well cared for and was healthy. She was not old enough to have been weaned; so there was a big problem.

"Seriously Lavender", asked Ananya, "what is to be the fate of this baby girl?"

"Oh, let's keep her. Can't we keep her?" pleaded Cally.

"Do you know her name, father?"

"A woman among the neighbours called her Matilda".

"We had a Matilda in our class at school, known as Tilly" said Polly.

"So she is meant for us – Cally, Polly and Tilly," Cally sang this to an impromptu tune.

"We are to have a baby sister."

"Stop girls!" Mother, who was rarely so emphatic, shocked the girls into silence. "Your common sense is running away from reality.

"I am too old to mother another child."

At this, the girls were crestfallen. Before they could resume their excited speculating, Mother said, "I am too old, but you are both old enough to be mothers. You have told me of mothers among your married friends.

"I see that thought has struck you both dumb and understandably so. Harsh reality can come as quite a shock.

"Before your excitement bursts out again, think about it. This is too important for recklessness.

"This baby may have a father, living somewhere in Africa. Only her dead mother would know and so the reality is that Tilly will grow up, if she survives infancy, with no parents. The place for an orphan is an orphanage.

"Oh, no," pleaded Cally, "An orphanage would be a cold-hearted, dismal place, especially as this would probably be the only black child present. She would feel lonely and might be ill-treated.

"You say, Mother, that we are old enough to be mothers. Yes, we know of girls of our age who are married and with babies and so couldn't we keep her?"

Ananya was by now exasperated and showed it by her impatience, verging on anger.

"Mothered by one of you, who neither wanted nor expected, to be a mother and has no experience or knowledge of childcare, this baby would probably not survive.

"She is not yet weaned and neither of you can produce breast milk. The best place for her is an orphanage, cared for by a wet nurse." Mother sat in silence and nodded at her girls, indicating that she required them to respond to her weighty words.

"Added to which," interjected Lavender, "You are both deeply involved in your good works, your politics and your studies. Your readings in coffee houses and taverns are increasingly important to the cause you support. You have precious little time to spare for a baby. And you must not underestimate the stares, the whispering, the ostracising that either of you would experience as an unmarried mother of a black baby.

"I know you are both brave. Are you brave *enough*?

"There is a good alternative for this child. She would not be left on the street. There is the new East London Orphan Asylum in Cannon Street Road. It was opened not long ago by the Rev Andrew Reed – no relation, as far as I know.

"And, as this baby is a foundling, there is the Coram Hospital for Foundlings. From there, she might be adopted. Her mother was a prostitute and so the sad truth is that this child may be destined for a better future, now that she is motherless."

"Lavender, please advise us", said Mother. "What does the law have to say about keeping a foundling?"

"The full details of this murder will be reported to the Bow Street magistrates, including the fact that it leaves an orphan child. I fear the magistrates will be happy to accept any arrangement that relieves them of any responsibility for the child's future, be it orphanage, or adoption, or even abandonment. Our magistrates care nought for the scores of babies left at night, wrapped in rags, on doorsteps around London. Let's face it: Until a few years ago, in this benighted country, the child could even have been sold into slavery, profiting the Bow Street Bench and helping towards the Runners' salaries.

"Any orphanage releasing a child to adoption would want to be sure that the child is going to a responsible family. On the other hand, most orphanages are over-flowing and only too pleased to pass children on. To answer your question, Ananya: regrettably, the law has nothing to say on the matter".

The girls had been all ears, while changing the baby's soiled clout and improvising something clean, bathing her in a wash basin and feeding her warmed milk, which she instinctively sucked from Polly's fingers.

"You see, girls", said Mother, "This is the process you would have to repeat at intervals each day: changing and washing her clouts, bathing and feeding her and do not expect to be undisturbed at night. And there would be costs. This would be another mouth to feed and a little body to clothe.

"As I have said, this child has been fed from the breast and this will have to continue for months yet. That presents a considerable problem.

"You must give serious thought to this matter".

"Up to now you have only had to look after yourselves. Now you would have responsibility for a vulnerable baby. She is not a doll; she is a real person, at the most demanding stage of her life"

Cally was impatient to speak, but Mother silenced her by holding up a hand and addressing her husband.

"Lavender", said she, "Could we postpone the orphanage visit until the day after tomorrow, so that Cally and Polly have more thinking time?"

"They are on the verge of taking an impetuous step in their lives and they are too old simply to be expected to abide by an instruction from us. They are intelligent, free-thinking women. They have to resolve this matter for themselves. We must allow them time."

This was agreed and the girls, chastened, or merely thoughtful, withdrew to their room to ponder a matter which could re-order and even dominate their lives for the next several years.

Lavender and Ananya, too, had thinking to do.

On the following day, the girls sat with Mother, needing a sounding-board, before making a decision.

Cally started. "Mother, we are sure we understand, but we need your confirmation. A woman cannot produce milk until she has had a baby."

Ananya nodded and smiled. "I sometimes wonder whether my daughters are worldly women or novice nuns.

"Breast milk comes with child-birth and that follows pregnancy, for which the contribution of a man is essential. Polly, have you a man in mind to father a child for you, so that those pigeon's eggs on your chest will grow and yield milk?"

"Mother, dear, you know that will never happen." They were both surprised and smiling. This was the very first time that Polly had addressed Cally's mother – albeit, inadvertently – as 'Mother'. Knowing the importance of this moment, Ananya pulled Polly to her. They embraced and kissed and Cally made it a trio.

This was now women talking women's affairs. Tapping her forehead, Cally said, "Mother, I think I remember you breast-feeding me.

"I am sure you do, Cally, for you were happy to be at my breasts until you were five years old, eagerly augmenting what you were fed at the table. I admit that my enjoyment was as great as yours.

"That explains your being our only child; so long as a woman is breastfeeding, she is unlikely to become pregnant. Your father and I were happy with that position. You, my darling, were treasure enough and your birth was nearly the death of me; my body would allow me no more babies".

"It seems I have been a problem for you from birth," said Cally, looking a little woebegone.

"You have ever been a delightful problem. Keeping pace with your energy, wit and boundless curiosity has kept your parents young. For so many married women, pregnancy is almost their permanent state. Every year another baby and they have more children than they can afford, even though so many die in infancy. Many women's bodies are prematurely worn out by the stresses of the repeated bearing and birthing. But you, my darling have enhanced my life and doubtless lengthened it."

"So, have you solved the problem of Tilly needing breast milk for months yet?"

"We have an idea", said Cally. "Mrs Downing's daughter, Dorothy, called Dolly, lives just two doors away. She is nursing her latest born, as well as a neighbour's baby. Polly spoke with her this morning. If we can agree fees, she would be happy to nurse Tilly for as long as we wish. Tilly would, of course, be her first black baby and she is quite fascinated by the idea.

"It was meant to be. Tilly, Cally, Polly and Dolly." Cally clapped her hands together as if to settle the matter. "Tilly's lovely colour is shades darker than mine," said Cally, "But still I might pass as her mother."Which makes me her aunt, "said Polly. "On the other hand, there's no reason why we should not both be her mothers." That is how the matter was agreed.

At dinner on the following afternoon. The girls announced the details. Their small teachers' stipends will be sufficient to pay Dolly. They also receive a little in modest honoraria, from the penny subscriptions collected from members at the meetings they address, although these barely cover their postage costs, which have to be paid on receipt, rather than on despatch and depend on distance, as well as weight.

The new mothers collected Tilly at least once each day and Dolly lent them a baby carriage, so that they could walk the neighbourhood, showing off the new little resident. There would come a time when Tilly was old enough to be taken to some of the meetings her mothers attend.

Lavender, too, had an announcement. The settee and captain's chair were to be moved from the first floor to the second floor, making that the new combined sitting room and dining room. The first floor was now to be the girls' bedroom, for all three girls. The baby's needs will be more conveniently met if your room is close to the sluice, water pump and kitchen range. The top floor room could henceforth be an office for all the clerical work you two now undertake; although, freezing in winter and baking in summer, it may not be the most comfortable of offices.

"Already," said Mother, smiling, "This small body is turning the house upside down; like mothers, like daughter."

The notorious Reed girls now had a fresh shock for the parish. It became routine for the new mothers to collect Tilly each day, except in the most inclement weather, for an airing. There had been no indication of a marriage and no sign of one of them being with child, but here they are, pushing a baby carriage. In order not to cause too much apoplexy among the gossips, the girls were at pains to make it widely known that they had adopted an orphan baby. Shock at apparent immorality was thus turned to a modicum of admiration for their altruism. However, it remained a hot topic of conjecture. A child with two mothers? And it is a black child. Can this odd state of affairs persist? It has never been known.

Progress with the baby carriage around the local streets was slowed by repeated stops, so that the gorgeous little black girl with enormous dark eyes – the like of which had never been seen before – could be inspected, lifted, rocked and cooed at. All this handling she tolerated placidly. Her admirers included Mrs Onslow, the Rector's wife. When Rev. Brown, the curate heard about the new parishioner, his characteristically uncharitable comment was: "Unfortunately, the black baby in our midst will eventually become a black adult. Fortunately for Roland Brown, his comment never reached the ears of the Reed sisters.

In anticipation of being asked Tilly's age, it was decided to record her birth date as the momentous day on which it was decided to adopt her: 1st June 1818. Ananya approved this, as she was sure the baby was less than six months.

1819

Although not knowing, of course, what a historic event it would be, from the turn of the year, the sisters documented the build-up to the great demonstration on St Peter's Field, Manchester, in August of 1819. The manufacturing classes of Manchester and the surrounding towns, all working in the spinning and weaving industry, were held closely together by the fact of all being poor, living in the same place, working together in large numbers, cooperating in work and relying on one another in good times and bad. This fellowship, this solidarity was the strongest weapon of the working class communities and their trade unions.

Cally was often amused by the formality, bordering on ritual, of Hampden Club meetings. Even more formal procedures were followed at trade union meetings to which she was invited as a speaker or reader. The Chairman would demand strict discipline, hammering his gavel and bellowing, "Order, order", whenever anyone stepped out of line by attempting to interrupt a speaker, by referring to an earlier speaker in derogatory terms, wandering from the point, or lapsing into profanity.

A couple of days after 16th August, the Southwark Club met and the sisters were asked to report on the sensational event as the sole item on the agenda.

Polly explained that "This account has been pieced together from a report in *The Times*, reports in provincial newspapers and letters from our correspondents.

"Weeks ago, hearing of the preparations for a forthcoming special mass meeting in Manchester, Cally and I asked our contacts in the area to send us eye-witness accounts as soon as possible after the event. John Smith, a boot-maker, has responded with a report of the contingent organised by the Middleton and Stockport Union Society and other reformist groups.

I will read his own words.

"'We assembled at the appointed hour with a fife and drum band. We were led by the Bootmakers' Guild banner, reading 'No taxation without representation.

"'Marching behind the band were the teachers and pupils of the day school and Sunday School, all in their sabbath best. They were close to the recently-formed Women Reformers' Society, with their newly-embroidered banner, reading, 'SISTERS OF THE EARTH UNITE!.The most remarkable banner I saw in the parade read REPRESENTATION OR DEATH'.

"'We Stockport people, mainly weaver families, were the first to arrive on St Peter's Field, around midday, after our six-mile march'".

"By now", said Polly, "Anyone who can read and anyone who has ears, knows much of the detail of this shocking and historic event, which has become quickly known as the Peterloo Massacre, the biggest shedding of English blood since the Battle of Waterloo finally defeated Napoleon."

"'Army veterans, paid to show no pity, were among those let loose on the unarmed, peaceful crowd, including hundreds of women and children.

"'Mindful of the disorganisation of the 1816 Spa Fields demonstrations in London, the 16th August meeting was meticulously planned for weeks in advance, which makes the brutal outcome all the more undeserved and tragic'."

Polly was standing on a box, so that everyone could see the speaker.

"'Taunted by the press about the ragged and dirty appearance of people at reformist assemblies and ridiculed for the drunkenness and rowdiness of many demonstrators, the organisers of the Manchester meeting declared that this event must be marked by cleanliness, sobriety, good order and peacefulness.

"I am still reading from John Smith's report.

"'Some of our groups were drilled beforehand, army-style, responding to orders and polishing their synchronised movements. On the day, marshals dashed in and out of the marching ranks, encouraging straight lines and keeping in step. In the sunny weather, there was a good-hearted holiday mood. Young women marched arm-in-arm, singing popular songs.

"'People travelled to Manchester on horseback, two or more on one mount, some by farm-cart. The majority were on foot in the long winding parade. It was nothing unusual for some to walk ten or twenty miles, there and back, over the long day.

"'The principal speaker was to be Henry Hunt. In the days before the event, he called on the contingent organisers for quietness and order and a steady, firm and temperate deportment. This call was faithfully reflected in the leaders' instructions to their followers, coupled with the stern warning that there could be trouble-makers present and so ignore all attempts at provocation.

"Mindful of the bitter lessons of Spa Fields and Pentrich, Hunt had sent another, more pointed, warning to the contingent organisers: 'Our enemies will be seeking every opportunity, by means of their sanguinary agents, to excite a riot, so that they may have a pretence for spilling our blood. At the most minor disturbance, the magistrates will read the Riot Act and release on us the hounds of hell.'

"The mood of the crowd was optimistic. With such a massive turnout – sixty or a hundred thousand were confidently expected – surely some of the reforms we demand would at last be won.'"

Polly paused and there was "Hear, Hear" from around the room.

She resumed from the letter.

"'the City Fathers sat in full session, throughout the day, in a room overlooking the Field.

"'It was not the mood of the gathering crowd that alarmed them, for it was entirely peaceable. They perceived, or chose to perceive, the sheer numbers as signifying violent revolutionary intentions and they saw weapons where there were none. A minority of the magistracy, urging patience and caution, were scorned

191

and shouted down. The arrogant majority, full of contempt for the lower classes; brimming with haughtiness and brandy, decided that the immediate undemonstrative arrest of Hunt and the other intended speakers would be the best way to bring about an early quiet end to the gathering, forestalling trouble. This order was passed to Deputy Chief Constable Nadel – the most hated man in Manchester – who pleaded too much was being asked of his sixty inexperienced special constables, who had been signed up only that morning. So the order was passed to the officers of the Manchester and Salford Yeomanry, who relished the invitation to use force on an enemy which had no visible means of retaliation. The Prince Regent has described the yeomanry as valorous. I describe them as brutally cowardly.many of them guilty of murder or attempted murder

"In order to carry out the arrests, the mounted soldiers had to force their way through the tightly packed crowd around the platform. The entry of the soldiers, shouting orders and barging and trampling people, caused panic to break out. Some demonstrators tried to escape, while others tried in vain to stand their ground. All were subjected to indiscriminate sabre-slashing. A young man's hand was severed in a single swipe. He died slowly of blood-loss. Seeing the disturbance near the platform, without understanding its cause, the magistrates ordered the 15th Hussars and Cheshire Militia volunteers to join the action, although many demonstrators were by now seen trying to run away. Eleven of the crowd were killed on the field, or died of their wounds within a day or two. Over 400 others were injured, mainly by sabre cuts, or trampling by horses or panicking demonstrators.

"More than a hundred of the injured were women and girls.

"The aftermath has been described for us by Samuel Bamford, a Lancashire weaver, radical activist and poet. At our request, he has sent us this distressing eye-witness account. Cally will read it to you in full."

Polly stepped down and Cally took her place. Polly's delivery, in her girlish voice, had been rather matter-of-fact in style, as was appropriate for the purely factual content of her report.

In contrast, Cally read the several pages of Bamford's letter slowly and making no secret of her emotional response to its content.

"The soldiers' cruel frenzy and the crowd's bloody terror were over in a half-hour hellish whirlwind.

"The field was now an almost deserted space. Even the screams and sobs had evaporated into the sunny afternoon air.

"The platform still stood, as well as some staves, holding flags and banners, which had been slashed to ribbons, as if to show the soldiers' contempt for any manifestation of our cause. I saw an abandoned banner which named Bolton as its place of origin. Over the whole field I saw caps, bonnets, shawls, bags, shoes, a man's jacket, with a sabre cut and much blood on the shoulder, a couple of soldiers' shakos.

'I saw no abandoned weapons, because, of course, the victims had been unarmed. And there were no corpses or groaning wounded, because they had been dragged away. There were spills of blood on the ground and bloodied hankies. The screams, sobbing and groans had been carried away on the breeze. All was now peaceful, provided you closed your eyes to the evidence of death and destruction.

"'The only soldiers remaining were members of the Yeomanry, at the edge of the field, tending their horses, wiping clean their sabres and chuckling about their easy victory.

'I remain your obedient servant, Signed Samuel Bamford, Middleton, August 1819.'"

Cally brought her reading to an ironic conclusion: "For the crime of having planned to be a speaker at Peterloo, although arrested before he could utter a word, Mr Bamford is currently in prison, awaiting trial.

"Within a day or two of the event, all of England knew about it. The gory details have taken a little longer to percolate and have been reported, discussed and fretted over in tap-rooms, coffee houses, chapels, work-places and parlours. Such a weighty matter continues to be at the forefront of our minds. Talk of this cruel event and possible vengeance will continue". The Club members sat in stunned silence.

Cally took a long draught and resumed. "Thank you, Polly and thanks to your correspondents for their reports". Then, with palpably intense irony: "Oddly, although at least a hundred valiant warriors wielded their weapons on St Peter's Field that day, not one of them was subsequently heard boasting of his exploits and no medals have been awarded.

"The readiness with which police and soldiers batter their own always distresses and puzzles me.

"Is it simply a matter of employment and payment for doing the Devil's work? Or do they derive enjoyment from their blood-letting?

"A man leaves the street of his family and neighbours as a member of that community, perhaps known to all from childhood, sharing their suffering and hardships; he sheds his everyday clobber, and his kinships are cast off with it; decks himself out in the livery of authority and changes his nature to a police batterer or army slaughterer, fully prepared to arrest, assault and even kill his own" By now her voice was an angry growl.

"How can men so speedily morphose? Is it simply the Judas shilling? Or do they additionally relish the thrill of superiority, of power, of control? Unless he was a beast from birth, what is it that made him ruthless, merciless, pitiless, a slavish creature for his commander?

"Following orders, they do the most despicable acts. Has the man had his conscience excised, in order to leave him a brute?

"How heroic are these warriors? The *Manchester Observer* has a low opinion of the Manchester and Salford Yeomanry, whose members it describes as 'The fawning dependents of the local great, with a few fools and a greater proportion of coxcombs who imagine they acquire considerable importance by wearing regimentals'."

Cally waved the sheet of paper from which she was reading and continued:

"'The Yeomanry', the *Observer* continues, 'were middle-class men, who had to be able to afford their own horses and dragoon-style uniform, dark blue with frogging on the jacket and facings on the lapels in white and all topped by a black patent leather shako, with a white hackle. They each carry a carbine and a sabre and consider themselves too grand to need much training'.

"Mindless murderers have little need of training", said Cally, again waving the paper, "Just let them loose on unarmed folk and see what valiants they are.

"If we could rid society of such weak-willed men, our reformist cause would advance more quickly and with much less undeserved imprisonment, torture, bloodshed and death."

"Is beastliness deep within men's nature? From earliest times, men have fought one another like ravening dogs. The Old Testament is full of accounts of blood-letting by the ancient tribes. My father believes it is down to the unrecognised, underestimated cardinal sin of greed. Those who have more, greedily fight to retain it. Be it more land, more food, more gold, more slaves, more status, more kudos. Having more bestows a readiness to fight to retain it and often a desire to dominate those with less. Those who have less are driven by instinct to self-defence.

"Perhaps this propensity so easily to resort to violence has come down through the ages and is in-born. But as a creature with reason, surely, we should be able to curb our animalistic urges."

Cally had wandered off into the realm of philosophy, and in a world of her own, she knew not whether she took any listeners with her.

Polly brought the audience back by picking up the story.

"Standing by at St Peters Field were troops of the 15th King's Hussars, complete with two six-pounder guns, under Major Thomas Dyneley, battle-hardened by the Peninsular War, 'whose report to the Home Office illustrates the kind of man Cally is talking about. He wrote as follows: 'The first action of the Battle of Manchester is over, and has I am happy to say, ended in the complete discomfiture of the enemy'.

"Note the belligerent reference to the Battle of Manchester. We reformist demonstrators never planned for this to be a battle. Our peaceful intentions were clear from our obvious lack of any weapons and the majority of us being women and children. Nevertheless, as far as the soldiery, magistrates and government were concerned, this assembly of citizens represented their enemy.

"Major Dyneley's report continues: 'Principal speaker, Hunt, appeared at half-past twelve and in less than a quarter of an hour the magistracy thought it right to take him into custody. This the mob attempted to resist, by crowding around the platform, but the military were at hand and rushed upon them. The number that were rode over might have been very great. I saw several carried very badly wounded to the hospital. We have taken Hunt and others of their sort, with two reform ladies and lodged them in Manchester's New Bailey Prison. The whole business was settled in five minutes'."

"I will repeat what he coldly wrote", said Polly, "'The number that were rode over might have been very great'.

"We know that Hundreds of poor people had serious lacerations on their heads from the slashing sabres. The trampling horses' hooves caused many deep cuts, bruising and broken bones.

"Dyneley's callous report shows him to be of the hesrtless remorseless variety Cally has described.

"He concludes his report: 'I was very much amused to see the way in which the volunteer cavalry knocked the people about during the whole time we remained upon the ground; the instant they saw ten or a dozen mobbites together, they rode at them and leathered them properly.'

'I must not say the pleasure of seeing the field of battle covered with hats, sticks, shoes, laurel branches, drum heads etc.; in short the field was as complete as I had ever seen one after an action'.

"He was very much amused to see the cavalry knocking people about.

"This crime was witnessed by the magistrates, whose duty it is to uphold the law.

"The only law they uphold is their own self-preservation, protection of their property, their position and their power. Only when they and their class are displaced will the rest of us enjoy the reforms we seek." This conclusion drew applause.

Cally returned to the floor: "The blood spilled at Peterloo won no concessions from the government. On the contrary. Since Peterloo, any pressure for constitutional reform has been met by more ferocious application of the Six Acts, the arrest and imprisonment of reformist writers, editors and publishers of newspapers, pamphlets and books.

"Among those detained for their factual accounts of Peterloo in the radical press are Richard Carlile, John Knight, our regular Oldham correspondent and John Saxton of the *Manchester Observer,* another regular source of intelligence for our information exchange.

"Mary Fildes, who founded the Manchester Women's Reform Society in July, 1819, in order to enrol women for the demonstration, was on the Peterloo platform, but made her escape, avoiding arrest and imprisonment and lay low with friends until the heat died down. She is a stalwart reformist, now responsible for establishing women's political unions and enlisting many women to the cause.

"The arrested speakers and contingent leaders, without charge, languish in gaols all over the country, awaiting their trials. Alongside them are men whose only offence was to report the facts of Peterloo in the radical press. The usual charge is seditious libel, or suspicion of preparedness to commit seditious libel, which magistrates have interpreted in such a variety of ways that our defence lawyers have had enjoyable times teasing and defeating the all too easily befuddled Bench".

Just two days after Peterloo, the sisters Had ridden on Alexia, with Polly riding pillion, to a huge rally at Smithfield. The principal speaker was Arthur Thistlewood. A Spencean militant and ex-army officer, Thistlewood, a man in his 40's, had a reputation as daring, to the point of recklessness. For his part in the Spa Fields riot in 1816, he was arrested, held in custody and sent to trial, but released. Seeking revenge for his time in prison and the confiscation of some personal possessions, he challenged Lord Sidmouth to a duel. This challenge gained much press attention, but Sidmouth scornfully ignored the matter.

Polly was fearful that the tragedy and humiliation of Peterloo would plunge her sister into despondency, in her dark desert, as after the major set-back at Pentrich.

Cally did lose her appetite, both for food and any sort of amusement, but she was persuaded to keep busy, spending time writing letters responding positively and encouragingly to their correspondents in the North. She was found one afternoon, shedding a tear over another letter from Bamford, which told of the permanent maiming of some of those injured at Peterloo, including a woman who was blinded by a horse's hoof trampling her face. the sisters were too busy for the self-indulgence of despair. Both were in demand, in the aftermath of Peterloo, to attend reformist meetings across London and the country south of the Thames. Additionally, of course, there was now Tilly to look after, who became more active, inquisitive and captivating with every passing day. Contrary to Lavender's prediction, her first garbled word, Which came earlier than is normal, was not "reform", but "Mama", with arms outstretched, repeatedly addressed to Cally, or Polly, or Ananya, whichever one of them came near. To her great wonderment and delight, she had now joined the Reed women's weekly bath day.

Every hour spent with the baby brought new achievement. Pee-pot training had resulted in the urgent signal of "Pee, pee," several times a day. A few weeks later there was a more discriminatory garbled plea, which the mothers could translate as "Bottom empty". Ananya declared the child to be twice as advanced as average for her age, obviously as a consequence of having twice the average number of mothers, providing double the expected amount of attention.

A month after Peterloo, the sisters had ridden to an open-air meeting in Westminster, leaving their horse in the care of the groom at the Albert Inn. Henry Hunt, on bail, and John Cartwright were among the speakers. The report in *The Times* estimated that 300,000 crowded the streets that day. The mood was agitated, but orderly. A local mounted militia battalion was present, but the soldiers kept their distance, dismounted throughout, as if chary of giving the least impression that they were of the ilk of the butchers of Peterloo.

Over the following weeks, the Reed sisters' correspondence was heavy with reports of protest meetings and demonstrations in all parts of the country, registering anger, indignation, compassion for the stricken and great impatience for an adequate response from the reformists.

In the Manchester area there were calls for vengeance. As before the Pentrich rising, farm implements were sharpened, pikes were made and collections of weapons were hidden, but cooler heads prevailed. It was among the trade union members that the bitter lesson of Pentrich had been learned best. The cry was still for vengeance, but the constitutionalists swayed the meetings and channelled the spirit of militancy into the establishment of trade union branches in more work-places, new Hampden Clubs, radical societies and reading circles.

In the autumn of 1819, The sisters were excited to receive a report from a group of pitmen in Northumberland. This corner of the North had long appeared quiescent, notwithstanding the formation of trade unions by the colliers, forgemen, stevedores` and sailors. Peterloo had spurred a group of tradesmen and artisans, friendly societies, trade unions and reading circles from passivity to action for reform.

Properly prepared in every detail, with permission from the Mayor, a demonstration was planned for 11th October on Newcastle's Town Moor, where the great Thomas Spence had addressed many a gathering during the previous century.

From inland and coastal villages, six-a-breast, drums and bugles playing, they marched to Town, mustering fifty to one hundred thousand. Out of this demonstration were born tavern discussion groups, reading circles and a reformist spirit that energised the area for another decade, Newcastle and Durham coming to match

Manchester and Birmingham as centres of trade union and reformist activity.

The sisters' voluminous correspondence had documented the build-up during 1819 to the massive turnout on 16th August. On the same St Peter's Field on 16th January, 1820, there was a big audience for Henry Hunt on his usual themes: condemning the Corn Laws and the hunger they caused and calling for universal suffrage.

Hunger was still rife, especially in the countryside, where labourers and others were least organised to demand higher wages.

The Speenhamland System had been introduced in rural areas, in 1795, at the height of the war and following failed harvests. It topped up low wages and poor relief, with a few shillings, according to the size of families. It was always inadequate compensation for the wages kept at poverty level by the employers and by now its benefit had worn very thin.

Making matters worse was the influential intervention of the Reverend Thomas Malthus. He criticised Speenhamland for topping-up parish relief according to family size. This, he claimed, tended to encourage early marriage and larger families, although policy ought to be aimed at curbing the demand for food and limiting the population. Whenever the Corn Laws and poverty arose in meetings, Cally took the opportunity to attack the Malthusian ideas. Here was another Anglican cleric who espoused the ideology of Christianity in the pulpit, while hypocritically embracing its opposite in practice outside the church.

That there were so many women, particularly young women, at the January, 1820 St Peter's Field meeting, was read by the authorities as an artful ruse to distract the militia. That the crowd initiated no violence was interpreted as part of a deceptive Machiavellian plot to obscure insurrectionary machinations under the surface. Even the mildest of demands for reform was taken as proof that thousands were engaged in conspiracies and bent on revolution. "*If only 'twere so,*" thought Cally.

For the bloodshed at Peterloo, the government attached no blame to the magistrates, nor the Yeomanry; those who were attacked, killed and wounded were to blame for the spilt blood. They were guilty of making unrealistic demands aimed at undermining the State and thereby giving the the authorities no alternative but to take stern action. "They brought it on themselves" was the conclusion of the Old Corruption.

Whenever Cally spoke about this, she ridiculed the government for attempting to turn the world and truth upside down. During the Civil War, the Levellers were condemned for wanting to achieve the aims of the revolution by turning the world upside down, putting the people on top and the mighty subdued. Now the Regency has created a fantasy world in which the innocent, the unarmed, those killed and maimed are the guilty parties and the government, its spies and the militias are pure as driven snow. When speaking about this, no matter whether addressing a meeting, or in conversation with her father, or the Rector, Cally's voice quivered with barely contained anger.

Across Surrey and Kent, the readings most frequently requested of the sisters were from Cobbett's *Political Register*, published weekly since 1802. He targeted every enemy of the poor, raging furiously against landlords, enclosures, the conspiracy of the rich against the poor and – a cause particularly close to Cally's heart – the hypocritical clergy.

Cobbett particularly addressed the country people, those who were least likely to be literate, most likely to be isolated, robbed of their ancient rights of common and robbed of fair wages. Small surprise that during the French war and beyond, so many had resorted to the ancient crafts of poaching, a source of meat for sale, or for the table, and a measure of revenge against the landowners who had stolen the country folks' strip fields, which had sustained their families for centuries.

Deployed against the poachers were armed game-keepers and viciously mutilating man-traps anchored to the ground, hidden in the undergrowth. Additionally, the government revived the 18th century Black Act, which specified 200 minor offences for which the death penalty could be applied.

On 15th September, 1819, a month after Peterloo, while still on bail, Hunt was triumphantly received at a rally in London. Cally and Polly rode in the procession from the Angel, Islington, to the Crown and Anchor, off the strand. The whole route was lined with cheering crowds. The sisters introduced themselves to James Watson and his son, Jem, both surgeons and well known radicals, veterans of Spa Fields and many another demonstration. After the meeting, the sisters accepted the Watsons' invitation to join them for chilled champagne at the Rising Sun Inn. Cally said nothing at the time, but could clearly see that young Jem Watson had set his cap at Polly and so had Watson senior, although old enough to be Polly's father. Small wonder. She is a pretty and vivacious woman, but should she ever be interested in a man, she can do much better than these specimens of the sex, who are well known for reckless behaviour, notwithstanding their commitment to the cause.

There was never an official inquiry into Peterloo, although a Whig MP said in the House, "An Inquiry is loudly called for and is indispensable for purposes of justice. The dispersion of the (Manchester) meeting was unnecessary, illegal and cruel".

Inquests on the dead were delayed until forgotten. The Prince Regent, as unthinking and club-footed as ever, publicly congratulated the Yeomanry and army on their 'valiant protection of the nation's interests at the Manchester riot.'

At a meeting of the local Hampden Club, in September of 1819, Cally and Polly were invited to report their news from the North on reactions to Peterloo. Polly quoted the *Manchester Observer* as the first known ironic naming of Peterloo. She went on to the paper's bitter comment on the gross hypocrisy of the Manchester bench of justices of the Peace, including clergymen, summoning "privileged murderers" to engage in acts of bloodshed against unarmed men, women and children. "Those magistrates know nothing of justice, nor of peace", declared Polly.

"How much more must the people suffer in order to achieve the equal rights of nature as Tom Paine defined them?

"Most of our correspondents' letters are dripping with caustic anger about Peterloo. Many of them talk of vengeance. *Black Dwarf* sums up the overwhelming feeling:"' If the people were ever to rise up and strike back at their enemies, is this not the time?'

"'The people of Lancashire have been brutally attacked by representatives of a callous government, which continues to impose on them the evil Corn Laws, adding hunger to their burden of distress."

"John Cartwright has put his case starkly,'If our meetings are to be ridden down, then we should attend them with the means of self defence. If our opponents are armed and act unconstitutionally, should not every citizen exercise the right to bear arms?'" Cheers around the room.

"After all, the 1689 Bill of Rights allowed Protestants to be armed in self defence against the armed Papists of the day. Standing against us we now have a far stronger enemy, militias, equipped and trained by the government, with no expense spared.

"Cartwright continues,'Are we brutally whipped hounds, or are we merely sleeping dogs, yet to be wakened?'" More cheers.

"We are posed these questions:'Where is the boundary between wisdom and careful consideration on the one hand, and folly on the other hand?'

"'When does prudence become cowardice? And when does submission become criminal passivity?'"

Polly's speech would not have been so well received had it not contained much that could be considered seditious. There must have been a police nark present, someone in need of both money and integrity, who went running to Bow Street to collect his florin for shopping Polly.

Although her name, her *nom de guere*, was known by the nark – Polly Mouse – the address of her home was not known by anybody at the Club, apart from Cally. She could therefore not be easily apprehended until the next meeting, when she was accosted by a squat lumpy-nosed man in the familiar police uniform, who checked her name and identified himself as a Bow Street Runner, name of Ruston. Cally introduced herself as Mrs Calpernia Wright, housemaid Polly's employer. Ruston hailed a gig and the unlikely trio rode – in haste, for some unexplained reason, to Bow Street, where the Court was as crowded, chaotic and noisome as usual. There Ruston led them to stand below the Bench. The sisters were mildly amused and too mystified to be nervous. A magistrate, from his lofty perch, first had their names recorded and their address, which Cally concocted on the spur of the moment as Datchet Street, Newington. The Beak drew towards him a dog-eared sheet and read out a number of accurate extracts from Polly's report to the September meeting of the Club. The text was as accurate a record as the Club's own Minutes secretary might have made

"Do you, Miss Mouse, deny making these seditious statements?" asked the magistrate, having to recapture his voluminous wig as it slipped forward under the effect of gravity when looking down at this rather small woman.

"Certainly not," said Polly, "I did read out those quotations and I must congratulate your informant on the accuracy of his note-taking."

"That's as maybe. These utterances contravene the recently enacted Blasphemous and Seditious Libels Act and collectively constitute a sufficient offence for you to be sent for trial."

Cally brought a chair to the Bench and helped Polly to mount it so that she was now almost on a level with His Honour.

"Sir, I do understand your concern; some of the statements might be looked on as challenging. They are dealing with a very serious matter.

"But blasphemous? Seditious?". Her large innocent eyes were brimming with distress and her voice, as always, was that of a ten-year old and quivering. "There is much here that is mischievous to say the least, said the beak, tapping the paper.

"But those words are not mine, Sir. I neither composed them, nor published them." Her pretence of fearful distress was impressive, even to her sister, who was familiar with Polly's acting skills.

"Surely, It is the author who should be standing before you, answerable for any offence."

His Honour was more than a little nonplussed by this unexpected turn, but overridingly he was hungry for his dinner and an overdue quaff. His frown indicated the need for more explanation.

"You see, Sir," said this child-woman, "I was reporting to the meeting Statements printed in the Manchester Observer. For merely reporting the troublesome words of an unknown person, I do not think I can be held as any more culpable than your most conscientious note-taker, who by recording the suspicious utterances, was repeating them and spreading them."

The magistrate's face was exasperation writ large. He gave an impatient, vigorous shake of the head as if to rid himself of a troublesome fly or this tiresome business.

"Do you regularly attend such meetings as this, Miss Mouse?"

Cally intervened with: "I should hope not, Your Honour, Miss Mouse's duties as my housemaid are too onerous to allow it. She remains under my close supervision at all times"

Addressing Cally, he said, "So be it, good day, Madam," and his hand rudely waved them both away.

In celebration of this lucky escape, they ran to the extravagance of hailing a gig to travel home.

On their way, they agreed it was advantageous that the limited intellect of Lord Sidmouth's intelligence service left the magistrate unaware that the two women before him were both daughters of Bow Street Runners. Polly was wondering which Club member she had offended sufficiently to warrant being victim of such betrayal. "We'll probably never know," said Cally, "Best not to ponder it. It may be a pathetic churl who resents his passion for you being unrequited, because you are unwinnable.

"You are a beauty and so there will be more such. Take from it what pleasure you can, my precious love, but let's hope not all your swooning swains are police snitches."

Dinner that day was riotous, as the sisters recounted their encounter with the Bow Street Beak. But they knew it was important to reassure their parents that they were aware that this was a lucky escape and that their political activity made them vulnerable, especially following the passage of the Six Acts. Any meeting of more than fifty persons could not take place without a magistrate's prior approval. Further, publishers of blasphemous and seditious libels were subject to imprisonment or transportation.

The even bigger news of the day was that Mother had seen Tilly's latest trick. The clever little body, had sat up unaided, turned herself over sideways on to all-fours and crawled a couple of yards. All declared that this child is very advanced for her age.

It was soon after this that Dolly declared the baby was ready to be weaned. Accordingly, Tilly spent more time each day with her mothers, although, for the time being, still spending nights with Dolly. Oatmeal stirred in warm milk was Tilly's first solid food, served using a tiny spoon. Seated in a high-chair at the head of the table, with a mother on each side, she dominated the conversation at dinner each day, although emitting no more than meaningless burbling.

The appearance of successive teeth was celebrated over a period of weeks.

With Cally attending a lesson with the Rector, Polly went on her own to collect their baby for her morning airing. Tilly was busy suckling and looked so contented at Dolly's breast, that Polly sat staring as if mesmerised by the scene. The spell was broken when Dolly said, "open your bodice", and placed the baby against Polly's chest. As soon as Tilly's cheek touched her mother's skin, her head instinctively turned and her mouth latched on to the nipple. Her tongue now began its suckling motion and Polly felt a delightful sensation.

The magic did not last long. Tilly sensed that the breast was dry and opened her hungry mouth to wail in protest. This new thing was a milestone for Polly. Her daughter, unknowingly, and her lover, enticingly, similarly cause an ecstatic sensation, evoking her tenderest feelings for each of them.

Before the year's end, there came the Tory government's response to Peterloo. Predictably it came not in the form of concessions, but further repression. The Six Acts were hurried through a Parliament frightened of what might come next. Firstly, the Blasphemy and Seditious Libel Bill, 1819 was moved by Lord Castlereagh, who was hated throughout the land for his instant resort to new repressive measures whenever he and the duet of Liverpool and Sidmouth sensed new reformist moves. The authorities now had the power to search, without a warrant, any property where it was suspected arms were hidden. Writers and publishers could be sent for trial if their words offended the sensibilities of the government. A stamp duty of fourpence was placed on all newspapers and pamphlets, in order to diminish their sale and, as one MP put it, 'diminish the evil they are inflicting on the country'. One Whig MP spoke against the Bill, describing it as "The most alarming attack ever yet made by Parliament on the liberties and constitution of the country."

His was a voice in the wilderness.

While some still held the hero of Waterloo in high esteem, others knew Wellington for his contempt for the lower orders, as for his ragged army. A James Gilray cartoon at about this time, depicts Wellington standing before the scales of justice. Weighing down one side are the scrolls of the repressive Six Acts aimed at silencing the entire reformist movement. That is the side on to which he throws down the additional weight of his sword. That put the Iron Duke roundly on the side of the most retrogressive Tories, a record he went on to maintain during his two periods as Prime Minister.

From the time of Peterloo, the government took every opportunity to claim the Manchester demonstrators had been armed and bent on insurrection, inspired by the revolutionaries across the Channel. Any publication giving the true story and asserting that the Yeomanry and Hussars were the instigators of violence, bearing the only arms on the field, was suppressed and its writer and publisher were arrested. There can be only one truth and that is the truth owned by the ruling class.

The Prince Regent was eager to clamp down on any dissent and reformist ideas and pressured his ministers accordingly.

When the Southwark Club met in October, the minutes of the September meeting were read, including key parts, which had brought cheers and table-thumping around the room at the previous meeting. This part of the agenda is usually a boring formality, with most of those present not bothering to listen, This time, the minutes secretary's droning monologue brought forth applause for the repetition of certain parts of Polly's original report. Clearly, the members relished the repetition of her seditious libels, such as "How much more must the people suffer?" and "If the people were ever to rise up, is this not the time?"

The most enthusiastic clamour was for the rhetorical questions: "Are we brutally whipped hounds, or are we merely sleeping dogs, yet to be wakened?" and "Where is the boundary between wisdom and careful consideration on the one hand and folly on the other hand?" and finally, "When does prudence become cowardice? And when does submission become criminal passivity?"

"Are we to be weak victims of history, or shall we *make* history?

The sisters had noted, in the correspondence received following Peterloo, that even those who were normally most sober and restrained in their views, had taken a more radical turn and this had been reflected in Polly's report to the September meeting.

A member, called Bourne, who was known for his constitutionalist and cautious reformist position, indicated a wish to speak and was given the floor. He argued that Polly's report to the previous meeting was incautious and failed to learn the lesson of Peterloo. Talk of that sort would lead her into prison. There is poverty and distress around the nation, but it has ever been thus. The majority of the people are loyal to the Regent and do not support radical reform. The best course is to seek modest improvements, without demanding such changes as votes for all. Keep the request for bread separate from the demand for votes. It is not votes that assuage hunger. Bourne's comments were heard by those present in complete silence. The only reaction was an assembly of sullen-looking faces.

Cally indicated to the Chairman and was given the floor.

"I think I can speak for most of those present," said she. "It is astonishing to hear such loyalist sentiments as those from Mr Bourne, uttered in a Hampden Club meeting.

"We all know that votes do not fill the belly, but it is those who have votes to wield who brought in the Corn Laws and taxes on other comestibles, creating hunger and the misery of the poor.

"Power must lie with the people; so long as it is held only by the rich, there will be no fair shares and no justice.

"We must have universal suffrage if we are permanently to eliminate hunger as a weapon of the rich for the domination of the poor.

"It is the threat and reality of hunger which is used by the merchant and landowner class to threaten and coerce the working class. Cally sat to loud applause.

1820

The death of George III and accession of his son brought Queen Caroline to the fore. She was variously described as beautiful, graceful and intelligent, as well as ugly, dumpy, dim and smelly.

George found her physically repugnant from the day they first met and they permanently lived apart. On the day of his coronation, he had all the doors of Westminster Abbey barred against his putative queen. All of this was wonderful grist for the cartoonists' mills. Cruikshank portrayed the royal couple in their gargantuan obesity, George's gouty swollen toe being soothed in Caroline's ample lap, with predictable coarse *double entendres* being exchanged in speech bubbles.

At a meeting of the Hampden Club, in the late spring of 1820, Cally asked for the floor, in order to make a statement. With Polly's encouragement, she had taken more than usual trouble over her appearance. The weather being warm, for the first time at a Club meeting, she was wearing a sari, crimson in colour, with a green scarf. Some members had never before seen a sari and so there was quite a stir as she walked in. She pulled the drape down from her head, on to her shoulder and started.

"Within days of Peterloo, I wrote to Percy Shelley, asking whether he was moved to commemorate the tragedy with a poem.

"After some weeks, a reply came from Mary, his wife. She explained there were postal delays because they were living in Italy.

"She told me that on hearing of the Peterloo massacre, Shelley immediately put pen to paper and posted a long poem to Leigh Hunt, the editor of *The Examiner* magazine, for publication in the issue of January 1820.As a subscriber to the magazine, I knew that no such poem had appeared and so I wrote to Mary Shelley again.

"Mary replied that Leigh Hunt had decided not to publish the poem at this time.

The reasons he gave she found entirely specious, as do I. She was kind enough to send me transcriptions of both the poem and Hunt's letter declining publication. It is a long poem, called *The Mask of Anarchy*. I will recite for you selected verses. You will see that he does not call for precipitate vengeance – an eye for an eye and a tooth for a tooth – meeting blood with blood, after the tradition of the Old Testament.

He considers us to be better than that. The slayers of Peterloo will be shunned by their own.

"Addressing the victims of Peterloo and their reformist supporters, he proclaims,'Rise like lions after slumber/ In unvanquishable number/Shake your chains to earth like dew/Which in sleep had fallen on you/ Ye are many – they are few'"

Cally projected her voice more loudly, in repeating the lines

"'Rise like lions after slumber/In unvanquishable number.

"'Ye are many – they are few'.

Then, turning towards each part of the room, as she pounded out: "In other words, our day will come."

Shelley was known to be an ally of the cause and so his words were warmly received by the meeting.

Cally continued.

"That the poem has yet to be published is disappointing, especially as Leigh Hunt is a reformist, who has even been gaoled under the government's ridiculous law against seditious libel. Shelley is not the only great poet to have fallen foul of Leigh Hunt's editorship. John Milton called The Examiner's editorial office a nest of vipers.

"Hunt gave as his reason for withholding publication, his thought that 'the public at large had not become sufficiently discerning to do justice to the sincerity and kind-heartedness of the spirit that walked in this flaming robe of verse.

"He clearly implies that in the immediate aftermath of Peterloo, the effect of the poem would have been too inflammatory on the victims of Peterloo and their many sympathisers.

"'Days of outrage have passed away and with them the exasperation that would cause such an appeal to the many to be injurious'"

Polly handed her sister a sheet of paper and Cally continued, "I wrote the following letter to Mr Hunt.

Dear Mr Hunt,

Please do not be tempted to chastise Mrs Shelley for allowing me pre-publication sight of The Mask of Anarchy and sight of your letter explaining why the poem has been withheld.

"Nobody can blame her for wanting to be rid of my pestering.

"I consider your reason for sitting on the poem to be patronising of the people of the reformist movement and the victims of Peterloo, for whom it was written. We do not need you to protect us from our righteous anger.

"'We have not sunk to the animal depth of the Manchester Yeomanry. We have not been guilty of any bloodshed, although wickedly provoked. Now and for a long time to come, this poem will be seen as a call for non-violent, iron-willed protest; determination not to mirror the violence of a blood-thirsty government; a pledge of steadfastness in the face of unbearable provocation, until we choose our own time to react.

'You have misread the reform movement, denying us the consolation and inspiration of Shelley's poetry. You have assumed, without any evidence, that our anger and hatred arising from Peterloo were out of control. You have exceeded your authority as Editor and betrayed the reformist movement, of which you have been part.

"I have decided to cancel my subscription to The Examiner.

"Yours etc."

"I have yet to receive a reply."

Cally sat down to shouts of "Well done and "Hear, hear."

Tilly's second birthday was marked by her being almost proficient at using the pee-pot. Now, several times a day there would be the frantic plea, "Pee,pee. A few weeks later came the more discriminatory announcement, "Empty bottom" in a garble that only Cally or Polly could translate.

"Having twice as many mothers has made this child twice as advanced as others of her age", was Ananya's judgement.

It started with Polly thinking aloud and then both sisters took a notion to travel. So far, north Kent and mid-Surrey were the furthest points to which they had ventured, always in response to Hampden Club or trade union invitations.

"We have yet to see one of these expanding industrial centres, William Blake's dark, satanic mills. Much of Yorkshire is often in turmoil and yet we know about it only from letters and newspaper reports. Yorkshire is not on the other side of the world; why can't we go and see it for ourselves? Tilly is not yet old enough for a long journey. Let's see if Mother and Dolly would between them look after her for a few days.

In truth, because their journeyings to date had been so limited, both sisters were nervous about a long expedition. Then Cally tried to see their challenge in perspective. "Mary Shelley recently travelled halfway across Europe with a new-born baby. We are planning no more than taking ourselves 200 miles within the bounds of England."

They engaged Bevis Brown, the groom they shared with the neighbours, to accompany them. He would be a sort of protector and, as one more worldly wise, he would advise them on the complications of the journey. His costs would be paid, plus a half-guinea on top of his usual wage. He would borrow livery from a friend, in order to look as if he worked for gentry. His first task was to go to the Angel Inn at Smithfield, in order to check the departure times of the York stagecoach. They would travel in June, when the turnpikes and other roads are in best condition.

Tilly's second birthday was celebrated on 1st of June and the sister's travelled north the following day. They hired a gig to take them to The Angel. The York coach was due to leave at seven in the morning. The four-in-hand was standing in the courtyard, the horses finishing their breakfast from nosebags. The sisters had paid for inside seats for themselves at six pounds each. Bevis was to ride up-front with the driver for a lesser fare. As the complement was not yet complete, their luggage stowed, they took coffee in the dining room until the coachman called them. Eventually they were called to board and found they still numbered only five out of a complement of six.

Confined in such a small space for the next three or four days, introductions were important. Miss Cally Reed and Miss Polly Reed, sisters, were taking a little holiday in Yorkshire. The Reverend Ebenezer Crawford, accompanied by his wife, Mary McLeod and daughter Catriona, is visiting York, prior to taking an incumbency there.

"We wonder where our missing sixth passenger is", said Cally. That is also the concern of the coachman, who is fidgeting by his horses, repeatedly looking at his pocket watch. He is eager to make good time. On the first turnpike, up to Hatfield, there will be several coaches meeting a bottleneck. With no possibility of overtaking. The first coach there is at an advantage.

At last, breathlessly apologising to everybody in general, a man arrives, hands his portmanteau to the coachman and clambers in. Cally is surprised to recognise Dr James Watson senior. He bows his head and smiles recognition to the sisters, "Miss Cally, Miss Polly, delighted that we are re-acquainted and to see we are travelling together." The coach has pulled away and above the metallic rumbling over the cobbles, introductions are completed. Dr Watson is sitting opposite the Crawfords. Leaning across the narrow aisle and shaking hands, he introduces himself as James Watson, surgeon, on his way to Edinburgh via York.

For the present, there was interest enough in gazing at the passing London sights, most of them new to the sisters. Then came the countryside and occasional villages. The up and down rocking and side-to-side swaying movement of the coach was a new experience and sometimes violent enough to be disconcerting.

Thankfully, neither gentleman was a tobacco smoker. The sisters tried reading. Between them, they had a novel by The Lady and another by Sir Walter Scott, but they were not used to reading constantly moving print. Cally resorted to conversation. Trivial comments on the weather and the dancing of the coach were exchanged among the passengers. Then to something more consequential. "Reverend Crawford, Sir, tell me, which branch of the church is yours?"

He smiled at Cally, clearly pleased to expatiate on this topic. "I am a minister of the Unitarian Church."

"Am I right in thinking, Sir, said Polly, "That Unitarians do not accept the Trinity concept of the Church of England?

"You are correct," Crawford responded.

"We see God, the Father, Christ the Son and the Holy Spirit, all of them to be manifestations of the one God?"

"I must admit," continued Polly, "That I always found it difficult to understand how Jesus, if also God, could sit on the right hand of God.

"When asked about that oddity by a child in my class – how could God sit beside Himself? I was at a loss."

"Being from the Christological branch of Unitarianism,"explained Mr Crawford, "I believe that ChrIst is not God. He was a divine being who was placed on earth as a real historical figure and, after crucifixion, he was taken back into heaven."

"Christ is both divine and human."

Cally and Polly exchanged quick glances, marking their joint decision not to voice their scepticism. Best leave the matter at that. People have a right to believe in fairies and in God, whatever makes them happy. They knew that, as a Unitarian, Mr Crawford would be on the side of the angels on the great issues of widespread poverty and the need for constitutional reform.

"May I ask what church you attend?" Mr Crawford's question was addressed to Polly.

"My sister and I attend no church, Sir. We are both Quakers."

"How very interesting."

That he was not being indulgent was shown by his next utterance. "I have met Mrs Elizabeth Fry, a most formidable champion of social reform, a true Christian. I wonder, do you know her?"

"As a matter of fact," said Polly, "My sister And I work alongside Mrs Fry at Newgate Prison and the nearby compters. We teach imprisoned mothers and their children, doing our best to make them literate."

"You are right that she is very strong-willed," added Cally, "She has won concessions from the Home Secretary and prison authorities, in the face of apathy and sometimes downright opposition from members of Parliament and the Church."

There followed a discussion about prison conditions, the further reforms demanded by Mrs Fry and John Howard and the notion of prisons being for rehabilitation and education, rather than mere confinement and punishment. Mr Crawford was clearly a humane man, as were his wife and his thoughtful, reticent young daughter.

Dr Watson was asked the purpose of his journey and he explained that his destination was Edinburgh Medical School, where he was to study developments in surgical operation techniques under Professor Bell, returning to London after a few days.

Mrs Crawford was looking at Cally somewhat quizzically and, glancing at her husband as if to obtain approval, she clasped her hands together and mustered the boldness to broach the subject. Addressing Cally, she said: "Miss Reed, please forgive me – where do you come from? I fear that may sound very rude."

"Not in the least," Cally gave her questioner a reassuring smile. "I was born in this country and my father is from Yorkshire, but my mother is from India."

"So, from your mother –" Mrs Crawford was again very hesitant – "You have inherited your beautiful appearance, including, again forgive me, those remarkable and unique eyes.

"But", attention was now drawn to the young Miss Crawford, who was gazing at Polly and trying to assemble the appropriate words, "your sister has not …

"Let me save your blushes," jumped in Polly, "We are, indeed sisters, but not by birth. I was adopted by Cally's parents."

Shoulders relaxed and there was a release of breath as the tension subsided, that little mystery being resolved without embarrassment or rancour.

The coachman was sufficiently familiar with the route to know where comfort stops provided the ladies, in particular, with discreet roadside bushes.

The overnight stop was at the George Hotel, Stamford, reached at seven in the evening. The passengers shared a table for dinner. Not wishing to be troublesome, the sisters compromised their principles by taking fish for their meal, baked tench from the hotel's own pond, while the others had haricoed mutton and pigeon. There was Burgundy and small beer and apricot tarts.

On Bevis's advice, the sisters took a room at the top of the house, as far as possible from the noise of night coaches coming and going, passengers alighting and boarding, and all the clatter of changing horses. Unused to long journeys, they were exhausted and slept well. Fortunately, in consideration of sleeping passengers in the stage inns, at night, the coach horn was not sounded as a warning of arrival and departure,.

Their coachman had them all roused at eight for a nine o'clock departure. The passengers assembled in the courtyard, breakfasted and yawning, where the coachman, with Bevis's help, was backing his fresh team of horses between the shafts of the coach, which was newly spruced up. So far, the journey had been uneventful; no lost or broken wheel, no snapped suspension strap, no lame horse, no lost shoe and no armed and demanding footpads. When they reached Newark, they found the road through the town had been newly macademized and so, as the coach virtually glided along, the passengers took to their books, but not for long. Soon the coach appeared again to have taken to a choppy sea.

Yesterday's conversation may have exhausted the exchange of factual information. Today's talk started with anecdotes and gossip, moving on to speculation and polemic.

Apropos conditions in prisons, Cally recounted the story of the successful effort to improve the transfer of women prisoners and their children from Newgate to Deptford for transportation. The Rector of St Mary's had enlisted the support of the Bishop of London in easing conditions on the transports and an unexpected bonus won by Mrs Fry was a grant from Sir Robert Peel, the Home Secretary, for the provision of small libraries on the convict ships.

"Our ultimate aim," explained Cally, "Is to end the cruelty of transportation, which usually amounts to banishment for life. On arrival in Botany Bay or Virginia, the convicts enter a life of virtual slavery, at the beck and call of convicts who arrived earlier."

"Of course, we Quakers stand for the abolition of slavery across the whole of the British Empire. Members of the working class in England surely stand in solidarity with slaves in the West Indies and Virginia. We are underpaid and overworked; slaves are paid nothing at all and are worked to death. Inside each black slave is a real human being, deserving of the same rights as all of us. The rich of England, in their grand mansions, are living off the profits of slavery.

"The Church of England has individuals who oppose slavery, but the Church as a body remains complicit in the trade."

Dr Watson changed his seat and addressed Mr Crawford. "Please tell me, Mr Crawford, what was the response of your church to the massacre at Peterloo?"

The Rev Crawford sat back in his seat, interlocking his fingers on his lap, while clearing his morning throat. "Firstly, let me say that we Unitarians, in common with other dissenting and independent groups, have ourselves fallen victim to violence; not as brutal as Peterloo, thank God, and not at the hands of the agents of the state.

"Our services have been disrupted by mobs, our meeting rooms damaged, our libraries sometimes burnt and our people abused. The crowd has frequently been screaming the loyalist slogan, 'Church and King'.

"Peterloo was an appalling event. The actions of the Manchester authorities were totally inexcusable. Nobody has yet been brought to account. That should happen before memories fade and the victims are forgotten.

"You refer, Sir", said Cally, "to the attacks on dissenters. The rampaging mobs of the cities are as often unpredictable as they are irrational. Targets might be Baptists one day and Unitarians or corn merchants another day. What is the solution?

She offered an answer to her own question: "I put my trust in achieving constitutional reform, so that the people's will has civilised means of expression, with no need to resort to remonstrances on the streets."

Dr Watson leaned towards Cally and spoke challengingly. "Madam, do you denigrate the demonstrators you categorise with the pejorative term, 'mob'?

Cally strove not to match her interlocutor's disputatious tone. With a kindly smile and a mild voice, she said. "I have sometimes been bold enough to think I might one day be able to write a novel, but I lack the literary skill of the anonymous lady and I have not the imagination to make up stories. Perhaps I might be able to write a factual history, in which case, I think my chosen topic would be – the role of the city mob in history.

"Although often regarded with contempt, the mob, in ancient Rome and in modern Paris, has been responsible for forcing changes, some of which have marked real human progress.

"Shakespeare knew the London mob well; it formed a large part of the audience for his plays.

"He knew the mob to be fickle. Boisterous, eager for holiday fun, often inebriated and ever capricious. He valued their attendance at his plays, but he was not such a romantic that he failed to recognise their ignorance, belligerence, excitability and unpredictability.

"In the opening scene of Julius Caesar, if my memory does not let me down, the plebeians, the ragged multitude of Rome, is chastised by the tribunes in the Forum, derisively addressed as, 'you blocks, stones and worse than senseless things.'

"They deserve the insults. They are so easily swayed. Sometimes for Caesar, sometimes for Pompey, sometimes for Mark Antony, favouring Brutus and next minute calling for his blood. They have all the hallmarks of a capricious, easily bribed, mercurial mob."

"In Verona, Mercutio and Romeo are inflamed into their murderous encounter by the mob of idle youths on the Rialto. Had they been apprentices. Like so many of the boys and young men in London, owing allegiance to their artisanal masters, they would not have been at a loose end and out to cause mischief. They would not have coalesced into a mindless mob challenging their friends to spill blood."

Temporarily out of inspiration, Cally took a rest to catch her breath, while her fellow passengers clapped their hands in appreciation of her recollection of Shakespeare's plots.

"Let's face it," Cally soon picked up the thread," the collective mentality of a crowd can overpower the thoughts and intentions of its individual members."

"But, Miss Reed, in describing them as ragged and blockheads, you are being contemptuous of the poor who are meeting, marching, protesting for their basic rights." Dr Watson's tone was still earnest and demanding of a response.

"Some of those words, Sir, were not mine; I was quoting the Bard. I would not underestimate or insult the people seen by Tom Spence and William Cobbett as potentially the vanguard for democratic change.

"And I must take account of the Englishman's relish for ritual and strict procedure. From the centre of any crowd can arise the call for order and the selection of a chairman. That is followed by a call for rules. Then with rules set, the next cry will be, 'Point of order.'

"I sometimes think that constitutionality is the English disease. I have attended so many meetings where arguments over custom and practice have consumed more time and energy than debate of parliamentary reform and the means to achieve it. There is something to be said for informality and a modicum of disorder."

"However, I will not dodge the issue. I do consider that the mood, the legitimate intentions of a crowd can be altered, misdirected by those with covert malicious intent, or by blatant provocators. I suppose one could say that a crowd of otherwise rational individuals, if manipulated by those of ill will, can lose its sense and behave in a way that earns it the pejorative term, mob.

"A mob is a stupid entity, made up of individuals who are permanently, or temporarily stupid. what dol I mean by stupid? a person is rendered stupid by being gullible, irrational and inconsistent. One does not have to be poor in order to manifest such characteristics as those.

"The descriptor, mob, is not limited to poor people. The yeomen, the sons of yeomen and merchants, who don elaborate uniforms and pick up sabres and carbines and mount their horses, leaving any ethical sense behind, become an armed force, a militia, a dangerous, a murderous mob".

Polly now contributed to the discussion. Her wide, innocent eyes and girlish voice lowered the temperature of the exchange. "My mind goes back to the Spa Fields disturbances, back in December of 1816. The entirely tenable plan to hear speeches and launch a petition to the Prince Regent was waylaid when a large part of the crowd, against the plans of the organisers, was led off in a crazy, fruitless adventure aimed at capturing the Royal Exchange and the Tower. The outcome was the reading of the Riot Act and the beating and arrest of scores of men. Supporters of constitutional reform had been misled and behaved irrationally, like a mob"

While Polly was delivering this anecdote, she was looking at Cally and the Crawfords, avoiding Dr Watson's eye. This seeming ingénue was aware of the fine line of artifice she was walking. "I have heard from more than one reliable source that the Spa Fields riot began when a man leapt down from the speakers' platform, shouting the well known words of Camille Desmoulins before the storming of the Bastille in July 1789: 'If they will not give us what we want, shall we not take it? Are you willing to take it? Will you come with me and take it?'

Thus a crowd of demonstrating reformists was converted into a looting mob by the incendiary challenge of one reckless man, goaded by government spies."

Cally gave her sister a conspiratorial wink and smiled at her arch audacity.

Dr Watson was silent and he would not meet Polly's eyes. His face indicated that he was ruminating.

Polly knew exactly what she was doing. From reliable sources, it was reported that the would-be embodiment of the Camille Desmoulin's legend was the doctor's son, Jem Watson, in his cups and probably carelessly allowing himself to be aided and abetted by John Castle, also known as Oliver the spy.

The driver pulled up the horses at a village pond, announcing that the stop was also for the passengers' comfort, gentlemen to the left and ladies to the bushes on the right. Noticing that they were at the foot of a steep hill, the passengers guessed the worst. Sure enough, on pulling away, the slow haul became a stuttering halt. The coachman apologised and requested that "We save straining the horses by the passengers walking up the hill." Thankfully, the weather was dry.

The climb separated the passengers according to their energy in tackling the slope. Dr Watson walked alongside Mr and Mrs Crawford. Cally found herself in the lead, with Bevis. Polly and young Miss Crawford walked all the way in close confab. Having first to finish their animated conversation, they were the last to mount the coach at the brow of the hill.

Pleading a headache, Catriona asked if she might sit next to an open window. This placed her on the seat next to Polly. For the next few hours, she and Polly, heads close together, were in quiet conversation, hardly above a whisper, despite the constant rumble of the wheels and the clatter of the horses' hooves. Cally asked Mrs Crawford whether she had any other children apart from Catriona. Two sons would have been younger than her daughter had they not died in infancy.

When Cally started telling Mrs Crawford that, together with Polly, she was mother to an adopted daughter, an orphaned child, all the passengers were attentive. Here was novelty – a black child with no father and two mothers, one of them brown-skinned and one white. Novelty, indeed. By early evening, the coach reached Doncaster for the overnight stop. The Coach and Horses Inn provided a disappointing dinner. Cally and Polly had to be content with barley bread, cheese and onions. In consolation for this rugged fare, they shared a bottle of indifferent Burgundy.

All being well, the next day would see them reach York.

"Do you think Catriona has set on you? Cally asked Polly while they were seated together at dinner.

Polly drew her chair closer, so that she could not be overheard. "She is a sweet girl. She finds you and me to be extraordinary, even exotic. She has never been to school. Her mother has taught her at home. She has no friends of her own age. She has been asking me the most childish and intimate questions, because she has nowhere else to turn, poor thing. It has never been explained to her what our monthlies are about, let alone the various practical ways to deal with them.

"Could you be lovers?" asked Cally. This bold question brought no embarrassment; the sisters were committed to total honesty with one another in all things. There was no topic under the sun that could not be candidly considered. Occasionally they had reviewed possible alternative lovers among their female friends and acquaintances and invariably came to the same conclusion. Chance had thrown them together and this circumstance could not conceivably be bettered. Neither of them was tempted by the novelty of a new intimate friendship.

"In another life," said Polly, "I could love such a pretty and innocent girl, but I already have the love of my life and cannot seriously imagine any other." They touched hands across the table and then took up their glasses and toasted, "Our everlasting love".

"It is no exaggeration," said Polly, "That I have been opening a new world for Catriona. She thinks I am a bas bleu, which I find flattering. I hope I will always be seen, like you, my darling, as a blue stocking among women. She finds my life and my ideas very exciting. By the time we get to York, I think we shall have a new reformist revolutionary. With her family settled in York, or nearby, we could have a new correspondent in the North Country.

"She was pitifully embarrassed to ask, but desperate to know whether we wear any under-garments under our skirts. She has heard say of that being a trend in London. I explained that short drawers, open drawers, or pantaloons, even ankle-length, are now fashionable among younger women. At the most recent comfort stop, my skirts pulled right up, I showed her my linen, my short drawers. She was shocked at my daring behaviour and delighted by my drawers.

"Having tested sensitive territory, I fear she may next want to know how babies are made. Of course, I could dodge the challenge by pleading that I cannot know, for I am unmarried. Or I could take the more courageous course. Or you and I might swap places in the coach, so that you have the educational task." Polly looked at Cally a little challengingly, who chuckled and emphatically shook her head.

Polly continued, "I assume her mother is too prudish to enlighten her daughter on intimate matters. I do not understand how people, in these enlightened times, can be so quaint. Catriona looks to you or me to tell her what she should have learned years ago, from her mother, or friends."

"No," said Cally, holding up her hands as if pushing the idea away, "You two have developed a rapport which Catriona finds so valuable, that it would be unkind to separate before you have to, when we get to York. She clearly needs you and she could have no better mentor. You are her Aristotle and this coach journey your Lyceum." Polly scoffed with a little puff of her lips.

Next morning, the coach about to commence its final stage, with more than a little pride, the coachman said, "I trust you all know we are now in England's biggest and best county, Yorkshire. In all directions you will see the hills of the distant dales. We soon pass through Sheffield, now one of the biggest towns in England." Cally recognised her father's boast about his birthplace, spoken in his dialect.

Dr Watson and Mr Crawford were continuing their conversation from yesterday's uphill trudge and Cally gave them her ear. "For a long time, stretching back into the last century, the greatest hostility to our Unitarian churches and other dissenting groups is found in Birmingham.

"Some of us have suffered because of our sympathy with the French Revolution and its original aim of establishing a more liberal society, some for being perceived as wealthy, some for their outspoken support for constitutional reform.

"John Dalton's home was destroyed and he was assaulted by a rampaging mob because his studies in natural philosophy were seen as ungodly.

"Attacks have become more bitter as the Church and King party has lost ground. It is weakened, because the cruelty of Peterloo was a big set-back for them. But Church and Kingclearly retains the support of Tory and Anglican magistrates, who fail to take action over even the most blatant offences against civil order committed by the loyalists."

"And assuredly, These same authorities readily pounce on we Spenceans and other radicals".Dr Watson was now speaking. "John Cartwright, in his newspaper, Black Dwarf, has put his case starkly. "He says that If our meetings are to be ridden down, as at Peterloo, then we should attend them with the means of self -defence.

"If our opponents are armed and act unconstitutionally, should not every citizen exercise the right to bear arms?

"Are we brutally whipped hounds, or are we merely sleeping dogs, yet to be wakened?"

"I agree with him," continued Watson, "Where is the boundary between wisdom and careful consideration on the one hand, and folly on the other hand?

"Those are important and difficult questions," interjected Cally.

"When do caution and prudence become cowardice? And when do compromise and submission become criminal neglect?" Learning from Pentrich and Peterloo, when too many of our people were sacrificed, we have to protect the followers of the reform movement.

"So much power lies with the opponents of constitutional reform.

"They have the police, soldiery and spies.

"They have the Treasury and control of the magistracy and judiciary.

"Unless our numbers are overwhelming, we will be labelled a criminal mob and dealt with accordingly. The Riot Act is nothing but a device for protecting the status quo.

"I apologise for bringing us back to the subject of mobs, but in giving the topic further thought, I realise that the ruling class frequently finds a mob, or rabble – call it what you will – most useful. A crowd is whipped into a frenzy by the rhetoric or bribery of malevolent persons above and outside of the crowd, which is thus turned into a belligerent mob to suit the objectives of a candidate at an election, for example.

"In London there are always malleable crowds on hand. Unscrupulous politicians know they can muster ostensible supporters by a distribution of free gin.Given more gin, the same mob can be quickly swung to intimidate the politician's opponents.

"The revolution in France, in 1789, won much sympathy and support in this country, strengthened by Tom Paine's book, *The Rights of Man*, but there was reaction to this, with riotous demonstrations, especially in Birmingham, where reformists and dissenters were cruelly attacked and the mob declared support for 'Church and King', as if the Civil War had never taken place. Ridiculous."

Perhaps Polly was scarred by the poverty, ignorance and injustice she had witnessed, because her patience and tolerance were sometimes worn thin. At this point, she said, "How to explain the motivation of the mob? There is illiteracy, ignorance, misguidance, but we cannot discount plain gross stupidity – for which there is no easy cure.

"Magistrates know they can rely on the mob to worsen the agony of a pilloried felon by pelting him with all manner of rubbish and ordure, forbidding only the throwing of rocks and brickbats, because that risks abbreviating the life of the felon and ending the sadistic enjoyment of the mob.

"The supporters of constitutional reform are drawn from the better educated citizenry. They have sufficient intellect to be won by rational argument".

"Thus they are elevated above the mob."

Cally was about to continue when the coach swerved and abruptly halted and there was raucous shouting from the road. The door was yanked open and a man wielding a pistol ordered the passengers to "Get out". Cally virtually leapt to the door and down to the road, shouting at the man, "Before you rob me, I need to relieve myself."

The astonished footpad had to step aside as Cally rushed across to the roadside undergrowth. There she made a fuss of adjusting her skirts and squatted down. Unseen by everybody, with her right hand she picked up a large pebble. She stood up, her clothes falling back into place and she hurried back to the coach, where the robber, his back to her, was still at the door, threatening the other passengers with his pistol.

In a flash, with her left hand Cally knocked off his billycock hat and swung her right arm smashing his head with the stone. While he was momentarily stunned, she hit him again. He bent over, holding his head. Cally grabbed up her skirts, lifted her leg and gave his backside a mighty kick, which sent him sprawling on the gravel. She was up and into the coach, shouting at the driver to move on.

It all happened so quickly that the passengers were not sure what had taken place, until Catriona, from her ringside seat at the door, enlightened them. she was in such a state of excitement, that her speech was flustered and she had to tell the story two or three times before her eager audience understood.

Cally was as much in a state of shock as the others, still trying to catch her breath. She was pleased with that kick. It was some time since she played football with her classmates, but she had not forgotten that essential skill. Dr Watson offered her his hip-flask. She gladly took it and swallowed some of the brandy. Unused to its harshness on her throat, she was left spluttering.

"Should we have arrested him?" Mrs Crawford innocently asked.

"Yes, madam," said Dr Watson, "but whose seat would he occupy on our way to York magistrates and how would we restrain him?"

"As it is, Miss Reed has administered instant and just punishment. He will have a sore head and gravel scrapes on his hands and knees for a few days.

"I most sincerely congratulate you, Miss Reed, on your astonishingly quick thinking and your bravery." By their reactions, the other passengers concurred.

"The man's big mistake," suggested Cally, avoiding basking in momentary glory, "Was to work alone. I am sure most footpads work in pairs or groups. I suspect he was unwilling to share the spoils with accomplices. It was his greed that let him down. Now he has nothing to show for his day's work but a sore head." "And the ignomy of having been floored by a woman," added Mrs Crawford.

Having left the footpad a mile or more to the rear, the coach pulled up and the coachman and Bevis came to make sure the passengers were recovered and that all was well. Bevis remarked that of all the ladies he knew, Miss Cally was the one most likely to floor a felon.

By and by, interest moved to the passing scenery. The rolling countryside, the many pit-wheels, the function of which Mr Crawford explained, and as their road passed Sheffield, their guide pointed out blast furnaces, tall structures belching out thick black smoke and flames, which must be a striking sight at night.

Early evening saw their coach pulling into the courtyard of the Roman Bath Inn at York. Here the sisters planned to take a room and stay for a few days. The Crawfords took their leave. They again thanked Cally for saving them from robbery. Their tearful daughter said a sad farewell to Polly, after they had exchanged addresses and kisses.

A bath was ordered. Unfortunately, it would not be in a Roman bath, but it would be hot. Soaking together in some luxury, with a maid topping up the water, Polly again went over the excitement of the footpad incident.

"You might have been shot. I don't know what I would have done, "pleaded Polly.

"I saw that it was a flintlock and I assumed he had primed it. Even so, it might have done him more harm than any of us. Father has shown me the types of pistol and explained the problems in handling them. Most of the deaths and injuries caused by flintock rifles and pistols are suffered by the users, not by the targets. The flintlock technology is weak."

On the following day, they took the post-chaise to Middleton, where they called on John Smith and

Samuel Bamford, their Hampden Club correspondents. Their guides took them to coalmines. They did not descend into a pit, but saw surface workers, mainly women and children, whose job was to sort the lumps of coal from broken rock and dust. The good coal was loaded into trucks which had to be pushed on to the wooden rails of a wagonway. Horses then hauled the trucks to Leeds. Coal dust, billowing everywhere, made the workers as black as chimney-sweeps. Samuel explained that families liked to be employed together, so that they could look after one another. Hence the employment of children as young as five, alongside their parents, for at least ten hours a day.

"For higher pay, some women and children worked underground, where everybody goes naked, or nearly so, because of the heat.

The obvious need was to have a shorter working week without loss of pay. A humane innovation would be bathing facilities at the pithead. At nearby Leeds they were shown the houses where the pitmen and mill workers lived.

Having seen how small, crowded and damp the houses were, Polly said it would be unspeakably cruel to keep animals in such conditions, let alone people. She had seen no London housing quite as putrid as this, apart from the worst of the St Giles rookeries.

The following day they took the post-Chaise to Manchester, where they hoped to meet John Saxton of the *Manchester Observer.* The growing cotton industry was so demanding of labour that the town's population was doubling every ten years. They had another two overnight stays in a farmhouse at Glossop.

The next visit took them back to Sheffield, where they met the Secretary of the Corresponding Society, Christopher Wyvill, a veteran of the cause. He recalled the establishment of the society in 1792, when there were massive demonstrations in the city in support of the revolutionary changes in France. The Corresponding Society quickly gained over 2,000 members, making it bigger than the London Society. Despite this evidence of the town's longstanding political awareness, it still had no MP. Perhaps it was precisely *because* of the evidence of the townspeoples' political views that Sheffield was left with no MP.

Their guides took them to out-lying villages, where spinning and weaving mills were sited near fast-flowing streams, which turned the mill wheels, which in turn worked the machinery.

Experiments were being conducted which might one day lead to water-power being replaced by coal-fired steam engines, burning coal from the nearby pits. Cotton cloth was now being made in such vast quantities that the mill owners were becoming richer by the day. Surely some of that wealth should go towards improving the lot of the cotton workers. They should not have to work for twelve hours a day, living like rats in conditions which spread disease.

Extending their adventure, the sisters decided to go back to London by sea. The journey would be quicker than by road and cheaper, because there would be no overnight stays to pay for.

They spent a last night at the York inn and on the following morning they took the post-chaise to Goole on the Humber estuary. The steam-assisted packet, *Resolute*, set sail on the tide around midday. The cabin had a couch and two armchairs, quite comfortable for Bevis and the sisters to spend the night, saving the cost of box-beds, which would almost certainly have unwashed damp sheets and bugs. They breakfasted at dawn. A crew member brought them curds and white bread, with which they drank the whey, followed by tea. Sailing conditions were perfect throughout; a steady breeze from the north, driving the ship southwards, on what the sailors considered to be a a calm sea, although the sisters felt increasingly queasy.

The steam engine was started soon after entering the Thames estuary and losing much of the wind.

They were allowed to watch the engine working, the first time they had seen this marvellous invention. They knew they were passing Greenhithe when they saw and smelled the miserable rotting prison hulks. The sound of rattling chains drew their attention to gibbets on the nearby shore. Several chained skeletons were dangling where the convicts had been hanged, probably years ago, their bones picked clean by red kites and crows.

The ship hauled up at Tower Pier about 24 hours after leaving Goole. The travellers felt proud of themselves for suffering no more than a little sea-sickness. They arrived home by gig. It was a firm decision that, should they ever again travel to the North, they would take advantage of their sea-legs. It was a happy reunion with Father, Mother and Tilly and there was much to recount at the dinner table.

Tilly now had a few more teeth and more words to gabble.

Future correspondence from the North Country, reported to the Hampden Club, would be enhanced by the extra colour the sisters can now give it, having met the correspondents and seen the places for themselves.

This little expedition, including the extra wages for Bevis, left the sisters temporarily penurious. They were lucky to be living with Father and Mother, but declined their offer of help, instead taking on the tutoring of more children of St Mary's congregants. As teachers, Miss Cally and her sister had the reputation of being knowledgeable, conscientious, patient and loved by their pupils. The size of their paying clientele was limited only by the hours in the day. But their priority remained the mothers and children in Newgate. They now headed a body, largely of women, who called themselves the Newgate Prison Visitors. They had regular meetings with the Governor, always accompanied by some of the convicts' elected monitors. Their latest petition was for the women and children to have a warm bath, with soap and towels, every week. The governor suggested this was probably more frequent washing than the Prince Regent himself. Unimpressed, Cally offered to write to the Prince offering advice on personal hygiene for himself and the reputedly noxious Caroline of Brunswick. The governor begged not to be associated with any such letter.

Although not subscribing to all of their radical views and never referring to their novel relationship, Elizabeth Fry continued to be their friend, admirer and inspiration.

Over recent years, conditions in Newgate had improved considerably, but Mrs Fry and the sisters considered there was still much to be done, because most people, like the government, continued to view the houses of correction overwhelmingly as centres for confinement, rigorous punishment and merciless retribution.

Writing in 1784, John Howard summarised the state of England's prisons as "Such as was calculated to counteract almost every purpose for which those buildings were intended.

"In consequence of the total want of attention to air, to cleanliness and whatever concerns the health of the prisoners, gaol-fever prevails to such a degree as to occasion the death of more persons than fall at the hands of the executioner.

"The morals of prisoners are as much neglected as their health", Howard wrote. "Idleness, drunkenness and all kinds of vice are suffered to continue in such manner as to confirm old offenders in their bad practices and to render it almost certain that the minds of those confined for the first time will be corrupted, instead of being corrected, being sent back into the world a worse member of the public than he was at the beginning of his confinement".

Howard and his supporters in Parliament sponsored several Acts, which set new regulations for the management of prisons.

In the interest of basic cleanliness, regulations required that cells should be whitewashed annually, that some means of sanitation should be provided, that there should be baths, soap and towels.

Gaolers were to be given an adequate wage in lieu of garnishing, bribes, keeping taps and their other corrupt practices. For those sentenced to hard labour, constructive employment and the necessary materials must be provided. When due to be discharged, prisoners should be bathed and pointed to means by which they may gain a livelihood in an honest manner.

Due to ineptitude, idleness or corruption, most of these legal requirements were ignored by successive Home Ministers and most prison governors. "Most governors deserve to be locked up in their own prisons", was Polly's verdict.

Reporting again in 1789, after further Acts were passed, during the reign of George IV, Howard wrote that," In consequence of these Acts and the exertions of many public bodies and public-spirited individuals new prisons were built in which the defects of the old ones were avoided. One positive result was that the incidence of gaol-fever was lessened."

"But at this point, the spirit of improvement seems to stop, scarcely touching upon that still more important object, the reformation of the morals of prisoners, which object remains as much neglected as their general health.

Cally's comment, at a Hampden Club meeting, was grim: "Judging by my familiarity with Newgate and the nearby compters, most of the defects in prison buildings and the management of prisoners remain with us.

"There has been no fundamental change. Much remains to be done. Gaol-fever may be less widespread, but the disease, usually called consumption, being endemic in the general population, especially among the poor, will be continually carried into the prisons in fresh infections, where the appalling conditions favour its spread. Overcrowding in our cities and the absence of sanitation and basic hygiene bring about disease. In that regard, there is little to choose between Newgate, the Seven Dials rookeries and the slums of ancient Rome of two thousand years ago, except that Rome had public baths and latrines and a cleaner water supply than much of London.

"The centre of the world's greatest ever empire, for all its grandeur and boasting, is a cesspit."

"And its politics likewise," chipped in Polly.

In sombre mood, Cally suggested to the meeting that, "At the present snail's-pace rate of social progress, we can be sure that, two centuries hence, in 2020, prisons and their problems will be just the same as now, in 1820.

"To be fair to Mr Howard, his frequent prison visits to Newgate, The Fleet, Bridewell, Tower Hamlets, Tothill Fields, King's Bench and Marshalsea – all known for their infamy – reveal what he describes as 'no alteration' – meaning no improvement since his previous visits – despite the regulations issued to the prison governors and sheriffs. The conditions of imprisoned debtors, Polly described as "Designed by the Devil during a fit of madness."

The debtor could be released only by repaying his debt, but whilst in prison, he was unable to earn money and so the sentence could last for decades. The debt inevitably grew as the prisoner was charged for food, for coal and even for the gaoler's work in turning the key to the cell door. A rich friend might clear the debt on the prisoner's behalf, or the debtor might obtain beer or gin and sell it at a profit to fellow prisoners, accruing funds by infringing the regulation against such liquors in prison.

One day, in Newgate, when Cally was in charge of a class of mothers and children, who were busy copying on to their slates, the calm was rent by frantic screaming from a nearby open cell. She rushed there and one glimpse was sufficient to grasp the meaning of the scene. She picked up a chair and brought it down on the man's head.

Was this becoming a habit? He was the second man she had battered within the year.

In response to the disturbance, guards arrived. They helped their injured colleague to his feet and grabbed the obvious guilty party, Cally, who grabbed Riva, the only real victim here.

All made for the governor's office, near the entrance, Riva sobbing and cursing her assailant in a mixture of English and Dutch expletives, with Cally making a loud song and dance about needing to meet the governor forthwith.

Riva Bakker, from a Spitalfields Dutch family, was well known to Cally, as one of the women's elected monitors. She was a cut above the usual run of prisoners, being literate, quick-witted and invariably noticeably clean, as well as having the natural gift of prettiness. She was the daughter of a de-frocked priest, who had sought his laicization on inheriting a famous coaching inn on the death of his brother. The taproom alone would bring far more income than a priest's stipend was his mercenary calculation.

And so it was. With his daughter in charge of the taproom, money came rolling in. It was by watering the beer and gin that Riva substantially raised the profitability of her enterprise. This was the worst of crimes; she was the woman who watered the workers' beer. But her tampering with the barrels was subtle enough to fool the senses of even the most epicurean of tastes. She got away with it.

Able to afford the latest fashions, perfume from Grasse and a coiffure freshened weekly, her followers were potentially numerous, but there was the one particular gentleman who offered not marriage, but something better than that, in the shrewd eyes of this bonne vivante: a small house, with stable, overlooking Regent's Park, a curricle and pair, a maid and a generous allowance. There could be no greater love. He came and went as he pleased and her only duty was to be at home of an evening, in order to please him.

Unfortunately, there came the day when her eye was caught by a man rather younger than her patron. She was entertaining her new gentleman one afternoon when her protector unexpectedly entered and found the pair in flagrante. In a fit of uncontrollable jealousy, he smashed the young man's head with a bronze statuette.

Runners took the murderer and his apparent accomplice to Bow Street and they spent time in

Newgate awaiting trial. Her patron claimed that he was protecting Riva from being raped by a vicious intruder and she claimed total innocence, as the victim of the attack. He was given ten years for murder and she ten years for complicity in the crime. Some lawyers found her conviction to be a travesty, but her funds did not run far enough to contest the verdict. Her erstwhile patron's highly placed and influential friends contrived to get him out of prison within a year. He was reluctant to risk tarnishing his reputation by assisting his ousted one-time paramour. She was uncomplaining, dismissing him as just a typical man. Standing before the Newgate governor immediately after the incident, Riva asserted that the guard had dragged her into the cell and was raping her. He had pestered her for weeks, touching her and making lewd suggestions.

The governor heedlessly dismissed her claim and when Cally asserted her right to speak as a witness to the crime, he warned her that her witness statement would be valueless without adequate proof. Rape was a capital offence and so there were stringent requirements of the evidence. There had to be proof of penetration of the alleged victim's body and proof of ejaculation by the accused.

He then sneeringly suggested that, "As an unmarried woman, you, of course, Miss Reed, would have no understanding of such processes".

Cally's anatomical and physiological knowledge had moved on apace since first discovering her passion for Polly. Recalling a remark jokingly made by Mother more than once, Cally glared at the man and shocked him to the quick. She declaimed, "Sir, you insult my intelligence. I am an unmarried woman, but not a nun and even a nun would equal you in knowledge of the mechanism of human procreation. And surely, your experience of the process is entirely one-sided.

"That guard is as guilty as hell.

"The victim stands here before you, with her prison smock ripped from collar to hem, her nakedness still humiliatingly displayed because you have yet to offer her cover".

The governor, flustered, handed Cally his own cloak from the stand behind him.

"As to penetration, why would he force Miss Bakker to lie on a table and why else would he be standing between her splayed legs, forcing them apart? The governor was muted in embarrassment by this explicit image, conjured for him by a woman, and looked away.

"As to ejaculation, have the prison surgeon or a local midwife immediately conduct an intimate examination of Miss Bakker.

"*Now*. It must be *done now*" she demanded, "Not a second's delay.

"Furthermore, I enter the contaminated remains of Miss Bakker's smock as evidence.

"The man is as guilty as hell. He should hang for this crime."

A lackey was sent for the prison doctor.

Most unusually, this alleged rape had numerous witnesses, as well as forensic evidence. Within the month, the guard was tried, found guilty of rape and given the prescribed sentence, execution.

The sentence was commuted to transportation by the Home Minister, who could not countenance a gaoler being hanged for raping a mere prisoner. In a fit of largesse, Sidmouth remitted the remainder of Riva's sentence and she was released.

For safety's sake, she did not resume tampering with the barrels. Her new notoriety kept the taproom flooded with customers and business was good enough without sharp practice.

Mrs Fry had long petitioned that the women and children should be supervised solely by women warders. Following this much publicised rape trial, at last, this was conceded.

On hearing this story, both from Cally and through the Runners' grapevine, Lavender congratulated his daughter on her grasp of forensic detection and unofficially admitted her as the second (Honorary) Detective Reed in the Bow Street Patrol.

Reminded afresh of the humiliation suffered by women prisoners in Newgate, watched at all hours by male guards, Cally went back to her reading of John Howard on prison reform and addressed the Hampton Club.

"In 1784, Howard published his first comprehensive report on his survey of conditions in the prisons, houses of correction and hospitals for the insane. His damning conclusion was that the state of the prisons was such as was calculated to counteract almost every purpose for which those buildings were intended.

"Howard was concerned that the morals of prisoners were as much neglected as their health.

"Idleness, drunkenness and all kinds of vice are suffered to continue in such a manner as to confirm old offenders in their bad practices and to render it almost certain that the minds of those confined for the first time would be corrupted instead of corrected.

"On Howard's recommendation, several Acts of Parliament have been passed for the better regulation of gaols and in consequence of the exertions of many public bodies and public-spirited individuals, new prisons were built in which some of the defects of the old ones were avoided. But at this point the spirit of improvement has stopped, scarcely touching upon that still more important object, the reformation of the morals of prisoners for their own long term benefit and to reduce recidivism.

"Gaolers have now been forbidden to keep taps, but in some prisons, the debtors sell beer in order to clear their debts and in some a neighbouring publican is allowed to supply prisoners with spiritous liquors.

"There is no employment or materials for work even for those sentenced to hard labour, who may be required to spend their days on the pointless treadmill, or may even languish in enforced total idleness.

Debtors should be kept entirely separate from felons and men from women.

"Because debtors are from the social classes – including professional and mercantile men – that can afford to accrue debt, they are generally considered to be a cut above the common felon and their more lenient prison conditions reflect this superiority.

Baths, soap and towels should be provided for weekly bathing for all prisoners.

"Gaolers must have a proper salary, so that they are not reliant on garnishes, profits from illegal taps, spurious fees charged to prisoners and theft from inmates.

"Prisoners should be required to bathe before release.

"When discharged, prisoners should be pointed to means by which they may gain a livelihood in an honest manner.

"Whilst interned, prisoners should be engaged in productive work, in order to profit the prison and themselves.

"As a civilised nation, we are called upon to ensure that an offender, while in prison, is not exposed to disorders which may destroy his health or endanger his life, or to any temptation from bad example, or bad society, which may render it probable that he will be sent back into the world a worse member of society than he was at the beginning of his confinement.

"Howard published another report in 1789, following further inspections of the prisons.

"In Newgate he found no alteration since 1784. It was still in 'very bad condition'".

"Speaking for Mrs Fry and her helpers, we are doing our best to ameliorate conditions, but we are constantly fighting a hard battle against the intransigent governor and Home Minister.

"Other London prisons were found to be equally bad, including Bridewell, King's Bench and Marshalsea.

"Overcrowding was still a major problem, worsening the spread of gaol distemper, owing to want of fresh air and cleanliness.

"Sick prisoners should be separated from healthy ones".

Acquainting the family with her thoughts on the problem of the prisons, Cally suggested that "In light of the snail's pace of prison reform, it is probable that two hundred years hence in 2020, prisons will be unchanged. The government and society will continue to view prisons as places for confinement, cruel punishment and for retribution.

"I suggest prisons will still be overcrowded and have little or no provision for re-education, reformation and rehabilitation. In other words, society will learn nothing over the coming two centuries and will remain just as cruel and stupid.

"There are no votes in prison reform, because the electors are vindictive and uncaring. Any would-be MP advocating prison reform at the poll will lose, just as any advocate of banning public whipping and public execution will be run out of town for wanting to prohibit such jolly entertainment.

"And they call this a Christian society. Blatant nonsense. Society is a mixture of heathen and hypocritical and likely to remain so."

Shaking her head in despair, Cally sat and resumed cuddling the squirming, protesting Tilly.

Polly remembered that Mr Howard had reported also on the conditions in hospitals, by which he meant the asylums for the insane.

"As we live so close to Bedlam – or to give it its proper name, the Bethlem Royal Hospital – might we need go and see it for ourselves? It is but a short ride from here, at St George's Fields, Southwark."

"You know who is its most famous inmate?" asked Father.

The sisters looked puzzled and so he told them the story. "Back in 1786, a woman made an attempt on the life of George III. As he was dismounting from his carriage at the Palace of St James', a woman stepped forward as if to hand him a petition. Instead she lunged at him with a knife. She was immediately apprehended and the King was unhurt. She had been wielding a blunt dessert knife which had not even penetrated the king's clothing.

"Of course, to make an attempt on the life of the King is high treason.

"Execution, without question. But investigation found that the woman, Margaret Nicholson, was clearly insane. She was sent to Bedlam and I imagine that is where she remains."

The sisters consulted Mrs Fry, who told them that a fellow Quaker, Edward Wakefield, had written a report on Bedlam in 1815, expressing alarm at conditions there. His report was passed to the House of Commons Committee on Madhouses. She suggested they might first approach the Chaplain, the Reverend Henry Budd, explain that they are not the usual run of gawkers, but Newgate Prison Visitors, with a genuine interest in the welfare of prison and asylum inmates. They did introduce themselves first to the Chaplain and then to

Dr Monro, the Principal Physician, who accompanied them on their tour of the hospital. They had read Edward Wakefield's report, lent to them by Mrs Fry, and so they had some idea of what to look out for. At the time of their visit, there were several obvious voyeurs, pointing and laughing at the more oddly behaved inmates. Dr Monro explained that he welcomed visitors, no matter what their interest, as they were a valuable source of income for the hospital.

Cally and Polly noted that some prisoners were naked, or virtually so, despite the cold, and many were chained. There were no obvious occupations or recreations for the inmates. Men and women were mixed and, in answer to a question, Dr Monro said that inmates with different conditions, or different degrees of insanity, were not separated.

All the warders were men.

There was no objection to being shown the most notorious inmate, Margaret Nicholson. She appeared to have a small cell of her own, where she had a bed and chair. Her ankles were manacled and chained to the floor. She could not exercise regularly or mix with other inmates because of her chains. She was calm and easy to engage in conversation and was entirely lucid and forthcoming. She voiced no complaints. It was as if she had given up on life and placidly awaited its end.

"Why are so many inmates chained to some degree?" asked Polly of Dr Munro. "To prevent them attacking the visitors," was the answer. "How many attempted attacks have there been in the past year?"

"None", was the answer, "Thanks to the restraining chains."

"Why do you not leave more docile inmates without chains, in order to see whether they remain non-violent?" asked Polly. No answer, merely a shake of the head, as if the question was nonsensical. She repeated the question and the doctor looked at her as if she were herself mad, but still no answer. She concluded that such a humane idea was too novel for him and beyond his understanding.

The sisters rode home from this visit in a state of some dismay. They had seen gratuitously inflicted suffering; human beings caged and treated like animals.

They wrote a long letter to Mrs Fry, with the request that she might pass it to her friend, Mr Wakefield, as they concurred with most of his findings and could see no improvements since he reported to the House of Commons Committee.

They decided there was nothing to be gained by mincing their words. Any reader of their letter who has some familiarity with the Hospital would know the truth of their judgements. They wrote as follows.

"Bethlem is overcrowded to such an extent that separation of men and women is not possible, so that women kept in a state of nakedness or near nakedness, with no privacy, suffer the humiliation of being supervised at all times by men, there being no female warders.

"There are simple ways by which the overcrowding could be of ameliorated. Some of the inmates should not be there at all. For others this is not a suitable place. Some are kept confined beyond the term of the court's sentence. They should be released. There must be some inmates who can now be considered cured of the condition which led to their confinement. They should be released. We asked for evidence of such releases. Our request was not met and so we suggested there were never any inmates diagnosed as cured and consequently discharged. We thought such a suggestion would be found brazen and disrespectful of the doctors, but it elicited no response. That lack of response we consider to demonstrate extreme arrogance on the part of the hospital's authorities.

"Most inmates are poorly dressed, regardless of the season and most were visibly unwashed. A few had no means of sanitation.

"There are different degrees of insanity, we were informed, and this we were able to adjudge by observing the inmates' behaviour. Similarly, there are different types of insanity, perhaps requiring different treatments, but all are permanently mixed together. Inmates who show hardly any disorder are placed in close company with others who demonstrate the most severe abnormality. This cannot be in the best interests of inmates.

"We have no medical qualification whatsoever and so our comments on inmates' treatment by the physicians may be naïve and misguided. Our concern is that inmates who behave in widely differing ways are uniformly treated by the physicians. Our lay opinion is that this cannot be for the best.

"Treatments include bleeding by leeches at the temples, presumably in order to draw blood from the brain. There may be cupping on the back, the neck, or the scalp.

An inmate may be subjected to immersion in a cold bath daily, regardless of the season. We were told this is to sedate them. It appears inhumane and drastic and likely to do more harm than good.

We saw a woman bound in a strait-waistcoat and she was kept in this condition for days at a time, whenever she behaved violently. Her violence usually took the form of anger and foul language. She had not lately attempted to attack anyone.

"For misdemeanours an inmate might be kept in isolation, or denied food. Surely, the denial of food is a cruel and unnatural punishment, which should never be inflicted on anyone in England.

"Many inmates were manacled at the wrists or the ankles, apparently regardless of their behaviour. We were told this was in order to protect the warders and physicians from attack. Unless an inmate has a record of violent behaviour, permanent chaining is surely excessive.

"We learned that the most common condition among the inmates is melancholia, closely followed by hysteria, among the women. There is also paranoia, epilepsy, dementia, delusion and mania. The sufferers of these conditions are not housed separately, although the seriously troublesome behaviour of some must surely be disturbing for other inmates.

"This institution is categorised as a hospital, where presumably some hope of cure back to health is the aim for some inmates. Therefore, would it not be better to term them 'patients', rather than 'inmates'?

"To our untrained eyes it appeared that there was a wide diversity of precise disease conditions among the inmates – and so we were informed – and yet the decisions regarding their treatment struck us as arbitrary and fairly uniform.

"The building lacked adequate warmth for the season. The building needs more windows for both light and ventilation.

"There were some present who were common felons. That they were here, rather than in a prison, was not adequately explained. Perhaps this was a mistake on the part of the court, or perhaps the definition of 'criminally insane' is too imprecise.

"The hospital needs adequate government funding, so that it does not have to depend on donations by inmates' relatives and it certainly should not be in the least dependent on entry fees paid by gawpers who visit Bethlem only in order to be entertained by provoking inmates into antic behaviour.

"Bethlem is an unhappy institution. The inmates, who tend to be there for long periods, should be able to enjoy more light, more fresh air, more comfort, more kindness, more entertainment and creative occupations. Such improvements would be more humane and surely more conducive to curing mental illnesses than the present harsh regime, which exerts repressive control, rather than aiming at cure or rehabilitation.

"Our Christian society should not be guilty of locking away and forgetting those whose illness baffles us.

When next they met, Mrs Fry thanked the sisters for their letter, every word of which she endorsed, based on her own knowledge of Bethlem. She held out little hope of a good outcome. For the sake of courtesy she had shown the letter to the Bethlem governors before taking it further. She described their reaction to the letter as 'explosive'. They dismissed its authors, whom, of course, they had never met, as 'obvious Jacobins'. The sisters listened in silence to Mrs Fry's report. When she had finished, both she and Cally were stunned when Polly burst into tears. Through her sobs and sniffing, Polly made plain that these were tears of anger, more than sadness. "I am angry that men given charge of Bethlem and its suffering inmates, educated men of some standing and, no doubt, hypocritical Christians all, could be so dismissive of the thoughts expressed in the letter. How dare they arrogate to themselves all power over vulnerable people?

"These men are evil. I cannot bear having to share the Earth with such monsters.

"Worst of all, I am powerless to do anything about them. And there are so many of them, in every walk of life."

Elizabeth and Cally tried consoling words, but Polly had clearly been struck deeply by this matter. Cally nodded reassuringly to Elizabeth, who kissed Polly's forehead and quietly left the sisters. Cally had never before seen her sister in such a wretched state of burning frustration, anger and dismay. She could do no more than hold her close.

During the recent wars, domestic food production was vital in order to mitigate the impact of the French blockade. Hundreds of Acts endorsed the enclosure of millions of acres of common land. Aristocratic owners and new farmers, exploiting the economies of scale and new scientific agricultural methods, became rich, while displaced commoners caused no end of discomfort, tearing down fences, burning haystacks, stealing animals, disabling farm carts and threshing machines. A call went out to Lord Sidmouth to send Bow Street Runners into the villages in order to help the local constables – popularly known and derided as Charlies – to track down the chief culprits and make an example of them by having them tried for capital offences.

Lavender Reed was despatched to a particularly troublesome spot, Coggeshall in Essex. He learned from Cally that this had been a Leveller stronghold in the previous century and clearly the militant legacy lingered on. He rode to Coggeshall and his first port of call was Broughton Padgett, his daughters' correspondent in the village, who called together a group of his friends. Meeting in the White Hart Inn, Lavender stood the drinks. His relaxed manner and bluff Yorkshire demeanour put the locals at ease. He told them he was no spy. Would a spy turn up in Runners uniform? He wanted no names. He simply wanted confirmation of their grievances, some of which he knew too well. It was clear that, as in so many areas, the enclosures had enriched a few and impoverished many, whose ancient rights in common had, in effect, been stolen from them and sold off to the highest bidder. The chief beneficiary was the lord of the Manor of Coggeshall, who had sold off his estate and withdrawn to London. Landless villagers survived on seasonal work for the farmers, the produce of their small gardens, poaching, with all its risks, and fluctuating parish support. Lavender arranged to meet the Rector, Rev. Edwin Mathew of the church of St Peter ad Vincula, who confirmed that the Vestry was embarrassed by the need to increase the Poor Rate each year, due to the dependence on charity of the growing number of landless villagers, who were either housed in the nearest workhouse at Witham, or received out-door relief. After consulting with Padgett and members of the local Hampden Club, who surprisingly showed no reluctance to engage in discussion with a Bow Street Runner. He went back to the Rector, who called in some leading lights of the Vestry, including two magistrates and the lord of the Manor's Steward.

Lavender started by explaining that he had been sent in order to explore ways of reducing the worrying level of violent crime in the area. He chose to call it protest crime, because people were demonstrating their extreme dissatisfaction with the distribution of land around Coggeshall consequent on the plethora of Enclosure Acts, which had taken away the peasants' strip fields, their grazing rights for sheep, cattle and pigs, and their right to cut turf and wood for their fires He pointed out that much of the common wastes remained vacant and unused and that the local oak and beech woods had mast rotting on the ground, which could feed pigs if a level of pannage were re-introduced.

He suggested that, if the bigger land-owners relinquished fractions of their holdings for annual rent to landless peasants, there would be, in effect, more small viable farms, more people with a vested interest in the security of their property, less sabotage and less call on the Parish.

There were the predictable groans and moans, but lavender's "tentative suggestions, made with all due modesty" were eventually agreed as an idea well worth trying. The Rector was to see to the drawing up of any necessary legal documents.

Lavender went back to Bow Street and gave the assurance that there would be less disturbance reported from Coggeshall.

Cally listened eagerly to her Father's story and declared that, "This is Tom Spence's ideas writ large and put into practice."

Father, dear, you deserve the highest commendation and an increase in salary."

On her daily airings, Tilly now insisted on using her own two feet, which meant progress was slow on such little legs, especially as this diminutive version of Cally, in exotic clothes which Ananya and Polly enjoyed making for her was an unusual sight, attracting the attention of passers-by, who wanted to examine and talk to this jabbering little object. Her mop of tightly curled hair was expanding and her mothers always embellished it with a silk flower or feathers, after the fashion of the day.

Around the turn of the century, when Cally and Polly were but babes, or not yet born, Southwark and Kennington Common – Much of which had lately been enclosed – had the reputation of being among the most radical parts of London. The agitation in the southern counties, between 1790 and 1803, was matched by disturbances in many centres in the North, arising from high taxes, low wages and food shortages consequent on the war with France.

The local radical tradition has left its mark. The Southwark Hampden Club, with as big a membership as any other in London, considered itself also to be a corresponding society. On behalf of the Club, Cally and Polly maintained links with clubs all over the country. When not teaching, or mothering Tilly, the sisters were dealing with correspondence, as well as being in demand to conduct readings for the illiterate or people who could not afford the radical papers and books promoting the reformist cause.

Lavender and Ananya, reformists themselves, gave the girls every possible support, but the sensitivity of Lavender's job has led to his sublimating his reformist zeal in sponsoring local charities, especially St Mary's Workhouse.

Between 1790 and 1803, in Lancashire, Yorkshire and parts of London, forced underground by the government's oppressive laws, secret organisations distributed handbills, recruited members, administered oaths of allegiance and held 'black lamp' meetings at night in secluded places, with scouts guarding the perimeter. Many such groups probably accumulated secret stashes of arms and defied the law against drilling and weapons training. Sidmouth's spies and hundreds of soldiers were kept engaged by the militancy of the reformists in the Midlands and the North, which also generated voluminous correspondence for the sisters.

By 1817-18, by which time Cally and Polly were well known activists of the Spencean trend in the reformist movement, members of the London Society of Spencean Philanthropists, the pompous title some adherents used for those who simply subscribed to the ideas of the late Tom Spence, which meant they were also disciples of Tom Paine, William Cobbett and Richard Carlile.

These people all knew one another, meeting whenever there was a large gathering of reformists.

They were far from being of one mind. After Peterloo, the most contentious subject was strategy for the way forward. Some despaired of constitutional agitation, seeing no hope but in a *coup de'état*, which would enrol the London poor, as well as organised groups, drawing in armed support from beyond the capital.

The leading exponent of this strategy – which Cally dismissed as too flimsy to warrant a minute's consideration – was Arthur Thistlewood, backed by that other veteran of Spa Fields, James Watson senior. The sisters were not comfortable in the company of Thistlewood, who always flaunted his Jacobinism. Edmund Burke's criticism of the French Revolution and the Jacobin dictatorship, was the position that coloured most people's view of 1789 and the Bastille. Burke had created a lasting image of the Terror, the guillotine and the hysterical bloodlust of Robespierre's Committee of Public Safety and credited all that to the Jacobins.

Being the leader of the conservative wing of the Whigs, it was not surprising that Burke's appraisal of the Jacobins ignored their positive achievements: the abolition of all residual feudal rights without indemnity; the improvement of small buyers' opportunities to purchase land forfeited by émigrés and dispossessed aristocrats, as well as initiating moves that led to the eventual abolition of slavery in the French colonies.

Controversies among the English Jacobins was a field of debate the sisters generally preferred to avoid. Although the French Revolution had given new impetus to the reformist movement in England, Cally would point out that, although it is insouciantly ignored by many, who ought to know better, we have the strength of our own revolutionary legacy, without the need to borrow from abroad.

The question that cropped up again and again, in various guises was whether the Hampden clubs should continue with educational gradualism, popularising reformist ideas by peaceful means, or deliberately diverge to underground revolutionary organisation. We should not consider becoming an entirely secret organisation, was Cally's view, unless compelled to do so, by even more oppressive government measures. "We win more support for our side by acting in broad daylight and demonstrating that we have as much right as the government to exist and to address the people."

Spending their afternoons and evenings meeting the demand for readings in taprooms, coffee houses and the backrooms of bookshops, Cally and Polly were probably better placed than most others to gauge the mood of radicals around the Metropolis. Between Thistlewood's overblown estimation of the militancy of the great mass of people and the reality on the ground, there was a widening gap. That he was one of several leaders making such dubious judgements was the biggest weakness of the reformist movement.

From August 1819, the policy argued by Hunt and T J Wooler in the *Black Dwarf* was for non-*violent* remonstrance at every opportunity and legal action against the perpetrators of the Manchester massacre. By October, with no successes to show, this peaceable policy was showing its ineffectiveness. There was clearly no prospect of bringing the Manchester magistrates and Yeomanry commanders to justice.

During October, with the movement was becoming increasingly restive throughout the country, the leading radicals, Watson and Carlile, put forward an alternative strategy, proposing simultaneous meetings of all reformist organisations, on a given date, as a demonstration of unity of purpose.

The date set was 1st November. Some looked on this as taking the constitutionalist position a step forward, while others, considered by Cally to be deluded by wishful thinking, hoped that simultaneous mass gatherings in all parts would lead immediately to insurrection.

Thistlewood was consumed by this ambitious idea and he travelled widely, canvassing the plan, but Hunt was unhappy about it and a public row broke out between them. The idea of simultaneous meetings did not work. The London meeting, for example, was not well attended.

By the end of December, 1819, the government's response to Peterloo demonstrated its defiance of the public mood and determination to strengthen its policy of repression, using its ample facility for concocting new draconian measures. Penned and promoted by Sidmouth and Castlereagh, the infamous Six Acts, 1819, better known as the Gagging Acts, prohibited any civilian body from conducting weapons training; prohibited any meeting of more than 50 people called to consider matters affecting the Church and State unless approved by magistrates. Writings deemed to be blasphemous and seditious libels would attract a sentence of up to 14 years' transportation. Stamp duty on periodical publications was increased to fourpence, the aim being to price radical papers out of existence.

The movement's response to this legislation was uncoordinated and weak. The dishearteningly quick dissipation of the righteous anger roused by Peterloo was more proof of the movement's confusion, organisational weakness, and lack of leadership. The government's spies had little to do; the deep divisions among the reformists was doing the spies' disruptive work for them.

In the summer of 1820, Hunt, Wooler, Carlile and scores of newspaper publishers and newsvendors were in prison. The sisters' busy correspondence with the industrial centres of the Midlands and North was now augmented by reports of militancy from rural districts, including Essex, Suffolk and Kent.

Thistlewood and Watson sought out Cally and Polly at the Southwark Hampden Club, in September and invited them to a secret planning meeting. Between themselves, the sisters ridiculed the idea of Thistlewood being capable of convening any gathering in secret. His circle leaked like a sieve.

They rode to the Black Lion in Water Lane, the appointed meeting place, which they knew to be the favoured watering-hole of Thistlewood and his cronies. They found it to be an unsavoury area. Opposite the entrance to the inn's courtyard, there was a stone wall against which several men were leaning. Kneeling or bending in front of them were women, all of whom, seen from behind, were unprepossessing, some of them pretentiously dressed in shabby cast-offs that marked them out as possible street-walkers and all of them apparently busily engaged. The sisters were unsure what was going on until Thistlewood came out of the taproom to greet them. "That's where the local whores serve their customers," he explained "It's cheaper than a room in a brothel." None the wiser, the sisters followed him into the room.

"You mentioned planning," said Polly, "Planning what?"

"We have in mind a demonstrative action in November, the biggest yet". With blank faces, the sisters exchanged glances. This sounded like another Spa Fields adventure. Could their early involvement possibly forestall another disaster?

Arthur Thistlewood could be an unwise man. But he was not ill-educated.

From a well-to-do Lincolnshire family, he had spent several years in the army and was reputed to be an excellent swordsman. His loyalty to the cause was beyond question. Impetuous and careless, he had landed himself in prison several times and had probably earned himself a permanent police shadower. His scheme may be madcap, but it must be heard.

In accordance with common practice, no proper names should have been used in such a meeting. Throughout the movement,Cally and Polly had always taken pains to ensure they were known only by their noms de guerre, Calpernia Wright and Polly Mouse.

Before continuing, Thistlewood introduced his colleagues, using their proper names: James Watson (whom they knew, of course), John Castle and George Edwards.

At this point, Cally interrupted Thistlewood, saying, "I'm sorry, I feel faint, would you please show me where the office of necessity is." She followed him, affecting to be a delicate maiden with the vapours. Once outside the room, she said," Surely you know that John Castle is an informer and so is George Edwards. I urge that nothing be voiced that should be confidential. Thistlewood angered Cally by smiling patronisingly and shaking his head in disbelief.

"I assure you I know from an impeccable source," said Cally, and you, of all people, should recall Castle, protector of a brothel madam and the chief provocateur, misleading Jem Watson, at Spa Fields. Thistlewood remained blasé and confident when they returned to the meeting, Cally, still seeming fragile, wafting her smelling salts and secretively winking at Polly, while shaking her head.

She was sorely tempted to demonstratively unmask Castle and withdraw herself and Polly from the meeting, but, by remaining, perhaps they could yet serve common sense.

James Watson gave his hyperbolic diagnosis of the state of the nation, all parts having a burning desire for insurrection. This meant that a lead from London would be compliantly followed. As the sisters feared, there was to be a repetition of Spa Fields, but as they were to find, planned to be more violent and inevitably more pathetic and potentially an even bigger set-back for the reformist cause.

The conspiratorial plan was to circumvent the restraints of the Six Acts by literally decapitating their authors and the rest of the government and establishing a Provisional Government composed of the leading radicals. Cally pointed out that many of the leading radicals were currently neutralised by being in prison. Undaunted, Thistlewood and the others were determined to proceed, on a date in November yet to be fixed. The plan was for nothing less than a revolution by coup d'etat.

"This is suicidal, was Cally's unspoken firm conviction, *"Our salvation will be the refusal of the reformist movement to fall in with this madness."*

Cally asked what part she and Polly were to take in the plan.

"In the French Revolution,"said Thistlewood,"The market women of Paris, alongside the sans-culottes, were a strong radical force, leading marches on Versailles and the Tuileries, bringing about the downfall of the king and queen. We see a similar role for women in this plan and we look to you, as the best-known women in our movement, to popularise our plan among women and win their support."

"I see," said Cally, "We are not just to be tricoteuses, witnesses sitting below madame la guillotine. "No. In short order, we are to muster hundreds of women, who will respond to news of the assassination of ministers by marching on the seats of power." In saying this she had to try hard not to sound sceptical or sarcastic, although knowing she was speaking unmitigated nonsense. She was confident that the worldly-wise women's leaders she knew so well, would see this vacuous plan for what it was worth, keeping their powder dry for another day with better prospects.

It was arranged that the sisters would meet with Thistlewood again, at the Black Lion, two days hence, by which time, the details would be finalised by the principal conspirators, who were now in permanent session.

"Father," said Cally at dinner, does the name, George Edwards mean anything to you?"

Lavender raised his eyes to the ceiling, while nodding. This was his way of expressing exasperation and voicelessly saying, "What on Earth are you up to now?"

"We Runners are rarely called together, but we did meet as a group this week. Of late we have been sent to trouble-spots outside London, as the repercussions of Peterloo and enclosures rumble on. As you know, I recently earned a commendation from you for my visit to Coggeshall. But we have now been instructed to refuse any calls to go outside of London during the month of November. We are on permanent stand-by, awaiting urgent orders from the Home Secretary.

One, George Edwards, addressed us. He is not a Runner, but I have often seen him at Bow Street. He explained that the jacks – his dismissive term for you two and your heroic, reformist trouble-makers – would be causing a major disturbance, in London, at some point during November."To answer your question directly, the name George Edwards means to me a spy and agitator highly prized by their lordships Castlereagh and Sidmouth.

"If he has crossed your paths, my darlings, do not tell me how, but beware. He is poison personified."

At the next meeting, the sisters were horrified to see Castle and George Edwards again present. The rest of the inner circle were introduced, all by their real names. Arthur Thistlewood was ignoring the most basic rules of security. He might as well have invited Sidmouth himself to attend. Why was this man being so reckless? With Castle and Edwards party to the planning, the government probably knew everything already, but why hand them the conspirators' heads on a plate?

Two master bootmakers were introduced, Charles Cooper and Richard Tidd, as well as John Thomas Brunt from London, James Ings, a butcher from Portsea, William Davidson, a cabinet maker originally from Jamaica and William Harrison, a radical Baptist preacher from Essex.

"It's no wonder that Hunt wants nothing to do with this enterprise", said Cally to her sister. "He is already awaiting trial and involvement in another Thistlewood fiasco could see him charged with high treason and at peril of his life."

In their room, with Tilly exhausted by her day's exertions and soundly asleep, they considered what to do. After a few hours with their daughter, like her, they were near exhaustion. Her energy appeared boundless, especially now that her walking was replaced by running and skipping. Her falls were frequent. However, with legs so little, her bottom was close to the ground and so there was not far to fall. No matter what happened, the child rarely caterwauled or shed tears. The bumps were taken in her stride.

"These men are all so stupid," said an exasperated Polly, returning to their main concern. Men are either evil or stupid and many of them are both; both wicked and brainless and yet they rule the world. Will we women never supplant such fools?"

"What can we possibly do? "Polly's shoulders drooped in despair.

"If ever we do have real power", said Cally, "Be sure to find that women can be just as evil and stupid as men, as witness Marie Antoinette.

"And Euripides's Medea murdered her innocent children simply in order to take revenge on their father, her husband, for his betrayal. Arguably, her stupendous pride and stupidity were exceeded only by her murderous evil.

"It is power that corrupts. Women have a cleaner historical record, because between them they have held less power than men."

"Being the ones who bring life into the world," Polly smiled and pointed at Tilly, "Women naturally have more respect for life and will be more humane and less violent."

Polly, more than Cally, found it easy to imagine that she had given birth to their daughter; the sense of attachment could be no greater.

"Let's not forget," said Cally, "That the community of women includes multitudes of outcasts in our hypocritical society: whores, dikes – women like you and me – outcasts considered to have fallen from the grace of god, by losing, or squandering, their sexual innocence."

"Oddly, I have never heard of a similarly fallen man, although there are the mollies, of course, as well as the clients of whores and the men who live off women's immoral earnings."

Rather than attend another meeting at the Black Lion, which by now must be a hopelessly compromised venue, probably under constant police observation, the sisters asked to receive their final briefing at the Elephant and Castle Inn.

There they met Arthur Thistlewood and George Harrison. They learned that the appointed day is moved from November to February, Wednesday 23rd. The place is 39 Grosvenor Square, the London residence of Lord Harrowby, the Foreign Secretary, who is to host a dinner for the Cabinet on that evening.

The conspirators' headquarters, where they will assemble before 7 pm and from where the operation will be coordinated, is in Cato Street, a fifteen-minute brisk walk from Grosvenor Square. A stable, with a hayloft above, has been rented by Harrison, who has told the neighbours that he is doing up the first floor and so they will see workmen coming and going.

An alternative gathering point for the conspirators is the Horse and Groom in Tottenham Court Road, less than five minutes away from the stable.

Thistlewood will station himself in Grosvenor Square, checking the arrivals at number 39. The whole Cabinet is expected to be assembled by seven o'clock and by that time all conspirators are to be in the Square or about other planned assignments.

"George Edwards gave us the date and place of the Cabinet dinner, which was confirmed by a notice in The Times." As Thistlewood divulged this, the sisters exchanged a glance, but made no comment. It was clear that, despite Cally's warning, Edwards was still trusted and was at the heart of the conspiracy. It was a doomed endeavour and their only hope was damage limitation, which must include self-protection. There would be nothing gained if they were arrested.

Hunt once described Thistlewood, after one of his several arrests, as 'a dupe of spies'. That judgement is about to be confirmed again, perhaps for the last time.

Once at home, "Now, to the task in hand," said Cally, letting out a despairing sigh. "She took up the notes she had been making, during their briefings." If this hare-brained scheme materialises at all, it is from women's groups around London that we might muster support. Here I have a list of them.

"I have written letters to several more distant groups, who need to know what is planned and may or may not materialise – a general mobilisation in early November – even if it is impractical for them to travel to London in short order – a difficulty that would never cross Arthur's mind. There is Mary Fildes at Heaton Norris, Alice Kitchen of the Blackburn Female Reformers, Mrs Hallsworth of the Stockport Female Reform Society and I have informed the Manchester Female Reform Society and those correspondents will pass on the message to all their out-lying village groups."

"And what precisely shall the Reed sisters be doing on the day?" Polly asked this question and herself answered it. Mother, bless her, will be looking after Tilly for the day.

"Although not liking this action, we shall remain loyal to the cause. We shall take up the position we suggested and the others agreed and do as much as we can to protect the conspirators from the enemy and from their own inanity."

"We'll do our utmost to avoid arrest," asserted Polly." The movement's objectives would be advanced not one jot by our being gaoled – and Tilly might notice our absence and take umbrage, as only she knows how.

"She would make a fearful and imperious ruler," suggested Cally, "If she ever came to power."

"No", Polly vehemently shook her head. "Her mothers will mould her as a beneficent democrat. As a ruler, she would be revolutionary and benign, bringing in an exciting and humane new order. Unthinkable ideals would become real."

"Back to the problem," demanded Cally. "Could a leaking boat make it to shore?

"Could a conspiracy as compromised as this make it further than Newgate Prison?

"Newgate for us would be easier than for those men," suggested Cally. "The women there are our friends. They would welcome us and fend for us." That was a slightly reassuring thought. "But still we must avoid arrest at all costs. We must not put our fathers' jobs at risk. We cannot count on the Bow Street magistrates being forever unable to link us with two of their officers".

"Their bevy of spies has, so far, failed to detect our true identities and in this regard, the Bow Street Bench is no better informed than the Hampton clubs, two of whose leading activists each happen to have a father in the police.

On the crucial day, the sisters were in the vicinity of Cato street, strolling John Street and Edgware Road, as if engaged in leisurely shopping, but watchful for the arrival of conspirators and men who might be police spies. They recognised some members of the gang going into the stable and some into the Horse and Groom. They noticed no arrivals of men who looked like policemen. By now, they had positioned themselves just yards from the stable. It was well into dusk when they saw a group of three or four Runners enter the end of the street. This spelled disaster. Polly rushed to the stable and started hammering on the door. Cally had brought a couple of handy stones. Her practice at throwing games came in handy. With her first shot, she smashed the upstairs window. Surely they had caused enough disturbance to warn the conspirators and give them opportunity to escape. Their alarum brought no immediate response from the men inside the premises. "Are they asleep or just dim-witted," cried Polly.

Meanwhile, at Grosvenor Square, Thistlewood had two pistols in his pockets and a letter for the Prime Minister, ostensibly from Carlton House, which would be his excuse for calling at number 39. He also carried a sword, with which he would run through the ministers, one by one, as they sat at table. His two professional butcher colleagues would then decapitate as many as possible, starting with Sidmouth and Castlereagh, whose heads they will carry away in sacks, for eventual triumphant display on the streets, rousing the labouring poor to a pitch of revolutionary anger. If, on Thistlewood's entry at number 39, the servants cannot immediately be enlisted to the cause, in order to forestall any opposition from them, they will be neutralised by grenades being thrown to detonate below stairs. Drastic action, but necessary.

It was a frosty evening, the winter dark being broken by one or two street gas lamps. Arthur observed the steady arrival of his colleagues to hiding places around the Square, although some were cutting it rather fine. Eventually came the local constable's call, "Seven o'clock on a cold and frosty evening. All's well." Little did he know.

It was clear that several of the ministers were going to be late. That was just as well because most of the conspirators had not yet arrived. Thistlewood started on the brisk walk to Cato Street where his colleagues must be assembled and dithering, rather than making for the Square. In his hurry and frustrated by the delay, he was unaware that he was followed. The invasion of Harrowby's house should have been well underway by now. Of course, like the rest of the conspirators, he had yet to discover that the dinner was no more than the bait in an elaborate trap. By seven o'clock, commanded by George Ruthven, there were eleven Bow Street Runners out of sight around the Square, outnumbering the conspirators.

The sisters had been strolling the area since mid-afternoon – Cato Street, John Street, Edgware Road and around again. They spotted no obvious police. They knew that most of the weaponry was stored in the stable and would have to be collected. There were more weapons and powder at Richard Tidd's house and at John Brunt's house. There was no shortage of armaments, all provided by John Castle, *"Just as at Spa Fields",* thought Cally, *"For a humble maker of dolls' houses, he has plenty of money, tainted money from Sidmouth. He is always well dressed and able to curry favour by standing drinks aplenty."*

Soon after dusk, some twenty recognised conspirators had entered the stable and several had left, presumably covertly armed and making for Grosvenor Square.

"This is all painfully slow," said Cally. If seven o'clock is the critical time, everybody should be in place by now, so that the deadly strike is swift, followed by the assassins' escape. Could gang members still be inside the stable? Sitting ducks? That way madness lies."

The original Thistlewood plan, as explained at the Water Lane meeting, was to have several assassination units designated to murder each of the king's ministers at their town houses. This would be done while the police and army were fully engaged elsewhere, drawn by various distractive tactics.

Fortuitously, the old mad, blind despised and fading king, George III, died on 29th January, 1820 and his funeral was to take place on 15th February at Windsor Castle. That would be the day of action. Every London soldier and many police officers would be at Windsor and would not hear of the assassinations until they had already been carried out.

Then it was heard from George Edwards that, with the king now dead and Prinny not inclined to sacrifice his busy social round by declaring a respectable period of mourning, cabinet dinner dates were to resume and the first such engagement was to be on Wednesday 23rd February, at the London mansion of Lord Harrowby, Foreign Affairs minister. This was confirmed by a notice in The Times. Excellent. All the prey were now to be gathered in one place, making the conspirators' task so much easier.

Conspirator John Palin had a diversionary task, disabling the platoon of Lifeguards in charge of the capital. He would go to Knightsbridge barracks and set light to the straw in the cavalry stables, below the men's living quarters. The soldiers would then be too busily engaged in saving themselves and their horses to concern themselves with news of insurrection.

It was known that there were fieldpieces in various locations around London, including the Tower and Holborn. Conspirator Cook's team was deputed to secure these cannons before they could be deployed against any conspirators. They were to be commandeered and directed against the Royal Exchange and the Mansion House, the lord Mayor's house being designated the centre of the revolutionary government.

Thistlewood had drafted a manifesto, addressing the nation, dated 23rd February, beginning, "Your tyrants are now destroyed. The friends of liberty are called upon to come forward. The Provisional Government has now taken power and there is to be a reformed Constitution".

In accordance with the revised plan, having collected arms from Cato Street, apart from the men assigned strategic tasks, the main body of conspirators were to go to Grosvenor Square, arriving soon after eight o'clock, making themselves as inconspicuous as possible in the shadow of trees, passages and porticos. Some of the gang were waiting in the horse and Groom, detained by theirdrinks. Others were simply bad time-keepers and yet others were not sure where to find Cato street. A few hopeless cases had simply forgotten the details of the plan. The inconsistency and lack of zeal among even committed reformists was a reality which Thistlewood found incomprehensible and for which he made no allowance.

Arthur had been in the Square for much of the day, observing the to-ing and fro-ing of servants and tradesmen, all of it consistent with preparations for a banquet. Observing Arthur's every move was a Runner, George Ruthven, out of sight in an upper room of number 39.

When the local Charlie called "Seven o'clock and all's well", Thistlewood took it as his cue to make for Cato Street, closely observed, as he had been all day.

Officer George Ruthven, who was in charge of the operation on behalf of Bow Street magistrates, assumed Thistlewood would gather his fellow conspirators and return with them to the Square, arriving at some time after eight o'clock.

Cally and Polly were out of sight in the doorway of number 22 Cato Street. They could just make out William Davidson, standing as if on sentry duty, at the door of the stable. He was far from inconspicuous, being black and armed to the teeth, with two pistols and a sword hanging from his belt and with a carbine at his shoulder.

Davidson was from Jamaica, having an African slave mother and an English father. He was well educated, but currently working as a rather lowly apprentice to a cabinet-maker. As a would-be assassin, he was no secretive conspirator. At his trial, he claimed merely to be an innocent by-stander at Cato Street, although he had no explanation for being heavily armed.

From her vantage point, Cally spotted the red waistcoat of a uniformed Runner, in the light of a gas lamp at the end of the street. The sisters immediately tried to raise the alarm by pounding on the stable door and throwing stones and smashing the ground floor and hayloft windows. The sisters' alarum brought about both the opening of the door and the police dashing down the street, followed by guardsmen, just arrived, better late than never. There was a crush at the door, with conspirators desperate to escape and Runners and soldiers determined to enter.

There was a narrow stairway, hardly more than a ladder, leading to a trapdoor, the sole entry to the dimly-lit upper floor. It appeared that no conspirator had the wit to control this obvious bottleneck. Runners were struggling to go up the stairs, while conspirators were determined to get down. There was close hand-to-hand fighting, but little use of weapons because there was simply not room enough to wield a sword or aim a pistol. Some conspirators jumped over the banister, in order to escape.

The first Runner to succeed in struggling up to the hayloft was Richard Smithers, who was confronted, in the half-light, by Thistlewood, with a cavalry sword drawn and at the ready. Arthur, the old soldier, instinctively lunged at the policeman, doing so with such momentum that he drove his sword right through the Runner's chest and fell on top of him. Smither's death was probably instant, as the post-mortem found that his heart was pierced.

It was later reported that one of the conspirators knelt beside Smithers, trying to staunch the bleeding, but such was the seriousness of the wound that this was clearly an effort in vain, for the man was smothered in the gushing blood

Still positioned at the outside door, Davidson suddenly woke to the need to obstruct the police and soldiers, so that his fellow-conspirators could escape.

He started firing his carbine. In the darkness and the confusion, his shots were indiscriminate. Hearing the shooting, Cally and Polly pressed into the cover of the doorway.

Above the noise of the turmoil, Cally heard a screech. She stretched out her arm to clutch her sister, but Polly was not there. In the dim light from candle-lit windows and the distant street lamp, She saw a bundle on the ground, in Polly's riding habit.

Kneeling by her sister, she heard Polly say, "I've been shot – in the back, I think."

There were now several runners and soldiers inside the building, grabbing and handcuffing conspirators while others were on the streets, giving chase to the ones who had managed to escape the building. By now, the commotion had attracted on-lookers from the nearby houses and beyond.

As if from nowhere, Lavender appeared, being one of the Runners' patrol. He swept up Polly in his arms and ran with the tiny woman to the Horse and Groom, with Cally weeping and running behind. He laid Polly, face down, over the saddle of his police horse, mounted and cantered off. He shouted at Cally, "Guy's Hospital".

Cally rode Alexia to the hospital, where she was led to the latest injured arrival.

Polly was lying face-down on a table, with her skirts pulled up to her chest and lots of blood. In her state of panic and grief, that was all Cally could take in. Father put an arm round her shoulders and explained that the surgeon was Mr Astley Cooper, "No better doctor in the capital. Polly will be safe."

Cally bent over her sister, stroking her hair and repeatedly whispering "Polly, dear, Polly dear."

Polly was weeping with the pain, but managed to whisper, "I've got a bullet in my bum."

Now they both giggled, as Mr Cooper, a tall, stern-faced man, curtly ordered a nurse, "Clothes."

The nurse, all in black and wearing a starched white cap, pulled off the holed and bloodied clothes. Cally took the bundle and committed herself to a day at the washtub.

Minus her short drawers and skirts, Polly was naked from the waist down, with no regard for her modesty.

"Forceps", another imperious order to the nurse. Mr Cooper was holding a vicious-looking instrument. He poured liquid on to a cloth from a bottle labelled Spirit and wetted the prongs. He held the forceps to a flame and allowed the spirit to burn away.

A young man, presumably a pupil doctor, put a pad over Polly's nose and mouth, held in place with a bandage wrapped round her head. Cally picked up the overpowering smell of the sweet vitriol from the pad, which would make Polly unconscious of some pain. The surgeon tied a scarf over his nose and mouth, presumably to reduce the vapour he would otherwise breathe in. Having a semi-conscious surgeon would be undesirable.

Cally could not help imagining the pain and wincing as Mr Cooper probed Polly's wound with the forceps. The poor girl started moaning and squirming and the nurse reacted by gripping her hips and holding her still, while the pupil doctor put a leather strap round Polly's legs and the table top and tightened it.

It seemed ages, but it was only a few minutes before the surgeon removed the prongs from the wound, gripping the iron ball, which clattered into a china dish.

The wound was cleaned with generous wipes of the spirit and Polly jerked with the pain. The pupil doctor now held a curved needle, with black thread. He made several punctures in order to pull together the sides of the entry wound. Despite more sweet vitriol being applied to the pad over her nose and mouth, Polly felt enough of this to make her grimace and sob. Cally was gripping her sister's hand and doing her best to keep control of her own reactions. Excessive weeping in sympathy would have been no help to Polly.

While the nurse wrapped a bandage around Polly's bottom and belly, Mr Cooper explained to Father and Cally that it was a flesh wound at the top of the buttock, not penetrating to the bone.

Polly stayed in the hospital for two nights, while she was observed in case the wound was infected. Cally was allowed to stay with her as nurse and companion. She assured her sister that she still had a very pretty bum, which would be loved all the more. "No bullet could spoil its beauty".

"The scar will be a battle honour. It's such a pity that so few people will see it."

When discharged by Mr Cooper, Polly was taken home, lying on her side along the seat of a hired coach, watched over by Cally and Ananya.

On that Wednesday evening of the Cato street debacle, after ten to fifteen minutes of confused struggle and chasing, the Runners and soldiers between them had seven men in custody and others still on the run, including Thistlewood.

Near the end of Kennington Butts stood a noticeboard on which parish notices and news broadsheets were posted. Pausing Tilly's walk, on Thursday morning, 24th February, Cally read the latest news in tightly packed text in its customary pompous style.

"In consequence of private information received by the Civil Power that it was in contemplation to make an attempt upon the lives of his Majesty's Ministers, whilst assembled at the house of Earl Bathurst in Mansfield Street to a Cabinet dinner yesterday evening,

"Magistrate Richard Birnie, with a party of twelve of the Bow Street Patrol, proceeded at about eight o'clock to the place which had been described as the rendezvous of the desperadoes in Cato Street, where, in a kind of loft, over a range of coach-houses, they were found in close and earnest deliberation.

"Officer Smithers was cruelly murthered by the conspirators' leader, one, Arthur Thislewood, who has escaped and is on the loose.

"Seven conspirators have been arrested and taken into custody at Coldbath Fields prison.

"During the disturbance, one of the gang was firing a carbine and an unfortunate passer-by, a lady, sustained a gun-shot wound and was taken to Guy's Hospital, where an emergency operation was conducted by Mr Astley Cooper, the Principal Surgeon. The victim is reported to be recovering".

The errors and hyperbole came as no surprise. The public valued these sheets for their melodramatic entertainment, rather than their accuracy.

On her way home, Cally saw another notice, the latest edition of the London Gazette Extraordinary, the Government's publication. Over the signature of Lord Sidmouth, it offered a reward of £1,000 to any person or persons enabling the apprehension of Arthur Thislewood and warned that any person receiving or harbouring him will be guilty of High Treason.

The only reasonably accurate text Cally read that day was the Gazette's description of the wanted man. He was caught within a couple of days, found asleep in a lodging house not far from Cato Street.

"High Treason?" Cally vented her fury on Father "Sidmouth is intent on making heavy weather of this incident. And the stakes could go even higher. I suppose it's not surprising. After all, he has probably invested a lot of money in this latest exercise in government chicanery."

"Father, as an arm of the law, please would you explain to me how Bow Street is able to justify the capital charge of high treason against the conspirators."

Delivered In that tone of voice, Lavender was aware that Cally would brook no evasion.

"After all," she continued, "Fatty Prinny, neither as Regent, nor as king, was even in the sights of the conspirators. I imagine they considered him to be largely irrelevant. He signs the statutes which we reformists find so objectionable, but has not the brains to frame them; he has his ministerial minions doing that."

"I know the law said, even when he was only the Regent, that harming him would count as high treason, as if he were monarch, but this conspiracy intended him no harm."

Lavender settled himself to deliver a comprehensive explanation. "The legal position is even worse than it appears at first sight. Firstly, there is the law of joint culpability. It looks certain that This man, who is variously named Thistlewood, Thistledown and Thistledon, will be found guilty of killing officer Smithers, the poor man.

"He just happened to be the first one of us to reach the hay-loft; It could have been any one of us. The law says that all of Thistlewood's confederates are equally guilty of murder, because they were with him at the scene of the crime."

"That is monstrously unjust, burst in Cally."Why, I've read a report that one of the conspirators knelt beside Smithers, trying to staunch the bleeding and was found soaked in the dead man's blood. That he should be hanged for the murder would be a crime against natural justice."

Lavender nodded his agreement and continued. "There are several counts on which the conspirators will probably be charged. The laws on high treason amount to a catch-all.

"I am thankful that you and Polly, despite your sympathies, had no part in this conspiracy and were merely by-standers, although I have yet to hear what bad coincidence took you near Cato Street that evening. Close enough for Polly to be nearly killed."

Cally thought it best to leave that truth for another day and urged Father to tell more about the treason law.

"It is high treason to commit adultery with the sovereign's consort, or eldest unmarried daughter, or the wife to the heir to the throne. I doubt that any such accusations will be laid against the conspirators, but it is arguable that they were conspiring to levy war against the sovereign, conspiring to murder divers of the Privy Council and preparing an address inciting the king's subjects to assist in levying war and subverting the Constitution. As evidence of that crime, the prosecution will adduce their large stash of weapons, their manifesto declaration of a new government and Constitution and their call to arms throughout the land.

"Unless the defence lawyers are clever enough to outwit the prosecution, there is enough to send all of them to the gallows." Lavender was shaking his head as if having not much hope.

"We know that George Edwards was up to his neck in all of this. If his trickery can be brought before the jury, It can only benefit the conspirators."

"Of course. Having Edwards questioned before a jury is the last thing the government wants. If necessary, the Home Minister will have his chief spy spirited away."

The guardsmen collected the remaining weapons from the hayloft – pistols, blunderbusses, swords, pikes and hand-grenades a veritable arsenal, all paid for by Edwards – and took them to their barracks for safekeeping. One newspaper report, stretching the truth, said the quantity of arms was "Sufficient to raze a city".

Smithers' body was laid out in the backroom of the Horse and Groom, where the post mortem was conducted by the police surgeon and where the body could be viewed by family and friends. The prisoners were first taken to Bow Street and then, having been transferred to Coldbath Fields Prison, they were examined by the entire Privy Council, precisely the men they were alleged to have planned to slaughter. Accused of high treason, the worst of crimes, the prisoners were now taken, in locked coaches, to the Tower. Thistlewood was in splendid isolation in the Bloody Tower and each of the others had a separate cell.

Lavender Reed told his daughter that, when he arrived at Cato Street, with the rest of his patrol,Officer

Ruthven had in his pocket a warrant issued by the Bow Street magistrates, naming precisely those men subsequently arrested or sought. "How were their names known even before their crimes had been committed?" asked Cally, and then immediately asserted the answer, "George Edwards, of course."

Polly had to return to the hospital for removal of the stitches and to have the wound checked for infection. This was carried out by a pupil-doctor, observed by several of his colleagues, gazing down from the raked seating of the the operating theatre. Cally subsequently mused to her sister that Polly's bare pretty bum could have been the year's most entertaining spectacle in London. This time Polly was covered by a sheet, which a nurse folded to reveal only the part of her body of immediate medical interest. The doctor described the nature of the wound, demonstrated the right-angle forceps, cut the cotton stitches and gently withdrew the threads. Polly had declined the sweet vitriol, as its earlier use had left her with a splitting headache.

A limp was the only legacy of the wounding. Each day since the removal of the bullet, with Polly gritting her teeth and her hand held by Mother, without fully knowing the wisdom of her action, Cally had bathed the area around the wound with brandy and had bound it with a fresh bandage. A poultice was the common cure-all, but Mr Cooper had used spirit and the wound had remained uninfected, so that appeared a good treatment to continue.

The trial of the Cato street conspirators was sufficiently newsworthy to displace the shenanigans of

Prinny and Caroline. On the death of George III, the periodically mad monarch, his profligate debauched son moved up from Regent to George IV, whose equally dissipated, estranged wife Caroline of Brunswick, thus became queen, in name, although never crowned.

Prinny's unpopularity and the scorching obloquy, in which he was held in the eyes of the people, he took with him to the throne. The reputation of his equally debauched wife benefited from the peoples' aversion to George. It was as if one's contempt for the new king could not be adequately expressed unless accompanied by support for his estranged queen.

The outcome of the trial was the death penalty for Thistlewood, John Thomas Brunt, John Ings, William Davidson and Richard Tidd. Five others were transported to Botany Bay and never known to return.

Some conspirators had turned king's evidence, making accusations against their co-conspirators in exchange for a more lenient sentence.

The standard sentence for high treason would have the pinioned prisoners dragged on a hurdle to the gallows, open to the abuse and missiles of the mob. After being hanged, but not necessarily dead, the prisoners would be eviscerated, then decapitated and quartered.

For some reason, it was at the point of pronouncement of the Cato Street sentences, that the Privy Council leapt from the seventeenth to the nineteenth century.

The traditional, ignominious hurdle was replaced by a wheeled cart, which took the condemned men from the Tower to Newgate, where a high platform had been constructed for this major public entertainment. The Court, in an apparent fit of mercy, also abandoned the sadistic butchery of evisceration and quartering. Consequently, the mob was to be denied the most sanguinary part of the spectacle.

The hanged men were left dangling for a half-hour, partly to confirm death and partly to enhance the ritual of execution. Some needed the hangman's assistants to heave on their legs in order to ensure the neck was broken.

The bodies were cut down and laid in coffins. This was an odd procedure, because it meant that the axeman could not remove the heads in the normal way. Instead, he had to kneel beside each coffin and cut through the neck using a knife. Thistlewood was the first to have his severed head held high, with the pronouncement, "This is the head of the Traitor, Arthur Thistlewood. The response of the crowd was subdued. The same procedure followed with each of the dripping heads.

Another innovation was that the heads were not then displayed on pikes at London Bridge or Tyburn. Instead they were immediately reunited with their respective bodies in the coffins.

Topped up with quicklime, the coffins were sealed and unceremoniously buried in an old drain in Newgate courtyard. Apart from the grisly butchery of the beheading, the Privy Council had ordered what was perhaps the least spectacularly barbaric public execution ever seen in England up to that time and then ensured that the site of the conspirators' burial was obscure and inaccessible. Their lordships of the Privy Council were striving to ensure that Cato Street produced no martyrs and no monument to the cause of constitutional reform.

The name, George Edwards, came up many times during the Cato Street trial, but there was no attempt to subpoena him.

When allowed to address the jury, John Ings claimed he had been duped into joining the conspiracy by Edwards and that lord Sidmouth had known about the plot for months, by virtue of his spy's penetration of Thistlewood's planning meetings.

Similarly, Brunt drew the attention of the jury to the mysteriously absent Edwards, saying he had been seduced by that villain, who is no doubt employed by the government.

At a meeting of the Hampden Club, in late November of 1820, in the Elephant and Castle Inn taproom, Cally was invited to give her analysis of the Cato Street conspiracy. It was known by some members that Polly was the unnamed woman reported as being a by-stander somehow shot during the incident, but apart from that, nothing was known of the sisters' involvement, although some present suspected they were not far from the centre of things.

This was the first meeting attended by Tilly, alongside her mothers. She was positively bubbling with excitement at being among so many new people, but bidden to be quiet and not fidget, she was as good as gold, sitting with a hand held by each mother, when they were not addressing the meeting.

The proceedings started with the chairman calling for three minutes of silence in commemoration of the Cato Street brothers who gave their lives for the cause.

"There is no consolation for us," Cally began, "We have suffered another major defeat. It is hard to see beyond blood, hunger and persecution to a brighter destiny.

Cato Street must be added to Spa Fields and Pentrich as defeats partially self-inflicted."

At this, there were groans around the room and a loud shout of"No! Shame on you."

Cally ignored the predictable interruption and continued. "I have it from an impeccable source that, when the Bow Street Runners arrived at Cato street, they had an arrest warrant, signed by the Chief Magistrate, listing the names of precisely those conspirators subsequently arrested and charged and brought before the Privy Council and sent to trial. Now, was this a case of magical clairvoyance, or simply the magistracy up to their usual tricks: mundane skulduggery? How could they possibly have a list of felons before the felony has been committed?

"The explanation is simple. The complex tale can be boiled down to the centrality of one character: George Edwards and his various aliases, venomous spy and *agent provocateur*.

"Several weeks ago, with my sister, I was invited by Arthur Thistlewood to a Spencean Friends of Philanthropy meeting at which his plan for a major demonstrative action would be revealed.

"Little of his plan was forthcoming at that meeting, but Arthur introduced his second-in-command, one

George Edwards. I found an excuse to interrupt the meeting, drew Arthur to one side and warned him that he was nestling a viper, that having Edwards present was no worse than inviting Lord Sidmouth to meetings. Arthur would have none of it and he has paid the most terrible price for his recklessness.

"During the trial of the conspirators, the name, George Edwards came up several times, but there was no attempt to subpoena him, neither by the prosecution, nor the defence, nor the Bench.

"When allowed to address the jury directly, James Ings claimed he had been duped by Edwards and that Sidmouth knew all about the conspiracy weeks before Cato Street, by virtue of Edwards, but the plot was allowed to run its course, in order to trap the conspirators. The Cabinet dinner, due to be at Lord Harrowby's house, was moved to Grosvenor Square at the behest of Edwards.

That dinner was merely the bait to catch Sidmouth's unknowing prey.

"When John Brunt had opportunity to address the jury, he referred to "The mysteriously absent Edwards", claiming to have been seduced by the villain, "Who was no doubt employed by the government".

"Shortly after the trial, Mr Alderman Wood MP was given permission to address the House of Commons. He made the following report, based on the account of an informant. Cally started reading a script she had copied from THE TIMES.

"'A resident of Fleet Street or King Street, whose name was said to be George Edwards, at times in the year 1819, was seen going from one public house to another, inviting persons to join with him in the execution of divers plots against the government, which he intended to bring forward. The plot was to bring into the House of Commons six or eight men with hollowed-out books under their arms containing gun-barrels cut down to the length of four inches which were filled with gunpowder, plugged at both ends and these implements being thrown down in the middle of the House upon some occasion of full attendance, would explode with great violence and cause much destruction.

"This Edwards, on one occasion, is reported to have said, 'Thistlewood is the boy for us; he's the one to do our work. He will very soon be out of Horsham Gaol'.

"My informant was introduced to Edwards at the house of Preston, the cobbler (one of the apprehended conspirators)who confirmed that Edwards did get those very books made for the purpose, that he procured the gun-barrels and had them cut up.

"At that time, too, according to my informant, Edwards was supplied with money all of a sudden, although just before, he had not enough to buy a pot of beer. All at once, however, he got supplied with cash and was enabled to buy aquaintanceship and purchase several weapons.

"He thought it clear that Edwards had become connected with the Cato Street conspirators at a very early period of their meeting together".

Mr Wood considered that Edwards should be called to attend at the bar of the House, although he may by now be abroad.

Mr Brougham MP addressed the house. He believed that Edwards, being employed by the government as a spy, like other persons employed in that capacity was not satisfied with merely giving information, and that he employeewoodself in inciting persons already guilty into the commission of further crimes.

Mr Brougham by no means blamed the government for employing Edwards as a spy, or for acting on his information, or for withholding him as a witness, or for abstaining from prosecuting him. He was of the view that, as long as men like Thistlewood and the others existed, the government was justified in employing persons to watch their proceedings.

"'The existence of such wretches as Thistlewood and Ings rendered the employment of spies necessary', he claimed.

"However", continued Brougham, "It does appear from the evidence that he employed himself not only as an investigator, but also as an instigator, inciting others to the perpetration of a grave offence. Justice would not be satisfied", Mr Brougham averred, "Unless Edwards was brought to trial. He was at the heart of the conspiracy to assassinate several members of the government. The plot was foiled by Edward's information and the ineptitude of the Cato Street gang"

"We know, that the government will not allow the examination of its own creature", continued Cally,

"In summary, my analysis is that the real Cato Street conspirators, those responsible for the plan to murder the members of the Cabinet, were the very ministers, who authorised and financed Edwards' espionage and provocation and connived in the Cabinet dinner deception.

"Our reformist organisations are riddled from top to bottom with spies and provocators. That fact has been demonstrated again and again, at a cost in blood and tears, but we appear to be incapable of learning the lesson".

Cally sat down and took a draught from her ale.

Polly stood, with the support of a walking stick, and was recognised by the chairman, who gave her the floor.

"I could despair," she said. "The Cato Street trial has passed without a murmur from the people.

On the other hand, from Carlton House there comes news of a right royal rumpus between the new depraved king and his dissolute queen. The talk is that he wants to divorce her. That will present a problem, even for the monarch. There may have to be an Act of Parliament giving effect to this sundering of the mightily meaty."

"God save the lean," shouted a wag, bringing uproarious laughter and table-hammering.

The chairman demanded order and Polly continued.

"Oh, the broadsheet publishers will have a lot of fun and will make lots of money. The London mob has all too soon forgotten Cato Street and will now be consumed by this salacious story. It has hardly begun and yet, already the petty-minded mob has demonstrated in support of Caroline of Brunswick, famed for sharing her bath with her butler. They say that, as she lowers herself in the tub, the water rises so much that the poor man has to swim or be drowned.

"Caroline's chief ally is Sir Matthew Wood, who has even offered her a home in London. Yet here is another MP who has criticised the government over Cato Street. He has said that the purposeful entrapment of the conspirators was in order to smear the legitimate campaign for parliamentary reform.

"Thankfully, London is not the centre of the universe.

"We know from our correspondents in the North that, while we were waiting for the Cato Street trial, big trouble was brewing in the weaving heartlands of Yorkshire and Lancashire and further north in Scotland.

"We have heard from Barnsley that, on the night of 11th April, an armed force, three hundred strong, marched north to rendezvous with a Scottish force that failed to materialise. Again, spies were the victors, their prize being the transportation of reformists and disillusionment and dissolution of reformist organisations. A battle between weavers and hussars at Bonnymuir, near Glasgow, resulted in three of our local leaders being taken and hanged by an English Court. Let us hope that one day Scotland will be free of the English yoke.

"My sister, Cally, has repeatedly argued that our righteous anger, caused by the hunger and oppression of the people has often been ill-directed and aimless. Some of our most vociferous leaders have wrongly judged the mood of the people. Their calls to action have been premature and reckless, leading inevitably to failure. Having control of the army, militias, police, judiciary and a network of spies, the government's overwhelming strength is bound to defeat our puny forces. But understanding that does not render us permanently neutralised.

"History has not stood still. Weavers, spinners, pitmen, dockers and seamen are increasingly aware of the means and extent of their exploitation by their employers. They, in their trade unions, will be the most politically aware and best organised of the allies of reformism. They understand that constitutional change is necessary if we are to see an end to the hunger and distress of the people.

"Let us repeatedly renew our pledges: universal manhood suffrage, without property qualifications, equal voting districts, Salaries for MPs, secret ballots and annual parliaments.

"These are such fair and clearly understood objectives, that allies will be won well beyond the working class. Parliamentary reform is the necessary precursor of workers' political power and essential for artisans and small manufacturers to trade free of the deadening weight of monopolies.

"Those aims should be the basis of a new Charter for the people, a Charter to be framed and displayed over every hearth, a Charter for which we canvass at every election, a Charter to be pressed on every MP."

Applause and hammering around the room.

Polly sat down next to her sister, sharing her drink.

There rushed towards them from the far side of the room, a young man. He was so excited that his scrambled words were at first hard to understand.

In a strong West country accent, he gave his name as William Lovett, come up from Cornwall in search of work, further learning and active involvement in the reformist struggle. The sisters confirmed their noms de guerre and introduced their daughter, Tilly, whose colour and remarkable bush of hair left the poor country lad speechless. He had never before seen a black woman or black child. Adored, generally forewarned and advised by her mothers, Tilly unashamedly enjoyed the man's amazement, but her smile was reassuring; more than a smile, a beam of joy and welcome.

Today her hair was not tamed by a turban, but it did support a hackle of white feathers.

He expressed how deeply impressed he was by the sisters' analysis of the Cato Street episode and inspired by their view of the way ahead.His excitement was infectious even for such composed and restrained veterans as Cally and Polly.

They could not guess that his arrival on the scene was to have major significance in the sisters' lives for years ahead.

1821

From time to time, Polly's lower back was still giving her some discomfort and so to another doctor, reputed to be one of the best, Polly was told.

"There is no need to examine the scar," he said, "Nobody could have dealt with such an injury better than Mr Cooper.

"The pain you often feel when walking is probably caused by the internal residual scarring in the muscles along the path of the entry wound. The problem will ease in time, but Miss Reed, you will probably be the lady with the slight limp for the rest of your days."

Unpleasant information, bluntly delivered, but Polly could live with that.

On the way home, recalling the Cato Street episode, she and Cally had curses aplenty for Thistledown's foolhardiness and for Davidson's irresponsible shooting.

"How can we make of this assortment of disparate reformist and radical organisations a cohesive body, united by agreed aims and methods?" said Cally, in a tone of despair.

"We do not give up hope," responded Polly. "We have a lot on our side. "Although there are crazy ideas on what to do, as witness Cato Street, there is agreement on our aims. The movement's obvious lack is leadership. Our allied reformist organisations need a national coordinating committee

"For the present, you and I remain at the centre of the network of correspondents essential to holding everything together.

"What is more, you and I are aware of all organisations' vulnerability to infiltration by spies and provocators.

"And we have our secret, impeccable source of information on the government's spies and any changes in their modus operandi.

"I am not suggesting we are utterly indispensable to the nation-wide movement for parliamentary reform, but I am not over-stating our importance by claiming that our judgement and activity may be crucial to the next stage in the movement's development. We must press the case for a charter, listing the movement's demands for agreed reforms. Such a charter must be popularised throughout the nation.

"We start from first principles. You, Calpernia Wright, must address the next meeting of the Hampden Club, making a major speech on the new direction the movement must take after Cato Street.

"There, my sweet girl, I have given you your marching orders".

Cally decided to start by going back to Burke, their leading opponent, not for a reassessment of her stance on reform, but in order to see whether the enemy identified weaknesses which the reformists have been too self-obsessed to detect.

Reflections on the Revolution in France Cally again borrowed from the Rector. She found that Burke did, indeed, assert that radical reformers are so taken with their concern for the *rights* of man that they have given too little consideration to the *nature* of man. It probably needed a believer in the doctrine of original sin to be as strident as Cally about human nature. Although not a believer, she found the well known concept of original sin to be a useful metaphor for the human condition.

Sometimes, in discussion with her radical friends, her criticism of the people of England has been considered so strident as to constitute misanthropy. There are those whose ignorance is in part due to their illiteracy, but there are so many whose ignorance is wilful. They may be able to read, but do not bother. Neither do they listen. Their misjudgements and stupidity are self-inflicted and unforgivable. They hold firm beliefs which are not based on real evidence.

Cally's thoughts go back to her late friend, Arthur Thistlewood and other radicals, who persistently misread the people, having an unerring capacity to deliver themselves blindly into the arms of any projector and every evil alchemyst and shallow charlatan. How otherwise to explain Spa Fields, Pentrich and Cato Street?

The sisters were sprawled on the settee, while Lavender and Ananya were still at the table. Tilly was exhausted by her day and asleep in her cot. Polly was running her fingers through Cally's hair and

Cally was stroking Polly's arm. Polly returned to the topic they had discussed during dinner. "Why are so many of our reformist colleagues so blissfully careless about the risk of spies within, despite our repeated warnings?

"Why are they so given to misreading the mood of the people?

William Lovett and Richard Carlile are the only close friends we can consider to be in our camp.

Additionally, like Elizabeth, they know us to be more than loving sisters.

At the first Hampden Club meeting of 1821, members had been given notice that the main item on the agenda was to be the Cato Street incident of the previous November and the way ahead for the radical reform movement. When Cally was announced as the speaker, there was warm applause. Members knew they were about to hear views that may be unsettling, challenging, or even infuriating. They could be enraged by her speech, but they knew that Cally never spoke shibboleths, never wasted her words on vacuity.

Given the floor, she removed her bonnet. There must be no barrier between her and her listeners. As a teacher, she knew the importance of eye-to-eye communication.

"Edmund Burke," she began, "Our principal critic and taunter, argues that we underestimate the frailties of human nature. I consider that criticism, although it comes from our principal enemy, to be valid. As a consequence of that fault, we have delivered ourselves, blindly, into the arms of every projector and reckless adventurer emerging from our own movement or planted by the crafty coercive state.

"It is true that, whereas we reformists are preoccupied with the machinations of the corrupt aristocracy and malign government, Burke's concern is what he considers to be the crude nature of what he contemptuously calls the 'swinish multitude'.

"I will remind you, in his own words, of his cynical view of Cromwell's Commonwealth. 'The occupation of a hair-dresser, or of a working tallow-chandler, cannot be a matter of honour to any person – to say nothing of a number of other more servile employments. Such descriptions of men ought not to suffer oppression from the state, but the state suffers oppression, if such as they, either individually or collectively, are permitted to rule.'

"Such contempt for the lower orders will echo down the ages and will, I predict, be just as prevalent two centuries hence.

"Cromwell had ideas in common with Burke. He abhorred the Levellers, of whose honourable legacy English Jacobins are the true heirs. He idealised the country gentry, of which he was one. He considered there was – I quote him – 'something peculiar only to the genius of a Gentleman that fitted him for governing states and leading armies.'

"At the end of the Civil War, the Levellers were concerned about the inequities in the distribution of seats in the Commons and talked of a franchise not limited to rate-payers. We are all familiar with these ideas. Translated into up-to-date terms, they are the backbone of our developing reform Charter.

"As Paine would have it, there are two distinct classes of men in the nation: those who pay taxes and those who receive and live upon taxes. In the latter class are the courtiers, placemen, eminent state pensioners and leaders of the parties. Despite their rich subsidies, our aristocracy is unable to breed a hereditary monarch of their own and consequently send to Brunswick for a king. We would have done no worse by going to a pawnbroker for a pledged spare princeling.

"At the expense of a million a year to the payers of taxes, we have a king who speaks not our language, understands not our laws and whose capabilities would scarcely fit him for the office of parish constable".

Laughter, cheers and stamping.

"And what are these tax-fed spongers kept for? For essential duties, no doubt. Any one of them would claim, 'I am doing the state some service.'

"Yes, we have the Lord of the Bed-Chamber, Lord of the Kitchen, Lord of the Royal Chamber of Necessity and Lord Overseer of the Sinecures.

"Take the House of Peers. Yes, please do take it and send it, in its entirety, to Botany Bay.

"What, pray, is it for? It is the pillar of landed interests. Were that pillar to sink into the earth, the same landed property would continue, and the same ploughing, sowing and harvesting would go on.

"The landed aristocracy are not the farmers who work the land. No, they are the parasitic consumers of rent.

"Lord Byron has told us the purpose of the peers of the realm: 'For what were all these country patriots born?' Cally looked around the room, as if seeking an answer, and then, with her hands beating the meter of the verse, 'For what were all these country patriots born? To hunt and vote to raise the price of corn.'

Cheers and hammering around the room.

"Tom Paine claimed to be a farmer of sorts. He said, 'I am a farmer of thoughts, and all the crops I raise I give away.'

"My thoughts of late have dwelt on the concept of property and how the possession of property is spuriously associated with intellect and civil rights. It was in 1816, during that dreadfully cold winter, that I first had the honour of addressing the Club on this subject. It is high time to revisit it.

"Our distinguished colleague, John Thelwall, great proselytiser for Tom Paine, damned Burke for stigmatising nine-tenths of the population as 'insensate, devoid of the power of reason, undeserving of a voice in public affairs, let alone a vote'. Here Thelwall was speaking as a teacher of rhetoric and elocution, as well as a radical and reformist.

"We followers of Spence and Paine believe in the power of human reason. The Enlightenment of the past two centuries, with its foment of ideas on philosophy, politics and art, has impinged on the common people, just as much as on the élite. The people demand freedom of expression, so that the opinions, not of a tenth-part, but the whole of the nation can be freely delivered and distinctly heard.

"The Enlightenment and Tom Paine have brought us clarity of thought and understanding of the limitations imposed on us. Compare what ye are with what ye have the right to be, is Thelwall's challenge.

"From the Middle Ages we have inherited the pervasive and oppressive reality of social orders. There are the rich, those who have money, land and rental income. At the other end of the scale are the poor, who own no such assets and the only thing they possess which can provide their wherewithal is labour, their capacity to work for others at a price.

"Unfortunately, neither the Enlightenment, nor the revolutions in France and England brought change in the contemptuous attitude of our rulers towards the individual who hires himself out for a wage, thereby subjecting himself to the control of another, in which lowly dependent position – so our rulers' thinking runs – he has neither opportunity, nor inclination to interest himself in the affairs of civil society.

"To its shame, the Commonwealth, too, despised those with no property.

"Even among the Dissenters, even among the Quakers – with the notable exception of Quaker Tom Paine – there persisted the notion that political ignorance and political incapacity are inevitable corollaries of propertylessness. Consequently, among the Dissenters, it was only the Levellers who included in their advocacy of parliamentary reform, universal manhood suffrage, regardless of property ownership. The Levellers demanded the franchise for all rate-payers, all who paid local property taxes. Rate-payers are entitled to attend meetings of the Vestry, which is responsible for raising money from local people for poor relief. During the 1820s, vestries increasingly stood in opposition to enclosures of common land and attempted to intervene, on matters of constitutional reform, much to the chagrin of the Church of England authorities, who deplored such unauthorised straying beyond the vestries' remit, considering such mischievous audacity to be a regrettable legacy from the Commonwealth.

"At this time, two centuries after the Civil War, the vote is held by about one in five men, mostly property owners of some substance. William Cobbett considers this to be fundamental to the Old Corruption fundamental to the graft, malfeasance and nepotism by which the ruling class hangs on to its wealth and power. This must be changed.

"We now have Cobbett, Henry Hunt, Richard Carlile and others arguing that a substantial extension of the franchise is long overdue, as is a redistribution of parliamentary seats and a wider cross-section of the population being elected to the Commons.

"The government has never been open to persuasion by rational argument. Most of its minions are too stupid and arrogant to engage in rational argument. They think they are untouchable.They understand only countervailing pressure, strength, or a threat to their grip on power. Nothing will change the Old Corruption until our demands for political rights are *forced* upon the reluctant ruling class. They will have to be *forced, to* concede to our demands."

By now, Cally's angry words had worked her into a lather of fury.

Tilly had never seen mother Cally in such a state. She was holding tighto Polly's hand, as if for reassurance.

"Polly and I have recently heard from our correspondent in Sheffield. She tells us of the growth of the Sheffield Society for Constitutional Information (SCI), which now has two thousand members, organised in two hundred tithe-paying groups. Each such group selects a delegate to the Central Council. Societies on the Sheffield pattern, are being set up in neighbouring towns and villages.

"Moribund corresponding societies are being revived or replaced by such organisations as SCIs. The future for the Peoples' Charter in the North is looking bright.

"The past 100 years have seen social changes of unprecedented proportion in the whole of human history.

"When, apart from the gentry, we were all serfs and all were engaged in subsistence farming, we worked without supervision by overseers, keeping whatever crops remained after the lord of the manor purloined what he considered to be his share. Wages had not yet been invented and profit as yet hardly existed as a concept in the minds of the landowners and other rich men.

"But with the arrival of manufactures and steam-power, a new and richer source of wealth was created. The mill-owner, to take an example, has income from the sale of cloth made by his workers. Of course, he has to spend money to get the raw cotton, linen or wool and he has to pay for machinery and perhaps rent. He also has a wages bill. He has to pay his workers enough to feed and house themselves and their families.

The workers' families are important, because they give rise to the next generation of his workers.

"If his out-goings exceed his income from sales, his business will not last long. He makes sure that his income is always greater than his costs. The difference between his total income and his total costs, the surplus, is his profit. Unless he happens to be Robert Owen, he is a greedy man and so he wants to maximise the surplus. There are various ways he can do that. He can join with other mill-owners in forcing down the price they pay for raw materials. He can invest some of his profit in new machinery that increases production. Or he can force his workers to work longer hours, with no increase in the hourly rate, or he can force down their wages, a measure which is more likely to succeed if all the local employers act together. Yes, try as they might to destroy our trade unions, they know the concept of solidarity and have their own employers' organisations.

"This is where the trade unions come in. Workers are aware that they are exploited. Their capacity to labour is indispensible to the employer and can be withdrawn at any time. That is the workers' powerful weapon. No need for pikes and guns.

"Hear, hear" from around the room.

Many of the serfs displaced by the brutal enclosures of common land, arrived in the towns and became factory workers, now subject to the discipline of industrial production; fixed working hours and a long working week, sweating under the figurative lash of the foreman. The workers soon realised that they have common cause and regardless of the oppressive

Combination Acts, they have come together in organised groups.

"Workers seeking economic betterment have become increasingly conscious of their weaknesses and their potential strength. They are aware that, having no vote, they have no influence over the membership of the House of Commons and count for nothing in local government. That political awakening has continued to develop.

"At the end of the last century, combinations of coalminers, sailors and shoe-makers were meeting, organising in groups, collecting subscriptions and loyalty oaths and threatening to stop work and actually striking, demanding higher pay.

"Pitt, the Prime Minister, reported to the Commons that barracks were being built in various parts, so that troops were readily available to magistrates in the event of extreme stirrings among the working class.

"The struggle for trade unions to be recognised by employers as legitimate representative organisations and the pressing need for economic successes have been increasingly coupled with the demand for political rights.

"At present, Although we are the majority of the citizenry, we have no voice in Parliament to demand an end to the Combination Acts. That is why we must win fundamental constitutional reform.

"The struggle for trade unions to be recognised by employers as legitimate representative organisations and the pressing need for improved wages and conditions have been increasingly coupled with the demand for political rights. Until the Combination Acts are repealed, they must be violated. That will result in men and women being brought before the courts. But non-violent opposition to unjust laws will eventually succeed.

Now the reformist movement potentially has a strong backbone. It is no longer a movement of easily ignored taproom and Sunday school gatherings, of readers and talkers on hypothetical matters. The movement now includes organised workers, with the muscular power of industrial action, able to persuade, or if necessary *force* their desires on a reluctant and obstinaterruling class. At last, there is room for us to hope that Tom Paine's Rights of Man will be realised in our lifetime.

"Our People's Charter now can be supported by a triumvirate composed of the existing reformist organisations, the potentially mighty trade unions and the more enlightened members of the merchant and entrepreneurial class, who grasp that their industries cannot run without the workforce and that their workers' eventual acquisition of basic political rights is inevitable.

"Cato Street and all our other defeats, have been bitter lessons. The crucial question is:Does our future look brighter than our past? Then, is there room for hope?"

Cally sat down between Polly and Tilly, taking a draught of ale. There was applause and the customary vote of thanks, during which, from across the room came a new face. He took Cally's hand without it being offered and in a most earnest manner he expressed his thanks and congratulations for what he described as a 'groundbreaking and inspirational address'. Then, "Forgive me Miss Wright, I am so swept away by your analysis, that I forget to introduce myself." Taking the hand of Polly and then Tilly, despite his excitement, he managed to give his name as "William Lovett, newly arrived from Cornwall."

"I have lodgings nearby and I am employed as a cabinet-maker. I intend to study and to be as helpful as possible in London's political life."

Cally responded by introducing her sister, Polly and their daughter, Tilly.

"Cornwall," piped up Tilly, "Is the most western county of England, where there is mining for tin."

Lovett was slightly taken aback by this diminutive sage, but found a response. "Yes, Miss, the most westerly and the most beautiful.

"I am delighted to meet you all and hope to do so often, as I attend these meetings."

Mr Lovett was as good as his word, appearing at every meeting, making short, modest contributions in discussions and readily volunteering to undertake even the most menial practical tasks, from moving chairs to officiating at workers' reading circles. The sisters viewed him as a shy man, whose excitement and animation in reaction to London's political turbulence helped him to overcome his reticence. Cally was amused that his stock was always too long and so it had two tails extending from his neck to his waist; an odd style, all his own. Polly admonished Cally for being harsh in her judgement of the man. "Coming from the deepest West country to the mad commotion of London can be no less disconcerting than being plunged into a foreign country. He is handsome by any measure, very presentable, intelligent. His marked accent does not in the least spoil his eloquence."

"From this pretty speech, it appears to me," said Cally,"That you have lined up for yourself, a very eligible bachelor. Have you given away your heart? Is our seraglio about to lose the rest of you?"

Polly took her sister's neck in a pretended strangulation. Then, nose-to-nose with her sister: "I think I know where cupid's arrow is truly aimed. When you are speaking at meetings, he is hanging on your every word. Has he ever expressed disagreement with you? No. Does he praise you? Yes, at every opportunity.

"I spy with my little eye, that his face lights up when you come into the room, or stand to speak. "Dearest sister, he is not the sort of man to be a love-sick calf, but his fascination with you, makes him your most loyal disciple. You are as abrupt and curt with him as you are with everybody, but his fidelity will never falter.

"Polly, mine. You have a vivid imagination and a propensity for creating crazy ideas." Cally was dismissive.

Polly was now stroking her sister's hair and face."Relish this admiration while you can. We are both getting older and one day we'll be faded old maids."

Lovett used the model of the sisters' nationwide correspondence network in creating an information exchange embracing all of London. He maintained a successful cabinet-making business and at one time was keeper of a coffee-house thought to house the best conversation in London. His occasional journalism earned him the accolade awarded to all newspapermen of note at that time, a spell in prison for seditious libel. He studied at the London Mechanics' Institute and found time to establish the London working Men's Association, campaigning for state-funded general education and constitutional rights for all.

Having been invited to dinner Chez Reed soon after his arrival in London, he knew the family's address. Some months later, he turned up at their door one day. He asked the maid whether Mr Reed was at home. Ushered into the sitting room, he introduced himself to Lavender and apologised for calling without warning.

"*Something of a stickler for quaint courtesies,*" was Lavender's inference. This was confirmed when Lovett gave the purpose of his visit. "I have come, Sir, in order to seek your permission to ask for the hand of your daughter, Cally.

"Since I have known her, she has grown in my esteem and fondness." Before Lavender could stem the flow, Cally's suitor rushed on with the speech he had carefully prepared.

"My business is sound and highly successful, so that I can provide my wife with comfort and complete financial security. On matters of politics and religion, we are of one mind, I know. I have yet to reveal my earnest hopes to Cally, considering it proper first to test my prospects before you, her father."

Confronted with such old-fashioned ritual, Lavender dared not show his amusement, but was momentarily lost for words. He would not have been more taken aback had the man sought to kiss his hand.

"Well, Mr Lovett, Cally and Polly often speak of you and so I know how much they both respect your commitment to the cause of parliamentary reform and advancement of the working class.

"I appreciate your respect for traditional courtesies, but I really think that Cally herself should take my place in this conversation. I think she is at home and so I will call her, if I may. At the same time, I will ask for some tea."

Cally was pleasantly surprised to see William. They shook hands and she invited him to sit down.

Without a word, Father gently withdrew from the room. Cally poured the tea.

Lovett fidgeted a little, took a breath, smiled at her and began.

"I will repeat what I have just said to your father. Over the time I have known you, you have grown in my esteem and fondness. You are beautiful beyond words, graceful and clever. It would realise the greatest hope of my life if you would agree to marry me."

Cally was now twenty one and a few tentative approaches had already been gently rebuffed, but this was the first formal proposal and from a man she respected, one from whom any woman would be honoured to receive a proposal. Oh, how she wished she had been given notice of this interview. It may turn out to be painful for William and it will not be easy for her

"William, I greatly value our friendship and our political collaboration. If this country were as much as half-civilised, you would be a Member of Parliament, nay, a government minister. I work for that day to come.

"I fear you do not yet fully understand me. I know it will not spoil our friendship – we are both too rational for that – if I reveal what you have not yet detected.

"Have you noticed how close are Polly and I?

"Of course, you are sisters."

"We are, indeed, sisters, Polly having been adopted by my parents, when she was about twelve years old. Our closeness is more than merely sisterly. I know you have studied the classics and so you will know of the ancient Greek poetess, Sappho, from the island of Lesbos. Little of her writing has survived, but sufficient to make clear that she composed a number poems expressing love and physical desire between women. The term 'sapphic love', or 'lesbian love', describes that love between two women, which can be as intense and carnal as the love between a man and a woman, although largely unrecognised by society and – to the limited extent that it is recognised – stigmatised.

"Polly and I are Sapphic lovers. We are as close and just as committed as if we were a married couple. We live in the same house and, being entirely candid, we sleep in the same bed, kiss and caress as lovers do."

"We even have a child. Tilly was an orphan until we adopted her. We are her two mothers."

William sat through this speech, his eyes fixed on Cally's lips. When finished, she smiled at him and he made a somewhat nervous smile in return.

"Not in rustic Cornwall, but here, in London, I heard of lesbian women, being spoken of disparagingly. I had insufficient knowledge to make a judgement of my own. I now find that I know two Sapphic lovers. I know them well enough to hold them in great respect. I regret that you cannot marry me, but, in this cruel world, I am happy to see true love, wherever I find it and even if I cannot be part of it.

"Would it be crass of me to say that I wish I were Polly?" They both smiled.

Cally felt sorry for William. "I trust," said she, "That our friendship and political collaboration can continue unabated."

That evening, Tilly put to bed, Cally did her best to give the family a word-for-word account of her conversation with William. Across the table, Lavender and Ananya took the hands of their daughters. His eyes were glistening a little as father spoke for himself and his wife. "Our two clever and beautiful daughters make us immensely proud. Your altruism and rationality have led you to rebel against every cruelty, inanity and hypocrisy in the book. I have deferred mentioning this, but I will now admit that I have known all along that you were involved in the Cato Street conspiracy and I have no doubt that you were on the scene for the best of reasons. One of the Bow street spies reported that two sisters (real identity unknown) were somehow implicated. From the whole of London, nay, from the whole of England, who but you could those two brave women be?

"Our rebel daughters are deeply loved."

1823

The painstaking work of Elizabeth Fry and her devoted band of Newgate Prison Visitors at last saw fruition with the Gaols Act, 1823. Promoted by the Home secretary, Robert Peel, it mandated the separation of men and women prisoners in all gaols, female warders for women prisoners and wages for prison staff, so that they should no longer be tempted ruthlessly to exploit the prison inmates. The use of brutal irons and manacles was to cease. Fry and her helpers knew better that to assume that all would now be well, especially as the Act made no provision for the official inspection of prisons. Prison Governors and gaolers were used to being a law unto themselves and so Elizabeth and her helpers had to continue their observation of prison conditions and their constant badgering of governors, MP's and Robert Peel.

It is Easter and there is to be a performance of Handel's Messiah, in Southwark Cathedral, by the orchestra of the Royal Philharmonic Society and the combined choirs of the Cathedral and all the local churches.

The family is there early, in order find seats at the front, in an open pew. For this special occasion, they are in their best. Ananya and Cally are wearing saris, Polly and Tilly are in their latest frocks, Tilly with her hair tamed by a traditional elaborate beaded headdress copied from a Benin bronze bust seen for sale in a Ludgate Hill shop.

Knowing that she was probably born in London, although her birth was not recorded anywhere, Tilly thinks it probable that her mother was a slave from Benin, like so many other Africans in England. Encouraged by her mothers, she has studied the tragic story of slavery and developed pride in her West African origin.

As the concert is about to begin, a lady of some importance, judging by her haughty demeanour, wafts in front of the Reed family, with her personal maid tripping along behind. Her ladyship pauses by Lavender, points at Tilly and says, "Please have your servant sit elsewhere, so that I may have her place."

Lavender is stunned, but quickly responds, "Madame, my granddaughter will remain where she is."

The grotesquerie is shocked by the lack of deference and to be so thwarted. Momentarily puzzled by the different skin colours of grandfather and granddaughter. She flounces onward.

There came a point during the oratorio where Tilly stood and stepped forward two paces to join the line of soloists on the dais. Her sweet, sturdy soprano filled the nave: "I know that my Redeemer liveth, and that He shall stand at the latter day upon the earth …"

As orchestra and chorus plunged into the theme, Lavender could not help looking round to see whether his nemesis recognised his 'servant'. Tilly's singing teacher is deeply impressed by her precocious talent. He has remarked that, hearing her pure high notes is like staring at the wonder of a full moon.

"For unto us a child is born." the line was begun by Tilly, with all the sopranos, in their delicate voices, joining her.

As usual, the Hallelujah chorus left the whole assembly uplifted and smiling.

As they left the Cathedral, Cally shared with Polly and Tilly, her thought that, *"Well, God, I am no closer to you than when I came in, but I freely admit that your church has given rise to some beautiful music."*

1830 brought the death of George IV, the one-time prince Regent. The new monarch was William IV, who continued the Hanovarian tradition of living with one of his mistresses, rather than with his wife. He was survived by 8 children, but none was legitimate and so his successor to the throne, in 1837, was Victoria, his niece.

The example of the London Working Men's Association (LWMA) was followed in different parts of the country. Various activists travelled out as missionaries for that purpose.

William Lovett kept up a correspondence with the radical members of parliament who supported some or all of the articles of the putative People's Charter, as constant debate took it through its numerous iterations, during the 1820s and 1830s. Having discussed the way forward with Cally and Polly and the officers of the LWMA, William invited all the supportive MPs to a meeting on the Charter at the British Coffee-House, in Cockspur Street, on 31st May 1837. It was a substantial gathering in this, London's best-known meeting place for reformists. The general mood was positive, but there were acerbic reactions to a few rancorous interventions from speakers who accused some MPs of professing support for the reformist programme at hustings, in order to curry favour with the crowd, then failing to give support in circumstances where they thought it might endanger their seats and prospects for advancement.

"This is not helpful," said Cally to her sister, "We are trying to retain friends and make new ones, not alienate anyone who cannot pledge total support, at all times, for every jot and tittle of our aims."

"The members of a large movement are bound to vary in their precise opinions and commitment to the cause.

Then in an impatient growl, "I have no sympathy for the holier than thou brigade."

Polly patted Cally's hand, whispering in her ear, "Patience, darling girl, let's see if good eventually comes out of the mix. You and I cannot be the only ones who can see what is necessary. Thankfully, wisdom is not solely our preserve.

William considered the Reed sisters to be his closest confidantes. They agreed on most things, although his too frequent blind spot was the importance of the movement in the Midlands and the North. It was in these industrialising regions that the working class and their organisations were to the fore and yet William took a patronising view of the rough and ready style of their correspondence and the speedy adoption of militant stands against recalcitrant employers. He wanted them to be more temperate and sophisticated in their approach, while the sisters valued the northerners' strident class consciousness, impatience for change, solidarity and courage.

Polly woke one morning with a ready-made idea." It is high time we travelled northwards again. In particular, could we not go to New Lanark, see that brave experiment for ourselves and, now that Robert Owen in back from America, we might be able to meet him, visit his model village and discuss his ideas."

It was agreed that Polly should look into possible travel arrangements and that is where her interesting idea could have come unstuck. To travel by stagecoach to Edinburgh, at least a day short of New Lanark, would entail ten days on the road and the cost of several overnight stops.

"But," pointed out Cally, "We agreed we would go by sea if we ever travelled to the North again. We could take the steam-assisted packet from here to Goole and then stagecoaches.

"And I read in the paper that a new ship, a paddle steamer, called COMET, operates out of the Clyde New Lanark is on the River Clyde and so by sea aboard the COMET. Tilly will love it. After all, she is now ten and she would find it a great adventure. She is our pride and joy and we want her to know there is a big wide world out there, beyond Kennington".

Polly looked into this idea and reported back."COMET is a newly built paddle steamer ferrying passengers on pleasure trips, back and forth on the Clyde. But it is not ocean-going and so there is no question of our taking it all the way from London to Scotland. On the other hand, the steam packet, City of Glasgow, operating out of Goole and London, is our alternative to the long, slow drag by road.

They took ship, the steam packet, at the New London Dock at Wapping. They had paid for a cabin on the foredeck, with a couchette for each of them. They each had a blanket from home and so it was sure to be clean. The fare included meals prepared by the crew, which turned out to be basic but acceptable. The late summer weather gave enough wind to speed them down the Thames, but not enough to create a great swell. All three were proud to find themselves good sailors, so far.

Tilly was of an age and of a mind to select her wardrobe for herself. Her growing pride in her Beninian heritage – influenced by the frequent discussions among the adults about the campaign to end the slave trade – led her to persuade Ananya – the chief seamstress of the family – to buy for her the most exotic fabric off-cuts to be found at the Spitalfields market stalls. Tilly and her grandmother assumed There would be a short skirt over calf-length trousers in brightly patterned cloth. Several bead necklaces and a turban completed the wardrobe of this precocious self-aware child. She was not pretentious, but enjoyed being decorative.

As they journeyed, the flow of Tilly's questions was ceaseless and her mothers were expected to have all the answers.

"What is the difference between a boat and a ship?

"Why is this ship called a packet? It would need to be in a very big parcel."

"Where is the steam engine and may we see it?

"Why is the water grey here and greeny-blue over there?

"Where does all this water flow to?

"What makes the wind blow?

"Today is Tuesday. We always have bacon on Tuesday. Shall we have bacon on this boat?"

Cally and Polly shared the load between them, trying always to be honest, never talking down to their child, but sometimes resorting to a little fabrication when their knowledge ran thin, sharing conspiratorial smiles without being seen, lest the rigorous interlocutor should become suspicious.

Two nights at sea brought them to the mouth of the Humber. At Goole they boarded a smaller boat, the Ouse ferry to York, where they took a room at the Roman Baths Inn. The sisters had stayed here before and the Innkeeper remembered them. He and his wife fell in love with Tilly and wanted to keep her. In serious businesslike terms, Tilly told them she would like to stay longer in York, but had to travel on to Scotland to meet Mr Owen and see his factory at Lanark.

By stagecoach, the party travelled to Housesteads on the Roman wall. The inn was very poor, but the compensation was seeing the impressive remains of the Roman fort. In response to her daughter's flood of questions, Cally had to discourse on the Roman occupation, Hadrian's wall and the reason there were now no centurions in residence.

The weather was cold, but dry. The rolling hills and vast skies of the border country were a revelation. The wall was not the only Roman legacy. The military road, parallel to the wall, was still as straight as an arrow's flight, although undulating, giving the horses alternating hard climbs and easy downhill glides.

The Fleece Inn at Alnwick gave a much better dinner and overnight stay, before the long haul to the White Hart at Edinburgh. All the way from London, the changing scenes had Tilly's eyes agog and the inquisitive chatter flowing. In Glasgow, they met Finlay Thomson, their correspondent from the shipyard trade unions. They were shown massive iron ships under construction. The contrast to Deptford Dockyard, where the boats were smaller and still built from wood, could not have been greater. The city's inn gave an indifferent overnight stop, before the one-day final stage, by the Clyde steamer, to New Lanark. A farmhouse gladly took in the little party, which roused much curiosity among the locals. A brown woman and an exotically dressed black child provided unusual entertainment.

New Lanark was approached from the top of a hill. At first, it could not be seen, because a fret had rolled in from the Firth of Clyde. As they descended, red and grey roof-tops gradually pushed up through the white mist.

"We have been higher than the clouds, but we saw no angels." Tilly's excited revelation was, of course, quite true. It became a glorious day. Whereas most ladies shielded their alabaster faces from the sun, fending off any risk of rustic colouration, Polly removed her bonnet and aligned her face to catch the full glare. She coveted the consistent brown and black of Cally and Tilly, in contrast to her own pale pastel colouration, that came and went with the summer sun. With sunshine came her freckles. It was Father who pointed out that she had the constellation of Orion on her nose, with the pole-star precisely between her eyes.

"If ever you are lost, Polly is your living compass."

"On matters of morality or politics, Polly is always my reliable compass," retorted Cally, planting a kiss on her sister's nose.

As they descended the hill, they could see that this industrial town was in sharp contrast to the black, smokey centres they had passed in Yorkshire, county Durham and Glasgow. The mills retained the colours of brick and stone of which they were built, rather than being soot-blackened. The streets were wide and there were many open green spaces. There were chimneys, but the well spaced buildings in a wide valley allowed the smoke to be blown away.

Cally pointed out the ash tree hangers on the far side of the valley. "They are giants walking down the hill," suggested Tilly. "Our daughter has a vivid imagination. She will be a story-teller, as well as a singer," suggested Polly.

Cally had arranged to meet Mr Owen at one of the schools. It was easily found by the hundred or so childish voices rendering Green Grow the Rashes. They went in through the open door and found the 5 to 10s in full voice. Tilly looked pleadingly at Polly and received a nod. She joined the end of a row and gave the song her all. Cally had taught her most of Rabbie's songs and she was learning to accompany herself at the piano.

The visitors' interruption of the day's routine was an enthralling experience for the children. Of course, they had heard of black and brown people and had seen drawings of them in books. The teacher welcomed the visitors, come all the way from London. That warranted another song, London Bridge Is Falling Down, with actions. The visitors joined in, Tilly providing descant.

Robert Owen arrived at this point. He was what the Scots described as a 'black man', having black hair and beard. He expressed his delight that the visitors had so readily thrown themselves into the children's activity.

"Every day," he explained, "The children spend much of the morning on singing, dancing and doing drill. By drill, we mean marching, running, jumping and swinging, all in a military way. We think that gives the children good exercise, precision, coordination and synchronised action, all good physical discipline.

"Unlike most Scottish schools, we have no corporal punishment, no slapping, no cane or strap.

"If a child does wrong, it must understand how its action has perhaps hurt others. There must be apology for harm done and, if appropriate, reparation. That is enough. Physical punishment only serves to promote the backward idea that in response to any offence, violent retaliation is acceptable.

New Lanark's mills, schools and houses all reflected the philanthropy of Owen and his concern for the welfare of the workers and their families.

That evening was spent with Owen at his home. He spoke at length on his idea of a socialist society, the essential characteristic of which is democratic control of the means of production, from which stems democratic control of the distribution of wealth. This utopian vision had not always worked in the townships he had established, but he remained committed to it.

It was possible to compare New Lanark with the other industrial towns in the west of Scotland.

New Lanark workers had a working day of no more than 8 hours and a working week of 6 days. They had an annual holiday of one week. They were healthier than the folk of nearby towns and there was less drunkenness and less illegitimacy.

The sisters' return to London was by ship, via Leith and Goole. Their sea-legs rather let them down as the packet buffeted its way down the east coast. Tilly, however, proved to be a sturdy sailor, as energetic as ever and taxing her mothers with the usual stream of questions and observations on the ship, the passengers and the restless sea. Undeterred by the rolling of the deck, she entertained the cabin passengers with song and dance. This exotic-looking little treasure delighted one and all.

At the first Hampden Club Meeting after their return, the sisters gave a report of their journey, embellished by thoughts on the significance of what they had seen.

Given the floor, Cally wanted to emphasise that modern industry created enough surplus to provide workers with adequate wages, humane working hours, healthy housing, open spaces for recreation and schooling for children. All this she had seen at New Lanark.

She was pleased to note that Owenite socialism in New Lanark had no place for religion. As throughout England, with the exception of poor Irish immigrants and some older people, most workers are not religious and do not attend church. There is complete indifference to religion.

The longer workers live in towns, the weaker become the threads of attachment to their rural roots and deference to the monied, the gentry and the clergy.

"A notable and positive development," said Cally, "A legacy of the Civil War and English Revolution is that, since the turn of the century, the grip of Church and King has been weakening year by year.

Cally's concluding remark was: "In comparing New Lanark with other industrial centres, the term, utopia, would not be entirely inappropriate.

"But in case anyone should consider the idea of a utopia to be too far-fetched, too idealistic, in the real world of 19th century Britain, with its dark satanic mills, let's use the word socialism.

"In our framing of the Peoples' Charter, let us be unafraid to detail what our socialist policies will be when we have the power to implement them. The people need to see our alternative to the backwardness of the Tories and the Whigs."

The sisters continued to be much in demand to attend meetings of reformist organisations and trade unions. Readings of the radical papers would typically lead on to lessons in political economy, history and English literature. The many autodidacts among the workers relished the inspiration for learning which Cally and Polly brought to meetings. Since their visit to New Lanark and their long conversation with Robert Owen, Their discourse invariably included promotion of the idea of socialism.

"It is nearly forty years since Mary Wollstonecraft published *A Vindication of the Rights of Woman* and it has had no more than the occasional mention at the Hampden Club. We really must honour her work by lecturing on it." This was Polly. Cally agreed and added that any lecture should include Mary's ideas on the education of girls, about which they had themselves accumulated considerable experience.

Polly was given the floor at the Hampden Club, the first of the duo to speak.

"The first writer in English, arguing for the rights of women, was Mary Astell. She was born in 1666 to a royalist family in Newcastle upon Tyne. At that time, over 80 per cent of North country women were maintained illiterate. I use the word maintained advisedly, because girls' education was virtually non-existent. They were given little or no schooling beyond domestic skivvying. Mary was fortunate to have a mentor in the family, Ralph Astell, a curate of the Cathedral Church of St Nicholas, who taught her some Latin, French, philosophy, mathematics and logic. She never married, but formed strong views on marriage by observing the unions of others around her. Being devout, she considered marriage to be an indestructible union, sanctified by the Church. Nevertheless, in her fifth book, *Some Reflections Upon Marriage,* published in 1700, she poses the challenging question, 'If all men are born free, how is it that all women are born slaves?' She goes on to point out the arbitrariness of views among the Whigs of the day, who although ostensibly more open-minded than Tories, claimed freedom to be the birthright of men and subjection as natural for women.

"Thomas Paine, author of *The Rights of Man*, had little to say about the rights of women, beyond noting the fact of their subordinate and inferior status. It remained for a woman to follow in his step, by applying the principles of freedom and liberty to the lives of women.

"Mary Wolstencraft published *A Vindicaion of the Rights of Woman* in1792. Although this was just a year after Paine's seminal work, it was not written as a direct response to Paine. Mary had her own furrow to plough. No doubt, her unconventional personal life helped to shape her views. She was most unusual for a woman of her class in 18th century England. She was an autodidact and well qualified to support herself as a successful journalist and author. She had no need of marriage to save her from destitution.

"She had affairs and bore children, out of wedlock, by Henry Fuseli, the painter and William Godwin, the philosopher and diplomat. Her daughter by Godwin, Mary Godwin, married Percy Shelly at age 16 and was widowed at age 22. She had started writing a gothic-style novel at the age of 18. *Frankenstein, or The Modern Prometheus* appeared in 1821, at first anonymously.

"Like Mary Astell, Wolstencraft was concerned that women were kept in ignorance by lack of education and in subjection by the tenets of the Church, derived from St Paul, who preached that woman is created for the man and therefore, 'Wives submit to your husbands.'

Our laws defining the rights of women follow the Church and are so reactionary that they might have been formulated by St Paul himself, based on the primitive mores of the first century. A married woman can legally hold no property in her own right and cannot claim any rights even over the children to whom she gave birth. People with influence and money enough are able to get round these anachronous laws, but for the majority they are implacable.

"Mary Astell proposed equal education for all children of ability and Wollstonecraft was scathing about the curriculum of the schools for daughters of the newly affluent, established in the 18th century and continuing into the present century. Daughters of the gentry and the aristocracy are taught how to while away elegantly their extensive leisure hours until achieving the essential goal of marriage, learning a little undemanding French, perhaps singing, but concentrating on fashion, etiquette, decorum, taste, dancing and bland conversation, facile activities, lacking any intellectual rigour.

"The placid life of the upper middle class young woman is wondrously satirised in the novels of

The Lady. The fictional mothers, exemplified by Mrs Dashwood and Mrs Bennet, spend their days fretfully seeking to match each daughter to a man in possession of a good fortune, preferably in the form of an estate yielding several thousand pounds a year.

Cally took the floor and claimed competence to speak about girls' education, "Having been engaged in teaching for many years.

"It has been argued by cynics that educating girls is a redundant exercise, because they will hold no office requiring learning. It is also paradoxically argued that women are not competent to hold public or professional office precisely because they have no learning.

"In reality, gIrls are just as capable as boys in learning languages, mathematics, logic and natural philosophy. These subjects make up the curriculum taught by my sister and I. We eschew the triviality and inconsequentialness of the typical curriculum for girls. Fed the same meaty education as boys, our girls suffer no mental over-load or stress. They leave school as competent women, just as capable as any man to hold public office, or to undergo training for a profession, such as law, journalism or – but for the barriers erected by men – entry into medical schools.

"Yes, women make competent nurses, so why not physicians?

"The unrealised potential of women has been likened to unmined gold, a precious entity left wasting in the ground. If that gold were released, it would enrich the whole of human society.

"Women are fifty per cent of humanity. Among the social reforms we demand must be included nothing less than the liberation of women from bondage, be it the bondage of illiteracy and ignorance, or the bondage of marriage and continual child-bearing."

I do not subscribe to the idea myself, having heard it said that it is men who start wars and deservedly are the greatest sufferers. They are mobilised as the armies and In their thousands they are killed and maimed on the battlefields. We women are largely spared that.

There was the routine vote of thanks to the speakers and applause, although it must be admitted that the applause was not uproarious.

"Clearly," said Polly, "Even in radical circles, there is some way to go before we achieve women's liberation. As usual, I wonder where we shall stand two hundred years hence, in, say, 2020".

The year's news was dominated by the effects of the severe economic crisis, as bad as that of 1816, which followed the Tambora volcanic eruption and failed harvests. Cally and Polly learned from their correspondents that, all over the North, trade unions were springing up like mushrooms in militant response to factory closures – notwithstanding the underlying exponential growth in the manufacturing industries – increasing unemployment and downward pressure on wages. Unsurprisingly, many organisations drew inspiration from the current revolutionary upsurge in France and Belgium.

England's biggest industry remained agriculture.

In lecturing on political economy, Cally explained that the enclosures of the previous century had largely turned arable land into more lucrative sheep pastures. The welter of enclosure Acts of the current century resulted in common land being turned into large farms on which the new, scientific mixed farming methods and the improved breeds of livestock, made agriculture more profitable and better able to satisfy the needs of the rapidly expanding urban population.

Nevertheless, England changed from an exporting to an importing economy, at a time when few countries had a surplus of corn and the Corn Laws were still in force. The price of bread, which fluctuated wildly according to the ups and downs of successive harvests at home and abroad, caused considerable hardship.

The rapid expansion of the coal industry figured largely in the sisters' correspondence, as new pits were sunk in South Wales, Scotland, Lancashire and Yorkshire.

1830 brought the death of George IV, the one-time Prince Regent. The new monarch was William IV, who continued the Hanovarian tradition of living with a mistress, rather than his wife. On his death in 1837, he was survived by 8 children, but none was legitimate, although all were sustained by the state, and so it was William's niece, Victoria, who succeeded him to the throne in1837.

The more seminal event of 1830 was the arrival of the railway in London. Crowds of spectators were drawn eo Euston Square, where a steam-driven locomotive drew wagons round a novelty track. Bigger things were quickly to follow. As railway lines were laid at ground level, or on viaducts, or in cut-and-cover tunnels, from the capital towards various destinations, thousands of the poor were displaced from their homes in central parts to out-lying areas, initiating the suburbs. The Reed family found themselves no longer surrounded by common land, fields, small-holdings and woods, but by ever-spreading streets of houses.

An 1829 Act of Parliament established the Metropolitan Police, absorbing the Bow Street Runners and the Thames River Police. Lavender took this as an opportune time to retire. He now spent his time as an adviser and helper to his daughters in their political work.

The sisters learned from their correspondents all over the north, that trade unions were springing up like mushrooms in response to factory closures, increasingly tenuous employment and the downward pressure on wages. Militants drew Inspiration from the revolutionary upsurge across the Channel in France and Belgium.

arpenter's Coffee House in Covent Garden piazza was one of the best-known gathering places for London's reformists in search of good conversation, friendly allies, exchange of information and energetic disputation. The sisters rode there one day in December, when a recent fall of glistening snow was now ravaged, lying in churned dirty slippery slush, preserved on the pavements and cobbles by night-time frosts. The brilliant, low winter sun had no heat, but was blinding, bouncing off the wet cobbled road as if it were a mirror.

No more than a large wooden shed, the sisters did not favour Carpenter's more than once or twice a year. Knowing the coffee to be execrable, they ordered a jug of rum and hot water to share with William Lovett, who had suggested this rendezvous. The air was thick with tobacco smoke and steam from the water boilers. One had almost to shout in order to be heard in the din from so many loquacious patrons. Above the smell of coffee, the sisters could detect the odour of unwashed bodies. Their own bodies smelled and tasted of scented water.

The trio were meeting to discuss the progress of William's project to establish a coordinating organisation for the trade unions of the Metropolis, a body they decided to call the London Working Men's Association. It was timely also to discuss the Bill about to go before Parliament, which was to become The Representation of the People Act (popularly known as the Great Reform Act) of 1832.

Although supported by the Prime Minister, Earl Grey, the Bill was expected to meet strong opposition from the Lords. The reformist movement was on the brink of its biggest-ever success.

At one point, Cally held up a finger to quieten her companions. She looked around the room and had her suspicion confirmed. She quietly urged a discreet look at the man near the door, in the purple Inverness with the large beaver collar, clearly a man of means. "By his voice and his face, I would know that man anywhere. I have not set eyes on him since the time of the Cato Street conspiracy.

"I know him to be John Castle, alias, George Edwards, alias Oliver the spy.

"Polly, when he leaves, may we follow him? With luck, if he lives within walking distance, we can find out his address. It was early twilight when their quarry left. He led them only a short distance to the door of a house, number 43, in King Street, which formed one side of the Piazza. Watching the house for no more than a few minutes, its nature became obvious. The constant traffic of over-dressed and over-painted women, frolicking with red-faced inebriated men, at this time of day, signified that number 43 was the infamous King Street brothel. Cally recalled Father disclosing that John Castle augmented his income as a spy by being the protector of a brothel's madam. Returning to Carpenter's to collect their mounts, they walked under the portico of St Paul's church. At the foot of the church wall there were two bundles of rags. First spotted by Polly, poking out from one of the bundles, there were two small bare feet. Investigation of the rags revealed two young girls, hugging one another. Hardly clothed, they were dirty, cold and doubtless hungry. London, the biggest and richest city in the world, had thousands of such starvelings, living by their wits. Such street-children are as commonplace as the sparrows and just as largely ignored, but these two were now on the hands of Cally and Polly, a responsibility they could not shirk.

Cally signalled to a parked gig and brooked no objections from the driver in putting the children, wrapped in their filthy rags, on the floor of the vehicle. The driver was silenced with **a** florin and the promise of another if he followed the riders to Kennington. The destination was St Mary's workhouse. The sisters used their assumed authority to override the objections of the governor to admitting the children without the prior direction of the overseers. Cally handed over a coin with the request that, "The girls be bathed, given more clothes, food and a warm place to sleep tonight.

"We shall be back here early in the morning in order to deal with the overseers. We take full responsibility for this irregular admission."

As Cally and Polly were about to leave, the smaller girl was overtaken by a seizure. Her arms and legs were jerking, her body was shivering violently and her teeth were chattering uncontrollably. Polly carried her to the fireplace, covered her with a rug and waited until the crisis was over.

The sisters ensured they were at the workhouse by seven the following morning, before any overseer might arrive and begin upbraiding the governor for housing the children overnight without proper authority.

The girls looked distinctly cleaner and better clothed and they now had shoes. The younger one still had a wracking cough. In better circumstances she would be confined to bed.

The bigger girl was distressed by this translocation from Covent Garden. "Farver relies on the money we gets by goin' wiv boys and men. Farver will whip us when 'e gets us back.". "What is your name?" asked Polly.

"It's May."

"And what is your second name?"

No response.

Of the other girl, "What is your name?"

"May."

But you cannot both be called May."

"Farver said, cos we is sisters, we 'ave the same name."

There was no point in arguing with this.

Neither of them could be older than eleven or twelve. Child prostitutes in Christian pre-Victorian London, were worth a lot of money to their keeper. Their lives were cruel and short. Many a small body was found in the Thames. Such finds, fished out before too far gone, could be sold as useful specimens for trainee surgeons. Such fishing was an unpredictable, but worthwhile business.

Of a sudden, there was a loud disturbance at the workhouse entrance. Cally immediately guessed the cause and cautioned the governor and Polly to … "Leave the matter to me alone. I will do all the talking, because I am the more practiced liar."

There burst on to the scene a man who would easily pass as a stereotypical member of the London mob. He brought with him the stench of stale beer and an even rougher looking compatriot.

"Where's my kids? I know you've got 'em. The gig driver tell't me this is where you brung 'em.

"This 'ere's Shiv and he'll use 'is shiv on you, lady."

Cally held up her hands in a demonstration of her total innocence. "My dear sir, there was one here before you. One who also knows the price of young girls put on the street to earn money. He took them away. You probably know him, being a member of the same profession. His name is John Castle. Do you know the address of his establishment?"

Rudely, without a word of thanks, the two ruffians took off. Cally suggested to Polly that they might ride to King Street, in order to witness the next chapter of the story unfold and possibly offering the children some protection. When they arrived at King Street, a noisy confrontation was already underway. They dismounted near St Paul's Church and, with Alexis and other spectators affording them some cover, they had a discreet observation post, overlooking number 43. From what the sisters could hear, it was clear that Castle neither denied possession of the girls nor agreed to concede their release.

Then came the shock of the grisly finale. Castle raised a pistol and shot the girls' putative father in the face. In immediate retaliation, Shiv drove his shiv into John Castle's chest. Just to make sure, he then lunged into Castle's belly. The pavement was now blocked by two apparently lifeless bodies and the slush was colouring with the gushing blood.

Cally mounted and hauled up Polly to ride pillion.

"We have kept our pledge," said Cally, sounding happy and self-satisfied.

"What do you mean?"

"No matter that it was not by our hands, but we have seen the demise of John Castle and his various aliases".

"Not by our hands, but by your lying serpent's tongue. But what is to be the fate of the two little girls?

"Polly, dear, listen to me, your sister, who is older and occasionally wiser. Relish whatever successes you have in life and remember that even the Reed sisters cannot solve every one of the world's problems."

1833

It was high time to consider Tilly's future. At school she is always top of her class. By invitation, she has sung in churches around London and as her name becomes known, she could probably make her way as a singer, but her aspirations are in other directions. Attending reformist meetings and listening to her mothers' discussions, she is familiar with the ideas and terminology of economics and politics. In school she has learned geography and history. Cally and Polly have been impressed and intrigued when Tilly has expressed the view that, instead of all these different subjects, there should be just one subject, embracing all of them. She elaborated this idea when her class was set 'A brief history of London' as the title of a composition, Tilly was being more than a little mischievous and challenging by making her opening sentence, "<u>Why</u> is London? Why does it exist and why is it where it is, rather than somewhere else in England?"

She went on, in the conversational styleof an innocent, to answer her own questions.

"I assume the first people to arrive here by land came from the south, arriving at marshland somewhere near present-day Kennington. In past centuries, the river

Thames was much wider, with marshes along each bank. These facts are part of the history of London.

"Well, these early travellers faced a conundrum. Do they find a ford and cross to the other side? Or, if they have some sort of boat do they go upstream? Or do they more easily travel downstream with the current?

"That may explain why London is here. While scratching their heads and discussing what to do, they make a little camp. As long as they stay in this place, they have choices. The grass may be greener on the other side. It is easier to travel on the water than on the land, provided you have that boat.

"By river, you can go faster and avoid wild animals and unfriendly tribes. You can travel westward, in the direction of the setting sun. Alternatively, you can float downstream in the direction of the rising sun. That direction has the advantage and disadvantage of being tidal, carrying you up and down at different times of day, because the open sea is not far away. These facts about the location can be called geography.

The river brings lots of travellers and many of them want to trade all sorts of commodities. Trade can be by barter or by the exchange of coins. Trade and exchange are studied in economics. People need all sorts of *things*; things to eat, things to wear, things with which to decorate themselves or defend themselves. People skilled in providing these things, settle in or near the camp. Our little camp becomes a village and the village grows into a town. There comes the day when one of the town-dwellers decides to take charge and ensure the town is organised as he (yes, it is usually a man) considers it should be, arranging defence against enemies, for example, or the price of corn Some people may be happy with his decisions and others may be unhappy, taking the view that they should be consulted, or that they have better ideas. The arguments that arise have given birth to politics. A bad harvest might be blamed on a vengeful god and the hungry people might be consoled by the promise of better times in the life beyond death. Londoners now have religion.

There. In a few sentences, by combining history, geography, economics and politics I have explained why London exists, why it is near Kennington and why so many Londoners want parliamentary reform and many go to church each Sunday. Have I made the world simpler and more understandable for you?

"I admit that there is something I do not fathom. The first people to arrive in England came northwards from Europe. England was not welcoming. Julius Caesar describes it as cold, wet, covered in horrible forest and infested with nasty uncivilised people. Why on earth did those early travellers stay here? If they had turned around and gone back, I would not have to put up with all our dreadful weather."

Tilly confided in her mothers that she wanted to go to a university, so that she could continue her education, but knew that to be out of the question, because girls were not admitted. She had worked out that the next best thing would be to study under an important writer, a writer of the sort of books she would study at a university. After mulling the matter for a few days, the sisters made their daughter a proposition.

"Tilly, darling, we think we know who might fit the bill."Mothers and daughter were at the table after dinner. "You may have heard us talk of Samuel Bowly. He is a prominent Quaker, well known throughout the West of England. He is not a writer, but he is a supporter of parliamentary reform and a campaigner, along with William Wilberforce, for the abolition of slavery. Being heavily committed to good works, including public education and the charity schools, as well as running several businesses, he may well be open to the idea of having an assistant. He is certainly not a poor man and so he would probably pay a modest stipend".

Tilly determined to write to Mr Bowly.

"Dear Friend

I hope I may address you as Dear Friend, as I, too, am a Quaker and you are well acquainted with my mothers, Cally and Polly Reed of the Kennington Friends' Meeting House and the London Working Men's Association. I was adopted by Cally and Polly in 1818, shortly after the death of my real mother, who had been brought to England as a slave from Benin. I have attended school for five years and additionally I have had lessons in Latin, ancient Greek and mathematics. I am proficient at singing and can play the pianoforte. My facility in handwriting and composition you are hereby able judge for yourself.

"Being now of an age to live independently, I am seeking a position. I am aware that you actively support many good causes, on top of your onerous business responsibilities. With due modesty, I offer you my services as an assistant, hoping that you may be able to offer me a small remuneration.

In due course, I can provide you with letters of recommendation from my mothers and from the Elders of the Kennington Friends' Meeting House.

Yours sincerely
Matilda (Tilly) Reed"

Quakers, among themselves, never used such titles as Mr, Mrs and Miss, nor Dr, nor honorifics, such as your lordship.

First and last names were used. In the sisters' Newgate schools they were always addressed as Cally and Polly by the children and their mothers alike.

Within a week, Tilly received a very encouraging reply. Samuel was shortly to be in London, for a meeting at the House of Commons about the Slavery Abolition Bill due to be debated in 1833. Tilly was given the date and time. First she would have a discussion with Samuel and then, if she wished, she could remain for his meeting with William Wilberforce and other MPs who were supporting the Bill. Samuel suggested it would be very useful for her to be present at this meeting with MPs, because if she became one of his assistants, he would want her to specialise in his anti-slavery work.

And so it came about that Tilly moved to Gloucester, where she had her own small room at the top of Samuel's house and worked in his study on the first floor, remaining with him for some five years in all. To begin with, her work was entirely concentrated on popularising the plan for an Act of Parliament putting an end to slavery throughout the British Empire. She composed letters and wrote speeches and letters to Samuel's dictation. She copied and filed correspondence with scores of individuals and organisations. She also became much in demand to address meetings, known to be black, the daughter of a slave and reputed to be an eloquent and entertaining speaker, sometimes bursting into appropriate song, and flamboyant in her Benin style of dress.

Very much the daughter of her strong-minded mothers, her blood boiled when she first read the full title of the Abolition Bill – an Act for the Abolition of Slavery throughout the British Colonies; for Promoting the Industry of Manumitted Slaves and for Compensating the Persons Hitherto Entitled to the Service of such Slaves.

She held her peace for a few weeks, until her work was well respected and her feet were securely under the table. Then, having ascertained that Cally and Polly wholeheartedly supported her view, at a meeting of the Bill's backers in the House of Commons, she gave controlled vent to her spleen.

"The chief motivation of abolitionists is the firm conviction that enslavement of fellow human beings is unethical. As slave ownership is unethical, then so is deriving income from that enslavement.

"All over the English, Scottish and Irish countryside there are great mansions, housing treasures from all parts of the world. These riches have been amassed by the centuries of unpaid labour of nearly a million abducted, traded and cruelly over-worked Africans whom we now seek to liberate.

"Slave-owners are among the wealthiest in the land. They neither need nor deserve compensation for the loss of their slaves.

"The Bill talks of promoting the industry of the freed slaves. Vacuous, weasel words. These people, who were torn from their families and homeland, have laboured for no reward. They have few possessions and probably no savings. If Parliament genuinely wishes to promote their industry, they are the ones who should receive pump-priming money. They are the ones who should receive compensation for the evil exploitation they have suffered."

There were nods and grunts in sympathy around the room, but there was no unanimity. The MPs and peers included many slave-owners, whose contributions in debates made it clear that their ethical support for abolition was not unlimited; their support came at a price. Tilly was disgusted, but appreciated that this unethical compromise was made long before her involvement. If the Bill was to become law, that despicable provision for compensation would have to remain.

Tilly became the ever-watchful enforcer of abolition and was destined to become the leading advocate of the African diaspora in Britain and the former slave states of Western Europe, Portugal, Spain, Netherlands and Denmark.

The three Reed women devoted a lot of time and energy to garnering the support of reformist organisations and trade unions for an abolitionist petition to Parliament, which had over a million signatures by 1833.The eventual Act took effect from August 1834. This was just two years after the Great Reform Act of 1832 came into force. At last the people were achieving successes. Slaves were being liberated all over the Empire and the Representation of the People Act, to give the Reform Act its official name, abolished the 'rotten boroughs', granted seats in the Commons to the big cities that had sprung up during the industrial Revolution and extended the electorate from about 400,000 men to 650,00.

"This is far from utopian," declared Cally at a Hampden Club meeting. "It does not fully realise our aim of universal adult suffrage. By defining a voter as 'a male person', women are explicitly barred and men qualify only if they own land, or pay a yearly rent of £10 or more, making no more than one fifth of men eligible to vote.

"It is not perfection, but the stern will of the people has forced the State, Tom Paine's Old Corruption, to concede the biggest constitutional advance we have ever seen in this country and sets a precedent on which we can build towards further reforms as we move onward to the end of the present century and into the 20th century.

"Brothers and sisters, we have much to celebrate, whilst also remembering our martyrs fallen at Pentrich, Peterloo and Cato Street and numerous other remonstrances, where magistrates or ministers turned out the army, militias and the police to assault and slay our brethren." Cally acknowledged the applause and the formal vote of thanks.

The sisters were known for their eccentricity of dress. They were resistant to the emerging fashions of the mid-century. Both of them stuck to the small spencer jacket. Cally favoured the conical skirt, but not the voluminous style that was on the way to the nonsense of the crinoline, with its ridiculous hoop or frame and furbelows. Polly, when more formally dressed, wore black velvet knee breeches and white silk stockings, with a short, hooded cloak, rather than a dress. Polly, in particular, was looked upon, by other women, as too bol. Despite the breeches, she did not look manly, because she was so tiny; some women found her boy-ish and were tempted to mother her, until she addressed a meeting or simply contributed to a discussion, when she was found to be assertive, ironic and challenging. Her girlish voice belied her steely nature.

Following Cally, William Lovett took the floor and reminded the meeting that the trade unions were increasingly committed to Owenite Socialism. The reformed House of Commons, he declared, would come to have a new socialist political party, born of the trade unions, which would eventually form a government and would take control of the means of production, distribution and exchange. That brought applause and cheering, but no response from Polly, Cally noticed.

Later that evening, Polly returned to the table after clearing the supper dishes and told Cally she had been thinking about William's idea of a socialist Britain, which is very much along the lines Robert Owen had proposed when they met him at New Lanark.

"But I have second thoughts about it", said Polly. Cally could tell by her sister's tone, that she was apprehensive about whatever misgivings she was going to voice.

"Your second thoughts are usually much more valuable than my first thoughts." Cally took Polly's hand and squeezed it, as if to prompt her into speaking her mind.

"Without a doubt, William's vision of the future is heartening. He envisages common ownership of the bastions of the economy and the best attainable system of democratic control of each industry and service. Some, like William, may consider this concept not be too utopian to be realised. He places his faith in a government formed by a new political party, a party which represents the interests of the majority of working people, to oversee this new society. This is where he and I part company

And possibly you and I, too." Polly looked at her sister and mouthed, "I'm sorry, darling Cally."

"We have experience of these political parties – the Whigs and the Tories and their liberal and radical wings, all of them exclusively male and devoted, above all, to the retention of their power.

"I suppose William, as does Robert Owen, envisages a new, ethical, humanitarian version of mankind to staff his new government and create his New Jerusalem.

"To borrow from the Bard: 'tis a consummation devoutly to be wished, but just a dream, a step beyond reality. From where has this new man appeared?

"The answer is that he has *not* appeared. You and I have discussed this for many a late-night hour. We are all of us moulded by the era and the world in which we live. We are shackled, like slaves, to the context of our lives. Some individuals are able to release themselves and define a new reality – Jesus and Tom Paine come to mind – but not, methinks, the average man, who is involuntarily of his time.

Polly took a sip from her tea and carried on.

"Who better understands coal-mining than pitmen and women?

"Who can possibly be fitter to run the fast-developing gas industry than the gas workers?

"The railways now being constructedcould not be better administered and operated than by the men building them and daily working them. The same applies to the canals and the same principle applies to the textile mills of the North.

"Our industries are currently in the hands of those rich men who invested capital in them.

"And how, pray, did they come by that capital? It was created by the sweat of the brow of each worker in those industries.

"So, who should rightfully own and control those industries?

"The answer is obvious: the workers organised in their trade unions."

By now, Polly was quite animated by her expounding, while Cally sat in silence, with a blank face.

Polly interpreted her sister's silence as a challenge, which she countered by elaborating her argument. "The workers in each industry will keep control in the hands of the rank and file, opposing inevitable attempts by full-time officials to wrest power to themselves, creating an unaccountable bureaucracy.

"There being no cohort of new men, honest, humane, altruistic and incorruptible, unless the trade unions are alive to the danger, there would be a similar assumption of power at national government level. The Old Corruption has not gone away; it is merely biding its time until returning to power."

It was now Cally's turn to speak. She walked round the table and sat close to her sister, stroking her face before starting.

"Do you remember last Easter, when you and Tilly went to an abolitionist celebration concert, I went to a London Working Men's Association meeting at William's coffee house, to hear a speaker from France, Pierre-Joseph Proudhon? I think his English and my French met about mid-Channel, with it blowing a gale." Polly giggled, knowing that French was not Cally's forte.

"But I understood enough to grasp all the essentials.

"Proudhon's theme was much along the lines you have been speaking. He called this trade union control *Syndicalisme.*

"His ideas did not go down well and I think I can recall the main arguments made against him.

"I risk again being charged with misanthropy, because I start by repeating my belief that most people are not sufficiently rational to see what is in their best interest. They tend to be most influenced by whoever spoke loudest or spoke last. Call me cynical, but that is my observation of one of the frailties of human nature.

"This irrationality leads most working people not to support socialism, but to stand by the one system they have experienced, capitalism. They have seen capitalism take us to the misery war. They have seen it create unemployment, the Corn Laws and gross inequality of wealth, but still they hold fast to it, despite its cruel buffeting, perhaps because it is cunning enough and flexible enough to amend its coloration from time to time.

"Church and King, the city mob's slogan of twenty years ago, has become King and Country. There is nothing as potent as patriotism to win the hearts of the unthinking.

"Tell me, Polly, if each manufacturing industry and service sector is controlled by its workers, will there be overall planning?

"I think we can agree that carefully considered planning would be needed in order to eliminate the evil of unemployment. That would demand the cooperation of manufacturers, banks and customs and trade officials."

"You and I are Quakers and pacifists, which puts us in a minority of the population. How, in your new dispensation, will decisions be made on the all-important matter of peace and war?

"I remember that Proudhon was asked how the government would be formed. His response was that there would be no central government, exerting its power by coercion and compulsion. Instead there would be voluntary cooperation.

"Unfortunately, the unions have demonstrated both solidarity and division. Even within a single industry there can be more than one trade union. Some workers consider themselves more skilled and insist on having a separate union and seeking better rates. They want to be the trade union aristocrats.

"Of course, there have been major advances. A generation ago, workers were subject to wage cuts, arbitrary dismissal and victimisation. No longer. The weapon of strike action is ever ready. Some iniquities committed by employers are now virtually unthinkable. Workers no longer see themselves in the condition of wage-slavery.There has been a revolutionary change in the balance of power between employers and workers. That change in industrial relations has diluted the appeal of radical political change.

"After battling for three centuries for parliamentary reform and having won it, the idea of forfeiting it for government without parliament is a step too far." Polly nodded, signifying her agreement.

The sisters smiled at one another. An unprecedented political row between the lovers had been avoided. They fell on each other in joyful abandon.

Milton Keynes UK
Ingram Content Group UK Ltd.
UKHW010639310823
427815UK00001B/3